GRAVESTONE

A NOVEL

TRAVIS THRASHER

David C Cook®
transforming lives together

GRAVESTONE
Published by David C Cook
4050 Lee Vance View
Colorado Springs, CO 80918 U.S.A.

David C Cook Distribution Canada
55 Woodslee Avenue, Paris, Ontario, Canada N3L 3E5

David C Cook U.K., Kingsway Communications
Eastbourne, East Sussex BN23 6NT, England

David C Cook and the graphic circle C logo
are registered trademarks of Cook Communications Ministries.

This story is a work of fiction. All characters and events are the product of the author's
imagination. Any resemblance to any person, living or dead, is coincidental.

2 Kings 6:16 in chapter 38 is taken from the King James Version of the Bible.
(Public Domain.) The first passage in chapter 88, Isaiah 59:9–10, is taken from the
Holy Bible, New International Version®, NIV®. Copyright © 1973, 1978, 1984 by
Biblica, Inc™. Used by permission of Zondervan. All rights reserved worldwide. www.
zondervan.com. The second verse in chapter 88, 1 Corinthians 4:5, is taken from The
New Testament in Modern English, copyright © 1958, 1959, 1960 J.B. Phillips and
1947, 1952, 1955, 1957 The Macmillian Company, New York. Used by permission.
All rights reserved. The third verse in chapter 88, Daniel 10:19, is taken from the New
Living Translation of the Holy Bible. New Living Translation copyright © 1996,
2004 by Tyndale Charitable Trust. Used by permission of Tyndale House Publishers.

The poem segment in chapter 8 is from Robert Frost, "The Road Not Taken,"
Mountain Interval (1920). The first poem segment in chapter 39 is from Robert
Frost, "A Ghost House," *A Boy's Will* (1915). The second poem segment in
chapter 39 is from Robert Frost, "Now Close the Windows," *A Boy's Will*
(1915). The third poem segment in chapter 39 is from Robert Frost, "The
Flood," *West-Running Brook* (1928). The fourth poem segment in chapter 39
is from Robert Frost, "The Road Not Taken," *Mountain Interval* (1920).

LCCN 2011923885
ISBN 978-1-4347-6419-5
eISBN 978-0-7814-0688-8

© 2011 Travis Thrasher

The Team: Don Pape, LB Norton, Sarah Schultz, Caitlyn York, Karen Athen
Cover Design: Amy Kiechlin Konyndyk
Cover Images: iStockphoto 3403969; 5000316, royalty free

Printed in the United States of America
First Edition 2011

1 2 3 4 5 6 7 8 9 10

032911

FOR BEN LIPPEN

I HEAR HER VOICE CALLING MY NAME.

THE SOUND IS DEEP IN THE DARK.

—*"A Forest" by The Cure*

PREFACE

Evil wears a mask, and I can finally see its face.

The rushing waters surround us as sunlight plays tricks on my eyes. Gold glitters in these woods, damp from the earlier rain, foggy from the temperature change. My legs splash in the cool stream that comes up to my shins.

He's standing on the edge where the water drops fifty feet to the jutting rocks below. He faces me with his sick smile. "What are you going to do now, Chris?"

I'm no longer scared, no longer running away.

"It's done," I say. "You're done."

The voice talking is not mine. The hand holding this knife doesn't belong to me.

Chris Buckley is gone. Long gone.

It's been six months, but I can still taste it in my mouth. The anger, the bitterness, the absolute hunger for revenge.

You don't have to do this, not here, not like this.

He smiles. "What do you think you're going to do?"

"Whatever you're doing to this place and these people—it's over. Right now."

His laugh twists into my skin.

"There are things you need to know," he says.

"I know enough."

"You know only what you're supposed to know. That's why I brought you here."

"I followed *you."*

"I could break your neck if I wanted to."

I smile. Because something in me says he's wrong. Something in me believes that if he wanted me dead, I'd be dead already.

"You're not going to do anything to anybody ever again," I say.

"So what happens after you kill the Big Bad Wolf?" he asks. "There are others lurking in these woods and in this town. I'm just the obvious one. Killing me achieves nothing."

My hand shakes, but I steady it as I walk closer to him. Streaks of sunlight circle us like a laser show.

You can't really do this, Chris, no matter how you feel and how right it is.

"So the pastor stands at Marsh Falls," he says. "How ironic. How fitting. And how utterly predictable."

"You killed her," I say to him.

He laughs and looks at me through his short glasses, and I want to take them and break them just like I want to break him.

"Six months and you're still seething," Pastor Marsh says. "That's good."

"People are going to know."

"Haven't these past months taught you anything? You're smart, but you're not *that* smart. You're not here because you're some bright young star chosen because of your intelligence, Chris. You're really rather unremarkable, to tell you the truth."

I inch closer.

He's now about five feet away from me. He looks behind him, then glances back at me.

This is the first time I think I see fear on his face.

Because maybe, just maybe, he doesn't see fear in mine.

One more step.

The echoes of the falls smother all other sounds.

Hell is not dying, Chris. It's knowing and living.

Whoever said that was right.

I think whoever said that is standing before me right now.

"Do you want to know the truth?" he asks.

"I *know* the truth. The new church. I know where it is. I found the folders. The pictures. I have proof. Everybody is going to know about Solitary. Everybody is going to know what's really going on."

"Have you ever been surprised, Chris?"

"You're a sick man."

"Have you ever believed in something with all your heart, only to discover it was an ugly little lie?"

"Shut up."

"Everything you think you know about this town and about your mother and her family—all those things are pretty little lies covering up the ugly, awful truth."

"No."

"Oh, yes, Chris. Maybe this has all been some elaborate test."

I move closer.

"Maybe we never wanted Jocelyn. That sweet but dirty little thing you professed to love."

I curse at him.

"Maybe all we ever wanted was you."

My hand is steady and I know it's because I've used a weapon before and I'll do it again. Even though a gun's a lot different from a knife, it doesn't matter.

I'm not Chris Buckley because that boy died on New Year's Eve along with something far more precious.

Stop before it's too late.

"We're watching, but all you see is the scene before you," Pastor Marsh says. "You don't see anybody but a face you hate and fear and a boy you hate and fear even more."

"I'm going to kill you."

He smiles. "If you do, Chris, we will watch and applaud and await."

Then the pastor opens his arms as if giving the benediction at church.

And that's when I plunge the twelve-inch hunting blade deep into the place where I imagine his heart might have been at one time.

I see Jocelyn's face as I move the knife and feel the softness of skin and hear the gasping, choking breath as I thrust down.

I let go and see him looking surprised. Not in horror, but almost in utter delight.

"You want to know the truth, Chris?" a draining, coughing voice asks.

And then he tells me.

And suddenly I realize that he's right and I'm wrong.

I realize this just as he staggers over the falls and drops below.

1. THE STATE OF A SIXTEEN-YEAR-OLD

Snow.

That's what the new day brings.

A white, cold cover-up.

Complete and total isolation.

Icy fingertips on the window.

And hot, raging anger.

The second day of the new year, and I'm ready to wake up from this nightmare and find myself back in Illinois. Where's my buddy Brady's game room with all the latest games and the ability to connect with twenty other players online? I can only connect with a dog that looks like a cotton ball dropped in chocolate. Everything else is impossible. Starting with Mom.

She looks like a survivor of a car crash. I didn't want to talk with her yesterday, but when morning came and she eventually woke up and I made an effort to communicate, I knew that something was wrong with her, too. Maybe she watched her own personal New Year's Eve bonfire and sacrifice. Maybe she got a call from Dad saying he wanted her back. Maybe she realized the mess the two of us are in and then proceeded to drink herself to oblivion.

I was going to tell her, but not in her condition of walking unconsciousness. Instead I made her coffee and waited until she could listen without dozing off into Slumberland.

Our phones don't work. Of course. Mom says they've been out ever since the ice falling last night turned to snow. If she's so groggy now, how can she remember what it was like in the middle of the night? All I can remember is the tapping on the window and Midnight snuggling next to me. I can't imagine the dog enduring a storm like this in the deserted barn where Jocelyn was keeping her.

Sure you can, buddy. You can imagine anything now. Anything.

The Internet doesn't work either. Yet our cable does.

I'd try a cell, but we haven't made it that far. Baby steps. Like my license. Like my sanity. Like my soul.

Midday, and the weather reports are wrong. This ice-turning-into-snow storm has tripled expectations, at least in the wonderful little vacation getaway of Solitary. *Come for the weekend, and you'll leave scarred and changed for life! Come for life, and you'll discover that life's not exactly worth living.*

I stepped out on the deck and saw a good seven or eight inches.

That was hours ago.

That means any thought of driving is no good.

No phone, no Internet, no car.

And no Mom.

I'm imprisoned with this rage inside me.

Still in shock, still out of my mind in awesome terror, still in this little cabin that once belonged to Uncle Robert before he disappeared.

A voice reminds me that oh, yeah, I'm still sixteen.

But I don't believe that voice anymore.

2. DÉJÀ VU

You leave, and we'll forget you. Do you understand?

Snowflakes hurl sideways as I make my way down the white, vanished road.

We can do this to your mother, Chris. To your father. We can do this to anybody who means anything to you.

I squint and look out the slit between my cap and the scarf covering my nose and mouth.

You'll live and you'll know, Chris. And you won't tell another single soul. Do you understand?

Each step I take is like one taken on the top of Mount Everest. It's not just the deep snow; it's that wind.

Do you understand?

I've been walking for at least half an hour.

Walking with that voice going off in my mind.

My answer has changed.

No, I don't understand.

And no, I'm not staying quiet.

There are two ways into town. Sable Road comes in from both the north and the south. Two roads that feed into a town the world has somehow neglected. So *snowed in* really means that. As I trudge through foot-deep snow, I realize it's going to take a while for them to plow Sable Road, and far longer to plow side roads like mine.

There's no way every single person in this town could be crazy psycho. No way. That's nice in zombie movies, but this is no Hollywood set.

If I can't find anybody in town, I'll keep walking until I get to another town. To another state.

To somewhere else.

The wind howls, and I swear I hear Jocelyn's voice in it.

Whispering *Be careful.*

Whispering *Be smart.*

But that's not her ghost because … because it's not.

Maybe I'll be able to see her with the help of some freaky old lady who does séances, but not here and not today.

I notice the tall trees that stand by the road like people watching a parade. Silent, towering sentries in white, guarding Solitary. I don't realize just how far the town is from our cabin. It sure doesn't help that I'm wearing tennis shoes. But snow boots are on the To Buy list along with a shotgun and some vampire repellent and an AA book for Mom.

Everything is gray, and I can't make out the end of the street. A dark cloud of doom seems to be stuck in this place, or at least stuck right over me.

When the road turns, I see the partially concealed sign of Solitary. Underneath reads the statistic that has never caught my eye until now.

Population 1772.

I think about how many people that is. Almost two thousand. They can't all own red robes and conduct sick rituals in the middle of the night. Not all two thousand. I refuse to believe that.

Population 1772—no wait, strike that. Now it's population 1771.

The wind howls, and again it seems to speak to me.

Not now, Chris, not like this.

But that's my fear talking.

I stood by the sideline and watched and waited when I should have done something. Anything. I should have gotten the car and forced Jocelyn to come with me. We could be in Canada by now. I could have forced Mom to come somehow.

No, you couldn't.

I could have saved Joss.

She could still be by my side this very instant.

No, she couldn't.

One thing the last twenty-four hours has taught me: I will never again be complacent. I will never just wait and wonder.

I'm going to seize the day, as they say. Or seize someone's throat. Whichever comes first.

The snow launches another offensive right as I pass the sign of Solitary. I can still only see dimming nothingness in front of me.

Until I see the figure.

I have a bit of déjà vu and remember a figure like this seeming to guard a town when I thought that town didn't need to be guarded. When I thought Solitary was just another little town stuck in the middle of North Carolina.

The figure stands in the middle of the road.

Then something else emerges at his side. Something low and dense.

A dog.

The dog has to be the German shepherd. The figure has to be that guy. The one I saw the day I rode my bike into town. The one I spotted at my driveway that one morning. The figure with a red mountain-man beard and a long trench coat.

I don't slow down.

The dog seems to jerk forward at me, but something keeps him restrained. He must be on a leash.

Flakes fly all sorts of ways as my footsteps feel weighed down, my feet no longer just cold but numb, my back damp with sweat, my nose a frigid Popsicle.

The man just stands there, facing me. I can see his face under a hood.

Is there anybody normal in this crazy town?

"Hello," I call out.

But the word gets sucked into the storm as soon as it comes out.

"Hey, can you help me?"

This of course is crazy, but I don't know what else to do. Nothing is as it seems in this town, so why should some dark, hulking guy with a scary dog necessarily be bad? I'm already here, and running away seems to be a bit ridiculous considering I can't even—

"Chris, over here!" a voice says.

It's a guy's voice, but not one I recognize. It seems to be flying around the air just like the snow. I turn to the side where I thought it came from and don't see anything—just the side of the road and the forest behind it.

I turn again and see something coming toward me.

"Chris, watch out!"

The moving thing has to be the dog.

It's bearing down on me and flying over the snow.

I think of that other dog I saw in the woods. The dog-thing-creature that was after me.

What'd I ever do to dogs?

I turn to run, and this is of course stupid, but I don't know what else to do.

I slip but regain my footing and then race down the path I've been walking. I decide to veer right into the woods.

I don't look behind me, but I can hear it.

"Chris, over here!"

Then I see something coming out of the woods toward me over me on top of me and I don't know if I can—

3. SOMETHING WARM

I awake in a golden field, and that's when I realize I'm dead.

This is heaven, and an angel is looking over me. I see the outline of a head and long hair with a sun-crossed halo behind it.

"You're really stupid, you know that?"

I didn't think angels were supposed to say things like that.

"What are you doing, Chris?"

The head moves, and for a moment I'm blinded. Then I see her.

Jocelyn.

"What happened?" I ask.

"Are you always going to be this dense?"

"Are you there? Are you really there?"

"You have to be more careful."

I move to stand up, but then I feel like that one time I had too much beer with Brady and vowed never, ever to do that again.

"You have to know the sides, Chris. You have to find out who you can trust and who you need to stay away from."

She looks as beautiful as I remember her.

"I'm sorry," I begin, moving toward her, wanting to touch her.

"This isn't the place for apologies. It's a dream, dummy. You're just talking to yourself. You know that."

"This isn't heaven?"

She laughs, and suddenly she begins to fade away. "You're still very much in Solitary. And that very much is *not* heaven."

I hear her laugh before the field and the sunlight fade out.

"Chris?"

That's definitely not Jocelyn's voice.

I wake up and feel my body shivering.

"Sorry it's so cold. It'll get warmer when the fire gets going."

The view in front of me opens like a blurry film. I see waves of candlelight. No, it's a fire that's starting. I see some kind of lamp floating in the air. No, a lamp on a shelf. A flickering lamp, maybe a candle or kerosene.

"Drink this," a guy says.

I recoil and tighten my lips.

"Okay, fine, it's fine. It's just something warm."

I want to say that something warm in this place is probably poison, yet my mouth can't say anything.

"Look, just relax, okay? You almost got mauled by that dog, then you hit your head on a tree branch."

I still have a gash on my side from running through the woods and getting stuck with a branch two days ago.

These woods are treating me very well.

The world does a mini-earthquake as I try to sit up.

"Just take it easy."

I try to make out the figure sitting across from me. I'm on a sofa that seems like it's about ready to collapse. The walls seem to be moving around us, as if we're stuck in that trash compactor in the very first Star Wars movie.

"My name is Jared. I'm your cousin."

When the blurriness goes away and I can make out his face, I panic.

I see a boyish face with a faint beard and mustache. For a minute I try to remember if I've ever seen him before. My head hurts too much to think.

"Did your mother tell you about me?"

I shake my head.

There's quite a bit Mom's neglected to mention.

"Well, look—I can explain later. My father is your uncle."

"Uncle Robert?"

My voice sounds trippy and slow-mo. Like *Uuuuuuunnnnnncccc ccclllllllllleeeee Rrrrrrrrrrooooooooobbbbbeeeeeeerrrrrrrrrrttttt.*

"Yeah."

"Where is he?"

The guy looks at me with a solemn stare. "That's what I want to know."

"But if you're his—What are you doing—Where are—"

"Take it easy, Chris. That hit on your head was quite a knock."

"The dog did that?"

Jared makes a face—some kind of weird expression that I don't get—then shakes his head. "That wasn't any ordinary dog."

"Are there any ordinary dogs around here?"

He just laughs and then hands me a cup again.

"Drink it. If I were here to hurt you I would have already done so."

I hold it.

"Drink."

So I do. The warm liquid that is probably tea, though it might also be Dream Juice, not only tastes wonderful but seems to both revive me and warm me up.

"Let me tell you a story, Chris."

"About what?"

"About my father. About his disappearance."

He pauses, looks at the door as if someone might be coming in at any minute.

"This could happen to you, too. So listen carefully."

4. TRUST

"What do you know about my father?"

"Uncle Robert?"

Jared nods and waits for an answer. The cabin we're in only has a couple of windows, and they're iced over, so it appears to be the middle of the night in this darkened room. I can hear the purring of wind outside. I shiver as I start to feel my toes again.

How'd I get here? I blacked out and then—then what? I recall an engine. Like a motorcycle. Or maybe ...

"Did we ride a snowmobile to get here?" I ask.

"What else could we have ridden in this weather? I had to strap you around me to keep you from falling off."

Part of me thinks he's making that up, just like the fact that he's Uncle Robert's son.

"I didn't know—Mom didn't even know he had any children."

"He never quite got around to sending out a birth announcement, not to mention staying around after I was born. Calling him my father—well, that's stretching it a bit. I only learned his identity after I turned twenty-one. By then, it was too late."

"Too late for what?"

"He was already missing. That's why I want—why I *need* to know everything I can about him. I need your help."

There's a part of me that doesn't like this. That doesn't like sitting here in another cabin with someone else I don't know, wondering what exactly is going on.

At least there are no dogs around here.

I think back to Midnight, who was curled up in a ball when I left her.

"All I know is my mom and Uncle Robert lived around here when they were younger. They moved after their mother died. Moved to the Chicago area, where my mom stayed. According to her, Uncle Robert went off to college but dropped out after their father died."

"And you've never seen him since?"

"I remember seeing him a few times. A few weekends. I remember jet-skiing with him when we went up to Michigan. Doing stuff like that."

"Why'd you and your mom come back?"

"What happened to him?"

"Answer my question first," Jared says.

"I'm tired of not knowing anything around here."

"Look, Chris, I'm only trying to help."

"Then tell me—"

"I don't know." The voice echoes off the walls. "I have no idea. That's why I need your help. Anything you know about where he might have gone."

I think of the items I found in Uncle Robert's closet. The gun, the iPod, the zip drive.

Don't tell him too much.

"Have you talked to my mother?"

The guy shifts his eyes in a way that isn't too settling.

"No."

"Why don't you?"

"Listen, Chris, you might not believe anything I'm saying, and that's fine. I get it because of—because of everything. But I know. I know what happened to her."

"What happened to who?"

He shakes his head as if he's already tired of this conversation. Or of me.

"What happened to Jocelyn."

"You know?"

The guy curses. "Yeah. A lot of people around here *know*. But you're never going to hear about it again."

"We have to get out of here and tell somebody. Anybody."

"Is that what you were trying to do?"

"Yeah."

"Were you able to dial 9-1-1? Or shoot off an email to someone? Anyone?"

I shake my head. A knot seems to be forming on the back of my head.

"The town is in shut-down mode. It's been like this before."

"Shut-down mode."

"The snow's only made it easier. Listen to me—there's nothing you can do."

I start to go off about what I think we should do, but Jared interrupts me right away.

"There's nothing you can do *now*."

"We have to talk to my mom."

"We can't do that."

"Why?"

"Because she's with them."

The firelight in the cabin illuminates the partial scruff on his face. I see the earnest look in his eyes; a guy not much older than I am, staring at me for help and answers.

"Look, man, I understand," he says. "My mom couldn't handle stuff and moved right after telling me about my father. Sometimes I think—I don't know. I think that something really bad happened to her here. The way it happens to a lot of people around here."

For a moment I get up and hold the coffee mug as if it might be a weapon I'm going to need any second. "You're lying."

"Chris, sit down."

"You're just another person in this crazy town who's trying to lie to me."

"And why would I do that? Now, especially?" His voice is calm and assured. He waits for me to sit back down and listen to him. "They don't know about me. And maybe—I don't know. I'd like to think that somehow that's why my father had nothing to do with me. He was protecting me. Wishful thinking, maybe. I'm not trying to do anything here but help you and find my father."

I'm tired from the overload on my brain.

"What do you mean, Mom is with them?"

"She knows. She knows everything."

"She knows about Jocelyn?"

He nods. "I'm not saying she wanted it to happen. There are a lot of people around here who don't like what's happening, but they have to put up with it. She's probably protecting you."

"There's no way."

"Why did you guys come back here?" he asks again.

"To get away from my father."

"Really? Why here? Why Solitary?"

"Because that's the only place my mom knows. She wanted to find Uncle Robert."

"Did you ever think that maybe she knew he was already gone?"

I sit in silence. The wind howls, and I feel like finding the nearest blanket and burying myself under it. I don't want to go outside anymore. I don't want to go anywhere.

"All I know is that your mother knows, Chris. I'm just searching for my father. And I'm worried—I'm worried that he still might be alive. For now."

I shake my head. The world feels dizzy.

This isn't really happening, is it?

"I don't get it," I said. "What's going on here? With this town? With everything?"

"I think it all got worse with that pastor. Pastor Marsh. When he came back, things started to happen."

"Came back from where?"

"I don't know—from exploring the world or something. He moved back to this town with ideas and plans. Big plans."

"For what?" My voice sounds hoarse.

"I think that an evil has hovered around this area for a long time. And he was the reason why it suddenly came back. With a vengeance."

"Why haven't you gone for help? Gotten out of this town and tried to get help?"

"Because my dad is missing, man. Plus, I tried. I went a few towns over to a guy that I know. Who's been in our house and eaten at our table. A guy I knew I could trust. And they'd gotten to him. I told him everything I knew—this was half a year ago. I told him about my father missing and then my mother taking off. And about others missing—high school students. The stories—stories that are shared in the middle of the night when nobody else is around. I

told him all this, and what does the guy do? He ends up reporting a
break-in at his house and claims it was me."

"What?"

"Yeah. And I—there's nowhere to go. Not yet. If I knew my
father wasn't alive, then I'd leave here. But that's what they do, Chris."

I think about what they told me. The warning on New Year's Eve.
That's what they do, Chris.

"So what are we going to do?" I ask.

"Listen to me, okay? You have to lie low. For a while."

"Have you been leaving me notes at school?"

He looks surprised at my question, then shakes his head. "What
kind of notes?"

"Just notes saying the same thing. To keep to myself. To stay out
of trouble."

"Not everyone around this town is like that pastor. The problem
is that you don't know who you can trust."

"Yeah, I know."

Jared shifts in his seat and hovers on the edge of it. "Listen,
Chris. You gotta trust me. We have to trust each other. Okay?"

For a moment I'm spiraling, doing somersaults down the side of
the mountain.

Then I nod.

I have to trust someone.

5. THE GHOST IN YOU

This should be our conversation:

"Where've you been?" Mom asks.

"I tried to go into town to reach the authorities to tell them about the ritualistic killing of the only girl I've ever loved in my sixteen years."

"And how'd that work out for you?"

"The big guy guarding the town sent his dog to attack me. Knocked me out, and when I came to I met my cousin, who told me not to trust you."

"Is that right? Hmm. What would you like for dinner? Campbell's soup or a bologna sandwich?"

Instead, our conversation goes something like this:

". . . . ."

Because when I come home, Mom is sleeping.

I think she was sleeping when I left.

Of course, in the world I'm living in, I check to make sure she's breathing. She is. I can smell that sweet sickly scent in her bedroom. The bottle of wine must've gone really well with her lunch.

Maybe that's why she's drinking so much. Guilt.

It's late afternoon, and the snow has died down. Jared drove me back home on his snowmobile, which should've been a lot more fun to ride. He didn't say much after we left his place or after we stopped at my driveway. Whatever sun is behind those clouds is already starting to fade away.

Like hope. Like peace.

I'm starving and think that soup and a sandwich sounds really awesome. For an appetizer.

I go into the kitchen. It's really narrow. I think back to our house in Libertyville. The one with the large island in the middle of the kitchen. The new appliances and the open area that fed into the family room. Perfect for entertaining.

This place is perfect for hibernating.

Back in our old house, I could escape my parents by going into the basement, which had a big television with a big couch in front of it. Even though this cabin is resting on what looks like stilts on the side of a mountain, there's no basement to escape to. There is no escape, not from here.

The silence gets to me. I don't remember there ever being a time when it was so dang quiet up north. The television was always on. I was always playing a video game or watching a show or listening to music or talking to my friends. Now the only echoes I hear are my own thoughts. And they're ones I really want to shut up.

The burner is the kind that slowly turns red instead of lighting up with gas. For a long time, I stand and stare at it. The silence feels like Styrofoam packaging surrounding me. I only wish I could be FedExed to a place far away.

My hope comes in Midnight.

The Shih Tzu belonged to Jocelyn, who kept her in an abandoned barn and went out once a day to check on her.

It's a wonderful thing, hope.

I can't believe she said that. And I still can't believe she's gone.

I hold the puppy as I lie in my room, listening to music. Still no Internet, no cable since it went out again, no lifeline to the rest the world. But I can lie on my bed with the angle of the ceiling showing just how narrow our rooftop really is, and I can listen to songs. I can escape with them. Or at least try to play them louder than my thoughts.

The album that's playing is The Psychedelic Furs' *Mirror Moves*. The lead singer has a heavy English accent, so heavy that it's hard to understand half of what he's saying. That's okay. I'll make up some lyrics that talk about an evil little town in the Smoky Mountains where ghosts whisper and zombies stroll about.

"Chris?"

Mom is standing at the door.

She's got a knife get out of here get out now!

My ludicrous thoughts are surely a result of some old cheese on my sandwich along with lack of sleep and lack of sanity.

I turn down the stereo.

"Where'd you go today?"

"Out."

She glances at me.

Mom doesn't look any different. Yet now all I can think about is what that guy Jared told me. It's crazy, but I really kinda believe him.

"Did you see Jocelyn?"

Her question seems honest and innocent.

I study her to see if I can detect anything.

If she knew, why would she ask that?

I nod.

"I'm surprised she can get around with the roads," Mom says.

"She has four-wheel drive in her Jeep."

She *had* four-wheel drive. She also had another four decades to live, if not more.

She had a life and a love and something special, and it was all taken away.

It was slit and cut out.

"Did you have enough for dinner?"

The subject of Jocelyn is passed over. Just like the storm outside. Just like everything in life.

"Yeah, I'm full."

"They'll probably call off school tomorrow."

"We won't know because our phone lines are down."

"Are they?"

I look at Mom. She really is clueless.

Maybe she knows something and maybe she doesn't. But this act of hers is no act. This is the booze show, and it's been showing up quite a bit. Slightly out of it, incredibly slow, massively disappointing. She makes some conversation that doesn't go anywhere, then says she'll be downstairs.

That's good, because I'm going to be here.

Right here in my room.

6. ECHOES

I dream of Jocelyn while I'm wide awake.

The wind whines outside while I'm stuck in this tiny raft in the middle of an ocean of darkness. I don't want to look at the clock to remind me how slowly time is passing. I can't imagine another day of this, let alone another year.

I remember riding next to her in her Jeep and listening to her talk over the music on the radio. I remember the day she drove me to the site where the old church once sat and where her parents were buried. I remember standing on the edge of the hill at the Grove Park Inn and looking out over the city and kissing her on the cheek and feeling like we were the only ones in the entire universe.

Something she said pricks me like a rosebush.

It's done I told her.

I thought it had been silly teen games and banter, but she was trying to tell me that it was more.

It's fine I said.

But her words haunt me. They laugh like an intruder in the closet, terrifying me but leaving me with no room for escape.

That's what you don't understand, she said. *It's not done. It hasn't even started yet.*

In the most forgotten hour of day or night, I remember.

And I realize something that's truly paralyzing: If this is how it all starts, where will it end?

7. TWO SURPRISES

The biggest surprise when I get back to school after a couple of snow days isn't some figure in a black robe and a pitchfork guarding the entrance to Mr. Meiners' classroom. It's not a bloody note in my locker saying *You did this.* It's not some clique of pale and glistening beautiful people that everybody and their brother should know are vampires.

No. It's when golden boy Ray Spencer comes up and asks me to try out for track.

What?

"Yeah, I heard over break that you were a pretty decent runner at your old school."

Of all the rumors that could have been circulating, *this* is what he ends up asking about.

I'm quiet and probably seem a bit standoffish because I still don't trust anybody, including this grinning homecoming king. Who once dated Jocelyn.

"What is it?" Ray asks. "Am I wrong?"

"Who told you I was on track?"

He laughs. He's wearing some new sweatshirt that's surely one of the fifty presents he opened on Christmas Day. "Is it some national secret?"

"I'm not a big fan of secrets," I say.

Ray chuckles and scratches his head. "Yeah, well, you moved to the wrong town. Okay—want to know the truth? I was looking you up online, and I saw some stuff on you at your old school. You ran track. Hurdles, right?"

"What were you trying to find out?"

It's the first time I've ever seen the guy look irritated. For a moment he looks like he might walk away, but then he shrugs.

"Look, I'm on the track team, and our team needs as much help as it can get. No big deal. I would have asked you over break, but I was traveling with our family the whole time."

"So you weren't around New Year's Eve?"

"No. Why?"

I try to see if he's lying. "Just curious."

"Haven't seen you at church either."

"Maybe the church thing isn't for me," I say.

"No big deal. So anyway, I was curious, so I googled you and looked up some info from your last school. Okay?"

Everybody isn't a criminal, Chris. Everybody's not to blame.

"Yeah, I ran hurdles. I'm fast but not that fast. My best event is the three-hundred-meter."

"That's awesome."

"Really?"

"Totally," Ray says. "That's a tough race. We haven't had anybody to run that. We're always getting blown out. And if you haven't noticed, we're not exactly into track. Football's the only sport anybody really cares about around here."

"I didn't even know there was a track team," I say.

"See—why do you think I was looking for another runner? I need more people who appreciate track."

"Are you the captain or something?"

He rolls his eyes and just then sees some of his buddies down the hall. "Just think about it, okay? Practice starts this week."

"Do I have to try out or anything?"

"No. If you've been on a team before, you'll be more than welcome on ours."

I see him walk away with the casual cool walk of someone who doesn't know failure.

I think I used to walk like that, back at my old school in Libertyville. It was easy to walk like that with a pack full of friends and a lawyer father who paid the bills even if he didn't pay attention to anything else.

I have to admit that I resent that walk. Quite a bit.

I wonder if I'll ever get it back.

One of the two people I've been waiting to see is walking toward me.

I wondered which one I'd see first. I was hoping to see Rachel, but instead I see her dark-souled sister.

I want to know if she knows. I want to see if she can see the truth, the truth that this school and this town and this air seem to be poisonous. But Poe looks away, as usual. She even appears to be heading past me without a hello.

I keep thinking that somewhere under the black eyeliner and pale skin and those fishnets and boots lies a girl who's just like any ordinary girl.

"Poe."

I stop as she keeps going.

Naturally.

· I turn and follow her and call out her name. When she finally turns, I see tears in her eyes.

She knows.

"Are you happy now?" she snaps.

The words bite. I would have been more prepared for her to slap me.

"Happy for what?"

"They're gone."

They? As in plural? Who's she talking about?

"Look—we have to—maybe we shouldn't—" I look around to see if anybody is watching us.

And yes, the usual audience is there. It's like this school employs a bunch of movie extras. *Okay, we'll pay you to linger and loiter around Chris and just stare and gawk and act like you have absolutely nothing else to do.*

"Get out of my face," she says. Or spits, more like it.

I notice a lip ring that appears to be something new.

"Poe."

"This is all your fault. I hope you're happy now."

I want to pull her back, but I know if I touch her I'll probably get belted.

So, two things I didn't expect on this first day back. An offer for track and all its glory. And being shunned by Poe, one of the only friends I assumed I had left.

There's Newt. Don't forget Newt.

I'm going to find that guy and sit him down and make him talk.

And then … well, then I'll figure something out.

Like what the heck Poe's talking about.

8. Empty Canvas

There is a gift in my locker.

No note this time. Not like the others I received, warning me, teasing me, messing with my mind.

No gun either. That nice little gift got me kicked out before the principal and the rest of the school realized that someone planted it.

I still don't know who did that. But that's only number 72 on the list of questions needing answers.

Today the gift is a picture.

I take it out and glance over my shoulder to see if anyone is watching me. Not that I can see.

It's a creased page from a magazine. A photograph of an ordinary road going into the woods. It looks like a colorful fall day. Could have been taken somewhere around here.

At the bottom of the page is something written in black ink. In Jocelyn's handwriting.

> *Two roads diverged in a wood, and I—*
> *I took the one less traveled by,*
> *And that has made all the difference.*

I'm pretty sure that's a famous poem, but I don't know who wrote it.

This was in Jocelyn's locker.

So why is it suddenly in mine?

As I close my door, I wonder what happened to the rest of her stuff.

More than ever before, except maybe on that first day of stepping into a semester already halfway through, I feel eyes on me. Watching and waiting. Wondering when I'm finally going to give up.

I think back to Jared's parting words when he dropped me off.

I'll be in contact with you. That's the way it has to be.

I wonder when I'll see him next.

All I know is that I'm supposed to say and do nothing. Just go with the flow. And that's what I'm doing.

It takes half the day before I find Newt. At lunch I finally sit across from him and give him a look that I hope conveys what I'm thinking.

A look that says *If you don't give me answers I'll do exactly what Gus Staunch did to you that first day I saw you being smeared across the school hallway.*

"Lunch might be the worst place ever to talk about stuff," he whispers as he smells his white-bread sandwich.

"Do you know?"

He looks one way, then the other. "I know enough."

I shake my head and motion my hands in a *So what now?* gesture. He takes a bite of the sandwich and then makes a face.

"Well?" I ask.

"Lunch is a time to eat."

"So when do I get the decoder that shows me how to look at the map to our secret meeting?"

"Don't get annoyed."

I laugh in disbelief. "This isn't 'annoyed.'"

"I didn't do anything." He's still talking in something barely above a mumble.

"I'm way past being annoyed."

As Newt's head moves up to face mine, I see his scar under the hard lighting of the cafeteria.

"I hope that doesn't mean you're going to be stupid," he says.

"Newt, man ..."

"After school, okay?"

"After school what?"

"After school."

"I can't just swing by your house, remember? I don't have a ride."

"You won't need a ride. Just—just meet me at the lockers and we'll go from there."

"Go where?"

He shakes his head and keeps eating.

I look around the room that's full of conversation and laughter, and I see Poe sitting at a different table than usual. Sitting by herself.

I sit in the art room and wonder how in the world I'm going to learn anything about art in this little town and this dead-end school. This is a new elective I'm taking. Maybe I should have taken computers or shop class. The art teacher, Mr. Chestle, sure looks artsy as he goes on about something or other.

I glance around the room to see if there's anybody I know. I recognize some faces from other classes, but nobody I know by more than a first name. There are more girls in the class than guys. A few look like freshmen, or more like sixth graders who decided to visit the high school for the day. There's that loudmouthed redheaded girl I generally try to avoid because she talks all the time. The hot dark-haired girl with her friends on either side. I need to avoid any and all hot dark-haired chicks from here on out until the end of my life. Which may be sooner than I think. There's a blond girl with glasses who easily could be a librarian. Or a witch. A librarian witch.

The blond is staring at me. She gives me a closed smile. As if she knows something.

I don't smile back. I think I probably look confused, irritated, maybe even a bit offended.

She glances away, and I continue checking out the class.

I look at the empty canvases all around the room just waiting to be filled.

I totally know I'm one of them.

It's going to be a long semester.

9. A WAY OF MAKING THINGS HAPPEN

I need to look on the bright side. It's the end of the day, and I haven't
been bullied by Gus. I haven't been suspended. Poe hasn't yelled at me
anymore (though we haven't spoken either). The only notable thing is
the absence of the other member of the threesome that came up to me
on the first day of school last October: Rachel. I figure she's just taking
an extra day or so coming back from vacationing in Colorado.

I'm waiting by my locker, a little nervous that Newt forgot what
he said at lunch, when I see him coming down the hallway.

"Ready?" he asks as he doesn't slow down.

I follow him outside, where it's now brutally cold. The snow hasn't
gone anywhere. It seems to have settled in, determined and suffocating.

"Where're we going?" I ask.

"Come on," he says.

I know that, like me, he doesn't have a license. Only one of us is
sixteen, however.

Loser.

Maybe there's a car waiting for us. Maybe it's Jared. This will
be our first meeting of the secret underground something-or-other.
We'll meet at Jared's cabin and come up with crazy theories and eat
lots of really bad food and maybe play some video games.

Instead, we walk up to a station wagon waiting for us. Or, as it
turns out, waiting for Newt. The man behind the wheel looks way
too old to be Newt's father.

"Come on, get in," Newt says.

When I'm in the backseat, he introduces me to the driver. "Grandpa, this is one of my buddies. Sam."

For a second, I wonder if his grandfather is called Sam. But then the driver calls out my name, or what he thinks is my name, with a cordial Southern accent.

"Where are you from, Sam?"

Newt glances back at me just to give me some bit of a heads-up.

"Oh, I'm, uh, from up north. But now I live just outside of town."

"That right? Whereabouts up north?"

"New York," I say. It's just the first thing out of my mouth. I know I don't sound like I'm from New York. I'm trying to think of more of the story when Newt's grandfather starts talking to him about his day.

"Sometimes Grandpa picks me up when my parents can't," Newt tells me.

The more I listen to his grandfather, the more he sounds like any ordinary old guy. Slower and more reflective, without much of a care in the world.

Soon I find myself in Newt's basement, just like the other time I went over to his house to try and learn a few things. His grandfather is somewhere upstairs, babysitting or maybe just sticking around to see what he can find in the pantry.

"Do you know what happened to her?"

Newt shakes his head. The door to the basement is closed, and he must know that nobody is around. He's finally not telling me to hush.

"I know what happened," I say.

I'm like a convict who wants to confess to the judge and jury and get the crime off his chest.

"Chris."

"What?"

"Just—just listen. The less you tell me, the less I know."

I don't quite get that logic. "What's that mean?"

"You need to tell people who can do something about it."

"But—why'd you bring me here?"

"I know that Jocelyn is gone. That she moved."

"Newt, she died!"

He doesn't give me a white-faced, shocked glance. He knows.

This whole freaking town knows.

"She died. I saw her die. She died right in front of me. You don't get it. You don't understand."

I take a deep breath and wait.

"The official word is that Jocelyn and her aunt moved."

"She didn't move," I say.

"I'm just telling you this so you know."

I guess if you've been living in the insanity that is Solitary for so long, you'd be able to appear as nonchalant as Newt.

"The stuff that happened with Wade—people believe that her aunt had enough and disappeared."

"People really believe that?"

"Not everybody knows the truth, Chris. Not everybody around here is—"

"Crazy?" I say, then add a few more colorful descriptions.

"Not everybody knows. Not everybody is a part of them."

"We have to do something."

"I'm doing all I can," Newt says. "And this is it."

I look around at the basement.

So you told me Jocelyn's officially missing. Great. Fabulous. Thanks. A lot.

"Rachel is gone too."

For a second I think he means she's gone, like Jocelyn is gone. That someone killed Rachel.

"She moved with her family."

"What?"

Newt nods. "They have a way of making things like this happen."

"Things like what?"

"People disappearing. People moving. People moving on."

I think of what Jared said about Uncle Robert and his mother. One disappeared and one "moved on."

"Jocelyn didn't *move*. Do you get it?"

"Don't get angry at me. I hear you. But Rachel *did* move."

"Why?"

"Because she knows too much and cares too much."

"She's not the only one who cares."

"Caring is a dangerous thing around here," he says.

"That why you're talking like a robot?"

The guy with the messy hair and the face of a ten-year-old shoots me a glance that I actually admire. It's a look that's the equivalent of a curse word.

"There are reasons why I remain quiet."

I think of the scars he has on the outside. I wonder if he carries just as many on the inside.

"So, what? Just like that? Rachel is gone?"

"Just like that. It's that easy."

"She didn't say good-bye."

"She couldn't."

Now I know why Poe was so angry.

But I had nothing to do with this. It wasn't my fault.

"Do you know where she is?"

"No."

"But why then—I was there—I saw it happen. I was there, Newt. I saw them. I saw what they did. Yet they let me go."

"I know."

"That doesn't make sense. Why make Rachel and her family move? What about me? What about my mother?"

"I don't know. I really don't."

I think of telling him about Jared. But Jared told me not to tell another person.

Don't trust anybody, Chris.

There's no need to tell Newt about Jared.

"What are we supposed to do?" I ask him.

"There's no 'we,'" he says. "I'm not in this equation."

"Then what am I supposed to do?"

"If I were you, I'd get as far away from this place as I could."

10. TAKE A DEEP BREATH

In town, in the heart of this beating Zombieville, after Newt and his chauffeuring grandfather drop me off in front of the restaurant where Mom works, I still think about doing it. I can see the door just down the street, the one with the sign that says *Sheriff* on it, and I contemplate going through it.

Last time I went in there, one of the sheriff's deputies threatened me.

Maybe Sheriff Wells will be there now. Maybe his invitation to contact him if anything "funny" happens is still applicable.

Yeah, a lot of funny things have happened, Sheriff. A lot.

I still have his business card. I still have his cell phone number.

I also would bet a hundred bucks he knows more than I do and that sweet Southern attitude is nothing more than cologne doused to cover up the stench.

It's freezing outside, and that's what makes up my mind.

When I go inside Brennan's Grill and Tavern, I find things a lot more warm and cozy. Not just for me, but for Mom and the guy she's talking to at the end of the bar.

Is that what a hostess does?

Then I see her raise her glass, and I assume she's off the clock or else this place really has a good benefits plan. A couple coming out of the restaurant partially blocks my view, making me invisible for the moment. I think what a cool concept, to really be invisible.

Considering the fact that she's drinking it up without a word from me, I'm already halfway there.

I slip out the door and back into the cold.

It's already dark out, even though it's just around six. I have no idea what the forecast is except for doom and gloom.

I pause and glance down the sidewalk at the buildings lined together. Across the street in the darkness lie the train tracks. Maybe I'll walk down past the rusty railroad signal, head into the woods, and find the barn that Jocelyn showed me, the one where she kept Midnight.

Maybe Jocelyn's ghost haunts the old farmhouse. Maybe I'll just set up camp there for a while, just me and Midnight, until warmer weather comes and I can finally make sense of everything.

There's nothing to make sense of, Chris.

Am I going to live in this cold darkness for the next six months? The next year and a half? Enough's enough. I start walking toward the sheriff's office.

Night is coming. Night is coming for us all.

This is exactly like my father telling me not to do something. Every single time he did, I managed to go right ahead and do it. The same with my guidance counselor. The same with my friends.

I hear the warnings in the wind as I reach the door, expecting to find it locked.

It's open.

I hear the siren sound as I enter the building. I expect to find Deputy Ross chewing his gum and getting ready to backhand me before sending me back outside. Instead, I see the sheriff.

"Chris," he says.

He's standing with a cup of coffee in his hand. Busy day at work, obviously.

"I need your help," I blurt out before I can persuade myself not to.

"What's wrong?"

"Everything. Everything's wrong. Everything, starting with Jocelyn."

"It's okay, just relax. You okay? Your mother okay?"

"Yeah, I'm fine. She's more than fine. We're fine."

"And Jocelyn?" He looks at me with a grim face.

Whatever I say next could have major consequences.

Don't do it, man. Feel him out. See if he acts like he knows more than he does. Just wait before you—

"Jocelyn's dead. She's dead, and I saw it with my own eyes. I swear. I know that sounds crazy, but I saw it. I saw everything. I know it, and I don't care who I have to tell. I'm going to tell it if it's the last thing I do."

I take a deep breath and feel like passing out.

Way to think about things, buddy.

Sheriff Wells remains composed and cool as he puts down his mug and tells me to have a seat. I've seen enough cop shows to know that he's gotta be careful. He doesn't know if I'm high as a kite and did it myself.

"Look, I know how this sounds," I say.

"Do you?" he asks.

And I search to see if there is any sort of hint, any sort of tone, any kind of giveaway. Does he know? Could he know? Am I making a mistake?

"Go on, have a seat," he says in his thick accent.

The sheriff is wearing a short-sleeved uniform shirt even though it's winter and quite chilly even inside his office. He doesn't seem to mind. As I sit at a desk, I keep wondering if Kevin or someone else is around.

"This better not be some kind of joke, Chris."

He says it in a manner that seems to mean *especially not after the kind of day I've had.* He looks tired, at least from what I can tell. His thick goatee is unruly, the stubble on his face a few days old.

I think of the first time I saw him, the night when my mother was drugged and knocked out in her car after work. All so that they could prove a point and send us—and me—a message.

"Ross told me you were in shortly after Christmas looking for her."

"That's right." I can feel my heart beating against my tongue and gums. Maybe I should tell him about Ross threatening me.

I almost do.

"Why do you think something happened to her?"

"*Know.* I know what happened to her."

"How do you know?"

"I was there. It was New Year's Eve."

His gaze dims. "That was four nights ago."

I nod.

"What did you do, son?"

"I didn't do anything. I found her. It was a group of men. Or people, I don't know. Like some Ku Klux Klan meeting. Men in robes. They killed her. I found her not far from where she lived. On a mountain ridge. A place with a bunch of rocks. Her throat was cut and so were her wrists. She was dead. They burned her body and told me if I told anybody someone else would be harmed. Someone like my mother or my father."

"Slow down, Chris. Take a deep breath."

"I'm not making this up."

"Why didn't you come in here right away?"

"I don't—I couldn't. I tried. I mean—I was afraid. My mom—I didn't know what to do."

"Did you tell your mother?"

"No."

"Why not?"

"Because—because I was—did you just hear what I said?"

He nods. I don't see him strapping on a gun and getting a rifle and calling reinforcements.

Does he even believe me?

"I'm not making this up."

"So who did this? Who were these people you saw?"

"I have some ideas."

"Like what?"

"I don't know—I just—I don't know who around this place I can trust. People have told me not to trust anybody. Including you. So I just—I couldn't contact anybody. Then the storm came and just shut down everything. Almost like—almost as if it was deliberately done. And I didn't know what to do."

The sheriff gives me a serious look. "I've had a lot of strange stuff come through these doors in my time here, Chris."

"It's Staunch. I know it. It's gotta be. And—and a whole bunch of other people, too."

He nods and waves his hand. "Look, Chris. Let's do this, okay? Let's go take a drive."

"Where?"

"To this place you're talking about."

"But I—I'm sure it's gone. I mean, the snow. I'm sure she's not there."

"So what do you want me to do, then? Go chase down men in robes?"

"I'm not making this up," I say.

"I'm just suggesting we go for a drive and you show me. I can take a look around."

"Should you call anybody?"

He shakes his head without even thinking about it. The look he gives me is unsettling.

You know something, but you can't tell me, right?

I suddenly wish I hadn't come in here.

Just like I wish I hadn't waited until it was too late to save Jocelyn.

"Come on. I'll take you home afterward."

I'm about to say something like *You just don't get it* or *This is serious, this isn't some funny game,* but instead I just stand and follow him outside.

The door shuts, and I watch the sheriff lock it.

As if he's hiding something.

As if he's about ready to bury something.

Something, or someone.

11. STORIES AND TROUBLES

The evening swallows the squad car. We drive slowly toward Jocelyn's home. Toward the place she used to live. The place where she used to breathe and eat and sleep.

The sheriff has sports radio on in the old car that smells like cigarettes and old man's aftershave. The lights cut into the dark woods we pass as we drive in silence for a few minutes.

"And you've had no contact with Jocelyn since when?" He obviously is not buying what I have to sell.

"Since—since I don't know when. Right after Christmas."

"When you came in to report her missing."

"I found her. I know what happened to her."

"Yeah, okay, but let me just ask you this, Chris. You come to a new town and you fall for the pretty girl. In a span of just over a month, let's recount what happens. They find a revolver in your locker."

"Didn't belong to me."

"You have numerous run-ins with Gus Staunch. A reason not to like the Staunch family, who lives right next to you. Someone attacks your mother—chloroforms her, for cripes' sake. Could be anybody. Could be people just scaring off the newcomers. Then I come to find out that you've turned into some vigilante with another gun that you've fired to save the pretty little girl from her wicked step-uncle, or whatever that greasy little Wade was."

What are you saying, Sheriff?

I keep quiet with my face hidden in the darkness, looking at him.

"A lot of others, people like Ross, people who don't have patience like I do—a lot of them would've already handled this situation."

"What situation?"

"You, Chris. The situation of you."

"I didn't do anything."

"Why don't we find Wade and ask him? I'm sure he'd say you did something."

"So you don't believe me?"

"Ross gave me a nice little write-up about you at your last school. I didn't ask him to do that—he went snooping around on his own. But it seems to me that drama follows you around."

I say it again. "I'm not making this up."

The sheriff nods gently, then remains quiet until we pull up to the small house. It's dark and untouched, with snow covering it like a concrete casing. No tracks can be seen anywhere on the driveway. No footprints in the snow, nothing.

The sheriff keeps the car running as the headlights beam down on the door.

"I've been by this house several times now since you came in to see me, since your little talk with Ross. Nobody's been around. Jocelyn and her aunt disappeared. I've spoken with Helen twice. Once just today."

I feel like I'm back at Six Flags Great America on that falling chair ride. My stomach's still hovering in the air as I'm dropping to the ground.

"Where is she?"

"Not she, Chris. They. *They* are in Florida."

"No."

"Now look here." He turns to me, and I suddenly have the urge to open the door and run away. "I'm not from around here. Just like you, I moved when I was in high school. This was when I lived in Kentucky years ago. So I get it. I get it. These people—they just don't like outsiders. Many Southerners don't. They act charming with their 'aw shucks' attitude, but they can be cold and mean. But the days of the Klan are gone, Chris. They're not around here."

"I saw them. I'm not—why would I make up something like that?"

"Because teen love can cause you to do a lot of things. Some pretty stupid."

He thinks this is because of ... teen love?

Seriously?

Boy, you picked this wrong.

I wonder if Jared is watching me. Or if he knows.

I'm sure he's probably wondering what in the world I did.

The sheriff doesn't know. He really doesn't know.

Unless he's the best actor in the world.

"That place you're referring to—it exists. It's called The Grounds, and it's got a bit of a legend around it. With the stones and all that. Kids like to go there. And something tells me Jocelyn took you there. Maybe for something more than just ghost hunting, right?"

I feel my bottom lip grow heavy. I really want to tell this guy what I'm thinking. But I don't.

I keep quiet.

This is my fault.

"Now listen to me, Chris. Okay? If there is any more trouble coming from your direction—whatever it might be—I'm going to become the not-so-patient guy. People rarely see that, but they don't like it when they do. Do you understand?"

Someone else said those very same words to me.

"Yes," I say.

But I don't understand, and I've never understood.

That's part of being a teen. Not understanding, trying to figure it out.

"I mean it, Chris," he says. "I really mean it. You go about your business, and you leave your stories and your troubles to your imagination. I'm not saying that it's easy being a newcomer, but you gotta go with the flow."

"Okay."

Yeah, I get it.

Stay quiet and stay put.

Walk around like everything's okay.

Wipe the blood off my hands and mind my own business.

The sheriff pulls the car back out of the driveway and heads toward my cabin.

12. OPTIONS

The reminders only bring me down.

The leather wristband that I'm wearing.

The photo printout of the two of us on Christmas Day.

The last letter she wrote to me. Maybe the last letter she ever wrote.

I want a new story, a different installment, a new character, a change of scenery and score. How about a new producer and director as well?

That night after Sheriff Wells takes me home with a good-ole-boy threat, I try to figure out my options.

I torched option A, which was remaining quiet.

I burnt option B, which was telling someone I trust.

Option C, the Newt option, is gathering my things and running away.

Option D is doing nothing. Doing what pretty much everybody's been telling me to do from my very first step into this tiny town.

I'm going to write a book called *Choose Your Own Misery.* If you choose to go walking in the woods, go to page 54. If you choose to spy on the creepy neighbors, go to page 72. If you choose to sit alone in your room, go to page 38.

All the pages will have the same result, of course.

Misery.

I don't want to listen to any music tonight. I don't want to do my homework or read anything or try and see if the Internet is finally working.

I'm petting Midnight and realizing he's the only living and breathing thing I can trust.

I'm not scared.

Jocelyn's words are an anchor in this murky wilderness, weighing me down, imprisoning me.

This whole dark world needs hope.

I don't trust anybody or anything, and that includes the hope that she spoke about.

It's a nice little thought. It's sweet for a Sunday morning to tell to a bunch of kids right before giving them candy. But this is the real world, and it's not for babies. It's time I grew up and smelled the scent of reality.

The smoke rises in the distance and the voices hush and the darkness falls and the lies continue.

This has nothing to do with me. Nothing at all.

So I believe.

So I hope.

13. Utterly Ridiculous

Good-byes never go as well as you'd like them to. I know this from when I left Libertyville three months ago. Three months that seriously feel like three years.

Half of the guys I was friends with never even officially said good-bye. There weren't any fond farewells or moving hugs. I mean—we're guys. A few said things like "see you around" or "take it easy." Really moving things like that. The stuff of Hallmark cards.

Right.

Even Brady, who drove me home from school that last time and dropped me off in front of the house I'd be leaving the next day, had little to say.

"Well, later, loser. Give me a holler sometime."

So I'm not expecting the letter I get in the mail. I've already moved on. I've already said good-bye in my own guy way.

But I guess—well, I *know*—that girls are different.

The letter is from Rachel. One of the three who came up to me that first day. The most talkative of the trio. The most friendly. And the one who in reality got me together with Jocelyn.

I'm afraid to open it. I don't know if she knows the truth. If she doesn't, then everything I'm going to read will be missing that big, gigantic (and bloody) elephant in the proverbial room. Yet if she does, I don't want to hear what she has to say.

I don't want to hear anybody else's "sorry." I'm tired of saying it over and over myself.

It's Thursday, and Mom isn't home. Surprise. I take the letter to my room simply because it feels private. I can shut the door and at least hear someone coming up the stairs.

> Hey, Chris!
> I just wanted to write you a letter to say good-bye. I've tried calling half a dozen times and either have the wrong # or something's wrong with your line. As you probably have heard by now, my family has moved. I never thought I'd be this sad to leave somewhere, but I am. I'm sorry that I didn't have the chance to say good-bye.
> Jocelyn told me right before Christmas that her crazy aunt had had enough, and they

were leaving. She said you didn't know. I just hope and pray that you're taking everything okay. I can't imagine—coming to a school and then having your friends leave so soon after. Having Jocelyn leave.

I hope you stay in touch with her. I really do.

I'm going to leave you my email and address at the bottom, so I hope you stay in contact.

You know what I really hope? I hope you get the heck out of that place.

I still can't believe how sudden everything was. As if my parents didn't see this coming too. But my dad's getting a huge pay increase and we're moving back to Colorado. I've wanted that for a while. I'm excited. I'll be able to catch a few great months of skiing.

Listen—one other thing. About Poe. Behind the dark makeup and the crabby demeanor and all that is a really beautiful girl. Inside and out. I say that because she's on her own too. She's not too happy—not with me or with life in general. And I know that for some crazy reason she blames you. But she'll get over it.

There's more to Poe than meets the eye.

Drop me a line sometime.

Stay cool. And don't let the place drag you down.

Rachel

I hold the letter and reexamine the words.

They mock me.

Just like this place and everybody in it.

I hope you stay in touch with her.

It's ridiculous. Utterly ridiculous.

Maybe I need to get a Ouija board and communicate with the dead. Or, better yet, I can find whatever those weird cards were that the students were playing with at Ray's party and join in and perhaps get a joker card that explains all of this.

I glance at the address and the email at the bottom.

Then in one swift motion, I tear up the letter. Again. And again. Until I have it in as many little pieces as possible.

Then I go outside onto the deck and toss the paper flakes into the angry winds, watching them disappear to the shadowy grounds far below.

14. THE SIGHTING

The next day, Friday morning, one more day before a mini-break that to me is the equivalent of a smoke break outside the prison doors, I find a note in my locker.

Of course I do.

Whenever I get a cell phone, maybe in like ten years, I'm going to be flooded with creepy and strange texts.

But for now, it's good old-fashioned pen and paper.

Turns out this note is signed. That's good because most of the notes I get are from Anonymous.

> Take a walk down your street and head toward town tomorrow morning around 10. Maybe someone will come pick you up.
>   Jared

So school isn't off limits to him.

I wonder if I can wait until then. I have a lot more questions I want this guy to answer.

Turns out someone else has some questions for me.

I'm approached by the poster child for the model high school student. Ray comes up to me and barely says hi before asking me about track.

"Oh, yeah." I'd totally forgotten. "Yeah, I'm thinking about it."

"So why didn't you come? We need you, man."

"Next week, then."

I'm so assertive. So strong.

"Monday. Hey, you coming to church?"

And for some reason, one I can't really explain, I nod.

Nod as in saying yes.

Nod as in saying *Yes, I'd love to come back to your place for crazy people.*

He tells me he'll see me then and leaves. For a moment I wonder what I've just done, then I realize that I want to go. I really *want* to go back to the church.

Maybe some of my questions will be answered. Maybe they'll be answered without my having to go search and find them.

After my class gets out for lunch, I see Jocelyn.

She's walking in the crowds.

I'm not imagining this. I see her. Same height. Same dark hair that falls below her shoulders. The way she moves through the other students.

I almost shout out her name.

Instead I grab the arm of the guy in front of me to move him aside, then I bolt past a few girls.

It's her, I know it.

But when I tug at her arm and see the face turning toward me, I know.

It's a mirage in the middle of a desert.

A ghost in the middle of a dream.

The girl who turns has a more round face, different eyes, different everything. She's cute, and she looks perplexed and amused. Her hair is different—not even the same color.

What are you doing, Chris?

She looks at me like I have a fungus, and I recoil as if I do. I see others looking my way, surely wondering and thinking the same things they've always been thinking.

There's the new guy, still fumbling around and acting loony, still attracting attention.

"I'm sorry," I say to the girl who is definitely not Jocelyn.

She walks on, and for a moment I stand in the middle of the hallway, a rock in the center of the stream. Then, as I turn to head to the cafeteria, I see Poe.

Watching me.

"Hey," I call out.

But she disappears down the hallway and into the girls' room. And as much as I'd like to talk to her, I've already made a fool of myself today.

"Is that yours?"

I don't even notice the girl in front of me asking the question. At first I wonder if she's even talking to me, then notice the eyes behind the little glasses looking my way.

"What?" I blurt.

"The painting—is that yours?"

She's got her hand on the mess that's my painting. Monet would roll in his grave.

"Oh, yeah, sure, thanks," I say, reaching to grab it.

She seems to want to help, but instead I jostle it away from her and somehow I end up pulling the canvas over her arm. She's wearing a very ordinary pink sweater that suddenly doesn't look very ordinary with the black streaks on the sleeve.

"Oh, man, I'm sorry," I say.

"It's fine. Really."

Her face is splashed just like her arm, but with a distinct color of red. She shakes her head and acts like a mouse just wanting to scamper away. She takes her painting, which was right next to mine in the shelves, and walks to her place.

I roll my eyes and sigh. Even when I don't try, I do things to make people not like me.

"Can I …" I start to say, but I don't really know what I can do. She's not going to take off the sweater. Not in class.

I watch the girl go to her spot in the room. A few minutes into class, I glance her way.

She's a quiet girl. All I know about her is that her name is Kelsey Page and she's a junior, like me.

Wonder if she lives in Solitary. Wonder if she knows.

I wonder if any of these kids know. Maybe they all do. Maybe they're walking around and thinking, *There's Jocelyn's guy, the poor sap that was pulled into her little web, the guy from Chicago who doesn't belong here.*

Kelsey brushes back her blond hair gently with the arm that I painted. I almost want to laugh. I still feel awful. I'm surprised she didn't go try to clean it.

My painting is supposed to be of a cabin in the woods, but it looks like a candy bar that's been sitting in the sun for an hour. It's one big goopy mess.

At one point in class, as I get some more paint, I see Kelsey passing by me.

"Hey, sorry, really," I say.

"It's okay."

She looks away. I can tell that she doesn't talk to guys much. Or maybe she just doesn't talk.

"At least it looks better than my painting," I say, trying to be funny.

"What does?"

"Your arm."

This gets a smile.

I notice for the first time that she's got braces, the clear kind but visible enough to probably cause her to try and hide them.

It's more than just a smile, however. For me it's a peace offering.

I don't want every single person in this building to think I'm a moron.

The glance I get from Kelsey makes me think that no, she doesn't think so.

Then again, the smartest thing for her or any other girl in this school to do is to stay far away from me.

15. LOST

When I get home, I can't find Midnight. It takes me five minutes of calling out her name and looking around the house before I admit she's missing. It takes another five seconds for me to go completely bonkers.

Mom's not home. This is something I already knew. I race up the stairs and go into my bedroom again, looking in the closet and under the bed and in the covers. I scan the bathroom quickly again, then look in the small room that's used for storage, even though we have nothing to store.

Midnight's nowhere to be found.

I call her name. Over and over and over again. Each time I get louder. Each time I sound more terrified.

"Midnight!"

I look everywhere. In my mom's room, in her bathroom, in our kitchen, in the laundry room. It's not like this is a huge mansion or anything.

I search the kitchen cabinets. I even find myself opening one above the counter, and then I stop myself when I realize that dogs can't fly.

Maybe they can in Solitary.

"Midnight!"

I go outside on the deck that is cleared but still a bit slippery, and I call out her name. It's getting dark. I scan the road below.

For a second I begin to think bad thoughts. Awful thoughts.

I picture Jocelyn.

No please no.

I begin to hear the thoughts. The judging, condemning words. I see the pointed finger. The eyes of shame and blame.

"Midnight!"

The ten minutes feel like my body being stretched out ten more inches. My hands and legs are attached to separate chains, and they're being pulled separate ways.

If she got out and roamed away I might never find her again.

I feel sick. Really physically sick.

I shout her name over and over like a crazy person, and in fact I'm shouting so loud I don't hear the noise until I stop to take a breath.

A scratching sound.

It's the last gasp of a dying dog before she departs.

Then I hear a little whimper of a bark.

That's outside. No, wait, it's inside.

I go back inside through the open door. The scratching is coming from the kitchen.

Then I realize that it's coming from the back door. I grab the handle, and it turns—something it doesn't do when it's locked.

Dogs can't open and close doors.

When I open it, I see the black little Shih Tzu standing there wagging her tail and looking up at me with a mischievous face. I pick her up and bring her face to mine.

She's fine, besides feeling a little cold. As she licks my face, I realize that she's also licking tears.

16. DON'T

Chris.

The voice hovers, yet isn't audible. It's in my head, in my dream. I open my eyes to familiar darkness, to familiar silence. I move and sit on the edge of the narrow mattress—one day I'm bound to turn and fall right off of it. I sit and wait.

Chris.

It's Jocelyn's voice, crashing in like a wave at high tide. I'm half asleep still, my eyelids shutting and staying shut, then opening again.

I need to talk to you.

I get up and walk down the stairs. Somewhere in the darkness at the foot of my bed, Midnight must surely be wondering what I'm doing. I wouldn't be able to tell her if she asked.

The steps creak, but creaks can't awaken the dead or the drunk. Actually, I'd bet that I'm more likely to talk to the dead. Ritualistic killing is one thing, but bad vodka is another.

You're growing so cynical and so mean.

It's her voice, but it's really mine warped into the memory of her words. It has to be. I'm awake, and I know what's going on.

You don't have a clue.

I stand for a second, wondering if I'm supposed to go out. She sounds like she's outside on the deck, outside in the cold night.

As I reach for the handle, I feel a gust of wind, and I shiver.

Get a coat, stupid. And some shoes.

So I do.

Then I go outside.

The air isn't just cold. It's hard and empty. It's so cold that it's hard to breathe, hard to think.

I can see the deck and the dropping terrain underneath me just fine in the light of the liquid moon. I don't see a ghostly apparition hovering anywhere. I don't see someone flying on a broom. I don't see anything unusual.

Except the shadow of the approaching figure.

And I turn and see Jocelyn walking toward me.

"Jocelyn?" I ask.

Her face hides under a fur-lined hood, the smile impossible not to see. A scarf covers her neck, her face so beautiful and angelic. I guess ghosts or visions or dream dates still have to wear warm clothes. Wouldn't want to catch a cold.

You're not dreaming.

I'm so cold and the voice sounds so real and maybe I'm not dreaming, maybe I'm really outside talking to myself or whoever this is.

It's me.

I go to touch her, but she pulls back.

Don't. Just—just look at me and listen.

"You're so beautiful."

Listen.

"What is this?"

There is a place that is somewhere between every day and every dream, a place like this.

This doesn't feel like either every day or every dream.

Not everybody can see it, but when you can, you have to take the light with the darkness.

I shake my head and reach out to touch her, but this time she shouts an emphatic *no!*

I can't help you in any way or give you anything you don't have or don't know.

As I glance at her, I can't help thinking that of course she can't give me anything I don't have or don't know because this is a dream.

Your mother needs you.

I nod. That's nice to hear. The whole world knows that.

No, she really needs you, Chris. Don't.

I wait for more.

"Don't what?" I eventually ask.

Don't.

I'm still waiting.

It's good to see you.

"Is this all—is this happening?"

Don't let anybody tell you you're not.

"I'm not what?"

She smiles, reaches out her hand, and goes to touch my lips with her finger.

Then I blink, and just like that, she's gone.

But I felt something, a slight little tap on the edge of my mouth.

I don't wake up in bed.

I'm still here, standing on the edge of the deck. I stay there for a while, watching the moon and feeling the chill and desperately longing for Jocelyn to come back.

17. REACHING OUT

"Have you thought about getting a job?" Mom asks me the next morning as I'm wolfing down a bowl of cereal.

"Sure," I say.

"Have you thought long and hard about it?"

I nod, but we both know I'm lying.

"You're going to have to start saving money, Chris."

"For what? A car? Gotta get a license first. And I'm still waiting to take a driver's ed class."

"You have to plan things out."

Oh, like you plan anything out.

"Yeah," I say.

"I want you to start looking, okay? It'd be good for you."

Oh, okay, and you know what would be good for you? Sobriety.

As I get ready to head out the door, she asks me where I'm going.

"Just out. Hanging out with a guy from school."

"What's his name?"

"Jerry," I say.

Yeah, that's a lie. Kinda maybe. I mean, maybe Jerry is short for Jared.

"What are you going to do?"

"When did you get home last night?" I ask.

"I don't know. Late. Brennan's was packed."

"Did you stay later?"

She looks at me with a confused and hurt and slightly irritated look. "Chris—"

"Questions are great, aren't they?"

"Don't be like that."

"Then you don't," I say.

"I'm just asking what you're going to be up to."

"I don't know. Maybe just hanging out."

"Be careful," she says.

My mother has never been the type to say things like that, not with me.

But Solitary has changed everything.

The sun seems to be helping melt some of this snow and ice. The temperature from the middle of the night/morning when I had whatever sort of thing I had with Jocelyn seems to have been a dream. I walk on the street just like I'm supposed to and wonder when everything's going to get nice and mushy.

I've been walking for a while and see that it's ten minutes after ten, and I'm just wondering if I've gone down too far and should turn back when I hear a vehicle—the first I've heard today.

A blue truck pulls up next to me. Sure enough, I see Jared at the wheel. I open the door and get inside.

"How's it going?" he asks.

As if we're going into town to shoot some pool and pick up some chicks.

"Haven't been threatened yet today, so things are looking up," I say, trying to sound like I'm taking all of this with humor and coolness.

Jared doesn't smile.

He probably knows that deep inside, underneath this really cool and composed exterior, is a teenager who is pretty much freaking out beyond anything his mind and heart can comprehend.

"You have breakfast?"

"I could eat more," I say.

"Good. There's a little diner that serves awesome food."

"But?"

"But what?"

"But there's gotta be a catch. Around here there's always a catch."

"The catch is that it's cheap and I've been eating there all my life and their omelets are to die for."

"That's not my favorite expression."

He glances at me and chuckles. "You're a witty one this mornin', aren't you?"

"I used to be a lot more witty." I think of my mother and of our last conversation and realize she's not the only one who's changed.

"Just relax, okay? We got some talkin' to do."

He turns up the radio, and a country singer belts out a loud and wild song about a loud and wild night.

When I grow up I want to be this singer and have his life. I want to sing about the ladies and the long nights.

Maybe I'll move to Texas. Or Alabama. Or Tennessee. Or Georgia. Anywhere but here.

Anywhere but this tiny ugly town.

I guess I'm hungrier than I realized. The meal isn't just food. In some weird way, it's relief.

"You like grits?" Jared asks.

"With butter on them, sure."

"Sometimes I wonder what life would be like if I had never tasted grits. You ever think about things like that?"

"Grits?"

He shakes his head. "Life. Destiny. The big-picture stuff."

"What's that have to do with grits?"

"If I'd been raised in California or New York, I wouldn't know the wonderful and mesmerizing thing called grits."

What is he saying?

"Do you ever think what life would have been like if you'd been raised around here?"

I swallow and laugh. "Maybe I wouldn't know any different. Maybe I'd be like the rest of them."

"I don't think so."

I wait for him to say more, but he just sips his coffee and watches me.

"Tell me about school."

"You've been there," I say. "You've seen the place."

"I used to go there. What I mean is—anything strange going on?"

I tell him about Rachel's disappearance, though I don't tell him about her letter. I mention that Poe is blaming me for her two friends disappearing. "They don't know that she's dead."

"Want to hear a story, Chris?"

I shrug.

Honestly, I'm not sure, because stories around here are not the warm and fuzzy kind that make your heart go boom boom.

"I never bothered to go to college, but I read a lot. You don't need school to learn. I was reading this book about World War II. Did you know that a lot of Germans—the good Germans, the ones who weren't with the Nazis, the ones just trying to live their lives— still knew what was happening in their backyard?"

"With killing the Jews?"

"With the Holocaust. People who couldn't do a thing about it. People who had to just keep living."

"You can always do something," I say. "I don't believe you just sit by and watch something like that happen."

"That's what heroes say."

"Is that bad?"

"Heroes end up dead."

I'm about to snap back at his comment when a heavyset woman interrupts our conversation to pour Jared more coffee. He lets her walk out of listening distance.

"Look—I can't say it's *bad*," he says. "But *foolish*, well … it's something that my father probably said. And now he's missing."

"What was he trying to do?"

"I don't know. Have you found anything on him in that house? Any information?"

"Lots of eighties records," I say.

Why don't you mention the other things?

"Any clues will help. I know that somebody was helping him, giving him information."

Why don't you also mention that lady in the shades who picked you up in the expensive SUV and told you she was a friend of your uncle?

But again, another voice, or maybe not a voice, but a feeling or premonition prevents me from saying anything.

This guy across from me seems trustworthy enough.

But I need more time to make sure.

That woman, the movie-star lady who gave me a ride and directions to the clearing in the woods on New Year's Eve, said she wasn't sure where Uncle Robert went. Nobody seems to know.

"I'll keep looking around," I say. "But what should I look for?"

"Names. Addresses. Details. He just disappeared."

"Do you think—?"

I don't want to finish the statement because uttering it seems wrong.

I want to ask if Jared thinks his father might be dead.

He nods, glances around. There is only one other patron in this restaurant, an older guy eating his breakfast and reading the paper. Nothing too suspicious.

"I think that if he's alive he's in trouble. Maybe he's like me, hiding. I don't know. I just know that if he's still alive and can come back to this town, he'll do it. And he'll contact you."

"Why me? Why not my mom?"

I receive another hard look from the guy across from me. "Would you contact your mother?"

Does he know about my mom's condition, about her state of mind?

"I don't know," I say.

"If my father is going to reach out to anybody, it's going to be you."

18. THE DISCOVERY

This place feels cold.

Maybe it's me and my imagination. But my skin is not making this up. I can feel the prickles all over my body as I step through the doors into the large foyer. A voice keeps telling me to avoid the creepy pastor at all costs, to sprint and get out of there if I see him coming. But of course I don't always heed my voices, and there he is, the guy with the frosted and spiked hair, zeroing in on me with his beady eyes behind the black-frame glasses.

I freeze, both my legs and the half smile on my lips.

I'm not fooling anybody with that look. I'm probably white as a ghost.

"Good morning, son," he says to me.

"Hi."

"Is it just you today?"

The way he glances at me really feels weird. Creepy in a way I can't explain. Not creepy in an axe murderer way, or creepy in a guy-living-next-door-doing-icky-things way.

It's just …

Creepy.

"Yeah, just me."

"I'm glad you came, Chris. I really am."

Then I wait for something new. Something else. Something bizarre. Something like "I will be roasting the cat in five minutes, son" or "I will dedicate the Marilyn Manson song to you." Something like that.

"The tension will go away eventually," Pastor Marsh says. "It's a battle of spirits, Chris. You might not understand this—you might not believe it—but it's true. Maybe someday I'll be able to show you."

I wait for something else, for something more, but it doesn't come. Instead, he goes to greet someone else.

He's just like any pastor, you idiot.

But I don't buy it.

I'm not making this up.

And I'm here this morning because I want some answers.

I'm doing what I'm supposed to do, going with the flow. Ray's invited me here because he wants me here. Or maybe *they* want me here. For some reason. So I'm here.

Maybe I'll discover that this church is really covering a secret network of terrorists that oh yeah also happen to be undead.

I stop my ridiculous thoughts and go to find a restroom. I see a set of wide steps going downstairs. Couples and families are walking up and down them. I follow suit, curious.

And going with the flow.

There is nothing sinister or even mildly strange in the church basement. A large hallway opens up to two more, where there are rooms for the nursery and for Sunday school or whatever they call it. Dad brought me to a few churches like this in Illinois. Once I sat in a big, open room that had several hundred high school students singing and praying and hanging out. I felt really out of place and told my dad afterward that I wasn't about to go back.

If only you could have known what would await you in Solitary.

I find a restroom and then get turned around when I walk out of it. Instead of finding the steps, I find a door that leads down another hallway. This one is different. There are no tables with pamphlets and sign-up sheets. No paintings and crafts from kids adorning the walls. No pictures or friendly messages like "God Is Love" or pictures of Noah and his big boat. This hallway is stark, even with the lighting. There is one door at the end of it.

For a minute I consider going back. I know I'm not heading the right way.

But what's behind this door?

I'm curious, and I'm safe because I'm not a cat. Right?

I get to the door and try the handle. It opens easily.

For a brief second, as my eyes see nothing but darkness in the room in front of me, I picture figures in robes standing in the dead of night.

Stop it, Chris.

It's very cold inside. I take a breath and can taste the musty air, as if nobody has stepped foot inside here in a while.

I move to the edge of the doorway and feel against the wall. Nothing. Then I try the other wall and find a light switch. Dim fluorescent lights fill the space before me in a strained glow.

It's a large room, apparently used for storage, though the first thing I see isn't extremely comforting.

It's a long black coffin.

I do a double take, thinking it's just my eyes playing a trick on me. But no, it's really a coffin, placed on some kind of stand that looks like an antique.

Okay, enough seen, now it's time to go bye-bye.

The door closes behind me.

I look around with wonder and fascination and quite a bit of fear.

I suppose the stuff in this room could be found in a church anywhere, though I've never heard of keeping a spare coffin on hand, but then again it all feels just a tad bit off.

There are several thick wooden pulpits all in a row. A painting on its side, about as big as I am, that depicts what looks like a couple being interrogated by an angel. A bunch of chairs, all different types from different years. Some instruments.

What is that?

Beyond the coffin in the dim light of the corner of this room is some kind of—

Is that a statue?

I squint my eyes and try to make it out.

I think of crazy Aunt Alice who Mom and I visited, and remember that mannequin sitting in her living room.

This isn't a mannequin or a statue. This is more of a wax figure.

How do you know it's not real?

But the hands are outstretched and not moving and it looks exactly like Pastor Marsh.

I laugh. Who would make a wax figure of the pastor? And why?

I step closer to the thing. It's standing in the corner, the arms firmly in place as if he's making a point, the smile just like the one I saw a few minutes ago, the black glasses the same.

I inch forward a little more, expecting to see the smile bend or the hands shift.

Get out of here, Chris.

I reach the thing and touch it, expecting to feel warm skin. But it's just hard plastic or whatever the material is.

I study it, trying to see if this is some kind of joke, wondering why someone would go to the trouble of making this.

Behind me something shifts.

Then I hear a sucking sound, and I turn and see motion behind me. A few feet away, the top of the coffin is open—

And that's when I bolt without seeing or hearing anything else.

My shirt gets stuck on something, and I howl because I half expect it to be the wax figure grabbing me. But it's just a coat rack.

The sucking sound, it's someone gasping it's someone choking desperate for air.

I reach the door and tear out of the room without shutting off the light. By the time I reach the end of the hallway, I try to get composed and calm.

But I'm soaked in sweat and probably look like a possessed man.

I go back into the bathroom and close the door to a stall and stand there for a few minutes, breathing in and letting my heart slow down and shaking my head in disbelief.

19. THE END OF THE ROAD

This road is called Heartland Trail. I wonder if the founders were playing a practical joke with that one. Or if it has a deeper, more sinister meaning.

Or maybe it's just another street name.

I'm walking to warm myself as I head away from the church, away from the pastor and the greeters and the music and the smiles and whatever the heck I just saw downstairs in the storage room. I'm walking down Heartland Trail, the opposite way from where it comes in through the forest off the main road. If I were forced at gunpoint to show on a map exactly where I was, I'm pretty confident the gun would end up going off. I don't know if Heartland Trail leads to anything other than a dead end. But I don't want to chance heading the other way and being picked up by someone asking me why I'm leaving.

The road drops away from the cleared-out section of trees and the hill the church stands on. Soon I find myself following the road through dense forest again, leafless trees that are massive and ancient looking.

What are you doing, man?

I don't know.

I really don't know.

I wanted to go to church to get some answers, and I only scampered out with more questions.

If you had a little more guts maybe you would've stuck around.

But the guts thing hasn't been working so far, has it? I got a gun and tried to do what I was supposed to do—warn away the gang of hooded weirdos in the middle of the countryside. I tried to stop them. I tried to get to her.

I tried. I really tried.

I feel tears on the edges of my cheeks and claw at them to get them off my face. I'm tired of tears. I'm tired of this. I'm tired of this moping, this sad sadness.

After walking for twenty minutes or so, as the paved road becomes a dirt lane, I have a feeling of déjà vu. I don't know why. But this looks and feels familiar.

I soon reach the dead end of the road at the edge of the forest. For some reason, even though it's sunny out today, the woods in front of me appear darker and denser. I'm half tempted to head into them to see where they take me, but I have no idea if they'll ever end. I can see myself getting lost and wandering around for days.

Doubt many people around here would mind.

It feels colder where I'm standing, the wind a little stronger. I shiver and look into the shade of the trees in front of me.

I wonder if someone is in there, watching me.

Someone or something.

I turn to head back down Heartland Trail.

Maybe by the time I make it back to church, the service will be over and I can still catch my ride home with Ray.

Something itches at me to turn around one last time before the road veers around the corner.

As I do, I suddenly recognize where I've seen this before.

The magazine clipping from Jocelyn's locker. The one that turned up in mine with the handwritten quote on it.

The line from the Robert Frost poem.

I looked it up. Should've recognized it. If it had been a song lyric, maybe I would have.

This is the image. The only difference is the time of year the photo was taken.

Why did someone take a photo of this place? And more importantly, why was it in my locker?

So many questions, I think, as I see the church nearing.

So many questions and so few answers.

20. BELOW

The cabin feels quarantined. Midnight is there on the couch, but Mom is nowhere to be found. It takes a while to find the note.

Hey Chris.
Will be home late. Helping out at work.
Mom

I look at the note for a while, find a pen and doodle little happy faces all over it. It soon resembles a crowd of people laughing. I can't tell if they're laughing at me or at my mom.

I find some lunch and eat it while I watch television. But I don't really pay attention. I'm staring at moving pictures and hearing noise and voices, but I'm really somewhere far away.

My eyes move to the windows. I can see the sky and the mountains in the distance. I scan the room, feel the hard couch, move the cushion to get more comfortable, flip through forty channels.

I wonder about this restlessness. The way I feel. Trapped. Wounded. Hurt. Imprisoned.

God wouldn't do this to someone, Jocelyn. He couldn't.

If this were a postcard sent to heaven, I'd add a third rhyming line.

He shouldn't.

But I don't know anything. I look at the walls and wonder if somehow my life is getting smaller, duller. Most definitely sadder.

I close my eyes and picture Jocelyn.

Love doesn't go away. It's always there, like the sun and the moon and the stars. It's always there even if it's cloudy or if it's daytime or if you're inside and you can't look up to the heavens. It's always there, hovering and beaming and brilliant.

It's there, and it won't go away.

The pounding wakes me up.

At first I think I'm back home, hearing my father in the garage working on something. But my father never worked on stuff in the garage. Not when he was a lawyer and worked on so many other things that made him stay away from the family. Come to think of it, I've never seen a hammer in my father's hand. Even after becoming born again and quitting his job to go into "ministry."

In the darkness I think and worry about Mom. I can't see my clock, but I know it's gotta be twelve or later. I realize that the noise is coming from above me, on the roof. Hail.

But part of me doesn't believe it—can't, in fact—because it sounds so loud and so violent. I've been in a few hailstorms back home, but never have any of them sounded so …

Dangerous.

I leave Midnight tucked in the corner of my bed and go downstairs. I see the opened door to Mom's bedroom and know she isn't there, though I still call out her name and turn on the light. Or try to turn on her light.

No power. Once again.

I look outside the front window and can see the blurry motion outside. I open the front door, but when I do, the hail tries to force its way inside. I hear things cracking, the icy bits flailing against tree limbs and anything else they can find. I cringe as I hear the sound of the cracks on my deck, like baseballs being ripped against the wood and the railing and the rooftop.

I wonder how Mom is going to get home.

I shut the door and really, truly feel imprisoned now.

The wind howls as if it knows, as if it can feel my tension inside. The hail mocks and surges into an avalanche of racket and wreck.

I move to the middle of the room and then I drop to the floor.

The pelting continues. Pounding, banging, beating away.

I start to shake, putting my hands over my ears.

The whole house seems to be rumbling. I wonder if there's a chance that it could slide off the mountain like those houses in California mudslides.

That's crazy stop it Chris.

But my imagination is the only thing to occupy my thoughts and hold my hand. The lawyer-turned-quasi-pastor is gone. The mother-turned-quasi-barfly is gone. The girl-turned-quasi-love-of-my-life is gone. Everybody is gone.

With my hands now holding my head, not my ears, but my head as if some part of it is cut and bleeding and leaking, I hear it.

Laughter.

It's loud—it's gotta be loud—because I can hear it amidst the blaring storm outside.

Then I realize something.

It's not from outside.

I hold my breath and move my hands and listen. It's not from upstairs or from somewhere in this room. It's beneath me.

I look at the dark carpet underneath me, so worn it no longer feels like anything resembling carpet, and I try and think what's under it. What's beneath this floor.

There's nothing but dirt there, and that laughter is all in your mind.

But I think of the house on the sloping hill.

I suddenly realize something fascinating and terrifying.

This house *does* in fact have a basement.

The laughter I'm hearing is coming from it.

And suddenly I get up and sprint upstairs, biffing it on the third step and landing hard on my chest and arms, then getting up in stride and moving and getting in my room and locking the door.

Then waiting.

Waiting for the storm to go away and the sun to come back.

Waiting for the noise to let me be.

Waiting for silence.

21. AT YOUR DOORSTEP

Four men surround me by the table. It's a sparse room, very white with dull and cold lights above us. The table is bare and basic; the chair I'm sitting on hard and cheap. I look around and know what they're saying, but I wonder why they're saying it to me.

"What are you doing here?" one of the men asks.

It's like four detectives on one of those old cop shows I used to watch. But why four? There never used to be four. Only one, two at the most.

"Where am I?"

"You do not belong here," another says.

"Where is 'here'?" I ask.

"No," says a guy with a beard, probably the oldest. "Not now, not like this. Not here."

I feel like I'm in trouble, but I don't know why. I look around me for someone I recognize—my mother, maybe Sheriff Wells, some-body else from Solitary that I know.

"How did you get here?" the man in the beard asks me.

"I don't know."

"You have nothing else on you?"

"Like what?"

"Any papers or documentation?"

I shake my head and then reach into my pocket. Maybe I'll find a silver passport or a golden ticket or my school ID or something. I don't find anything but lint.

There's a knock, and then the door opens. A woman stands in the doorway and glares at the men, as if they're wanted, as if they're in trouble. They all turn, and without saying anything they file out one by one. The bearded man glances back at me and pauses.

"Stay here, right there in that chair. Can you do that for me?"

"Yes," I say.

When they're gone, I wait for a few minutes.

I'm sure I'm being watched, though there is no one-way mirror that I can detect.

I get up and try the door handle.

It turns, and I open the door and step through.

I told the guy yes when he asked, "Can you do that for me?"

And I *could* physically do that, if I wanted to. But what I need to do is get out of here and find out where I am.

As I step outside the small white room, the lights go out like a fuse box bursting. I step ahead to find a wall or something to guide myself with, and instead I find myself falling backward, doing somersaults as I'm dropping, the wind whipping my face and my hair, and my stomach lost a hundred stories above me as I suddenly and completely find myself back in my bed.

I don't wake up with a gasp. It's more like I brace myself for impact.

I wake up to the sound of cracking life outside of me. I look out a fogged-over window that I wipe down only to reveal a distorted crystal spiderweb covering the outside. The world outside is one big icicle.

I open my bedroom door and holler out for my mom. Nothing.

That answers the school question. No Mom, no school. I seriously doubt the bus is going to be out on a morning like this, but even if it is, I'm staying here. If Mom is playing hooky, so am I.

Hopefully she'll call soon to let me know she's alive. Which is always a nice thing to know.

I think about last night—the hailstorm and the strange sounds and the even stranger dream—then I randomly pick out an album to crank.

Beastie Boys' *Licensed to Ill* does the trick.

I blast it away and cause Midnight to look up from the nest she made in the corner of the bed.

This is what it feels like to be single.

This is what it feels like to be on my own.

And I gotta say … I like it.

That all changes in an hour when I hear a knock on the door.

About time she showed up.

I have a mouth full of ancient Cheerios that taste like soft mush after being drowned in milk. I glance at the door and wonder why it's not opening, then get up and reach for the handle.

Before I open it up, I can see him in the window.

The ugly round face, troll-like and irritated as usual.

"Come on, open up."

For a second I consider not opening it, but my male pride lets me down. I swing the door open and finish swallowing my cereal.

Gus glances at me with disinterest. I didn't see him at all the first week of school. Maybe he just got back from vacation or from the cave he sleeps upside down in.

"Nice little storm, huh?"

"What do you want?" I ask.

His hands are free, which is good. I look down and see a black Humvee waiting at the bottom of the hill.

"I always knew I'd be knocking on your door one day."

"Where are your boys? And your baseball bat?"

Gus laughs. He seriously couldn't seem to care less about the way he looks, the oiliness of his skin, the just-got-out-of-bed hair.

How can someone look that oily in the middle of winter? Especially after an ice storm.

"This isn't my idea, you know. My father figured this would be the ideal opportunity to meet you."

"Uh, no thanks."

"No, Chris. If you're smart, you will walk down the hill with me and get in the car."

"So, what? School is open?"

Gus nods. "They don't have many snow days, and they've already used a couple. Half the school won't show up."

"Good to see how dedicated you are."

"I was in Florida all last week. That's my dedication."

"Where's your tan?"

"What are you talking about?" Gus says. "I'm a vampire. We don't like the sun." He laughs and then tells me to get my stuff together. Fast.

In a weird way, I get the feeling that he knows I'm by myself.

I recall the voice laughing underneath me in the middle of the night.

Maybe it was him.

22. ICHOR STAUNCH??

I brace myself for this meeting with a man I know I've seen before. Yet when I look inside the Hummer, I wonder if my eyes are playing tricks the way everything else seems to be.

"Hello, Chris."

I know that voice I've heard that voice in the darkness.

Bold, bright eyes look at me in a way that Gus can't and will never be able to. He kind of looks like Gus, though.

"Why don't you have a seat?" the driver says as he pats the empty seat next to him. The SUV smells new.

This is Ichor Staunch?

The guy is wearing a blue dress shirt and a black sports coat. He doesn't have fangs and a Count Dracula cape.

"Come on, I'm freezing," he says.

I do what I'm told. I shut the door and figure that I couldn't run away from him if I tried. I buckle my seat belt in case we tragically veer off the side of the road after I grab the wheel in a brave act of stupidity.

Stop it, Chris.

The guy behind the wheel is not Gus's father. No way possible. Even though he sorta looks like him, there's no way. I saw Ichor Staunch that day I walked downstream, the day I spied on the lawn of their house.

You weren't sure that was his father. That could've been anybody.

"Late night last night?" the man says.

He's got graying brown hair that's still thick and combed to one side. He doesn't look like some evil businessman or dark Sith Lord or the Boogeyman. He looks like just another grown-up on his way to work.

"Gus, does this boy talk?"

The Southern accent is strong but seems to be held at bay, as if it could go off when necessary.

"Oh, he talks all right. Talks way too much if you ask me."

"It's impolite to not reply to people, Chris."

That voice belongs to the one I heard in the hole when I was abducted and shoved in the middle of the cabin. And it belongs to the voice that warned me about Jocelyn, the one that threatened me and my family after they took her.

"Sorry," I say.

"Ah, you *can* speak. That's good. I'd like to hear what you have to say."

I nod.

"So I've heard from Gus that you've had a difficult time adjusting to Harrington High."

"No."

"No, sir," he says.

"Excuse me?"

"No, *sir.*"

I repeat his words. His order.

"I wanted to make sure that you realize that Gus is harmless. And Gus, you *are* harmless, right?"

"Right."

Gus sounds timid, like a little puppy. I glance back and see him sitting there in complete and utter obedience.

"Here's the thing about being me," Mr. Staunch says. "I've earned the right to bully people. Bullying doesn't have to stop when you become an adult. You know? But as for my son, he doesn't quite understand the logic and etiquette of bullying. You are the new student, so he sees you as fresh meat and thus decides to terrorize you. Most students would have backed off, but I get this feeling that you're not a 'back off' sort of guy."

"No. Sir." I emphasize *sir* in a way that I might spit out tobacco. My fear is settling in and turning over into something else.

It's the same man I heard that night of Jocelyn's death. I'm certain.

"Gus doesn't realize that you don't mess around with desperation. You can't. Eyes are watching him, and so far, he's been quite stupid, haven't you, boy?"

"Yes, sir," Gus says.

There.

The way he said *boy.*

That's it.

My skin itches with bumps, and I feel the back of my neck. It's wet with sweat.

"I still have a reputation to keep up. If Gus is out of line then that means I'm out of line, and I can't have that. But you, Chris, Christopher, whatever and whoever you claim to be—you need to understand that you can't wave a red flag at a bull. Do you understand?"

I glance at him and shake my head.

"My son—my wonderful if sometimes extremely arrogant and ignorant only son—is a bull. God bless him. I love that about him. He is so much his mother, though he will never know because she's no longer alive. But she was a bull, and he takes after her. And what do you not do with bulls?"

"Wave red flags at them?" I say.

"You don't taunt them in any way. You stay away from them."

"That's always been my plan."

"Keep it your plan, Chris. And you'll just make it to the end of the school year."

We're not far away from school. The roads are a little better closer to downtown Solitary, but not much.

Nothing else is said for the rest of the drive. The SUV pulls up to the stairs leading into the school, and Gus gets out without saying good-bye to his father. If it really is his father. I'm about ready to get out when I feel a strong grip on my wrist.

"Chris, hold on for a moment."

I wince even though I really try not to. I don't want to show fear or hurt or pain in front of this guy.

"Remember this, Chris. Remember my words. And remember that when I tell somebody something, I mean it. You do not want to mess with me."

I nod.

"I meant every word I said to you. You're on very shaky ground right now."

He lets go, and I take a breath as the world darkens a bit. It's hazy, and my head is dizzy.

"Have a wonderful day at school," he tells me with a salesman's smile. The phony smile of someone who wants to eat your soul.

23. Some Kind of Misery

"Come on, Chicago! My grandmother can run faster than you, and she's dead!"

Good to know that the track coach is keeping with the Solitary theme of Abuse Chris at Whatever Cost.

I'm finishing up a two-mile jog on a track that is still icy and that rests on the other side of the hill that Harrington High sleeps on. This is the first football field I've ever seen with a line of bleachers dug into the incline. Right now it's loaded with crystal land mines, the kind that'll make you slip and break your neck—not that Coach Brinks seems to care anything about that.

That's one reason I'm at the back of the pack today. The other is that sleep deprivation does not help when you're running a timed two-mile for the first time in a long time. I never was good at long distances, and I told Ray that. Of course, he's leading this group of ten students, most who I've never met during my brief time in Solitary.

When I finally cross the finish line, the man standing there with a timer glares at me. He resembles a ruler, tall and thin and ready to whack you on the back of your butt.

"Chicago, get over here," he yells.

It's still cold, and I'm wondering why we're running outside.

"What do you run again?"

"The hurdles."

"That was not the most impressive two-mile I've ever seen."

"Sorry—I haven't been running much."

If you don't include running away from ghosts and evil people.

"Your time makes me wonder if you've ever run at all."

"I was avoiding the ice on the track."

Coach Brinks scoffs at my comment and looks me over. He's got the kind of expression that doesn't back down. It's not wild, but rather icy calm. Just like the ice on this track that will let you fall and crack your skull and lie bleeding.

"We've run in worse. Sure you're from Chicago? Maybe I oughta start calling you Miami."

I smile. If this is what track is going to be, then thanks but no thanks.

He gets the team to line up in the middle of the field for a pep talk.

"Look, people. We stunk it up here last year, and all I ask of each and every one of you is that you don't stink it up this year. Got it? Just give this your all. I'm not expecting any championships or any boom boom pow, but make things interesting at least. That's why we're here, Chicago. That's why we're practicing in this God-awful weather. Because we need as much help as we can get."

I scan the people around me. There's a really tall, skinny kid who looks like a freshman. A muscular girl. A boy and a girl hanging on to each other in a way that suggests they're a couple.

Now I can understand why Ray wanted me out here. There's nobody out here to begin with. When the coach divides us into short and long, Ray pulls me aside.

"Don't mind him. He's a great guy."

"I'm sure."

"He's a bit—crazy. You never know what he's thinking. And I'd like to say he'll warm up, but he won't. But that doesn't mean he's not a good coach."

"I don't know about this."

"Come on," Ray says, tapping me on the back. "Can't wait to watch you do hurdles on this track."

"I'm doing them now? Today?"

Ray runs off toward Coach Brinks as I stand there in my sweatpants with holes in them and a sweatshirt with a hood that's a bit too small when I put it around my head.

I glance at the stands above us. Empty seats covered with snow and capped with ice.

I have a feeling those seats are going to be lifeless all season.

Ray curses as he drives down the street a bit too fast for my liking.

"You're really good," he says.

"I'm really out of shape."

"Yeah, but you can get in shape. You can't teach talent."

"I have a lot to learn."

Ray laughs. The beams of his Jetta cut through the gloom, the car riding smoothly on streets that could stand to be salted and plowed half a dozen more times.

"You shoulda seen our hurdler last year. I mean, the guy jumped up, no fluid motion, no grace. It was like he'd run and then stop and jump. He couldn't do the high hurdles, of course. But the three hundred were just as tough for him."

"Why'd he even do them?"

"We needed someone. I run the four hundred. I can't do hurdles."

"Yeah, well, I'm not promising anything."

"You get in shape, and I bet you'll be something."

It's only a few minutes before we reach my cabin, and I want to bring up something that I've been holding back.

Let it go. Don't say anything, Chris, just let it be.

"Hey—can I ask you a question?"

Ray nods as he fumbles with his iPod, which is playing a song by Kings of Leon.

"You ever hear from Jocelyn?"

The question doesn't produce any notable reaction. He doesn't slam on the brakes and start screaming in horror. He doesn't give me a creepy, mysterious glance or a creepy, mysterious smile. He doesn't even shrug and look away as if he's hiding anything. He just shakes his head and keeps doing what he's doing and then notices me studying his every move.

"Thought you would've heard from her."

"No."

I don't say any more.

If he's hiding something, then he's really good at it.

But if he's been used to hiding stuff, maybe he's a pro. It's like running—the more you do it, the more in shape you'll be and the better you'll perform when it comes to your race.

Remember that Ray is not from around here. Maybe that's the difference.

I thank him for the ride home. He tells me no problem and then gives me the same advice that Coach Brinks gave us all: "Eat your carbs!"

"I'll be lucky to eat anything," I tell him, knowing my mom hasn't gone shopping for a while. Except to buy booze.

I go into my cabin wondering what to expect, feeling a deep, sinking feeling suddenly coming on.

I suddenly realize that for the past two hours, I've had some other kind of misery to think about. It's been track and Coach Brinks and my aching legs and lungs.

I'd take a few more hours of that to avoid this.

Going up these stairs. Getting to the door and seeing if it's unlocked.

Opening it, afraid of what I'll find.

Or what I won't find.

24. As Imaginary as Laughter

Coach Brinks would be happy. Lots of carbs tonight for dinner. Homemade spaghetti, garlic bread, salad with the works on it, including thick homemade croutons.

Amazing how food can transport you back to another time and place.

Mom used to make this all the time back in Libertyville. Back when Dad would come home late and immediately sit down and devour his food and wine while Mom tried to get nuggets of talk from him.

Libertyville isn't just a place I used to live in. Not anymore.

It's now a life I once had, a place I once belonged, a world I once understood.

I died when I had to move.

But food and the flavors and the aromas all remind me of that past life and past love, even though love wasn't something that flowed much in our house.

As I finish dinner, I grow conscious of something that's been at the back of my mind. We're watching television while we eat, so I didn't really even notice Mom much until she cleared the plates.

She looks younger, prettier.

I think it's makeup. And something with her hair. She must have gotten a haircut.

I don't say anything because I don't know what to say. But I wonder if it's for her job or maybe for someone at that job.

After dinner, she's cleaning up, and nothing much is on television except some news shows about celebrities I've never heard of doing dumb things nobody really cares about.

"I'm going to take Midnight out," I say.

It's cold, and I bundle up. Mom still seems focused in her own little world. She's sipping wine and busy, and that's fine. She won't ask me any questions or notice what I'm doing.

I take a flashlight with me as I put Midnight on a leash. She's so tiny, not even the size of a football, and the leash seems to weigh her down so much that she just stands there wondering why she's attached to some chain. When I get out on the deck, I put her in one arm while I turn on the flashlight and walk down the steps to the driveway.

Since our cabin was built on the side of a steep mountain, there's a story and a half of concrete propping it up underneath the base. The deck has long wooden beams that help hold it up, though my mom said it doesn't really need them since the primary support is built into the deck and attached to the house.

I've never spent a lot of time underneath the deck, looking at the base of the towering concrete wall. But that's what I'm doing now, scanning it with my flashlight to see if there's any sort of entry. A door or a window or something, anything.

Because I know I heard a voice. I'm positive I heard laughing the other night.

I spend a few minutes underneath, aiming the light at different sections of the concrete. Nothing. I bundle Midnight up even though it's not too bad out. It's cold, but the wind isn't too strong, so you don't feel the cold as much.

I do the same on each side of the house, but most of the concrete is in the earth. No door can be seen, no trapdoor in the ground nearby, no lever or handle to pull.

Wait a minute.

I have an idea. Somebody could have built a tunnel into this house the same way they built that tunnel or passageway under the little cabin in the forest above us.

Christopher, come to me.

I hear that voice in the echoes of my memory, and I shiver. The voice I heard when I was at the bottom of the hole.

The voice you thought you heard.

The more time that goes by, the less I think that I imagined it.

I didn't imagine that hole or that passageway in the ground, just like I didn't imagine the blood on Jocelyn's neck and wrists.

Colored syrup, Chris, the kind any halfway decent makeup artist on a movie could whip up in two seconds.

I didn't imagine that hellish scene around the rocks on New Year's Eve.

Just like I didn't imagine any of this, including the laughter I heard the other night.

I feel my body beginning to tremble because of the cold and realize I'd better get back inside. There are only two possible explanations for the sound I heard coming from beneath me in my house. Either there is a passageway leading to the basement from somewhere around the house, or there is an entryway into the basement through the house itself.

At least I can hunt around inside for the latter.

As I walk up the steps and reach the deck, I look out to the woods around me. Somewhere far below is the creek. Somewhere down the road in the distance is the Staunch residence.

And somewhere, maybe, just maybe, lying in the shadows of the trees or maybe even looking at me from somewhere unseen at this very instant, is Jocelyn.

It's a nice thought. But it's probably as imaginary as the laughter I heard. And as the sanity I would really like to have.

25. GIRLS

I don't get girls. I really don't.

Maybe Solitary isn't the place to get girls. Either getting the girl at the end, arm in arm and heading into the sunset, or *getting* the girl, understanding and figuring her out. Maybe this place just isn't designed with either of those things in mind.

Then again, maybe boys aren't designed to figure girls out. And that's why the girls always win in the end. Because we can't say or do or think enough to keep up.

I'm heading to my locker, trying to figure out the conversation that just took place between Poe and me. Goth girl, one of the misfits or "outcasts" as she once called them, the only remaining link I have to Jocelyn. I examine the interchange to see where it all went terribly wrong.

"Poe, hey, can we talk?"

Maybe this was a bad way to start, going up to her with a question, offering her a way out.

"No."

"Look, I just want a few minutes. I mean, are you going to keep this up all semester?"

I guess no doesn't mean no with me, because I keep talking. And those blue eyes rip me a new one as they dig into me with a ferocity that scares me.

"Keep what up?"

I guess Poe doesn't know what I mean because she hasn't been thinking about me at all.

Wasn't she the one who came up and talked to me on that first day? Where'd it go bad? Why'd it go so bad?

"Can we just—can you just stop for a minute—please?"

"What do you want?" she asks.

One might glance at this girl in front of me and put her in a box. Dark girl, creepy, thinks about witches and listens to Evanescence, avoids the sun but doesn't avoid the eyeliner. But when I look at Poe, I see a girl who's probably just as confused and scared and bewildered as I am.

"You have to let me talk to you."

"Isn't that what you're doing by blocking my way?"

"No. I mean, really talk." I say it in a hushed tone. "In private."

"No."

"Why?" I ask.

"Because. I'm done with you."

"It's about Jocelyn."

"Oh, really?"

I nod.

"That's great, because I just got an email from her, and she's loving life there. Happy?"

"No."

"*Yes,*" Poe says in a way that feels like someone punching me in the gut. "She said you keep sending emails and texts and that you can't get the point."

I look around us and wonder if this is real, if what she's saying is real, if the ground I'm standing on is real.

"Poe."

"Yes, *Chris?*"

She says my name the way she might say *fungus*.

For the first time I notice how pretty Poe is, those blue eyes standing out in the white and black picture that is her. I don't understand why she wants to hide it. The dark dress with long sleeves and the thing around her neck—I don't even know what that is. The strange high-heeled shoes. The spiky, multi-colored short hair.

I don't understand why she has to act so ugly when I just want to help.

"Look, all I want to do—"

But as I go to finish my sentence—each word collapsing like chunks of a concrete bridge during an earthquake—Poe nods and mocks me with a *just finish it already* glance.

I stop midsentence. Probably looking red-faced, humbled, and pretty stupid.

"Don't," Poe says.

"Don't what?"

"Don't anything."

Then she walks away.

The Poe-and-me-versus-the-world story line isn't going to happen the way I might have imagined.

I reach my locker and wonder how I can fit my entire body into it. I open it up and see a photo slip out.

What now?

I pick up the picture, annoyed that someone or maybe everyone has the combination to my locker.

It could've been slipped in through the holes, Chris.

I look at the picture of a smiling guy.

He has messy hair that seems lit up and lighter because of the sun. He's laughing, with one hand rubbing the back of his head in a nervous sort of way.

I study the picture because it shocks me.

Not because the guy looks so carefree and happy.

But because the guy is me.

"Hi," says the mouse on my right.

It's not really a mouse, but the way the blond talks, sometimes it seems like she's auditioning to play the part. Everybody in the art room goes to the same place to paint their masterpiece. Somehow Kelsey has managed to be right next to me, always standing on my right. She always says hi first, usually about five or ten minutes into the class, as if she has to build up the courage first.

"Hey," I say, not really interested in talking.

She's a girl, and she might look harmless now, but I know. Those glasses and that round little face and the braces may make her look sweet and innocent, but I know. She's a girl, and I'm watching myself around her.

"I saw you talking with that girl."

"What?"

"I don't know her name. But I know you're friends with her."

"Poe."

"That's her name?"

I nod. "Not sure if she'd call me a friend."

"Why?"

"Maybe you can ask her that. Haven't quite figured that out."

She keeps working. Her painting is symmetrical and logical and very bright. Mine is like an ugly face plastered in mud and smeared over the high school hall.

"What's that supposed to be?" I ask her, changing the subject, wanting to change the mood.

This usually happens, where she'll break ice that doesn't really need breaking and then we'll go on to chat and I'll do 75 percent of the talking. I'll leave the class wondering what all I was talking about and why I was talking so much. I guess art class makes me realize just how badly I need to talk to someone. Even Minnie Mouse here.

Kelsey describes the porch on the back of her grandparents' house, and I see her painting with new appreciation.

"What about yours?"

"This is what I first thought and felt when I walked the hallways of Harrington."

She laughs in this cute way that makes me want to keep joking around. So I do. Saying nothing really; she's just being polite, and she's easy to make laugh. But laughter never gets old to listen to. Ever. And someone smiling at you never gets old either.

It's a nice break. It's nice not to be glared at. It's nice not to be ignored.

It's nice to just have something …

Normal.

"Do you live in Solitary?"

"Lowden, technically," she says.

Maybe not having a technical address is a good thing.

"Do you think you're going to be here next year?" Kelsey asks.

"I really hope so. I mean, I don't know what I'd do at a school where people actually like me."

"It's not all that bad."

I give her a *really??* expression, and she laughs. Maybe she's not laughing with me but more at me and my expressions.

"It's not bad all the time," she says.

"Yeah, right."

"People can't help where they're from."

She says this in a slightly defensive manner, and when I glance at her she's looking at her painting.

"I know that," I say. "Really. It's just this place, that's all."

Kelsey nods, but I think I pushed it a little too far.

The joking stops and my attempts at conversation stall, and I leave the class feeling like the dork I felt like when I walked in.

Like I said, girls.

I mean, come on.

What is their deal?

26. THE PRISONER

I'm in the restroom when I see Gus and his boys walk in. I think it's the same one that we were in when they cornered me in the stall and forced me to go militant all over them.

"Relax," Gus says. "You look like you're auditioning for the next Karate Kid movie."

"What do you want?"

Gus looks back at Oli and the two other clowns he's with, then comes and stands next to me at the sinks. He washes his hands and watches me.

"So we're all cool, right?" he asks. "After that nice little chat with my pop?"

I nod. Oli is looking at me but giving away nothing.

It seems like Gus is biding his time. He moves and checks down the line of stalls, then nods to the guys. Oli goes and stands by the door. Burt goes over to make sure I don't hide in a stall while Riley stands close to Oli.

Gus looks at me, laughs, then darts in my direction and grips the top of my T-shirt with his hand, bringing me forward and off my feet. He pulls me down, and in one motion I crash against the floor and then feel him pulling me back up.

Something's in his hand it's a knife.

Then something pricks at my temple.

It's not a knife but the edge of a very sharp pencil that digs into my skin.

He presses hard as he moves his head to my ear. "Now you listen and you listen good. We're not finished, you and I. And just because my pop said that everything's fine and dandy doesn't mean it's fine and dandy."

I yell as he digs the pencil in further.

"I could take this and put it in your eye just for starters. And don't think I won't. I will."

My eyes are closed, and I'm wondering what's next.

I hear someone else speak, but Gus curses over the voice. "When the time comes, when nobody is looking, I'm going to be there."

"What do you want from me?"

"I don't want anything. Not a thing. I just want to watch you bleed."

I howl as he thrusts the pencil deeper, then lets it go.

"You tell anybody about this and it will just get worse for you. But I don't want you walking around thinking you're safe."

He lets go, and I grab the side of my face and hold it.

He leans over me. "I don't care what your last name is or what you may or may not do. When this—all of this—is over with, you're mine."

He spits in my face, and I feel it splatter on my forehead, nose, and cheeks. I wipe it and watch Gus walk out, followed by the boys in boots and jeans and then Oli.

I look down at my hand, which is covered in blood and spit. Then I glance at the doorway.

Oli is still there. He looks like he's about to say something, then he leaves.

The dark prick on the side of my head is bleeding. I wash it with warm water that doesn't really stop the bleeding; it only makes the pain worse.

I glance briefly at myself in the mirror, my hair a bit wet, my face a bit red, the piece of tissue on my puncture.

Chris.

I open my eyes wide but don't see myself anymore. I don't see anyone. Instead, I see an image of something real, something alive, something like a scene in a movie.

What ...

I close my eyes and open them again.

There I am.

What was that?

I realize I just imagined a cabin or a small house with a porch on it. A swing. Sometime in the afternoon. Just like that girl's painting.

I'm seeing things, and it's because I can't control my head. I can't control the earthquake going on inside it.

I leave the bathroom, remembering the first time an altercation like this happened. That was the day I lost the letter for Jocelyn, a letter that would change everything.

I'd give anything if I could go back and be given one more night, Jocelyn.

I'm walking around with a bloody piece of toilet paper on the side of my forehead, but nobody cares. I could have a missing limb, a squirting and bloody stump like the kind in funny horror movies. I could be spraying these kids around me, and they still wouldn't care. They'd go on laughing and leering and looking my way. They'd keep ignoring me, keep wondering what my name is and why I moved from Chicago and why I am so stuck-up/full of myself/quiet/shy/snobbish/fill in the negative blank.

I am a loaded gun, full of blanks.

When I enter Mr. Meiners' room for history a bit early, he surprises me by asking about the wound.

"What happened, Chris? Who did this to you?"

"Oh, you know," I say.

"No, I don't know."

"Just the same old story."

"Hold on." He reaches into his briefcase and pulls out a white handkerchief. "It's clean."

I pick the dried clump of bloody tissue away from my skin and apply the soft fabric.

"Thanks."

"You're getting close, Chris."

"Excuse me?"

Mr. Meiners shakes his head. I can see the smile underneath the beard, the friendly smile and the open eyes.

I go to my seat and know there's absolutely no way I'll be able to learn a thing the rest of this day.

The bus rumbles like some old mule carrying too much weight up a hill. The outside resembles the Russia of World War II that Mr. Meiners was talking about. Cold, lifeless, in a state of shock. We're prisoners on our way to a prisoner-of-war camp.

I can't do this anymore.

It's only January.

The bus jerks to a halt, sending all of us against the backs of the seats in front of us.

I need a license and then a car and a map, and I can leave.

I'm near the back of the bus and see a curly-haired guy with glasses eating a candy bar and watching me. I nod.

Then he stops chewing, as if something is wrong, as if somebody actually noticed this strange weird eating trance that he's in.

He looks at the rest of his candy bar, a Milky Way, and shoves the whole thing into his mouth. He chews it quickly, as if he's in a contest. Or as if he thinks I might try and grab it from him.

I gotta get out of here.

My hand rubs the edge of my temple where there's a nice, healthy scab.

"How was your day, son?" an imaginary mom might ask me.

"Same old story," an imaginary son might say back. "Got stabbed with a pencil. Insulted by a couple of girls."

"Why aren't you at track practice?" she'd ask.

I curse to myself.

I totally forgot about it.

Too late now.

I can hear Coach Brinks. "Where's Chicago? Somebody tell me where Chicago is! We're running a five mile for no reason other than I hate you all, so where is Chicago?"

Candy-bar boy is still looking at me.

"Buddy, come on," I say.

Unfortunately, he doesn't seem to understand English, because he just keeps watching until, fifteen minutes later, he stands up for his stop.

He leaves me a parting gift before he gets off. The wrapper for his Milky Way.

Nice.

27. GHOSTS

My future is waiting for me on the counter when I come home.

"Some drunken fool came up to me and passed it along."

Are you talking about yourself, Mom?

"He said that she pays really well."

Then maybe you should take the job.

I pick up the tiny, cut-out block of paper with a typed job listing.

Wanted: Strong teenager who works hard. Groundskeep, maintenance, indoor and outdoor work. Flexible hours.

There's a number at the bottom of the sheet.

"You trust the guy who gave it to you?"

"Al validated it. This guy who gave it to me likes me. He knew I was asking about a job for you. Said that the owner, Iris, pays well. If you don't mind the reputation of the place she owns."

"Oh boy."

"Do you have any other ideas?"

"There's a mountain man with big dogs who wants me to take care of them. Says he'll pay me in raw meat. That may or may not be human."

"That's not even funny."

"I'm not joking," I say.

And a part of me isn't.

"Did you already call?" I ask her.

"You have a job interview this weekend."

"Oh, come on. Where is this?"

"It's a place called the Crag's Inn."

I lean against the couch as I watch my mom, who seems a bit lost in the kitchen. "Are you serious?"

"Very."

"The Crag's Inn? Mom."

"What?"

"What do you mean, 'what'? The name alone sounds creepy. Like the hag's inn."

"You're going to go unless you give me an alternative."

"Why this sudden rush of me needing to get a job?"

"You need to keep occupied."

"Track's not enough?"

"Aren't you supposed to be there now?"

"Yeah. I forgot."

"You need to keep busy. Or else you'll get in trouble. Like back home."

"Why are you bringing that up now?" I ask.

I look in the fridge for something to drink and grab a can of generic diet soda that tastes exactly like generic diet soda.

"Chris, this job pays very well."

"Where is this Crag's Inn?"

"A twenty-minute drive."

"You going to take me?"

She smiles. "We need to think about getting that license, and then maybe you can drive yourself."

"In what car?"

"First things first."

I put the note down on the counter and stare at it.

I have a bad feeling about this.

Turns out I *should* have a bad feeling about it.

Turns out that everybody knows about the Crag's Inn and the lady named Iris who runs it. How many ways can you say haunted house?

Ray confronts me to see why I missed practice. I tell him I got sick, which is true because I did get suddenly and violently sick of Harrington High. I bring up the Crag's Inn.

"A job? There? Are you high?"

"My mom was told it pays well."

"I'm sure selling crack pays well too. Doesn't mean you should do it."

"Why? What's wrong with it?"

He just shakes his head. "Man, being new sucks, doesn't it?" He laughs and walks away.

Thanks a lot, Ray.

I ask Newt about it over lunch, since Newt is my one and only lunch buddy again. His eyes grow big behind the spectacles; his mouth opens slightly.

"What? Is it haunted or something?"

"No, not something," Newt says. "It is haunted. Without question."

"Come on."

"It's true."

"Have you been there?"

"No. It takes forever to get to. Some dirt road that winds around like a coiled snake. It's on the edge of the mountaintop. A cliff."

"And what's wrong about it?"

"Do you just *want* trouble, Chris?"

"I didn't have anything to do with it. Someone recommended it to my mom."

He shifts in his chair. As usual, he peers around to see if anybody is watching. Then he lowers his head and talks in a whisper.

"The lady who runs this inn—it's kinda like a bed-and-breakfast—they say she's crazy. Iris. Years ago lost her husband, and her children abandoned her. Turned into a recluse. They say …"

"What do they say?" I know I've seen a lot around here, but I still can't help being cynical.

"People who have stayed there don't leave."

I make an oooohhhhh sound and exaggerate the look on my face.

"I'm serious."

"So, what? Does she eat them or something?"

"A couple went there on their honeymoon. They were driving across the country, staying at quaint little inns. The wife slipped off the side of the mountain and died."

"And you think this Iris pushed her?"

Newt is undaunted. "A guy in my gym class last year went up there with some buddies one night. He said he saw weird things—lights flickering in the windows even though no car was parked there. All these animals coming out of nowhere, like groundhogs and foxes and birds. And they weren't scared, not up at this place. And then the guys were freaked out by some ghost. They said it was Iris herself, who isn't alive but is a ghost of a woman who was killed by her husband—"

"Newt, come on," I say. "Are you making this up?"

"No. I swear. It happened. The guy said they were attacked by the animals, too."

"Okay."

"I'm telling you—everybody knows it. That place is haunted. And that lady is crazy. That's why nobody wants to work for her."

"Isn't this whole place haunted?" I ask. "Isn't everybody around here crazy? What's one more?"

"Shh, keep your voice down."

"Maybe all ghosts aren't bad. Maybe there are some ghosts that I want to talk to."

Newt squirms in his seat and gives me an exasperated look. "Why?"

"Unfinished business," I say.

28. IN MY SLEEP

I haven't forgotten.

Not in the least.

It wakes up with me like a hangover. It's in the mirror like a black eye. It walks with me like a pulled muscle. It hears the same silence I hear. It sees the same glances I see. It comes home to an empty house. It needs answers like an unfinished crossword puzzle. It kisses me to sleep like the bite of a spider hiding under the covers.

I have not forgotten.

What I'm trying to do is make sure I have a plan and make sure I have my sanity. Maybe just not in that order.

My hope lies in this stranger named Jared. Not Newt or Ray or my mom or my uncle or, God forbid, Poe.

It's in someone I don't know and can't find but who's out there.

I just have to bide my time.

But I haven't forgotten you, Jocelyn.

I'll never forget.

The sound downstairs doesn't awaken me because I'm not asleep.

It's the middle of night, and I'm thinking of Jocelyn. Mom got home before I went to bed, and she was in a decent enough mood. Everything seemed normal. She asked me if I'd finished my homework and asked about school and seemed genuinely interested to see if anything out of the ordinary was happening at Harrington High. Of course I said little, but we still managed to have a halfway normal conversation.

So the screams coming from downstairs really freak me out.

I jerk out of bed and topple over Midnight as I open my door and practically tumble down the stairs.

I don't need to ask who these screams are coming from.

Tonight they're louder than usual.

I go to Mom's bedroom and shout her name and turn on the light.

She's in the corner on her knees, clawing at the wall. Clawing like she's trying to get out, clawing like she's trying to get something off of her.

"Mom, Mom, come on, Mom, it's me, Mom!"

She waves her hands around her head as if she's fighting off mosquitoes. Her hair is messy, and she's wearing a long T-shirt. Her white arms and legs look skinnier than I remember.

"Mom," I keep saying.

Finally the glazed, possessed eyes blink a few times and come back to reality. She's breathing heavily, as if she's been running.

"You're just dreaming, Mom."

She puts a shaking hand over her eyes and nose as if she wants to hide underneath it. The bed next to her is a mess of wadded-up sheets and blankets.

"It's okay, Mom."

"No," she says.

"You're awake now."

"He comes to me in my sleep."

"What?"

She looks around the room as if someone might still be there. I can feel the cold bumps crackling over my skin. I realize how cold I am, standing there in only boxer shorts.

"He comes into my room in the middle of the night. He crawls into my bed."

I don't want to hear this.

"Mom, you're just dreaming."

"He's real, Chris. He's real, and he's been coming ever since we got here."

I shiver and shove the fear away. One of us needs to be sane and strong. It's gotta be me.

"It's just a nightmare, Mom."

"No."

"Remember when I found you outside that one night?"

"This is different."

"What do you mean? How is it different?"

She tightens her mouth and seems to try and swallow but can't. I go into her bathroom and get her a glass of water. I hand it to her as she sits on the edge of her bed, looking at the wall across from her. A bare and empty wall. No pictures, no art, nothing.

She takes a sip. A little bit of water is still on her lips and dribbles down the side of her chin.

She's like a child. I swear this is ridiculous.

"He's real and I feel him."

"Come on."

"I'm not trying to frighten you, Chris."

"You're not frightening me. At least not with what you're describing."

Your insanity's freaking me out.

"I wasn't drinking tonight."

"I know."

"I swear, Chris."

"Mom, I know."

"I saw him. I felt him. He's real. He's real and he has red eyes that glow in the night under the covers and he came for me. He wants me, Chris."

I go to open my mouth, but then I feel it tighten. I feel my eyes water up and my soul get showered on, and I feel like I'm about ready to just unleash a really seriously embarrassing bout of tears. I slide my hand over my mouth and then bite my skin to get some reality back.

Mom rubs her arms like they're dirty, like she's cold.

"Can I make you something? Something warm?"

She only shakes her head. She leans back on her bed, and I try to uncoil the blanket to put it over her. I see her profile on the edge of the pillow. Her eyes are still wide open, once again looking at the wall.

Can you see something I can't?

I want to ask her what I should do. I don't know.

You gotta call Dad.

"Mom—"

"Lock your door, Chris. And keep that dog by your side."

For a second I look back through the door. I can't see anything outside it.

But I wonder.

"He's real, Chris. He's real."

I wait for a while and watch as her eyes close. Then I shut the door and make sure our front and back doors are locked. I stand in the family room in the pitch black, and I wait. I listen. I stand still to see if I can hear anything. Something moving in our house. Outside our house. In Mom's bedroom. Maybe even below us.

But I don't hear anything.

I only feel cold and creeped out.

I go upstairs and do what Mom told me to do. I lock the door. Then I bring Midnight up by my chest and stroke her with my hand as I wait for the night to be over.

Sunrise always takes too long to come.

29. THE WARNING

The Crag's Inn is impossible to find. The bumping, twisting road starts to make me carsick.

After reading the map Mom gave me and telling her no road exists out this far on this stretch of dirt road, we stumble upon it. A side road to a side road. One going slightly upward and the next going straight up as if it's daring you to try to drive it.

The thought of doing this every week is insane.

But what isn't insane, Chris? You gotta go up the hill to fall off it.

"This map must be old."

"It's the latest they had," Mom says.

"Maybe someone doesn't want this road on a map. Think about that?"

"Perhaps, but someone *does* want some part-time work."

"It's part-time work to get here."

"We just got turned around."

"I swear," I say, trying to fold the map and then just crumpling it up and tossing it into the backseat. "There are twice as many roads around here as that map shows."

"Some of these roads might not even be listed. Who knows."

"I think Solitary isn't listed. The town people forgot. Like the evil little child in class."

"Stop it."

The road we're on is bumpy with several large gashes in its center.

It coils upward, going straight along the hill and then veering around and continuing the opposite way.

"Those are from rain and snow draining down," Mom says, meaning the ruts in the road.

"Great. I really don't feel like barfing right now."

"We're almost there."

"You don't even know if we're on the right road."

But we both know. There doesn't have to be a creepy sign for creepy to be all over this.

After we going back and forth like a yo-yo, my nausea seriously getting worse from the road and from reading in the car, the road takes one more turn and then levels out. The trees are denser here than anywhere we've passed so far. The sky is blocked from view. The road ends in a dead end, with no driveway or parking place around. It just ends with a house nearly hidden amidst trees.

"That looks abandoned," I say.

"That's why she needs help."

"What? Cutting down trees?"

"Be respectful, okay?"

"Am I ever not?"

"Even with your mother."

I roll my eyes as she stops the car. I can hear the sound of birds here. They're loud, and it seems like they're everywhere, like we're standing outside an exhibit at Brookfield Zoo back in Chicago.

"You first," I say, only half joking.

We're facing the side of a dark log cabin with a giant stone chimney arched in its center like a church steeple. It's hard to tell the size of the inn. The cabin is oddly shaped, with a slanting dark tin roof on one side and a porch on the other, an upstairs window and then slightly off to one side a bottom window underneath it, then another deck on the left side of the house. It looks like a kid put it together with Legos and made it uneven and out of whack.

"Come on," Mom says.

I get out and stare at the trees around us. They're so dense I can't see any end in sight. I turn to try and find a door, since there's no sidewalk or driveway or walkway.

Mom is heading toward the deck on the right side, which has some remnants of steps going up to it. I pass something that at first resembles a mailbox, then I see it's a wooden sign with a faded emblem on it.

On top of this sign is the most brilliant blue bird I've ever seen.

Amidst the dark shadows under these trees and the faded gray of the cabin we're walking toward, this ball of rich blue paint is just sitting there, not making a sound. I walk a little closer, but it just sits there, perched and watching like a suspicious stranger.

Mom is already a few steps ahead of me. I don't want to make the bird fly away by calling her name. I slow down and then stop.

The bird's head moves, so I know it's real. For a minute I was beginning to wonder.

Maybe it's a pet. Maybe it's been trained to be around humans.

The bluebird's chest is a lighter blue while its feathers and head are a vibrant turquoise. The black eyes and beak face me as I reach out my hand, knowing the bird is going to fly away but still mesmerized by being so close to it.

Then it bites me.

I howl as the bird keeps tapping away at my hand.

It's not like it hurts. It just shocks me.

"What is it?" Mom calls back at me.

"Ow. Get out of here. Go on."

I bat the bird away, and it flies off. For a second it seemed like it was going to come back at me, but then it disappears.

It wasn't going to come back, come on, man.

I look at my hand. One of my fingers is bleeding.

I go up to my mom. "That bird bit me."

"No, it didn't."

"Yeah, it did. That pretty bluebird—just sitting there looking peaceful—it took a nice little chunk out of my finger."

"Why'd you reach for it?"

"Most birds fly away. At least the kind I'm used to."

Mom has a smile on her face. "Maybe it doesn't get many guests."

"Thanks for your understanding. Glad it wasn't a bear."

"If it was a bear, I think there wouldn't be time for understanding. Just running."

I'm rubbing my finger, still irritated that something so striking had the nerve to bite me, of all things, when I hear a voice above us.

"You're late."

Standing on the deck is a gaunt figure dressed in black.

I see her eyes, and I almost turn around and start running back down the hill.

"Come on inside," she says, then she steps through a door and disappears.

Mom motions her head for me to hurry up.

That bird was a warning. It was a sign.

I stare at my index finger and see the speck of blood on it, then wipe it off with my other hand.

That's just a sign of what's to come, Chris.

30. IRIS

I look at her shriveled bone of a hand marked with spots and bruises, which shakes as it takes the teacup off the table. I'm guessing Iris is old. Like maybe a hundred.

"This is a hard place to find," Mom tells her as we sit on a sofa covered with tiny white hairs that belong to either a dog or a cat.

"Not if you're looking in the right spot," Iris says in a raspy but dignified voice.

She's got an accent. A *proper* accent, almost British or something like that. Or maybe it's just that I think anybody who talks proper sounds British. She's sure not from around here.

Even her outfit makes her look … different. She's wearing a black turtleneck and black pants. Perfectly matched and fitted, strange almost for someone so old to be so fashionable.

She didn't offer us anything to drink and barely even suggested we sit down. I can already tell that I don't want to work for her. The only difference between her and a crabby old man is her gender.

"I don't suppose you were told the job description? Most of the time that's what scares the children away."

Children?

"I was just told that this would be a good job for someone who needed work," Mom says as she shifts on the couch. "Chris is willing to do pretty much anything."

"Chris, is it?"

I nod.

"I'm Tara Buck—Tara," Mom says.

She still isn't used to using her maiden name of Kinner. I still like the sound of Buckley myself even if I don't like who it belongs to.

"It's good that Chris is willing to do, as you say, 'pretty much anything.' Because every day and every week there is something new to do at the inn."

"How long have you run this?"

"My dear," Iris says to my mom, as if she's a child too—maybe we're all children compared to her—"the inn keeps me, not vice versa."

The room we're in is modest and orderly, nothing too strange or weird. Everything is very woodsy in terms of colors and decorations and feel. A painting above the fireplace sums up this room and probably this inn—a picture of a tiny log cabin perched at the edge of a very high cliff.

That's this place, dummy. Someone drew this from far away, as if they're taking a bird's-eye view of it.

The woods must hide how high up we are. Which is a good thing because I don't particularly love heights.

"When are you available, Chris?"

"Well, I'm not sure—I can't drive—so I mean, it's up to my mom."

"When would you like him, Miss …?"

"It's Iris. And does he finish sentences, or does he have a speech impediment?"

"I finish sentences," I say.

"Good. Just wanted to know what to expect."

"When will you need him, Iris?" Mom asks again.

Iris brings the teacup to her mouth and takes a long time to sip it. Then she sets it back down and looks at us. Her hazel eyes are a bit unsettling in their steady stare, as solid as super glue.

"This Saturday, to start. Eight in the morning will do."

"That's fine. And for how long?" Mom asks.

"As long as it takes."

I wonder if I get a say in any of this.

"And what will he be doing?"

"Tara, you must understand. This inn is a special place for special people. It's hard to get to for a reason. It is a place to rest. A place to hide. We have unique guests here who sometimes want to be left alone and sometimes need tending to. My job is to do whatever is required of me. And I need someone to do what is required of him."

I glance at my mom to see if she is as confused as I am.

Thanks, Mom. Great job choice. It's going to be nice when Iris "requires" my left thumb for her creepy experiments in her dungeon.

"Yes, I understand—we understand. It's just—any ideas to share so Chris knows what to bring or what your expectations are?"

"Chris already looks strong and fit. That's one thing. He seems to do a good job keeping quiet, which is another thing. Chris?"

"Yes?"

"Can you keep secrets?"

I want to laugh. This whole town is built on secrets. I'm carrying a backpack of them myself.

Yeah, I can keep freaking secrets.

"Yes," I say.

"What does that mean?" Mom asks.

"As I said, we have unique guests who stay here, Tara. And discretion is wise when it comes to them."

Mom sits on the edge of the seat and shakes her head. "When you say 'unique,' what do you mean?"

"You don't have to worry."

"Chris is respectful, if that's what you're going for."

"Respect and caution are two different animals," Iris says. "They're both wise for a place like this."

"I can keep my mouth shut, if that's what you're asking."

Iris seems surprised by my sudden answer. Yet I see a slight smile on her face.

And for some weird reason, I think of another smile. Another slight smile that popped up surprisingly. The first time I saw Jocelyn smile.

"I don't want to have to worry about my son being around strangers," Mom says.

"There is no need to worry. Chris will be safe and sound in this place. Nobody will harm him here."

I think of the bluebird and want to beg to disagree, but this time I keep my mouth shut.

"But Chris cannot bring guests to the inn. That is unequivocally forbidden. Is that understood?"

I nod. I'm doubting that Newt's going to want to come up and stay the night at this place anyway.

"Chris is a hard worker," Mom says.

"Then he will be able to earn the money. For Saturdays, I pay two hundred dollars."

What?

"Two hundred, for—is that for the day?" Mom sounds as shocked as I am.

Iris just nods, not even bothering to watch our expressions.

Judging by this place, where everything seems old and outdated, I can't see Iris having a lot of money.

Two hundred bucks for a day? Can I start now?

"We'll see how this first Saturday goes and proceed from there. How does that sound?"

"Great," I say.

Iris smiles again. Maybe she likes my outspoken nature. She gives me this look, and for a second I think I've got her wrong. She's not a crabby old woman. She's just—

Careful?

My mom thanks her, and then Iris stands as if she's got other things to do than chitchat the day away. That's another difference between Iris and other old people, especially around here. Most of them have plenty of time to burn. Iris acts like she's got other duties to attend to.

I look down a hallway and wonder if anybody else is staying in the house. If someone "unique" is back there.

When we get outside, we hear rain falling above us onto the covering of trees. Even though it's winter, the trees are still dense enough to cover us.

"When did it start raining?" Mom asks. "The sky was clear when we came up here."

"This mountain never ceases to surprise me," Iris says. "The longer I'm up here the more accustomed I am to seeing anything."

"Do you go into town much?"

Iris merely shakes her head. Maybe that's what she needs me for, though she knows I don't have a license.

"I look forward to seeing you next Saturday, Chris. Be safe."

As we walk to the car, I scan the area and find it—the bluebird, surely the same one that bit me, perched on the edge of a limb not far from our car.

I watch it carefully before getting into the vehicle.

I think of Iris's last words to me.

Be safe.

I wonder exactly how she expects me to do that, and if she has any clue about the mess that's waiting for me off this mountaintop.

31. BELOW

There's gotta be a way to get to it, if something's really there.

I'm searching the cabin, not that there's much to search. Mom is working tonight, and I have no big dates or parties to go to.

I plan to see once and for all if this house has a basement.

My hunt begins in the back of the cabin, in the laundry room. There's an old washer and dryer back here, probably installed when this house was built thirty-something years ago. I check them out, look behind them, see the mounds of dust and cobwebs, think it might be nice to clean those one day just for our health and well-being. There's a tube going out of the wall, but that's nothing unusual.

I examine all parts of the wall and the floor. Not much to examine except faded paint and cracked tile and dirt and grime.

There's a small closet that I've never really noticed by the back door. A half closet for coats. Maybe this is an elevator.

And maybe Batman's going to come out and show you his hidden lair right under your house.

There are a few coats in here. A pretty cool hunting coat, another hip-looking denim jacket. I'm guessing these weren't installed with the washer and the dryer. Again I check out the walls and the floor. No type of door or opening or anything unusual. Just some dirty boots on the bottom of the floor.

I keep this up, going into the kitchen and inspecting each of the cabinets and the dishwasher and the back of the oven and all of that. Nothing. I look underneath the stairs that jut up right in front of the main door.

Nope.

I've been scouring the cabin for an hour and am starting to feel pretty stupid. Maybe there's an empty area below this floor that was never intended to be used. Or maybe there were never any voices or laughter in the middle of the night.

You heard them and you know it.

I check the only other room downstairs, my mother's. I move a dresser but find nothing. I move her bed but find nothing. For a minute I sit on the edge of the bed and listen. It's getting darker outside, and another storm is supposed to be coming.

There's still the bathroom.

Maybe the bathtub has a special button you push that allows you to be sucked down the drain like at some big water park.

You know it's sad when your own thoughts mock you.

I turn on the light and glance around. A tub, a toilet, and a sink. I might as well be thorough. I kneel and open the doors to the cabinet and look at the handful of towels and toiletries belonging to Mom.

There's nothing unusual.

I'm about to close it when something makes me pause.

Every cabinet I've seen has pretty much looked the same except for this one. I take out the towels and notice that the plumbing for the faucet is strangely warped, like it was built around something. It's bent and goes around the edge of the interior of the cabinet, allowing more space.

The thing that caught my eyes was the scuff marks. The scraped sides.

Then I see it.

No way.

I see the square outline of something—I don't know what. The back of the cabinet is the same color as the rest, but the four sides of it look—

Detachable.

I nudge it. Then nudge it a little harder. There's nothing behind it.

After a few tries, I shove it hard with my palm.

This time a portion of the drywall gives.

This isn't drywall. It's a door of some kind.

Right now I know that maybe I should call Mom or call somebody, but I doubt that anybody can help me.

I insert my hand into the opening and feel the cold.

For a minute I think. But it's not a very long minute.

I run out of the bathroom to find a flashlight.

And maybe something else.

Something for protection.

The knife belongs to Uncle Robert, just like the gun I found in the same duffel bag. The gun is lost somewhere on the side of a mountain close to the place Jocelyn died. I think about that gun and what I should've done with it. What I could have done. Instead, in my grief and terror, I dropped it.

One of the ten thousand things I regret.

The knife is a folding kind, but that doesn't mean it has a small blade. This is the kind you can cut a deer open with. I touched the blade once and felt it cut my skin. It's that sharp.

The knife is in my pocket. I'm wearing a sweatshirt because— because to be honest, I have no idea where I'm going to go after I slip through this opening. Maybe I'm going to find something like the hatch from *Lost.* Or maybe it's going to be an alternative universe like *Donnie Darko,* because really, I'm dead. I died on that hill just like Jocelyn. Or maybe I'm going to see a white rabbit and follow it and end up finding Johnny Depp smiling below, wondering what took me so long.

I'm a product of the culture, or at least I used to be. Now I really do feel like I'm in a time warp, an alternative universe, a black nightmare.

I've pushed away the covering to the back of the cabinet and am about ready to climb in through the narrow enclosure when I hear Midnight barking. Her bark is more like a little cough. She never does this, so I go out to the main room to see what's wrong.

Midnight is on the couch, just barking. I pet her for a few minutes and tell her that everything's fine. Maybe she can feel my fear. Or maybe she smells something coming through that opening.

Yeah, like the smell of death.

I go to the fridge and get the little baggie full of treats for her. I've been feeding her little cut-up hot dogs. I saw this on a program once. One of those dog-whisperer shows where a kooky guy gets the dog to do anything. His trick: hot dogs. Lots of them.

"It'll be fine, girl, just stay right here."

Back in the bathroom, I pause for a moment as my flashlight scans the opening. All I can see is a black wall. It doesn't look like there's much of a passageway there.

I slide in and then put my arms and head through the place where the piece of panel was. It's a door of sorts, a kind that swings upward and only can be opened from the back. Once I'm through it will fall back in place.

I slide in a little more and then slip.

For a second, I'm falling headfirst into some dark hole.

I know dark holes. I've become pretty well acquainted with them.

This time I grab on to the edge of the opening and prop the rest of my body up. My legs and gut are still propped in the cabinet so I'm able to balance and not fall in.

I bring the flashlight over and aim it down, my head drooped over some opening where the cold air is coming from.

This really is a hatch.

There is a square hole that's large enough for a person to fit through. Along the side of the wall facing me is a set of metal rungs going down. I see the bottom. All I can see is dirt.

Maybe a lot of people would stop now. And I realize the people in scary movies do idiotic things. *Hey, let's go for a late night swim. Hey, the moon looks great if we go to that abandoned cliff. Hey, I know there's a serial killer around, but can't we still just make out a little longer?* Those idiots are all goners, and you know that the moment they do something so stupid.

But I can't remember seeing this in a horror movie. I seriously doubt Desmond is going to be in my basement, and if he is, then maybe that will explain everything.

I think back to the little cabin I found in the woods above our place. The opening I fell through, the one with a similar ladder attached to its side. The passageway leading into the darkness below. I wonder if the two are connected in some way.

After trying to see if I can fit in the narrow tube going down, I stop moving and have an awful thought. If someone or something's down there, they'll be able to grab me before I can see them.

Nothing's down there, just like nothing was in the cabin above the house.

I wiggle backward and force myself through the cabinet. I can just imagine Mom coming home now and seeing my head sticking out below the bathroom sink.

Are you really that bored, Chris?

My legs arch, as does the rest of my body as I struggle to find the rungs of the ladder. Soon I have one hand attached to a cold strip of metal while the other has the flashlight. I scan the bottom to see if anything is moving.

Before I'm too far down, I check the door and make sure it's secure. In case Mom sees it and suddenly has the crazy idea of trying to go through it herself.

Only one of us needs to be that stupid.

The ladder ends as the hole opens to what must be our cabin's basement. On the opposite side of where I'm climbing is a wall that has another built-in ladder on it. I swing like a monkey from one side to the other and then finish climbing down on the opposite side, which I presume is the edge of our house. It's cold down here, and I know that I'm now underground.

When I get down I scan the area with my light, trying to keep my hand from shaking. I pat my jeans pocket and make sure the knife is still there. For a moment I just take in my surroundings.

There's really nothing to take in.

It looks like an unfinished basement. The walls surrounding me are cement, the ground a soft dirt. There are no doors or windows or openings coming in. Except for the rather large and ominous opening on the other side of where I'm standing.

I try to figure out which direction is what. If I'm guessing right, the opening is toward the back of the house, which means it's a couple stories underground.

What if it connects to the other passageway?

There's a part of me that thinks this is pretty cool. In the same way I think a movie that gets me to stop breathing is pretty cool.

There's another part of me that wants some answers.

I listen and can't hear anything. No voices, no laughter, no wind.

Then I hear Midnight barking.

That's when I realize that it's pretty easy to hear what's going on above.

That's also when I realize beyond any doubt whatsoever that the laughter I heard the other night was real, and it came from where I'm standing right now.

32. SOME UNDERGROUND
LABYRINTH

I've been walking for ten minutes, and every step I take makes me wonder if I should turn around and run back out. It's cold and black. I mean, absolutely deathly black. But that's not what terrifies me so much. It's not claustrophobia. I don't get crazy in confined spaces. And this tunnel isn't like a foxhole. It's not quite six feet—I know this because I'm about six feet, and I have to bend a bit to keep from scraping my head. The width seems to vary as I move along. Some places might be five feet across, some just wide enough for me to fit through. The light shows nothing but dark earth and stone that somehow and in some way was carved here. It's definitely man-made.

What for is the question.

For the first few minutes, I pound my fist into the side walls and the roof above me. They're hard, maybe because of the cold but also because of the hard earth. Some of it feels like clay, or really hard dirt, while in other places are chunks of rock. There are lots of rocks.

I doubt it's going to crash in on me. The only thing that could do that is an earthquake, and I don't think they get those around here.

No, what terrifies me is wondering what's ahead. The passageway has gone straight with only a few slight turns. At first, after I stepped into the tunnel from my basement, it descended quite a bit, but it's leveled out and just heads straight.

There's nothing I've seen—no lights or cables or candy wrappers or Egyptian symbols or signs that say *Go Forward at Your Own Peril!*

And again that makes me nervous, because I have no idea where this is going.

My flashlight seems strong, but I wonder what I'd do if it went out. I could find my way back, no problem, but pitch black and musty air and cold dark underground …

Don't think that. Don't go there.

When I reach an intersection with another tunnel in the shape of a T, I'm forced to make a decision.

If there are more of these decisions and passageways, you might end up getting lost and confused in some underground labyrinth.

But it's just one turn. That's all. I can remember that.

The question is which way.

I stand there for a second, my imagination going into overdrive.

If someone comes out of nowhere chasing you, you're in trouble. Especially if he's short.

That makes me laugh, but I think I do that because I'm so jittery.

What if these are tunnels for letting out water from some dam or river? If these filled up there'd be nowhere to go to get out.

These and a hundred other scenarios swirl around my head.

Yet I want to know. I want to find out where these go. Are they all interconnected? Do they all lead to one place, and where would that be?

I turn right, then begin walking steadily and quickly.

I have no idea which direction I'm going. North, south, east, west. It doesn't really matter.

I reach another intersection, this one looking more like a Y, and again I go right. That way I'll just have to remember to go left on my return. I wonder how long I've been walking. Half hour, hour, longer?

I feel cold.

A bark comes out of nowhere. I jerk and stop and then listen.

I can't tell if it's in the tunnel or somewhere outside. I wait for several minutes, then keep going.

There it is again.

A loud bark, and deep. Not some tiny puppy.

It's in the tunnel.

Oh come on. Not more dogs. No more crazy dogs.

I feel itchy and sweaty and cold and numb at the same time. Suddenly I just want to be out of here.

When the next bark comes, this time sounding as if it's directed *at* someone or something, I stop and aim my light ahead. The passage just keeps going. I can't tell where the noise is coming from, behind or in front of me.

This little adventure was nice and all, but it's time to go back inside.

I turn around and head back down the tunnel.

I hear the barking again.

I feel more nervous walking back, because I feel like something is behind me. As I get to the point where one passage goes right and the other left, I turn behind and aim the flashlight to see if anybody's there. Then I beam it back in front of me and then I see—

He's tall and hunched over and haggard with a long ancient face and his eyes look hollow just like his open mouth and he points at me.

I stop and then buckle backward as if something's on top of me. I run into the back wall as I keep the light on the man.

"Hello, Chrisssss."

The voice the dead eyes the wrinkles the spots the decaying skin the undead.

I don't realize I've tripped and fallen backward. I'm still aiming the flashlight at the man, who just stands there. Then I get up and run.

I run in the direction I was headed before I stopped. I don't know where I'm going, but that man or thing was real and I'm getting away from him.

The laughter starts up, and I know. This man or thing or beast or creature dwells in these tunnels. He was laughing in our basement.

As I run, the shaft of light going up and down with my hand, I have a terrible thought.

He's the vision my mom has been having. She's not been dreaming or having wild cocktail nightmares. She's been terrorized by this old man who may or may not be dead.

"Where are you going?" the voice calls out, like a stranger's tongue licking my ear.

I feel like centipedes are crawling all over my back, but I'm too petrified to stop and brush them off. I keep running. One tunnel morphs into two that morph into several more and by now I'm lost and running and thanking Coach Brinks for starting to get me in shape.

As I run, I think I hear other sounds.

More animals.

More voices.

The sound of rushing water.

And the sound of

No don't don't even don't go there because that's beyond creepy.

But it's true, and I hear it just like I saw the old man.

I hear the cries of babies.

33. Building Blocks

One might call me lucky for getting out, but I don't think luck should ever be applied to my name or my life.

Yes, I happened to keep running and make a wrong turn. Blame the grinning old fossil or the weirdo baby sounds. The tunnel I sprinted through got bigger and opened up into the mouth of a cave. And yes, I ended up in the woods in the middle of nowhere.

Nowhere being Solitary, nowhere synonymous with Solitary and everything around here.

And yes, sure, I eventually found a side road that I'm walking on right now.

But lucky people can stop shaking.

Lucky people don't encounter zombies in underground tunnels.

Only stupid people do, and I'm stupid.

The dirt road winds around, but I know it has to eventually connect with some other road.

Either that or morning will come and I'll eventually see where I'm going.

There's a part of this that should be fun. Investigating new places and secret passageways and hidden secrets and blah blah blah.

But that's fun in a video game when you've got your buddies next to you and your stomach is full of candy and soda and it's three in the morning and you know that tomorrow you'll be hanging at the beach or going to a party or living life.

I've been walking for several minutes when I stop and start breathing in and out and desperately try to keep my heart from racing and my body from shaking.

Every time I blink, I see his eyes. Or his lack of eyes.

For a while I'm a mess in the middle of this road. But I fight it and I win.

I fight it and I tell it to go away.

I fight it and I finally grind my teeth in anger as I start walking again.

So I know.

It's more than I knew yesterday or the day before.

I hear Jared's words again. *You have to lie low. For a while.*

I'm really tired of all of this because I don't understand any of it. I walk faster. I want to bolt up the opening in the bathroom and then

Then what?

I don't know.

I keep walking but I don't know.

The world turns bright and changes. Have I been dreaming?

I'm walking in a long, round passageway with glass above me showing the clear blue sky. For a second I try to stop, but the ground is moving. I glance at my feet and see the moving walkway below me.

My clothes are different. I feel different. Everything is vibrant and clear and quiet.

The walkway ends, and I get off.

I'm standing at the edge of wide, empty hallway.

Not a hallway. A terminal.

There are tall windows lining the terminal, showing off the clear blue sky. It's beautiful, almost like a painting. It's bright, too, so bright that I almost miss seeing the woman walking down the carpet several gates away from me.

She turns back, and I know without a doubt that it's Jocelyn.

"Hold on," I call out as I see her.

Her hair is still long and dark and full, the kind a guy dreams of running his hands through while staring into her eyes. She looks taller, but I notice it's because she's wearing heels. She's dressed up in a long black dress, the kind an adult might wear to go out for a fancy dinner. She doesn't look like the Jocelyn I remember. She looks grown up.

Something about this, about me, about us, feels different and strange.

I start running, but the faster I run the farther away she seems to be.

Then I blink, and the brightness and the blue turn to black.

I open my eyes and start to slow down and find that I'm still on some deserted dirt road in the hills of Solitary.

I didn't die and wake up in some weird airport. I didn't see some woman looking like Jocelyn heading out for a party.

I didn't see any of that. It was just—

It was just like those tunnels and her eyes were as real as the hollowed-out eyes of the man in them.

I keep walking, heading I don't know where.

I don't even believe the noise of the truck or the piercing beams of the headlights when they come from behind me.

It's only when the truck stops and a voice calls out that I realize that I'm not dreaming.

"What's your name?" the driver asks after he asks if I need a ride.

There are a lot more things in this life that I need besides just a ride.

Do you have a spare case of hope in the back? Maybe just a six-pack will do?

"Chris Buckley."

The guy seems ordinary enough. Maybe my mom's age, maybe younger. He's got a friendly face that seems familiar for some reason. I decide to take his offer. The sports radio station he initially had turned up loud is now down. The cabin smells like Mexican food.

"Where do you live, Chris?"

"Solitary."

"This is quite a ways from the downtown."

"Yeah."

"Everything okay?"

"Yeah."

I can't help thinking about what I just saw in those underground tunnels and about the fact that Mom might be coming home. I see her standing at her sink after taking a shower, and a grisly, aged hand reaching out to grab her legs from the cabinet below.

He's got a laid-back Southern drawl that relaxes me. "Do you know where you are?"

"Not exactly."

The man keeps looking at me as if he's trying to figure out if I'm high or drunk or just stupid.

"I take this way whenever I'm heading to Greenville. It's a short-cut if you don't mind the weaving roads. Not a lot of people know about it."

"So where are we?"

"Technically we're still in North Carolina, though South Carolina is really close," the man says. "We're closer to the older town of Solitary that was burned down years ago. They moved the regular town closer to the tracks, and that's where it stands now. Not a lot of people know about the original town because it happened years ago. I'm a bit of a historian in my spare time."

"Do you live in Solitary?"

"No. We live nearby in Lowden. My name's Jack. So I assume you go to Harrington?"

"Started before Halloween last year. I moved with my mom from the Chicago area."

"That's quite the move."

"Yeah."

For a second it looks like he's about to tell me something, then he remains quiet.

"So you going to tell me where your house is?" Jack eventually asks.

"I would if I knew where we were."

"If I get to the center of town, can you tell me?"

"I can walk from there."

The guy laughs. "Come on. Looks like you've walked enough already. You're still sweaty."

I absently wipe my forehead.

"So, you like Harrington?"

"Sure."

Jack laughs. "That was convincing."

"It's more like Harrington doesn't like me."

"High school is shorter than you realize. I tell my kids that."

I nod, but there's no way I buy it.

"I'm forty-two, and as I get older I see life as these chunks. Blocks of time. Sometimes you just have to get through the block in order to keep moving. That's what I tell myself when I take odd jobs like the one I just did in Greenville. Strange hours, but it's money, and nowadays that means a lot."

I don't know what to say, so I don't say anything.

"Harrington is one of those blocks," Jack says. "You make it as strong as you possibly can, and then when you're finally ready, you climb on top of it and step to the next box, whatever that is."

"So you travel a lot for your work?"

"Yep. Would move if we could, but we can't. Selling a house is hard these days. And moving to a place means you've got something to move to."

"Yeah," I say.

"Building blocks. That's what it is. Keep that in mind."

34. THE CAMERA

The next day, Mom is quite angry. Not because I disappeared last night and almost lost my life. She doesn't know anything about that thanks to my decision to close that magical trapdoor below her sink. It's because of Midnight's upset stomach. And it's not even that she's furious about having to clean up a trail of puppy vomit from the couch to the back door. No, she's furious because of *why* she needed to clean it up.

The conversation goes like this:

"What have you been feeding her?"

The little tuft of black on the couch obviously doesn't know we're talking about her.

"I don't know."

"I buy her dog food."

"A dog wouldn't eat that generic stuff."

"So what has she been eating?"

"I don't know. Sometimes I give her hot dogs and stuff."

"What?"

"I saw it on one of those shows. That's how you train dogs. You give them little hot dog treats."

"What show was that?"

"I don't know."

She looks in the fridge and discovers the pack of twenty-four hot dogs missing.

"Chris!"

Yeah, so maybe the dog whisperers don't give their dogs that many hot dog treats.

Hey, if that's the only drama for the day, I'm happy.

It's Sunday night, and it's been a productive day. While Mom went to work and I was given a reason not to do much of anything, I found a hammer and some nails and bolted that door in the cabinet down.

Do you really think that's going to keep away the boogeyman, you moron?

I don't answer that voice because there's no answer I can come up with. I'd need to find a special store dealing with ghosts and spirits in order to answer it.

So you gonna tell Mom?

No. Not quite. Not yet. I will.

I spend the rest of the day searching the cabin. I don't find anything.

I do, however, decide to finally check out more on Uncle Robert.

It's about time, Chris.

Yeah.

To be honest, I'd forgotten about the flash drive and the digital camera and the letters I found in my room some time ago. I've been borrowing T-shirts like The Pixies one I'm wearing or the Interpol one I'm going to wear tomorrow. I've been listening to his music and sleeping in his bed, but I haven't looked closely at Uncle Robert's personal stuff.

Tonight I decide it's time.

I start with the camera. It's an expensive digital model. I turn it on and find over a hundred photos waiting to be seen.

I see pictures of the cabin as if they were taken when Uncle Robert first moved here. Then I see snapshots of my uncle, first outside on the driveway, then on the deck, then inside. He looks older and heavier than I remember him. He also looks amused in the first few shots, like he's laughing at whoever is taking them.

The first twenty-five pictures are all like this.

And then I see a shot of my uncle with someone.

The woman. The lady who picked me up in the silver SUV.

She's holding a hand up in front of her face as if trying to shield it. I still can't see her eyes, but I know it's the same woman. She looks attractive, and from the way my uncle has his arm around her, it looks like he thinks so too. A few shots following are blurry, as if they were taken of someone who didn't want to be photographed. The lady perhaps? The mysterious woman in hiding? Who was she hiding from?

It dawns on me to look at the dates. I scroll back and see that the photos of my uncle and the woman were taken a couple of years ago.

The next dozen shots are of scenery, landscapes and hills and forests and flowers. I scroll through them quickly until something makes me stop.

There it is, just like it looked the first time I saw it, just like it looks in the magazine page I was given.

Maybe it wasn't a magazine page.

On the small screen of the digital camera, I can't be positive that it's the exact same shot, but I believe it is.

I'm looking at a photo—maybe *the* photo—of Heartland Trail, the road I took by the church that dead-ends in the woods.

Following it I see more pictures of the woods themselves. There is one that looks like a trail. Another that shows what might be an opening to a cave that looks like a mouth of a giant on its side. Another few shots are dark and blurry, and I can't make out anything.

Then I see something else that makes me pause.

Hanging off what appears to be the limb of a tree is an upside-down cross. It's the cross itself that makes me feel deep dread. It resembles two carved-out blocks of wood, carefully whittled down in a very crude fashion. Both pieces appear to be dipped and covered in something dark and shiny, and they're fastened together by some type of metallic coil.

It looks ancient, this cross. And it looks designed specifically to be hung upside down.

I don't know much about the occult and people worshiping the Devil, but I know this is one of their symbols.

Maybe it's the town logo for Solitary, too.

The next few photos are of something that resembles a tall, spiked tree. Since it's so big and it looks like the pictures were taken at night, they're too hazy and gray to make sense.

The next twenty or so shots are of the woman, and this time she's not hiding behind glasses. She's beautiful.

There are a few more shots of her with my uncle, as if he's holding up the camera.

I see a couple of shots that appear as if the woman is hiding underneath covers, as though my uncle woke her up holding the camera.

That's the bedspread on the bed my mom sleeps in.

Then the photos end.

I try to remember that brief car ride I had with her.

The movie star.

I try and remember her words. *I was a friend of your uncle.*

They appeared to be a little more than friends.

Maybe she knows why Uncle Robert disappeared.

I suddenly wonder if Jared knows about this woman. Crazy, soap-opera-like thoughts go through my mind.

Is this Jared's mother?

But Jared is older than I am. And this woman doesn't look anything like him.

I'm too tired and too fried to check through the flash drive. I don't want to know what's on it.

But I need to find the woman in these photos and ask her what happened to my uncle.

35. One Puzzle Piece

I wonder how many people around this school know me. Or know *of* me. The new guy, the guy from Chicago, the kid who started liking Jocelyn, the idiot who wouldn't listen, the moron who wouldn't learn. I wonder how many notice the cloud covering me as I walk around. Probably fewer than I think. Probably very few. But I still walk around like Pigpen from Charlie Brown, a dusty mess circling over me.

There are times when I want to just go into an empty room and wait it out. The periods between periods, when you actually have time to talk and notice and interact. Those are the times I hate the most. Sitting in class and trying to listen to the teacher is okay. At least I know what I'm supposed to be doing. At least I know that I'm protected. Maybe, hopefully. But the periods between the periods are the worst.

They're bad because they remind me of Jocelyn.

I don't know how this works. Nobody's told me, and I doubt anybody will. I watch how Mom is coping with everything with Dad, and that's not a way I want to go. Not that I'd be allowed to drown my sorrows anyway, but I don't want to escape my memories. I don't want to let them go. I don't want to forget what she meant to me.

These hallways don't necessarily remind me. Instead, they mock. They taunt me and howl with laughter.

This school, just like this town, is twisted. If I were to dig deep, I'm sure I'd find warped and sickly roots.

I just wonder what they'd be attached to.

"So I hear you met my father."

For a moment I don't even notice her there. I'm in a bubble, a little place of bliss behind this canvas of blue. It's a chance to get away from everything else even if I have no business trying to paint.

"What?" I say.

"The other night. He said he picked you up on his way home from work."

"That was your dad?"

She nods.

I shake my head and laugh. "He didn't tell me he had a daughter who goes to Harrington."

"He's a bit protective. He said he met someone who had just moved here in October, and I knew who it was right away."

"Tell him thanks again for the ride."

"What were you doing?"

The other students in the class are talking and painting. Mr. Chestle is laid back in a way that makes you wonder if he smokes a lot of pot on his time off.

"Just walking around."

"In the middle of a freezing night?"

I just shrug. For a moment she looks as if she's going to push me for an answer, but she doesn't. She goes back to painting something that could be displayed in a museum.

"That's really good," I say.

But it's lame. It's like cutting her off with my car and then slowing down to make sure she's okay.

"There's a lot of land to check out around here," I finally say.

A lot of land to check out? What are you, some kind of surveyor?

"My dad was pretty concerned."

"Why?"

"The same way he's concerned for me. He's overprotective about everything."

Kelsey continues to paint, holding her brush so naturally it seems like she was born holding it.

"They say that the big cities are dangerous places to go out after sunset, but my father disagrees. I sometimes think he would feel better about living in one of those big cities than around here. At least there, you're surrounded by people."

He's got a good point.

"He just wanted me to let you know to be careful, okay?"

"Yeah, sure."

There's more to be said, of course. There's always more to be said. But Kelsey doesn't seem to be a more-to-be-said kind of girl.

And for the moment, I appreciate that.

We're in an indoor track that's forty minutes away from the school. Occasionally we go practice indoors like this, just to get a good workout. I'm bending over, feeling dots twirl around as I try to get back my breath and my bearings. I've just completed my first officially timed 300-meter hurdles. I don't know what my time was, but I know how out of shape I am.

Coach Brinks is behind me and belts my back. Then he curses at me in a way that sounds like an abusive father. This is his way of telling me I did a good job.

"What were they feeding you up there in Chicago?"

I'm still sucking in air, so I don't say anything.

"You keep that up, and we're going to be competitive, I'm telling you what."

He tells me my time, but I don't pay attention. For a minute I stand and look around the indoor stadium with the mini-track. Thankfully I have my track shoes from my former life to make running a little easier and quicker. The track belongs to a school around Hendersonville.

As the coach tells me to work on form and steps and all that wonderful stuff, I see Jared in the stands just sitting and watching me. Not trying to hide, not trying to be subtle. He waves as if he doesn't have a care in the world.

"Come on, Chicago. We gotta get that suburban flab fit to run in the springtime."

I shuffle back onto the track and prepare to work on my form.

Of course, when I look back at the stands, Jared is gone.

"Got a ride home?"

The voice comes out of nowhere as I'm walking toward the doors of the high school. I see Jared standing at the edge of a darkened hallway leading into the school.

"I was going in the van back to school."

"I'll take you home."

I see the guys walking out and call after one to tell him I've got a ride. Then I wait until they're gone and follow Jared the other way.

For a while we walk down a shadowy hallway that looks like it's gone to sleep. I walk a few steps behind him, wondering where he's taking me, wondering why we couldn't just go out the front door.

"Come on," Jared says. "There's a parking lot to the side of this school."

"How'd you know I was here?" My words echo in the otherwise still corridor.

"Knowing stuff is easy."

He finds a door and leads me outside. The cold air is a nice relief against my sweaty skin. I see his truck waiting and get inside.

"Nice work on those hurdles."

"Thanks."

"I used to play football myself."

For a few minutes, Jared talks about his football days. It makes it seem like any ordinary conversation, like any ordinary friendship. My big brother talking to me as he takes me home. Then he changes the topic without any hesitation.

"Any leads? Anything unusual going on?"

"Every day is unusual around here."

"Give me specifics."

There's still a hesitation and a doubt. I don't know why. I really don't.

But I tell him first about the passageway I found under the house. He listens and doesn't give away whether it's a surprise to him or not. I don't mention the creepy old man, because I've started to think I might not have seen him. I don't know. All I know is that I did discover a hidden passageway under our house.

"It was just like one I found in an old cabin above our house."

Jared nods.

"What are those? Who built them?"

"I don't know," he says in a matter-of-fact way. "I've heard rumors of such things but have never seen them myself. You said the tunnel you were in led out to the middle of a country road?"

"The middle of nowhere."

"How'd you get home?"

"I walked."

A lie. A simple lie. For some reason, I can't tell this guy the entire truth.

You have to trust someone, Chris. You have to or else you're never going to trust anyone.

"Did you tell your mom?"

"No."

"Good. Don't. Don't say anything until I'm able to check it out."

"I'm not going back down there."

"Did you see anything strange?"

Yeah, I saw Scrooge looking for the ghosts of Christmas but wandering around like a blind man.

"The whole thing is creepy," I say. "The fact that there's a secret passageway that leads into the bathroom. It makes me think—I'm wondering if people have been slipping in and out of our place."

He doesn't react to this. It doesn't seem like anything is going to surprise Jared.

"I found pictures," I tell him. "A camera with pictures of Uncle Robert. Many of them with a woman."

"What'd she look like?"

"She was blond. Pretty. Older."

"How old?"

"I don't know," I say. "My mom's age maybe. Maybe a little older."

Jared sighs.

"What? You know who she is?"

"Maybe."

"I was thinking—I mean, she didn't look like you."

He laughs. "If you're wondering if that's my mom, no. No way. She's out of the picture. That all you found?"

"Yeah."

Again with the lie.

Maybe if he gives me more to work with, more to believe, then I'll do the same for him.

"You see anything else at school? Any strange or weird things happen to you? Any calls or emails coming in? Anything?"

"Why do I feel like you're interrogating me?"

Jared slows the truck down and pulls to the side of the road. We're in winter darkness in the middle of the country.

"Listen, Chris. I don't know what it's going to take to get you to totally trust me, okay? There are reasons why I'm not telling you everything. Other people might want that information and might end up getting it from you. The more you can tell me, the more I can help you. The more I can keep you out of trouble."

"Who was the woman?"

"Her name is Heidi."

"What's she have to do with your dad?"

"I think they fell in love. And that's a problem. A big problem."

"How come?"

"Because she's married to Pastor Marsh. And whatever happened between her and my dad, it ended up with both of them missing."

"But I saw her. She's the one—she told me about what was going to happen to Jocelyn. She warned me and tried to get me to help."

"Chris, listen, okay? If you see her, you have to tell me. You have to let me know right away."

"Why?"

"Because I have a feeling she might know what happened to my father. She might even be the reason he's missing."

36. MAYBE

That night I try to find out what's on the zip drive that belonged to my uncle. But all I find are files that I can't open after an hour of trying. The next day, I find Newt and ask him if he's any good at computers.

"Why do people automatically think I'm good at computers and electronics?" he asks me, as if it's a question he's been asked a hundred times.

"Are you?"

"Well, yeah. Of course."

I shake my head. "Here. Take this home and see if you can do anything with it."

"It's an older model."

"It can't be that old."

"A couple of years at least."

"See why I asked you?"

"Whose is it?"

"You just tell me if you can open it, okay?"

"Did you steal this?"

"No. But make sure nobody steals it from you. Okay?"

He slips it into his pocket and walks away from me as if I've just given him drugs.

Maybe this zip drive holds all the information I need on this town. Maybe it has one of those "If you're reading this now, then ..." letters from my uncle.

The maybes remain with me in my classes and in my breaks and in the hallways and in the vast canyon of my mind.

I see Poe, but she still continues to ignore me.

Maybe she's with them and knew all along.

But that doesn't make sense. She suspected something was wrong when a guy she liked went missing the year before Jocelyn did.

Maybe that's when she went over to the dark side.

I try and tell myself that this isn't Star Wars and that there's no Darth Vader reeling me in. I already know who my father is, thank you very much. I don't need to scream *No!* as my father asks me to join him, because I've already been there and done that.

Maybe it's time to tell your father.

But I can't and won't. There are people out there to ask for help. The problem is they'll want proof. I have nothing. I have nothing but stories that seem made up by a new kid who's been nothing but a problem since he got into town.

Maybe she's still alive.

That question comes up daily and gets shot down right away. I saw Jocelyn there, dead and lifeless. She's gone. I know it.

In history, as Mr. Meiners smiles at me while most of the other students seem to be drifting off, I make a list of names.

> Don't Trust:
> Pastor Marsh
> Sheriff Wells
> Kevin Ross (moron deputy)
> Anybody with a last name of Staunch

NOT SURE:
MOM
POE
RACHEL (THOUGH SHE'S GONE, SO WHATEVER)
RAY

PROBABLY:
NEWT
JARED
THE BLOND WOMAN (HEIDI??)

I glance at the list and see how pathetic it looks. I don't trust my own mother. My father doesn't even make the list. As for friends and family—nope. None are on it.

I decide to add one more name to the probably list. Just to make it even. Just to make it seem like I'm not a complete and utter loser.

Kelsey

I don't know her any better than most of the people in this place. But it just seems like if there's someone I might be able to trust, it's the shy girl who blushes several times a period every art class.

I have to start somewhere.

This is where I'm starting.

And as Jared told me when we first met, I need to lay low. Or lie low. Whichever one really works. That's what I'm going to do.

For a while.

Just a while.

37. A LOCKER LOVE POEM

I think this place is preparing me for prison, if I ever do something to deserve to be imprisoned.

It's like that Bill Murray movie *Groundhog Day* with the same things happening over and over.

I see the same girl named Harriet every day on the bus, and she does the same thing. As I walk by, she makes sure that no part of her body touches me, not her leg or her arm or anything. It's like I have the plague. And this girl Harriet is—well, I don't want to be mean, but she's a big girl. And it gets me because I'm like *What did I ever do to you, and why are you rejecting me?*

Every day I see Newt, his shifting eyes, the scar so evident on his face, his body always two seconds away from bolting from the limited conversation we have. Every day I ask about the zip drive, and every day he gives me a long and detailed reply that I never quite follow but that makes it obvious he's working on it.

Every day, at some point, I see Poe. Every day is Halloween for her. It appears that her Goth tastes have taken over. Her skin seems to be getting paler and her makeup darker and her sneer snarkier. I've given up trying to talk to her, and I'd give up passing her by if I knew where she'd be walking. But she pops up at the most random times. The thing is, I always see her. Every day, without fail. It's like she's there to remind me of what's not there. Like she wants to rub it in my face.

Then there's Gus. He hasn't gone away. It's obvious that he does what his father tells him to, because he's been staying away from me, but I have to see him just as I have to see Poe. It's not *that* big of a school. You can't hide from everybody and everything.

In this dark gulag, with the weather bleak and cold and gray, I find myself looking forward to something surprising: art class. Not so I can project something deep inside that I don't even know is there onto the canvas. Hardly. It's so I can step out of the bleakness and the cold and the gray and see something that's the opposite of all those things.

I realize this is happening, and a part of me finds the biggest frying pan it can to whop me upside the head.

That's the last thing you need, Chris.

I know. And it's not like there's anything between us. Kelsey's harmless and she's cute, but that's all. She's so shy that I still have a hard time talking with her. She could be schizophrenic as far as I know. But it's nice. That's all I can say. It's a nice breather. It's like those short breaks to get water during track practice.

Even if she's harmless, you're certainly not. Look what happened to—

But that's crazy, because this isn't Jocelyn and it never will be.

Still, I gotta say that it's nice to hear laughter here. It's nice to hear someone laughing with me and not at me.

It's nice to see a smile.

The days groan by, and I mark them on the stone wall of my mind like a prisoner who's lost track of the date.

Yet even prisoners have surprises. Mine come every now and then.

Most of them are unexplainable. And most of them seem to pop up in my locker.

First there was the picture. The one of me that I can't remember being taken, the one with an expression I can't remember ever having. I have that picture at home in my room, hidden from view and also hidden out of curiosity and for safekeeping. Then there was the photo of the woods—the photo that seems to keep coming up, the one that seems to have some kind of meaning that is lost on me.

Now today, my Groundhog Day is broken up by something new.

A Hallmark card.

Actually, it's not a Hallmark card. It's too unusual to be one of those.

It's in my locker, and it has my initials on the front. Written in black ink in a very precise matter.

The card is funny. It shows a funny-looking guy with spiked hair surrounded by a circle of people yelling and screaming at him. All the people look like ordinary men and women, but they're all angry and crazed. The guy in the middle has a smile.

On the inside of the card is one line: DON'T LOSE YOUR SANITY LIKE THE REST OF US.

And underneath, no signature. Just a simple note: You're not as crazy as you might think.

I examine the card and make sure there's nothing else on it. But no.

Like all my locker love poems, this one is unsigned.

38. What Do You Believe?

I want to kiss her longer when she turns her lips away and gazes up at me in the field we're hiding in.

"What?"

"You've got to stop this, Chris."

I look at Jocelyn as the world around seems to drift slowly away like smoke into the air.

"Stop what?"

"These dreams. These thoughts. They'll confuse you."

"What do you mean, 'confuse' me? I know exactly what I want, and it's something I should've given into when I had the chance."

"Don't say that."

"I want to say that."

"You're dreaming. This isn't real."

I touch the edge of her cheek, and she feels real. This feels real.

"It doesn't matter what it feels like," Jocelyn says. "I don't want you getting this confused with other things."

"What things?"

"You have to let me go."

"So how do I do that?"

"You'll find out," she says.

As I move to kiss her again, she's gone.

On my first day of work at the Crag's Inn, Mom gets lost again and ends up making us half an hour late. It's not like this is some maze of streets in Chicago; there are only a handful of back roads weaving their way through these hills. But it looks totally different this time, as if new roads have sprouted like weeds in the backyard. Mom knocks on the door and sees Iris and apologizes for my tardiness.

"I certainly hope this is not a sign of what's to come," the proper-sounding voice says.

"No, not at all."

"Good. Then I will lead Chris to his first project of the day."

I scarcely say good-bye to Mom before I'm in the woods at the side of the cabin, cutting and hauling chunks of wood. There's a large tree that looks like it recently fell or was cut down. It's been chainsawed, and my job is taking those sawed bits and cutting them down into usable logs for the fire. An hour into the job I can already feel blisters under the gloves I'm wearing. I'm sweating even though the morning air is still quite cold. The dense woods cover up the sun that's slowly beginning to brighten up the area like lights on a Christmas tree.

Sometime, I'm not sure when, Iris comes outside carrying a plastic cup of water.

"I thought you might need a drink."

"Thank you."

She doesn't ask how it's going, doesn't scan my work. She leaves the cup with me and goes back inside. I look at the side view of the inn and notice that the only part that's not enclosed with trees and woods is the front. I can tell from the slanting ground that the inn is at the very edge of what appears to be a steep cliff.

I'm curious about the place, but not willing to snoop around too much. I have a job to do, and two hundred bucks sounds pretty good to me.

"Did you bring a lunch with you?"

"No."

I was hoping you'd have an all-you-can-eat buffet in the middle of your hotel.

"Okay, then. Finish what you're doing and come on inside. I'll show you where to clean up and where the dining area is."

"Okay."

I didn't hear her mention any food, but I doubt she's going to make me sit in the dining area with nothing to eat.

Maybe there will be guests? Special guests?

I finish cutting the wood and haul the remaining pieces over to the side of the cabin that now is almost entirely lined with a four-foot wall of freshly cut logs. I'm proud of my work and also know that come tomorrow I'm going to be aching all over.

I wonder if Iris saw my efforts, but I don't say anything about it as I walk inside and she shows me where the bathroom is. I walk down a hallway lined with old black-and-white pictures of people. Strange-looking people.

I stop for a minute to look at one of the pictures. It's of a man and woman standing next to a railroad car. It looks like it could have been taken close to the downtown area of Solitary.

The strange thing about this picture is the expression on the couple's face, if they're a couple. They're smiling. No, they're laughing.

Most of the pictures I've seen of people back in the old days, when pictures were still a new thing, showed people who looked serious and miserable. That's what's so strange about this shot. The people don't look serious and creepy and miserable.

But maybe that's the point. They're delirious and delusional. Like they've been sniffing something funny and drinking moonshine and getting ready to howl at the moon.

"Hurry up, please," a voice calls from behind me.

The bathroom is sparse, but something else surprises me.

On the back of the toilet is a small plate standing on a little holder. On that plate is a Bible verse: *Fear not: for they that be with us are more than they that be with them. II Kings 6:16*

I glance around to see if there are any more quotes or crosses or angel wings, but I don't find any. The Bible verse doesn't surprise me. Nothing surprises me around here. But it makes me curious to see if Iris is one of those kinds of people.

I go back into the main room where we sat with her that first day. She waves me on like a ten-year-old to a large open room with lots of windows filling it with a blanket of sunshine. There are half a dozen tables arranged in it.

"This is our dining room," she says.

I glance out the window. It looks like we're hanging over the side of the mountain.

"What do you like to eat?" Iris asks.

"I'm not picky."

"I have a lot to choose from, so let me know."

"Anything, really."

"Chris?"

"Yes?"

For some reason I think of the Joker's cheeks when I glance at the old woman. There are deeply etched lines on either side of her face, and I can't tell if they're from wrinkles or just from the sunken nature of her face.

"Please answer my question as specifically as possible. I don't have time or patience to try to read your mind."

"I like ham," I say, not sure why. It's not like I love ham or anything, but I'm slightly terrified by her straightforward statement. "And chips."

"See, that wasn't hard."

"I could've brought my lunch," I say to her.

"Part of working here includes meals. If you had come early enough, you could have had breakfast."

I nod.

She disappears, and I move closer to the windows. There's a door that leads to the deck outside, but I'm not going out there unless Iris asks me to. Still, I can see the deep bowl of a valley in front of us, with the tops of surrounding hills in the distance. When Iris comes back, I take my plate and thank her.

"Have you ever seen such a view?" she asks me.

"No."

I've been skiing in Colorado, but those mountains are different from these. These seems rounder and softer and …

More romantic.

If the guys could only hear my thoughts. But it's true. More romantic, but also more sad. More melancholy.

I take my plate of food and sit down at a table near the window. I just stare outside as I eat. Iris brings me a can of pop, which I thank her for. As I open it, I see a bluebird fly down and sit on the edge of the railing. I wonder if it's the same one that greeted me by biting my hand the other day. It sits there and faces me, as if it's watching me.

As if it's watching and waiting for me.

Add *creepier* to that list of adjectives fitting these mountains.

I eat my lunch, and the bluebird just sits and rests and watches.

I'm not sure how long of a lunch break I have, so I eat my lunch in about ten minutes and bring my empty plate and can into the kitchen. As I come back out, hoping to see Iris, someone else walks into the dining room. For a second I'm a little freaked out, since I didn't know anybody else was there. I wonder if this man works here or is a family member.

"Hello," he says.

For a moment I feel my muscles tense up and my body start to shake. I say hi as I pass him by. He's maybe forty-something and seems ordinary and friendly enough. I hear him go into the kitchen, and I'm glad that I don't have to make small talk. Something about the guy makes me want to run away.

"Feel like cutting more wood?"

I turn to see Iris coming my way. She has an amused look on her face.

"Sure," I say in a voice that wouldn't convince anybody.

She laughs. "I think you've cut enough wood to last me through the winter. Just remember—be honest, or I'll make your words come true."

"Okay."

"So, do you feel like cutting more wood?"

"Maybe not for another ten or twenty years."

The smile I see on her face surprises me. Even though she's ancient, there's something very youthful about it. Come to think of it, I don't think I've ever seen someone so old smile such a nice smile.

Maybe I just need to be around old people a little more.

"I've got some work for you to do inside. That sound okay?"

"Sure."

At the end of the day, after calling my mom and telling her that she can pick me up at five, Iris comes to me and hands me ten twenty-dollar bills.

"I hope you don't mind me paying you in cash."

"No."

I can't remember the last time I've held this much cash in my hand. Maybe never.

"Thank you for your hard work."

"Sure," I say again.

"Did you get tired of hauling those boxes of books down to the basement?"

For a second I'm about to give an answer that means nothing, then I remember what she told me earlier.

"They were pretty heavy."

"Hardcover books tend to be that way. That room was once a

library of sorts, and it's become a bit unmanageable. We're going to make it into another bedroom."

"Okay."

She smiles. "That's we as in you and me."

"Sounds good."

She glances at her watch and tightens her lips. "We have fifteen minutes before your mother comes. Let's sit for a while."

It's already dark outside, and there's only one window in the main room. I sit on the couch, facing her.

"Tell me something, Chris. What do you believe?"

After a day of working with little communication with anybody else, the question is baffling. For a moment I don't reply.

"Rather large question for simple chitchat while we wait, right?" she says.

"Believe about what?"

"About life and death. What do you believe?"

I clear my throat as I try to figure out an answer.

I don't believe in anything. Not a thing. Not now and not ever.

"I don't know."

Those eyes look at me like I've done something wrong. They make me want to climb over the couch and hide behind it.

"At the end of every day, I ask myself what it is that I believe. And I think that the sad thing about so many people is that they can go their entire life without asking that question. Or fully answering it."

I nod, nervous, wishing that Mom might be early, wondering if Iris is going to be all spiritual and holy with me every time I work.

"What if you knew you were going to die at midnight tonight?" she asks. "What would you do?"

"Maybe hold a big going-away party?"

"You don't have to do that. Not with me."

"Do what?"

"Use sarcasm to cover up the awkward feeling inside of you. It's okay. Talks like this—talks of importance—usually make people uncomfortable."

"I'm fine."

But we both know I'm really not.

"Chris, will you do something for me this next week?"

"Sure."

"Next Saturday I'd like for you to answer that question. Answer it the best way you possibly can. And don't worry—I can see it on your face. I'm not going to judge you or force you to hear about something you don't want to hear about. I've done that sort of thing before, and I … I'd just like to know what you believe."

"Okay."

I see the lights of what has to be my mom's car outside. Iris stands, and I follow her to the door.

"You surprised me today. It's not often that I'm surprised anymore."

I'm not sure how I surprised her, and I don't have any idea how or why, so I nod and say thanks.

This wasn't the day I was expecting.

I walk out in the cold, and as I walk to the car, I swear I hear a bird flying above me.

39. PROMISES TO KEEP

I should be doing my French homework because I'm really bombing the class. It doesn't help that I wasn't doing that great in French back home, and then I came here and ended up in a far more advanced class. The teacher, Mrs. Desmarais, who looks like she walked off the set of *Ratatouille,* is short and speaks with a thick accent. But I imagine that she goes home and cooks grits and talks with a Southern accent and sleeps next to a guy named Billy Bob.

Perhaps thoughts like this and not paying attention in class are why I'm bombing out.

So I should be doing my homework because all they do is talk French in the class and all I do is fear being called on. Instead I'm reading a book of Robert Frost poems that I checked out of the library.

As I read them, I imagine Jocelyn doing the same. In fact, I imagine her reading the very same book I'm reading, her hands holding the hard cover and her delicate fingers turning the pages. Even though I don't fully get what I'm reading, I'm moved because I imagine a connection.

Any connection now is better than none at all.

And all I want is a connection to her.

All I want is to see her again.

The Frost poems blend and merge like song lyrics.

I dwell in a lonely house I know That vanished many a summer ago.

The wind outside shakes the house, and the light in my room seems dim. I fumble through lines and scan pages and go over poems that seem a lot like French. Occasionally a line stands out.

No bird is singing now, and if there is, Be it my loss.

I read the words and feel sad and feel sorry. I just want to know. I want to know why they killed Jocelyn. Is it because some people around here are utterly crazy? Or is there some bigger conspiracy, some darker evil?

What do you believe?

I don't know. I don't know anymore. It was easy to tell Dad what I *didn't* believe. I didn't believe in him or in anything he believed in. That was the easy way out. But now I'm not so sure.

Jocelyn found faith before she died.

Was that why she died? Was it because she knew she was about to go?

Blood has been harder to dam back than water.

Maybe anything in life can be related to what you're going through. Song lyrics by The Cure. A Bible passage. A random reading in French. Or a poem by Frost.

I keep reading, but my random thoughts wander across the poems and into the darkness of the night.

I don't just want justice and for the bad men and women to be punished. I want to know why. Why did they have to do it to someone like Jocelyn?

I stumble upon another poem that sounds familiar and that seems easier to read than the others. After a line about lovely and dark woods I read this:

But I have promises to keep, And miles to go before I sleep.

I carry these words with me to bed, to the safe confines of blankets shared with Midnight. I think of Jocelyn and remember.

I'll never forget. I'll never let go. And I'll find out why, Joss. I promise. If that's all I ever do, I promise I will find out the truth and make them pay.

40. A DIFFERENT LANGUAGE

Newt looks especially disheveled today, like he just woke up from sleeping all weekend. I don't get what he's talking about at the moment. I'm taking a while to wake up from sleeping on the bus myself.

"The zip drive."

"Oh, yeah."

"Figured you'd be asking about it."

"Well, yeah."

"I spent all weekend trying to figure it out. I need to bring it to someone who knows more about computers."

"You have someone in mind?"

"Maybe."

He walks away, always secretive, always saying as little as possible even when the moment doesn't require it. One of these days I'm going to get his story.

As I head to my first class, I see the walking ruler that resembles Principal Harking.

"Good morning, Chris."

"Hi." Now I'm the one acting like I can't talk and need to run away.

"Everything going okay?"

"Yeah, sure."

"Glad to hear it. Glad you're staying out of trouble."

"Yeah."

Was I ever in trouble, or did trouble spill over me?

"It can be a long semester," her tight lips say. "One has to pace him or herself. One has to focus on the big picture."

"Okay."

She's blocking my path like a stick of dynamite ready to blow. "Do you see the big picture, Chris?"

I nod, but have no idea what she's talking about. Graduation? College? Career and a family?

"I've seen so many people who are narrow-minded, not understanding the big picture. They see the tip but they don't get underneath to find the depth of life and their situation."

I can't help glancing around. The spectators are there. They always are. A couple girls gawking and a few guys being nosy.

"Don't reach to judgment or conclusions. Just see the big picture and run the race. That's how you succeed."

A motivational speaker Miss Harking is not.

I nod and then nod again to say bye as she walks on.

Why is it that everybody talks in a different language here? Not the Southern accent, though that in itself sometimes makes it hard to understand. I just never seem to be in conversations that I *get*. Normal conversations. About things like sports and politics and the weather and food. Not heavy, weird warnings. Not eerie foreboding messages that mean absolutely something to everybody else but absolutely *nothing* to me.

I shake my head and am too tired to come up with a creative curse for this encounter. I head to my next class.

Maybe I'll find the big picture in there. A big fat picture that I can roll up and take back home.

41. HERE COMES THE SUN

Oh man.

"I can't tell you what I'm painting," I tell her.

"Why not?"

"Because it's personal. It's private."

"Your *painting* is private?" she says.

"It is."

"Why?"

"Okay, fine. You want to know what I'm painting? Seriously?"

Kelsey smiles. I've grown to find her clear braces cute just like her smile and just like those pretty blue eyes.

Oh man, come on.

"This is a family portrait. See, there, I told you."

"That bad, huh?" she says, going with my mockery.

"Totally. It's awful. Just dark. That's all I can say."

She doesn't know that there's some truth in my concept, even though the piece in front of me is not a family portrait but rather is supposed to resemble those woods in the picture from Jocelyn's locker. It looks a little more like a canvas that's been blasted by a passing car hitting a puddle of dirty water.

"Maybe I need to introduce you to some more of my family," she says.

Oh man.

Every day, every period I'm next to her, I find myself enjoying this banter. I like to see the smile on her face and love to hear her laugh at something stupid I said. I love the way she's watching for me as I come into class, usually the last one in. It's obvious, and I'm pretty sure she likes me and I know that it's harmless and fun.

But another voice tells me to stop. Immediately. Do not pass Go and do not collect one more dollar.

I need to stop this, all of this.

Because you know what happened last time, don't you?

When the crazy thoughts start going even crazier, I imagine things like Kelsey and me falling madly in love and then Jocelyn coming back, just like it happens in soap operas.

You're not going to fall in love with this girl. She's cute, but that's all. That's it.

I imagine getting close and then having something happen to her.

I imagine that maybe she's getting closer to find out secrets about me and to win me over so she can lie and steal from me. Not that I have any secrets or anything to steal from.

All I know is that this is harmless and safe and fun. It's like waking up in the cold fog every day and then for a single period, I'm allowed to go outside and sit underneath a crystal clear sky and soak up the sun.

Kelsey Page is that sun, and it's not just because of the color of her hair.

That's fine, but don't tell her that, because she'll roll her eyes and surely make a gagging sound.

Every day the sun comes out and shines down, and then I have to leave it and go back into the drab and the murk.

42. GROWN-UPS

It's obvious that Mom's been crying.

"What's wrong?" I ask. I've been home a few minutes before seeing her. Before *really* seeing her.

"Nothing."

"Did something happen at work?" I ask.

She's sitting on the couch across from me. "I didn't go to work today," she says.

I've come to understand that Mom has several looks. The drunk look and then the hungover look. The angry look. The don't-really-care-about-anything-look (which is a lot like the drunk look but more awake).

This is different from all of those.

This is the Dad look.

"Did you talk to him?" I ask.

"What? How did you know?"

"Did he call?"

She shakes her head and closes her eyes.

"Why'd you call him?"

"Because—because he's the only—" She stops herself. "Chris, not now."

I wait for a minute but then decide not to push.

"You want to go out to eat tonight?" she asks.

I shrug.

"Somewhere outside of Solitary."

I nod without hesitation.

Definitely. Like Mexico. Or Alaska.

"Anywhere you'd like to go."

"Why don't you pick," I tell her. "And I'll treat."

"Stop acting like a grown-up."

I want to tell her to stop making me, but I don't. "I've got money to spend," I say instead. "Let me spend it."

"We'll see," she says, standing up.

The thought of my father's face and voice makes me angry. I'm glad he's not here. And come to think of it, I don't want to hear what he had to say. The less I know about him the better.

Mom and I are doing just fine.

Or at least that's sure what I want him to believe.

43. FIGHT

It's interesting how life can work sometimes.

How one random comment can be followed by another random comment. How one plus one doesn't always necessarily equal two, but a number far greater.

I'm nearing the open area of the cafeteria when I pass Gus and his boys. I wonder if he even bothers going to class or if he really, truly is just a high school bully cliché.

"Miss your little slut?"

There's no chance that I misheard him. The words cut deep.

I'm carrying a paper bag containing an apple and a sandwich and some chips and a can of generic pop.

It takes me maybe two seconds to turn to my right and raise my hand and ram the bag against Gus's ugly fat pimply face. It lands somewhere between his forehead and his nose. I was going for the nose, but it doesn't matter because it did the trick.

A steady burst of blood splats out on the white floor as Gus goes backward, and I proceed to take the bag again and ram it against the side of his big flabby ear.

Then things get blurry, and I'm being both pounced on and pulled away and yelled at and smothered.

This melee seems to go on a long time, but it's just probably a matter of seconds.

When I finally see the light of day someone's pulling me back and I see that it's Oli and it's crazy how strong the guy is. In front of me is Gus buckled on the ground with a hand covering the geyser that's his nose as his eyes squint.

That can of generic pop sure did the trick.

His buddies are at his side while a couple of teachers are around us and a whole bunch of students are circling this circus.

I see Mr. Meiners, who shakes his head and jerks my arm and tells me to come with him.

As I do, I hear something crazy.

Applause.

"What do you think you're doing?"

Mr. Meiners is leading me to the principal's office, and I'm wondering why he isn't leading Gus or even seeing if the guy is okay.

"I'm tired of it."

"Tired of what?"

"If I don't do something, he's just going to keep it up."

Mr. Meiners tugs on my arm and pulls me to a stop. "Listen to me and listen good, Chris. Don't be stupid. Don't. Okay?"

I'm shocked, not because of his grip on my sweatshirt or because he's angry, but because he's talking in a hushed tone.

"You just don't get it, do you?"

I shake my head.

"Mind your own business and stay away from trouble, especially that kind."

"You don't know what he said."

"I don't care what he said, and you shouldn't either." He breathes out and looks up and down the hall. "Just stop bringing attention to yourself. Stop being a hero. You gotta see the bigger picture, Chris."

"You sound like the principal."

He yanks my sleeve hard enough to make me grimace. "And you sound like some ordinary moronic teen. The thing you just can't comprehend—that you can't see—is that you're not. You're different, Chris."

By now another teacher is coming down the hallway with Gus. Mr. Meiners leads me to Miss Harking's office.

Which stinks, because I was kinda hungry.

Like any ordinary moronic teen might be.

44. BELIEF

"So do you have an answer to my question?"

My body aches from the work I've done today. No woodcutting—it looks like Iris has barely touched any of the wood I cut last Saturday. But I've been cutting down weeds and cleaning up debris around the house. Do that all day long and you'll see how exhausted you can be, especially when you're going up an insanely steep incline.

I curse in my own head. I don't feel like answering some stupid question about what I believe. I've just come in and washed my hands, and I'm still sweaty even though it's freezing outside.

She stands at attention like a drill sergeant, waiting.

"No, I haven't—I'm still not quite sure."

"Chris. Please give me the respect to at least consider the things I ask. I'm sure you thought of my question at some point in the week. Yes?"

"This has been a lame week."

"How so?"

"Got after-school detention for three weeks for sticking up for myself."

"So you believe one should stick up for himself?"

"Yeah. If you need to."

"See how easy it is to answer the question."

"I thought you were asking about life and death."

"That too," Iris says. She goes away and then brings me a bottled water.

It's not quite time for Mom to come, but my work outside is finished.

"So what else has been 'lame' about the week?"

"I don't know."

"I think you do know, Chris." She waits, but I don't answer. "Is it the school, or the town, or your family?"

"How about all of the above?"

"Do you believe that you're watched over?"

I let out a chuckle. "Yeah, totally. Everybody's watching me. Everybody's telling me to lie low and go with the flow and stay out of everybody's hair."

"And are you?"

"I don't know."

"Do you believe that God watches over you?"

"No." I probably sound a bit irritated.

"You seem to know that without question."

"That's just what I believe."

"So you don't believe that angels watch over you?"

I think of Jocelyn and then for some reason think of Midnight. I don't know why.

Maybe because they're the closest things I've seen to angels on this earth.

"No. Why would they?"

I'm expecting an argument or her opinion, but I don't get either. She goes over to a table in the corner and takes something out of a drawer. She hands it to me—a square black-and-white photograph.

"That is Jason. My son. He died before he was ten years old."

I don't know what to say.

"I used to have this place as a mini-monument to him, but I've since realized that he's in a better place and that he does indeed watch over me. Not in any way that I can fully understand or observe, but I believe he's here."

"Sorry," I say. I want to ask how he died and when, but I don't.

"When someone we love dies, there are two ways to go with the empty hole inside of us."

Why's she talking plural?

"You can grow to love more and rely more. Or you grow to hate more."

I look away from her at the bottled water I'm holding. I'm feeling awkward and stupid.

"Death isn't the final stage in our journey, Chris. That's what I believe."

I feel my body wash over with tingles.

Does she know, like everybody else?

Does she know about Jocelyn?

"It took me a while to learn that," Iris says as she takes back the picture of the smiling kid. "It was a hard road. But we're all on our own journey, and death is but a part of it. It's the necessary evil of this ugly world. But it can also be perhaps the brightest part of it all, understanding what death truly means. Do you know what it means, Chris?"

I only shake my head. At least I'm being honest. I don't have a clue.

"Some people say it's the inevitable end. But they say it like it's the sad end of some story. In reality, death is just the starting point."

She puts the picture away and closes the drawer. My "lesson" for the day is over.

Strangely enough, I want to hear more.

45. UNINVITED GUEST

Why can't *I* drown my sorrows? Why are adults and rebellious teens the only ones who get to do that?

It's Saturday night, and I'm still sore and exhausted from the day of working at the inn, but I can't get to sleep. Part of me is worried about Mom, who is really sloshed downstairs. It's one thing if she's passed out or if she's not here, but she's here and she's awake and God knows what she might end up doing to herself. I worry about her going outside and falling off the deck and breaking her neck. So I lie in the darkness with my eyes wide open, listening and wondering and hoping.

I remember when Dad used to have bad days. He was gone so much that I didn't see much of it, but during the last few years before he met God in the parking lot of somewhere, I'd see him downing the heavy stuff. That's how Mom started, because they'd both drink together, casually at first at parties and all that other adult stuff they'd do. Then as the stresses of Dad's job as a lawyer increased, so did the dark stuff he'd drink in the clear short glasses. Mom never liked it and didn't like him drinking it either. Said he got mean when he drank, and he did. Mom drank wine and got tired.

Eventually, after Dad told us he'd been born-again and I seriously needed him to explain exactly what that meant (I'm still kinda wondering), he swore off the liquor altogether. I don't think he was/ is an alcoholic, but he just stopped drinking.

Mom sure isn't born-again, because she's only been drinking more.

I really have no desire to copy all that.

Yet—a very big yet—sometimes I want to escape. Not just this room and this shack, but this life. And I know that's one way to do so.

It's temporary, but it's still a tiny escape.

Eventually, as I'm half in sleep and half out, I hear running water in Mom's bathroom. She's getting ready for bed.

Good.

I wonder what Dad is doing. I wonder how that's going for him, how it feels to have been born-again and then to lose his family.

If that's part of the deal, then no thanks.

I think of Jocelyn.

You not only need answers, Chris, you also need hope.

It's easier to ignore my father's ramblings than hers.

A monster slipped into our house this morning when I was asleep, and he came through the front door.

I'm walking down the stairs in my sweats, and I see him standing in the living room. The narrow weasely face. The square cool-guy glasses. The short cool-guy hair. For a second I think I'm dreaming.

"Good morning, Chris," the politician—I mean piranha—I mean pastor says.

Mom looks worse than I do, because she's in clothes that she slept in and she obviously hasn't had a chance to do any of that fixing up that women do. I've always thought she was pretty, but she can't cover the out-of-it look from the wine last night.

"I was on my way to church and thought I'd stop to see you folks and bring you some breakfast."

He's already in a button-down shirt with a fancy pattern on one side and nicely pressed jeans. I can smell his cologne or hair product or his girly-man soap.

"Do you like coffee?" he asks.

"Sure," I lie, my voice and body and mind all hovering over this surreal moment.

I see a box of half a dozen donuts. Not Dunkin' Donuts, because this place is too weird to have one of those. These should be called Devil Donuts. Each one comes with its own hallucination.

"We began a new series of sermons at the start of the year. I thought you might be interested. Chris, you've been to our church a few times."

I think of the last time I was there, of the storage room, of the weird vibe I got stepping foot in the building.

"Yeah."

"Not trying to bribe you with donuts." He smiles his creepy smile. "But I believe that a church is about more than just a building or a pastor. It's about community. It's about the people."

"It's very nice of you to come by," Mom says. "I feel embarrassed that I was—"

"Please," Pastor Marsh says. "This is my big day, but it's your day of rest. I don't mean to disturb it at all."

I see him watching me so I take a donut, even though I'm not very hungry. I smile as my mouth is full.

"How are you doing, Chris?"

He hasn't done anything to me. Besides given me creepy, weird vibes.

So why do I feel like I want to run away every time he's near?

"Doing good."

What if I'm wrong? What if everything everybody's told me about this guy is a lie?

"Staying busy?"

I nod.

"Chris got a job at the Crag's Inn."

The eyes move to me, and they change. I swear they change. They do something weird. Not like change colors and suddenly widen in horror, but they seem to lock on me like a bird zeroing in on its prey.

Maybe it's just my imagination.

"And how are you enjoying it?" Pastor Marsh says without any change of tone.

"Good."

"Is the old lady still working there?"

"Iris?" Mom asks. "Yes, she's still there."

He doesn't stop looking at me. "Good to hear you're keeping busy."

Why does everybody want me to stay busy? As if what? As if I'm going to get bored and then suddenly build an atom bomb?

"My new sermon is on community. It's about building bridges and building relationships. No pressure, but of course I'd love to see you there. Both of you."

"Thanks," Mom says.

She's too tired and embarrassed to have her defenses completely up. If she did, she might tell the pastor what he could do with his community. Or where he could go with it.

"There are some great teenagers at our church, Chris. I think you'd enjoy getting to know them. In lots of different ways."

He smiles, and I feel like something's slithering down my back. I smile back, and it's gotta be the worst fake smile ever.

"Enjoy your day. And your donuts."

Mom thanks him as he walks to the door. Before he steps out, he turns.

"Oh, and Chris, next time just ask if you'd like a tour. I'll give you one anytime."

Then he's gone, leaving me speechless and Mom cursing.

"Why did he show up here? It's barely eight o'clock. I must look like a train wreck."

You probably smell like a vineyard.

"Did you invite him over?" she asks.

"Are you serious?"

"Well, why would he just show up?"

"Maybe Dad put in a call to him."

"Stop it. What did he mean about giving you a tour?"

I shrug and take a second donut.

"How are they?"

I nod. "If I die from poisoning, you'll know who did it."

Neither of us laughs.

As The Smiths say, that joke isn't funny anymore.

46. IN RAINBOWS

Sometimes the moments crawl by like a centipede. And sometimes they slip away like a plume of smoke. January turns to February, and I barely seem to notice. I stay busy, with the hour of detention every day after school ending at the start of February. Coach Brinks seems to think that I should be forced to run harder since I've been missing some of practice. Between studying and track and work on Saturdays at the Crag's Inn, I'm exhausted all the time.

I'm staying under the radar. No new notes visit my locker. Newt doesn't have any discoveries for me. He seems to have given up on the zip drive.

Time moves so quickly that I'm surprised to discover it's Valentine's Day. How could I totally forget a holiday like this one, even if some candy company and card company created it?

How can I be such a loser to have nobody to even give a card to, much less to give me one?

Everything's been going fine, but this is like the car hitting a deep pothole in the middle of the dirt road. The alignment seems to go out of whack, and I realize that I've been coasting and forgetting.

But not today.

Not on Valentine's Day.

During art I completely ignore Kelsey. We've continued our nice little banter every period, but suddenly I feel a cloud over my head and my soul. I feel empty and I feel afraid. I feel all these things and I can't begin to tell her. Nor can I play her little games today. I'm not interested, so why bother?

So I shut her down the first few times she tries to talk. Then we just work in silence.

There's a part of me that would normally make amends, but not today.

I'm feeling off base, like screaming is going on inside my head and I need to get out of here.

I glance at Kelsey's eyes behind her glasses, but she deliberately doesn't look my way. Her normally cheery face has a shadow over it.

Happy now, Chris? Happy now that you've infected even those who seem uninfectable?

When the bell rings, she gets her things together, then she turns to me like a robot and hands me a card. "I got it, so I figure I might as well give it to you. But I know you'll think it's stupid. Whatever."

She forces a card into my hand and then dashes away. It's not *that* dramatic, but still.

Valentine's Day. Of course she'd get me a card. Could it be any more obvious?

I feel like a tool.

I'm left alone in the classroom and open the card. It shows a girl standing on a palette of colors, like a messy rainbow or something. Her hair is flying out like she's being struck by lightning, and she has an expression on her face like she's laughing in a delirious way.

I open the card.

> *Every color is just a bit brighter when you're around.*
> *Happy Valentine's Day.*
> *Kelsey*

This is pretty much a perfect card.

The colors are just like the kind we paint every day.

I can't believe she got this for me. Then I think of what she said and how she walked off. I slip the card into my notebook.

I haven't had someone notice me like this since—

Since the world brightened to a point where it couldn't brighten anymore.

Since the world had a blackout.

I know I should go find Kelsey and apologize for being rude.

But I can't. I can't and I won't.

There are things I need to do. Things I need to do today.

And there are many other people that Kelsey can and should be around. Not me.

It can't and it won't be me.

47. GRAVESTONE

I've been wanting to do this for some time. Wanting and needing. I just haven't known how or where or when.

This isn't something for a movie or a television series. Maybe that's where I'm getting the idea, but that's not why I'm doing it. I'm doing it because—because I have to.

Because she deserves it.

Because despite how much I want to forget and move on, despite the insanity of it all that gets a little less insane as time goes on, I need to do this. For Jocelyn.

Mom let me borrow the car because I told her I'm just going down the road to a friend's house. She's letting me drive a little more with each passing week, for practice. Sometimes she's with me and sometimes not. She knows how remote these roads are and that nobody's around to give me a ticket.

She doesn't know exactly how far I'm driving, but she doesn't need to know.

It takes me longer than I expected to find it. The place Jocelyn took me, where she showed me the church and the cemetery that used to be.

The tall grass and weeds aren't as high as I remember, and the church seems more desolate than I remember. The ground is hard and it takes me a while to find them, but I eventually see the pair of gravestones.

I place a rock between them.

I'm not exactly sure what else to do.

Is she watching me from above or around like in The Sixth Sense?

It's a nice thought, thinking she might be seeing me, but that's not why I'm doing this. I'm doing it out of respect. And love. And need.

The rock is one I found down by the creek, thin and about the length of a football. I carved some crude markings on it with a small pickaxe I bought in town. They're undecipherable except by me.

And by Jocelyn.

At the top is a large J. Then at the center, resembling the cuttings of a caveman, it says December 31. At the bottom, a round thing that's supposed to resemble a heart.

I look at the flat rock between the two short tombstones. I breathe in and feel the cold emptiness of winter. Then I look up to the sky. "You once called me your guardian angel. Remember that?"

I'm talking out loud, unafraid of being overheard. For some reason, I think this is a special place uninfected by Solitary.

Then again, the church did burn to the ground. What do I know?

"You called me an answer to prayer. But I couldn't guard you, Joss. I couldn't save you. And I'm sorry. I'm sorry for not being there."

I look at the sky. I don't have tears, not anymore. There's just this big gaping hole inside, like the remnants of a dissolving asteroid plummeting to the ground and disintegrating. All I'm left with is a crater full of ashes and rock.

"You told me that you came here and asked God to send you a sign. As a reminder of the brightness. So I'm going to do the same thing. I'm going to ask. Maybe this is a magical place where God doesn't exist but wishes can come true. I don't know. I don't know anything except that you're gone and I failed you. I miss you."

Once again I glance at the rock I made, this ugly scratched excuse for a gravestone.

"If it's true—if what you believed is true—then you're okay. And that also means you can look out for me. So I'm asking you—I'm asking God—I'm asking whoever can hear me: Help me. Send something to help me out. Because I'm lost in this darkness and I'm not sure where I'm going to go or what I'm going to do."

The wind is slight and cold. I would love to say that I suddenly have a premonition, that I hear a whisper, that I see something. But there's nothing.

It's just a boy standing over the makeshift grave of the girl he loved, praying a prayer he doesn't really believe.

Faith isn't an easy thing. Whoever tells you it is, is just wrong.

I bend down and touch the rock one more time.

I know I'll never come back to this place.

When I'm back in my mom's car, I see it.

I wonder if it's the same wolf I've seen before.

No, this one is darker and not as tall. It's standing near the grave site. It doesn't sniff, doesn't seem to be looking for anything. It walks as if it's

That's stupid.

I shut my voice up before it goes further.

No wolf is patrolling these hidden graves.

It's just that this place is so remote that wolves and other animals seem to be everywhere.

Good thing wolfie didn't decide to bite like the birdie did.

It's getting dark, and the outline of the wolf makes me shiver for a second. I start up the car and drive away.

48. 1000 Reasons

My prayer is answered the following day.

I'm sitting in the lunchroom trying to make conversation with Newt, who's playing with an app on his iPhone and pretty much ignoring me.

Until he says, "Oh yeah, I finally got to see what was on that zip drive."

I stop chewing and just stare at him. If he was closer I'd hit him. Seriously. "What? When?"

"Yesterday. I asked my guy, and he finally emailed me the contents."

"And you were going to tell—"

Before I can finish my sentence I hear an *Oops!* and something slams straight over my head. Something cold and thick and gooey drips down on my forehead and nose and shoulders.

I smell it. The unmistakable scent of Thousand Island dressing.

I jerk back as the bowl bounces on the ground. I hear a snicker and Newt's "Gross" and the fat pig's stupid voice say, "Oh man, I'm *really* sorry."

Gus is literally beaming.

Here's my bright ray of sunshine. Thanks a lot, all you who hear prayers.

Riley is right next to Gus and asks if I'd like a little lettuce with my dressing.

I stand and wipe a thick slab of the stuff off my head.

Everybody is watching us.

"Great."

That's all I can say.

Gus stands there with Burt and Riley at his side, daring me to do something.

He knows that I can't. He knows that one more straw or infraction or anything will result in a suspension.

"I must've tripped," he says, his smile showing his ugly teeth. "I'm really sorry."

For a second I look at Newt, but he only looks away.

This all started with you, remember that?

I hesitate for a brief second. A really brief second.

Then I brush past Gus and head to the bathroom.

As I go, I hear the laughter and discussion turn into something even worse.

Applause.

I'm running water over my head in the sink when I sense someone standing next to me. I look up to see Poe.

I'm surprised, not because she's standing in the guys' bathroom, but because she's about the last person I'd expect to see. I'd probably be less surprised if Jocelyn were to walk in.

"What are you doing?" Poe asks, looking at the mess I've made on my T-shirt by trying to rub out the puke-color Thousand Island stains. "You have to take that off."

I want to ask her why she's bothering to talk to me all of a sudden, but I don't. I can use someone, anyone, at this point.

A kid walks in wearing headphones, takes one look at us, then promptly turns around and walks back out.

"I don't have anything else to wear."

"Just take it off and wait a minute, okay? I'll be right back."

For a second she glances at the shirt. Of course, it's another of Uncle Robert's. It says "All Cats Are Grey" and has a faded-out shadow on it. On the back is a picture of the band The Cure. "I really liked that shirt," Poe says.

She leaves me standing there, clueless. Suddenly I'm no longer thinking about Gus. I'm wondering why Poe decided to break her vow of silence.

When she comes back carrying a black T-shirt, she wonders why I haven't taken off my shirt. I do so with a bit of reluctance. I'm not the guy who loves being on the skins team. I'm pale and don't work out and have a nice collection of moles and freckles. I'm dripping on my bare chest and jeans as I take the shirt from her.

"That's all I have, but it's a guy's large. You know me—I like wearing oversized stuff."

It's a long-sleeved black T-shirt with the words *Sorry if I looked interested. I'm not.*

I look at myself in the mirror. My hair sopping wet, my face still lined with remnants of salad dressing, my pants and shoes speckled as well.

Poe laughs. "I love the shirt."

"What are you doing?"

"I can only go so far."

"What's that mean?"

"You need some new friends," Poe says. "I might not have a heart to loan out, but I'm not heartless either."

I'm standing there looking at her, still confused. "Look—just—"

Then she bursts out in laughter.

It's nice to see a smile on her face. Underneath the eyeliner and lipstick and all that other stuff she's hiding behind, Poe's actually really pretty.

"What did I do to you?" I ask her.

"It's done. I'm over it. Plus, Joss is getting on my nerves lately. It's fine, really."

For a second I thought she said *Joss is getting on my nerves lately.*

She's talking about someone else.

Something or someone that rhymes with Joss.

Either that or she's crazy.

"Just return the shirt to me after you wash it, okay? And Chris?"

"Yeah?"

"Just—just take care of yourself. Okay?"

She leaves me in the bathroom, still wet, still smelly, and still totally confused.

As I head to my locker, I see Newt there with my books. He wants to say something, but I just shake my head. He doesn't have to. This is a sad boat we're in. I never thought I'd be in any kind of boat with Newt, but here I am.

"What are you going to do?" he asks.

"Finish my conversation."

"With whom?"

"With you."

"Oh, yeah."

"What'd you find?"

"Just some Word documents."

"Did you read them?"

Newt shakes his head. "The less I know, the better."

"So, do you have them here?"

Newt opens his locker and produces a file folder. It's got twenty or so pages in it.

"You didn't read any of it?"

"The first page," he says. "Then I got a bit scared and stopped."

"What about your friend?"

"Trust me. He won't tell anybody. Last thing he wants or needs is to get into more trouble."

I take the folder and head to my next class.

I suddenly have a thousand more reasons why I hate this place.

49. EMAILS

They look like emails, copied and pasted into a document.

As Mr. Nivel drones on about something that I'm assuming has to do with Algebra II, I carefully slip out the first page and read it. It's not addressed to anybody, nor is there a name at the bottom. But it doesn't take me long to figure out that this must be an email *to* my uncle rather than one he sent.

THIS IS AN ACCOUNT THAT NOBODY KNOWS AND THE ONLY WAY I'LL BE ABLE TO COMMUNICATE. THEY CAN SEE WHO CALLS WHOM, WHO EMAILS WHOM, WHO TALKS TO WHOM. I DON'T KNOW HOW, BUT THEY KNOW. AND THEY SILENCE THOSE WHO TALK.

HE SAYS HE CAN'T DO ANYTHING ABOUT YOU BECAUSE YOU'RE SPECIAL. OTHERWISE THEY WOULD. BUT IT'S A CHOICE—IT'S YOUR CHOICE. I DON'T KNOW WHAT THIS MEANS. DO YOU?

ALL I KNOW IS THAT THE MAN I THOUGHT I FELL IN LOVE WITH AND MARRIED IS NOT THE SAME MAN. SOMETHING HAPPENED. SOMETHING OUT THERE IN THE DARKNESS. IT'S AS IF HE WENT OUT INTO THE WOODS AND CAME BACK A DIFFERENT PERSON.

I HAVEN'T SEEN HIM DO SOME OF THE THINGS I'M IMAGINING, BUT I FEEL IT. I JUST—I JUST HAVE THIS IDEA.

THAT'S WHY I CAME TO YOU. I THOUGHT YOU NEEDED TO
KNOW. I CAN GET IN TROUBLE FOR SAYING THESE THINGS.
BOTH OF US CAN. BUT YOU NEED TO KNOW THE TRUTH.

I'LL TELL YOU ANYTHING I FIND OUT. I MIGHT NOT BE ABLE TO
EMAIL YOU FROM THIS ACCOUNT. IF NOT, THERE HAS TO BE
ANOTHER WAY TO COMMUNICATE. I'LL LET YOU KNOW. SOON.

I slip the page back into the folder and then realize I can't keep reading these here. If I'm caught and this ends up in the hands of the wrong person, something bad might happen.

You don't know who it's from or who it's for.

But I would guess that it's from Heidi Marsh, the wife of the pastor. Jared was right. He keeps being right.

I decide to read the rest of the emails later tonight. And then try and contact Jared to share them with him.

The rest of the day I just get stares.

Including from my former art friend.

I'm so distracted and disjointed from the lunch incident and the emails that I forget to do the obvious. It takes me about fifteen minutes to finally tell a silent Kelsey thanks for the card.

She nods.

"It was really nice."

"Yeah, sure." She doesn't say anything else.

And you know, I don't blame her. I wouldn't say anything to me either. I'd stay far away. And I want her to stay far away. I belong on a salad bar with various ingredients that people pick from and pick at every day. Nothing that will amount to a hearty meal.

A few times I'm about to say something. A wisecrack. A comment on my shirt and messy hair. A statement that shows I have a pulse and a soul.

But I say nothing.

Nothing at all.

And the bell rings and Kelsey goes, and I figure it's probably better this way.

I see Gus by his locker at the end of the day.

"Love the shirt, Chris. It really fits you."

I want to say more. Do more.

But I remember Mr. Meiners' reaction, his jerking of my hand and his yelling at me.

Mind your own business.

I want him to see me like this, a portrait of me minding my business.

I just walk away from Gus, doing what Mr. Meiners says even though he's not around to see me doing it.

I feel a little more alone tonight. I used to be fine with this. I used to not even think about whether I felt alone or not. I could lose myself in hours of video games or watching television. If I really had nothing to do I could go online and see what people were posting on Facebook.

But tonight I have things to do. Homework, of course—the given in every high schooler's life. But I'm talking about things to read.

Maybe that's why I feel so alone. Because I'd like someone to be here when I'm reading them.

Mom is working (of course) and Midnight is sleeping (of course). I've been putting it off even though it's all I can think about.

I can hear the wind picking up and know that snow is coming. Just a sprinkling, nothing major, just enough to remind a person to stay inside.

I open the folder and pick up where I stopped, with the next printed-off email that only has the text and no addresses.

> IT WASN'T ALWAYS LIKE THIS. I'VE STRUGGLED TO BE THE GOOD WIFE, TO KEEP MY VOWS. WE MET IN CAMBRIDGE WHERE HE WAS STUDYING AT HARVARD DIVINITY SCHOOL. ALL I CAN SAY ABOUT THAT TIME—ABOUT THAT YEAR AND A HALF WE DATED—WAS THAT IT WAS MAGICAL. HE WAS MAGICAL. HE WANTED TO CHANGE THE WORLD, AND I WANTED TO BE AT HIS SIDE. I REALLY FELT LIKE HE LOVED ME. MAYBE HE DID. I DON'T KNOW. I DON'T KNOW MUCH NOW.
>
> THE ONLY REASON I'M SHARING THIS IS BECAUSE I'M SCARED. AND I THINK YOU NEED TO KNOW. I DON'T KNOW WHAT TO DO, AND THE FEW PEOPLE I'VE REACHED OUT TO HAVE CLOSED THE DOOR COMPLETELY. PEOPLE LIKE SHERIFF WELLS, LIKE GRETTA, LIKE SOME OF THE CHURCH PEOPLE. THEY IGNORE WHAT I SAY AND JUST KEEP GOING. I NEED SOMEONE TO KNOW.

IT ALL STARTED WHEN WE MOVED BACK HERE FIVE YEARS AGO. I DIDN'T UNDERSTAND WHY SOMEONE WHO COULD GO ANYWHERE WOULD CHOOSE TO COME BACK HERE. HE SAID THAT IT WAS ABOUT GOING BACK TO HIS CHILDHOOD HOME AND STARTING FRESH AND BUILDING SOMETHING TREMENDOUS. I WAS WILLING TO GO BECAUSE HE SAID THAT IT WAS WHERE GOD WANTED HIM TO BE.

I FEAR THAT THE GOD HE WAS TALKING ABOUT ISN'T THE SAME GOD THAT I KNOW AND BELIEVE IN.

EVERYTHING CHANGED FROM THE START. EVERYTHING. BUT I FIGURED IT WAS ALL ABOUT GETTING THE NEW BEGINNINGS CHURCH OFF THE GROUND. BEFORE WE CAME, THERE WERE NO CHURCHES. THERE WERE THE UNDERGROUND CHURCHES, OF COURSE. I WOULD COME TO DISCOVER THEM LATER ON, AS YOU DID. BUT THERE WAS NO OFFICIAL CHURCH. NOTHING. AND THAT WAS THE CREEPIEST THING TO ME ABOUT SOLITARY. HERE WE WERE IN THE HEART OF THE SO-CALLED BIBLE BELT, BUT THERE WASN'T A CHURCH AROUND. BUT HE WOULD ALWAYS SAY THAT WAS WHY HE WANTED TO START ONE, WHY HE DEEMED IT A NEW BEGINNING.

BUT FOR US, IT WAS THE BEGINNING OF THE END.
I NEED TO GO—THAT'S ENOUGH FOR NOW.

PLEASE DELETE THIS AND MAKE SURE NOBODY SEES IT.
WE CAN'T TALK ABOUT IT—EVEN AT CHURCH. NOT NOW.

SEE YOU SOON.

I put down the email and then shuffle through the pages. There's a whole book here, almost. This is going to tell me everything.

Never once in the two emails I've read does the woman mention a name. But there's no question she's talking about Pastor Jeremiah Marsh.

I go to the next one and begin reading.

And I keep reading for the next two hours.

I learn a lot of random bits of information about the town itself, about Heidi Marsh and how terrified she was, about the church. But several key things stick out.

The first is that as the New Beginnings Church grew larger, the pastor and his wife grew apart. She refers to the "baby issue," which makes me think they were trying to have one but couldn't. She never gets specific. Heidi mentions that she kept seeing less and less of her husband and felt alone and isolated in this place.

But I remember the pastor talking about his little girl the first time I heard him preach.

Then strange things started happening. She calls these "the visions." Again, she doesn't get too specific. The few people she spoke to about them, including her husband, didn't do anything. Just called it stress and told her to keep taking pills.

The seventh email is a big one.

THEN CAME FINN. I DON'T REMEMBER HIS LAST NAME. I'VE TRIED NOT TO THINK ABOUT HIM. BUT ALL I KNOW IS THAT HE WAS THE START OF SOMETHING BLACK AND HEINOUS

AND THE REASON WHY THIS PLACE AND THESE PEOPLE NEED TO BE EXPOSED.

FINN AND HIS FATHER CAME TO OUR CHURCH. HIS CHURCH, I SHOULD SAY. I NEVER KNEW WHAT HAPPENED TO FINN'S MOTHER, IF THERE WAS A MOTHER.

FINN WAS SIXTEEN YEARS OLD, A GOOD-LOOKING BOY. A NICE BOY.

MY HUSBAND TOOK A VERY PARTICULAR INTEREST IN HIM.

THIS TROUBLED ME FOR MANY REASONS.

I SAW THE TINY BIT OF FAME THAT MY HUSBAND WAS GAINING START GOING TO HIS HEAD. I BEGAN TO SEE HIM HAVE THIS POWER OVER THE PEOPLE. IT DISTURBED ME. THOSE WHO DIDN'T REVERE HIM ALMOST SEEMED FEARFUL OF HIM. INCLUDING ME.

OF COURSE, ONE OF THE MOST TROUBLING THINGS WAS HIS RELATIONSHIP WITH STAUNCH. I WASN'T ALLOWED IN THEIR CLIQUE OR THEIR WORLD. I THOUGHT "BOYS WILL BE BOYS," BUT IT WAS MORE THAN THAT.

THEN THIS FIXATION ON FINN.

AND THEN—THEN EVERYTHING STARTED TO COME TO A NASTY HEAD.

HE STARTED TO DO THINGS TO ME THAT I DIDN'T WANT HIM TO. HE HAD CHANGED. HE WALKED AND TALKED LIKE

A TORMENTED, POSSESSED MAN. THIS WAS AROUND THE
END OF THE YEAR, AND I JUST KNEW SOMETHING BIG WAS
GOING TO HAPPEN.

THEN FINN DISAPPEARED. AND THE REST OF THE
CHURCH—THE REST OF THE TOWN—WENT ON AS NORMAL.
I COULDN'T—I STILL CAN'T—BELIEVE IT. EVERYBODY ELSE I
TRIED TO TALK TO SHUT ME DOWN. HE PUSHED ME FURTHER
AWAY. AND HE CONTINUED TO HURT ME. I KNOW HE DID
SOMETHING TO FINN. AND TO THE OTHERS. AND I'M AFRAID
THIS IS GOING TO CONTINUE. WE HAVE TO DO SOMETHING.

I put the email down and feel my body trembling. I'm not cold.
I'm terrified. I'm about to grab Midnight and put her on my lap
when the door swings open, and I spring up, clasping the folder in
my hand.

"You're still up?" Mom asks, dusting off the light sprinkles on
her coat.

I'm needing CPR, but I keep my mouth shut and just nod in a
nonchalant way.

She looks wide-eyed and tired at the same time. She probably
shouldn't be driving. But that means she won't notice the white ghost
that's her son.

"I'm going to change," Mom tells me. "Are you hungry?"

As a matter of fact, I am. I could eat a boar.

I guess fear does that to you.

Learning something new every day.

50. All My Maybes

Maybe I don't want to learn anymore.

Maybe I don't want to try and fight.

Maybe I want to go to bed without a worry in my head or my heart.

Maybe I just want to forget about Jocelyn.

Maybe this pastor is a quack, but aren't most of the pastors out there?

Maybe I should just throw the rest of those emails away and never think about them again.

Maybe I should realize that Jocelyn is gone and Uncle Robert is gone and Mom is basically gone, just like Dad, and I'm on my own.

Maybe I should bolt up my curiosity just like I bolted up that piece of wallboard in the bathroom cabinet downstairs.

Maybe the wind wouldn't sound as menacing if I didn't have a dozen other things to worry about.

Maybe I need to just stop, drop, and roll.

Maybe all my maybes will eventually start turning to gibberish.

Maybe I need some sleep.

Maybe it will come.

TRAVIS THRASHER

51. Why We're Talking

Jocelyn sits waiting in the chair, surrounded by a hundred other chairs. She's alone, still wearing the black formal dress, still made up like a movie star.

She looks over at me and smiles.

I feel naked and silly. But I can't hide or run or do anything else. Plus, all I want to do is go over and see her.

I find myself moving closer to her. There's no sound in here other than the sound of my feet against the shiny, clean floor that reflects the sun from the glass windows around us.

I stop before getting to her.

She's no longer just beautiful.

I can't think of a word or a phrase....

"Hi, Chris."

Her voice doesn't sound like an echo or a distant muffle. It sounds real and warm and whispers in my ear. "Sit, please."

I rest in the bowl-like chair that faces her.

Jocelyn sits with one leg crossed over the other, looking so refined and elegant. She's older in this—this vision or dream or whatever it is—but she's also the same. The eyes that look at me are the same ones that looked at me in that classroom and that hallway and that love we shared such a short and such a long time ago.

"We don't have much time," she says.

"Time—what is this? Am I really here? Are you?"

"How are you, Chris?"

I don't worry about what I'm saying, not here, not looking into those eyes.

"Terrified," I say. "Lost. And like totally just—sad."

She nods.

I want to kiss her and grow old with her.

"The next few months are important for you. You need to know this."

"I'm sorry I didn't—that I wasn't able to help you," I say.

"Don't apologize for something you didn't do. That's not why you're here."

"What is this place? Is this real?"

"Yes. What you see and what you feel are real. Very real. This is not a dream."

"I'm sorry, Jocelyn."

"Chris. A hundred sorrys won't get me back."

"What will?"

She smiles.

I remember everything about her and how short-lived everything was and how she kept warning me—how the whole world warned me—but how I just refused to understand.

"How could you understand, Chris?"

She can read my thoughts? In dreams, or nightmares, or visions, or whatever this is, I guess anything is possible.

"Can I run away with you?"

She shakes her head.

I hear something shaking above us and see a plane taking off.

"You need to listen carefully."

"Jocelyn, help me to get out of Solitary."

"That's precisely why I'm here, Chris. Why we're talking."

"What do you mean?"

The adult Jocelyn doesn't smile or give me any sense of security or hope in her expression.

"There are those you can still help. There is still time."

"Time for what?" I ask.

"You have to stay in Solitary. You cannot leave."

52. AND SO

And so I stay.

Like I'm going anywhere.

Some ghost of an adult beautiful fantasy Jocelyn is telling me to stay, so yeah, I'm going to stay.

I just hope she doesn't tell me to fall asleep on the train tracks tomorrow, because chances are high that I might.

I stay and I endure.

Take a breath and hold it.

Keep holding it.

Keep.

Holding.

It.

53. The Hurting

The boy sits with his arms on his knees and his hands over his eyes.

Is it an horrific dream?

Yet somehow he does what everybody wants him to do.

"Listen to me, okay? You have to lie low. For a while."

So he listens to his newfound friend and relative Jared and lies low.

He ticks off the time, the class periods, the homework, the bus rides, the silence.

Say what you want.

"You go about your business, and you leave your stories and your troubles to your imagination. I'm not saying that it's easy being a newcomer, but you gotta go with the flow."

So he listens to his sheriff, who isn't being very sheriff-y, and decides to go with the flow.

No fighting back at the bullies.

No speaking out to others.

No investigating with Newt.

No investigating in the woods.

How can I be sure?

"Your mother needs you."

So he listens to the shadow of Jocelyn and stays around to try and help his mother.

Memories fade.

Avoiding the dreams.

Avoiding the memories.

Avoiding the pain.

The scars still linger.

"When I tell somebody something, I mean it. You do not want to mess with me."

So he doesn't mess with the man named Staunch.

Waiting but not relating.

And he walks the familiar halls and sees the familiar faces and feels the familiar fears and finds the familiar shadows. A host of secrets and lies and deception.

It's a very, very mad world.

The school doesn't know him and the teachers look through him and everything makes him sad.

"Don't lose your sanity like the rest of us."

So he tries to follow the card's advice from the unknown friend or mocker.

You can change.

So he tries to stay sane and tries to change and tries to fit in.

He tries to listen. He tries to change and not do anything.

"Mind your own business and stay away from trouble."

So he minds his own business and stays away from trouble and lets February become March.

I'll make no noise.

And he doesn't.

I'll hide my pain.

And he does.

I'll close my eyes.

And he does, every day.

He finally does everything he's told to do and he does it in silence
and fear and anger and numbness.

There's nowhere to run or go.

He stays away from anything bright or hopeful.

He closes the door and locks it and memorizes the albums that
detail his hurting.

54. GROUNDHOG DAY

I almost forgot about Aunt Alice. I'm just about maxed out with
creepiness until the moment Mom says, "We need to visit your
aunt," and I suddenly remember that *oh yeah I have an aunt named
Alice.*

Who likes mannequins.

And whose place smells like death.

And who looks like she's one séance away from joining the realm
of the dead.

"Thanks, but I have to go grave digging tonight."

"That's not funny. It's been a while since I visited her, and it'd be
good for her to see you, too. Last time, she asked about you."

"As in the size of my body? So she knows how much stuffing she
can fill me with?"

Mom laughs, but the joke of Aunt Alice doesn't seem as funny to
her as it did the first time we left her creepy cabin.

Soon we arrive at her place. It's a soggy Sunday afternoon with the rain stopped just enough so we're able to see the road that leads to my aunt's cabin. Right before we reach it, my mom drives over something.

"What was that?"

"I don't want to know," I say.

She stops the car, and we both get out.

Wedged underneath the car is something big and hairy. Mom freaks out and gets back in the car. I notice that the thing is not moving

hello nice little doggie hello nice little black smoke doggie from hell

and I also notice the smell.

That thing isn't going to move for a long time.

It looks gray but also seems to have glitter over it.

For some reason I think of Bill Murray. I have no idea why.

"Get in the car!"

"It's dead," I say through the window.

She rolls it down. "What's dead?"

"Whatever is under our car. Move up."

I wish I hadn't asked Mom to do that.

On the road is the body of a dead groundhog.

I say body because there's no head to the thing.

And I say dead because—well, there's no head to the thing.

If that thing jumps up and starts running at me, I don't care what happens, I'm going to be as far away as possible from the woods and Solitary and North Carolina and Bill Murray movies for the rest of my life.

Mom parks the car and then gets out. I walk her way.

"Just a dead animal."

"What?"

"A groundhog."

"You sure it's—"

"Yeah," I tell her as I block her from going any further.

Last thing Mom needs is any more reason to have nightmares.

Aunt Alice seems happy today. And when I say happy, I mean deliriously happy. Medicated happy. Or possessed happy.

"Come on in, come on."

Last time she wasn't as friendly. Her short, round figure seems to roll through the living room. The place is the same as I remember it before, dark and creepy, although there seems to be a bit more light this time. Maybe she has the drapes open or something. It still stinks. The black crow is still there. But thankfully, no mannequins.

"Just sittin' down for some lunch."

I follow Mom and look over her shoulder, and when I see the family at the table I stop and then get in a sprinting stance, ready to dash.

Sitting around the square table in the corner of the kitchen are four …

oh man

I see that Melissa the Mannequin has gone and found herself a family. A husband with blond hair and two kids. A boy and a girl.

Oh this is beyond creepy.

They're clothed, and their blank faces stare out like the rest of the things in this house, screaming *Help us, we're trapped with a short devil lady.*

"Sorry, I didn't know ya'll were coming."

"You're having quite the party, huh?" Mom says. She glances back at me. "Would you like anything, Chris?"

"No. But thank you."

She looks at me and gives me a "cut the crap" look.

Mom talks with Aunt Alice about the weather and about making jelly and about the weather while I feel claustrophobic. I look around the living room, and I see a picture of Uncle Robert in a frame, one I didn't see last time we were here. I'm tempted to take it and show Mom. But as I glance into the kitchen, she notices me looking at it.

"I gave that to her last time I was here," Mom says.

I nod. We don't have any pictures up in our house, not really. But Mom gives Aunt Alice a photo of Uncle Robert.

I'm standing and watching the crow when something catches my eye. It's the back of the girl mannequin's head, her dark hair unmoving and her shoulders stiff as my legs feel on a day off from track practice.

Suddenly, the head starts to move.

The face turns, and the eyes are blank and hollow.

No no no.

And worms and maggots suddenly start to pop out of them.

I blink, and of course I don't see this. This is in my mind, not a dream and not a fantasy. It's just me imagining something crazy.

I feel hot and dizzy and want to run in the woods for about five days.

"Mom—can I—bathroom?"

"Just down the hall."

I go down there and find a tiny room with barely space for a toilet, sink, and tub. A big plastic seat-thing sits on top of the toilet, like a basketball rim for a three-year-old. It takes me a few minutes to take it off.

As I'm washing and air drying my hands, I notice the shower curtain hiding the bath behind it.

Of course, I'm curious.

Of course, I can't let things go.

So of course, I pull back the grimy yellow plastic curtain.

In the tub sits the rest of the groundhog. I see the whiskered face looking up at me as if it's popping out of a goopy, bloody hole. But of course, there's no hole. Not in this tub.

I jerk the curtain back and half of it comes down. Then I curse as I turn on the faucet again and rinse my hands with cold water, then douse my face with it.

I look again, and it's still there.

I'm not imagining this.

I go back out to the main room, feeling woozy. "I need some air," I tell Mom.

I should tell her to maybe wait to use the restroom until we get back home, but I don't.

I can't.

I feel just—just not so good.

55. DOUBLE DATE

Spring comes, but it sure doesn't bring hope.

Sometime in March, as I'm minding my business and ignoring things like emails waiting to be read and missing students and the shadows of dead girls I once loved, I get approached by Dan something-or-other who is in my grade and has never acknowledged me once that I can remember. I'm surprised the guy knows my name.

"Hey, Chris, what's up?"

Dan says this as if we talk a lot.

"Hey," I say back, pretty confident he doesn't really want to know what's up in my life. How long does he have to hear my answer?

"Hey, I got a favor to ask you."

I'm wondering if he starts every sentence with hey.

"Yeah, okay."

I'm at my locker and can't help glancing around to see if this is a prank. He's not carrying anything from the salad bar in his hands, so I guess I'm lucky there. Not that I could see someone like Dan ever doing that. Dan's one of the midpack boys. I see him hanging around with Ray and his buddies. Or some of the jocks. Or some of the burnouts. I haven't really ever noticed Dan, because to be honest there isn't much to notice about him.

"You know Georgia, right? Georgia Wilson?"

I nod. Georgia is a pretty brunette I've seen hanging around with Kelsey. She seems a bit stuck up, but that's just based on her looks and on the fact that she's never looked or talked with me either.

"Hey, I got something to ask you, and man, I'll totally owe you if you help me out."

"Okay."

"Look, I've been trying to go out with Georgia for like ever, and she just gives me the cold shoulder. You know her, you know? I mean, hey, I get it, but still. I just want her to go out once, you know? So the thing is, I was with her and her friend Kelsey. You know Kelsey, right? Well, they were talking and Georgia was teasing her because she likes you but never in a million years would ask you out, so I kept on about Georgia going out with me, and Kelsey suggested a double date."

"Kelsey suggested that?"

"Yeah, totally. Not lying."

"She's asking me out?"

"No, are you crazy? Look, you can't even tell them that I was talking to you. She'd flip—Kelsey, that is. She'd die. I couldn't believe she even suggested something like this, but whatever. She must really like you."

"She's basically been ignoring me in art class."

"Yeah, that's girls. Georgia goes from talking to me one week to ignoring me the next. Whatever. It's their time of the month or week thing or whatever. Can't figure them out."

I might have expected some things to happen to me today, like falling into a black crater or seeing a life-sized bunny rabbit following me around, but I sure didn't expect this.

"So what do you want me to do?" I ask.

"Ask Kelsey out."

"What?"

"Come on, man. She's cute."

"I thought this was a double date."

"Yeah. Say that we want to double with them. Georgia will totally go for it, because she wants Kelsey to get together with you. She thinks you're like some mysterious guy or something." He laughs in a way that says *you're not mysterious you're just kinda a loser that I need to use for the moment.*

"Well, I gotta check my calendar," I say.

"Okay, you do that. But then let me know."

Dan apparently doesn't recognize sarcasm.

"So how am I supposed to do this?"

He slaps me on the back, and I feel like I've been permanently imprinted with his handprint. He might be middle of the pack, but the guy is strong.

"How do you ask a girl out? I mean, how'd you ever ask out Jocelyn?"

I look at him to see if he's joking. Or worse, to see if he's mocking.

"Man, a hundred guys wanted to go out with her. You had to be doing something right, huh?"

I nod, but carefully.

"Sucks that she moved, you know. But whatcha gonna do?"

Again I try to see if he's mocking me, but nothing I can see says that he is.

"Just let me know, okay? Talk to Kelsey sometime today. Let's do it this weekend if it works, okay, man?"

He takes off, and I'm left to wonder how I'm going to ask out a girl who no longer talks to me. We haven't spoken much at all since she gave me that Valentine's Day card. I've tried.

But you haven't tried that hard, have you?

And I wonder why I said yes.

Did you have a choice, really? And do you have any other pressing things to do, really?

I think about Kelsey. She's cute and fine, but I know that the best thing I can do for her is stay away.

It's one date. It's one thing to help a guy out. You could use some more friends, right? And you could have some fun. Right?

I'm surprised Kelsey wants to have anything to do with me.

I think back to not long ago, just a lifetime ago, when Rachel figured out a way for me to ask Jocelyn out.

Maybe one day eventually I'll grow up and learn to ask girls out on my own.

"Hey."

The universal word for teen boys everywhere. This can mean many things. It can be a sign that we're alive, or it can mean that yes we've just crashed our car into the tree, or it can mean absolutely nothing.

Kelsey no longer paints by me, but today I've brought my painting over by her.

"Can I—do you mind?"

Those eyes peer behind her glasses like a face hiding behind a window. She blushes.

"How're you doing?"

"Fine," she says.

I can't imagine a date because I can't imagine her talking enough to me to make it last longer than ten minutes.

"You like what I'm doing to my fruit?"

She glances at my canvas and nods.

"See, that was a test. That's not fruit. Those are people. That's a portrait of my family."

Kelsey looks at me, then back at the picture. "Really?"

"No. Just kidding."

She can't help but laugh, and that means I see her braces.

For a while I try to make some kind of conversation, but most of the things I say sound so stupid. It's really amazing this girl wants to go out with me. I'm still hoping that Dan wasn't pulling a prank on me.

"So, uh, hey."

There it is again. This time it means *Look, I'm about to go out on a limb when I've been hiding behind the tree for some time now, and you might laugh in my face but that's okay because I can always follow up your rejection with another hey.*

"Do you know Dan?"

I'd say his last name, but I don't know it because we're not quite buds.

"Yes."

"Well, I was just wondering—we were talking today—"

"You were talking to Dan?"

Already Kelsey sounds like she doesn't believe me.

"Yeah. And we were wondering about maybe—well, sometime maybe on Friday or Saturday—"

"He made you do this."

"What?"

"How'd he do it?"

"Do what?"

Kelsey looks annoyed, and suddenly she doesn't seem like such a wallflower.

"He's been trying to go out with Georgia since forever, but I never thought he'd do something like this."

"Something like what?"

"I didn't know that you knew Dan."

"Well—I mean—not really well, but—"

"So then why?"

"I was just—we were just thinking—"

"Chris, please. I'm not that stupid."

"What?"

"Do you do everything someone asks you to do?"

"No," I say, genuinely surprised. "It's not that."

"Then what is it?"

Yeah, Chris, what is it?

I'm not sure how to answer this. I'm also not quite sure why Kelsey is irritated. With me.

"Look, I'm sorry, I just—"

"Is this some joke or something?"

"With who? What? I was asking the same thing."

She nods, looks serious, then goes back to painting.

"I just thought it'd be fun."

"Hanging out with Dan?"

I laugh. "Are you kidding? I mean, seriously ... why would I want to hang out with Dan?"

"Then what are you talking about?"

"It'd be fun hanging out with *you*. And not by some stupid picture that looks like death that I'm painting while not even looking at you."

For a second, I really have no idea if Kelsey's going to laugh or sneer.

Thankfully, she lets out a slight giggle.

"I wasn't trying to do anything," I say. "I just—I thought it sounded like a fun idea."

"Okay," Kelsey says.

I nod. Then let the silence make me wonder exactly what she just okayed.

"By *okay*, do you mean—?"

"Saturday evening. You guys come over to Georgia's house by seven. We'll figure out the rest then."

"Okay," I say.

And yes, I guess it is okay.

Not sure how this will work out, but I'm not worried.

I'm just glad Kelsey's talking to me again.

It would sure be awkward if we weren't speaking on our first official date.

56. THE NEST

"That's a nice haircut, Chris."

Iris notices things like this. She's all about being on time and minding your manners and being *proper* (insert quasi-British accent here). But that doesn't mean she's mean or even cold.

"Yeah, decided it was probably time. Mom cuts it, so that's always a bit scary."

"It's nice to not see bangs dropping in front of your eyes. You have pretty eyes."

I'm not sure how to answer that one, so I nod and smile.

"I assume that means you have big plans this weekend?"

"Not really."

"Is that a genuine 'not really' or more of an 'I'm not feeling like telling you'?"

"No—neither—I mean, I have a date tonight, but it's nothing."

"Your date is nothing in terms of how you feel toward it, or rather how little you'd like to discuss it?"

"I'm doing a guy a favor—he likes this girl who's friends with another girl who kinda—well, long story. No big deal."

Iris is holding that leather journal again. It's thick and looks like it's from the Civil War or something. I always see her carrying it around. Occasionally I see her writing in it. She places it on the table as she sits across from me. I've only now stopped sweating from clearing weeds and bushes outside with a sling blade.

"No big deal for you, or for the girl you're going with?"

I start to say something, then suddenly feel this is one of her insightful traps. She does that every time we speak, trapping me with some idiotic thing I've said and making me eat those words.

"Do you know something, Chris? I met my husband on a blind date."

"Really?"

I knew that Iris had a son but had never heard anything about a husband.

"Stanley. He was tall and skinny and looked absolutely wrong next to me. We could never fit into a picture together, so how could it be? I did the same thing you are doing—a favor for someone. So you never know."

"That's a pretty big leap," I say, chuckling more out of nervousness than humor.

"Nothing is a big leap in this world. Nothing."

I nod. I know Iris well enough now to recognize this as her opportunity to share a little more with me.

This is the routine. I work and she feeds me well and pays me well and then we end the day with these chats. Usually I'm trying to suck in air because the elevation is high here and because I've been working my tail off. I'm drinking something, and Iris comes in her stylish pants and dark shirt, her long hair pulled back in a ponytail and those wide eyes staring at me in wonder, and then proceeds to tell me a story with an insight.

"If this is but a tiny drop in a vast ocean, isn't it sweeter if you get to share it with someone you love and trust?"

"I'm sixteen. I don't think Mom is going to want me to run off and get married anytime soon."

"I'm not talking about marriage. I'm talking about love and trust. I'm talking about the journey."

"Okay."

"Do you know how old I am?"

I shake my head. Mom has reminded me it's not polite talking about women's ages, including hers.

"I'm just a month away from turning ninety."

For a second I don't believe her. Iris looks old, but not *that* old. She still walks around with energy and life. Her face is full of wrinkles, but not that many.

Is she somehow starting to look younger the longer I'm around her?

"I've always been told I looked young. I can see it in your eyes—even you thought I was younger, though what's a decade or two when you're this age? I'm thankful for my time here. But as every day passes, I grow to understand that this is like a nest for a baby bird."

"This inn?"

"This world. This life. We're born, and we're warm and secure, but one day it's time to fly away. And some make it. Some birds are able to soar. Others aren't so lucky."

I think of that bluebird that bit me. I still see it every time I come here. It's like Iris's pet that guards the house.

"When you're sixteen, you don't think in those terms." Iris places a frail hand over the journal and brushes it as she might the head of a child. "But when you're older, you have to. When you're older, it's inevitable."

"What is?"

"Remember what I first asked you a couple of months ago?"

I nod.

"It's easy to put off deciding what you really believe when you're a teenager. Or when you're twenty or even thirty. By then, you're too busy living life to stop and figure out exactly what you believe. But when the shadow of death lingers, you are forced to think of it. And either you believe there is more, or you believe that this is all you have."

For a second I'm wondering how a double date turned into an exposé on life and death.

"Stanley died when I was almost forty. I couldn't believe it then. And even now, I can't believe it."

"I'm sorry."

"We'd tried so long to start a family. Times were different then. If it didn't work then, it didn't work. And that—that was painful. I was finally able to have Jason. But then he died. I still wake up wishing and wondering. Even though I know that this little nest will soon be gone, I still wake up wondering what it would be like to have birds of my own, babies I could have nurtured. But life doesn't always turn out the way you want it to."

"Yeah, I know."

Iris nods. "I know you understand this, Chris. Did you know that Jason and I came here after my husband died?"

"No."

"I decided to take the money we got from the will and from selling every single one of our possessions and build a fortress that was far away and high enough to get away from the world. I believed we could escape. I believed we could get away from everybody, including God."

"I thought you said this place was already here."

"Yes. It was. But I decided to make it my own. Yet the truth I learned—and I learned this the hard way—is that nothing in this world is our own. Everything we're given, big and small, is a gift from God. The moment we first see light when we're born. The oxygen we breathe. The food we eat and the water we drink. Everything is a gift."

"He gives more to some than to others."

"You're right," Iris says to my cynical comment. "And it seems random. But it doesn't matter. In the end, I'm not going to think and wonder what it would have been like if I had owned this or been given that."

I think of her husband and her son.

"I do think of them," she says, as if reading my mind. "But even if we only get a small chance to walk alongside someone we love, even for just a moment—isn't that a blessing? Isn't that in itself a wonderful gift?"

I think of Jocelyn.

Yes. It is.

"Tonight might be something fun and ordinary. It might be just another experience you will have in high school. But, Chris—it might also be the start of one of the most blessed and beautiful things you have ever known. So don't judge and don't dictate. Let whatever doors open swing open and then walk through them."

57. THE REST OF US

Oh man.

Or maybe I should say *Oh Dan.*

The guy driving the car used to be Dan the guy from high school. But a cologne-drenched, gel-spiked, brand-name-wearing Casanova has taken possession of Dan. This guy is a breath away from ridiculous.

"Hey, man, I got a great album to get the ladies in the mood."

The hip-hop song begins playing, and I realize Dan has already entered the land of the loony. I think this is 50 Cent's most popular song, but it makes me want to cringe and duck below the dashboard. Not because of the song itself, but because two skinny white guys in

North Carolina are riding with this tune cranking about makin' love and
drinking Bacardi and a whole lot of other stuff I can't even understand.

There are clichés, and then there's … this.

"Want some?" Dan hands me a black flask. "My father gave it to
me." He curses before I can ask if he's serious. "I put some of his gin
in there. Try it."

"I'm good."

"Come on. Drink up while you can. I know the girls sure won't
be drinking. Especially Kelsey."

I shake my head, and he takes the flask and sips it again.

I'm wondering how in the world I got to be sitting here in this
bad episode of the *Real World: Solitary* next to Dan the Man. If this
is any indication of how the night is going to go …

Needless to say, this won't be one of those beautiful and blessed
doors Iris was talking about.

When the door of Georgia's house opens—well, I might have to take
back my thoughts.

Beautiful and *blessed* are two words that come to mind.

Also *bewilderment*.

Where did Kelsey go, and who is this girl standing next to Georgia?

It's not like she did some dramatic Disney movie moment where
the Ugly Duckling suddenly becomes Jennifer Lopez. No, Kelsey's
already cute. A young-looking, sweet, innocent cute, the very definition of cute. But standing there, Kelsey's graduated to something
beyond that word.

Georgia says hi and acts more excited to see me than to see the dude I'm with. Kelsey still has her glasses on and still stifles a view of her braces with a tight-lipped grin, but that doesn't mean she doesn't look—

Older.

I'm wondering if Georgia gave her a makeover. She's wearing stylish jeans and a nice long-sleeved T-shirt. I'm not sure what else she's done. Makeup, maybe, or the way her hair is a little more stylized and wilder or something.

We make small talk and meet Georgia's parents, who also seem a lot more interested in me than in Dan. I'm wondering if I'm some special boy who's been granted a nice evening out because he's so … special.

We get outside, and Georgia says she's going to drive.

"I'm not going to leave my car here," Dan says. His black Altima looks close to new.

"Oh, you don't have to worry about leaving it here," Georgia says. "You can follow us."

"Isn't this a double date?"

Georgia smiles. "It's whatever you want to call it."

Then they get into her Toyota and don't seem to worry about waiting for us. Dan and I climb back into his car and race to follow them to wherever they're going.

Chili's has never taken on such importance, such surreality. I'm not sure if surreality is even a word, but if not I'm making it up. Because I don't quite feel like I'm here eating chips and salsa and wondering how in the world I got to be sitting at this table.

I mean, not long ago I was at a table with Jocelyn and Rachel and Poe.

Remember them?

Jocelyn is gone. Really gone.

Rachel moved away. For reasons I don't know.

And Poe might as well have moved away.

Now I'm sitting at a table full of strangers and glancing at Kelsey as Dan and Georgia exchange dialogue that seems a little more on the hurtful side than playful.

"I never did 'go out' with Brady," Georgia says.

I still can't decide if Georgia is full of herself or not.

"You *so* went out with Brady, at least for a couple of weeks. He sure talked it up anyway."

Dan, on the other hand, is totally full of himself. Full of that and a lot of other … stuff.

"What's your definition of 'going out'?"

Dan makes a face like he's going to say something crude when I decide to change the subject.

"How long have you guys known each other?" I ask Kelsey and Georgia.

They both laugh, and I'm wondering how that can possibly be a funny question.

"Sorry," Kelsey says. "Georgia and I used to *not* hang around with each other. It was really only at the end of sophomore year we became friends."

"She thought I was a bit of a snot, and I can be, to be honest." Georgia looks at Dan. "I have to be. At our school, the guys sometimes don't get the point."

"Are you going to be this way all night?"

"If I have to, yes."

"We started hanging around after a party," Kelsey continued. "Turns out we have more in common than we thought."

"Just like Dan and me," I say.

The girls laugh, and Dan looks at all of us, wondering what I said.

He's already acting a bit more animated and out of it. I'm thinking that flask isn't helping.

Maybe I can get a ride home with the ladies.

"So why'd you move down here?" Georgia asks.

I go into the story about my parents' divorce, but I make it short and sweet. I don't get into details about my dad finding God and my mom finding wine.

"But why Solitary?"

I can see Georgia's point.

"We wanted to escape from civilization. It was this or somewhere in Alaska."

They laugh again, and the more the girls laugh, the more comfortable I feel.

"I'd totally live in Alaska," Dan says. "Hunt wild animals and live off the land."

Georgia and Kelsey seem to be laughing with me and laughing at Dan.

"What?" Dan says. "I totally would."

"Have you ever gone hunting in your life?"

"I've shot guns."

"Yeah, I can totally see you gutting a deer," Georgia says.

After a while of this, when we're eating our meals, Dan seems to be bored with being abused by Georgia. He's busy playing with his phone and texting or something. Georgia is picking at her salad, while Kelsey doesn't seem too interested in her meal either.

"Not a fan of tacos?" I ask her.

"No—they're fine."

"You're going to have a lot to bring home."

She smiles in a way that I love. It's a shy smile, a kind of unsure smile that's nice to see when so many people in this world seem so sure of themselves. It's a smile that I can't remember seeing on many of the cute girls back home.

"Tweeting about what you're eating tonight?" Georgia asks Dan.

"Telling everybody how my date with Georgia is going."

"Dream on."

"The night is young. Lots can happen."

"If you noticed, we did drive separately. Chris, you're certainly welcome to come with us to the party later."

"Come on, that's not even fair," Dan says.

"Then mind your manners."

"What do you think I'm—"

"That includes shutting that big flabby mouth of yours."

Kelsey looks at me. Before I can get her to say something, she takes a bite to make sure she's safe from sharing her thoughts.

Dan is the kind of guy who doesn't talk with you but talks *at* you. I'm still not sure if he's heard any of the things I've said to him, so I've basically stopped talking. But when we arrive at the party, I'm able to get away from my chauffeur and hopefully not see him anymore tonight.

I could say the same about Georgia, to be honest. I'm not really warming up to her either.

Kelsey, however—well, she's a whole other matter.

The party is at the house of some senior. Lots of kids jammed into a small space with dim lights and loud music and lots of alcohol. Kelsey looks more lost than I probably do. After a half hour of wading through people and trying to talk to no avail, she suggests going outside.

It's cold but not frigid. Winter's gone, and the promise of spring is near. We walk past newcomers and get to the street.

"Do you mind?"

"What?" I ask.

"Just—staying out here? Getting away?"

"No."

Kelsey walks in the center of the street, confident that nobody's coming and if they do we can move to the side. For a while I just walk alongside her.

"Thanks for doing this," she says.

"What?"

"Tonight."

"Yeah, sure."

"Dan's a real winner."

"We're bonded for life. I think I've heard more 50 Cent tonight than I've heard my entire life."

"Sorry."

"Please. It's no big deal. It's kinda humorous."

"Do you like parties?"

"Do you?" I ask.

"No."

"So why go?"

"That was Georgia's idea. All of this—it was really her idea."

"Yeah, I can tell she's really crazy about him."

"They've been that way forever. I could see her marrying him. Like after she has all these relationships with all these other guys, I can see her finally settling down for someone who's crazy for her."

"Seriously?"

Kelsey nods. "I've told her that, but she thinks I'm delirious. I don't know. I just think it's nice to know that someone out there likes you."

There's a long pause as we walk.

"Do you—do you miss her?"

The question slaps me on the back of the head. For a second I really question if it's Kelsey who asked it. I don't need to ask her who she's talking about.

"Yeah."

We keep walking. I know I probably should say something else, or just say something about anything, but I can't.

She has no idea about the truth. She can't. There's no way she can know.

We get to a turn in the road, and Kelsey stops. I can't see her eyes in the darkness.

"Do you think we're all the same around here?"

"What do you mean?" I ask.

"That we're all just a bunch of rednecks who don't know anything."

"Who said that?"

"I heard you say something like that to Gus."

"When? Recently?"

"It was after a fight in the hallway. Just after you came."

"You noticed me?"

Kelsey laughs. "All the girls noticed you. Who wouldn't? The fact that you weren't from around here just made you more interesting. Chicago, too. That was all everybody could talk about. The girls, that is. And then—then suddenly you were with her. Jocelyn. Of course nobody was surprised."

I knew that people noticed us together, but I'd always assumed it was because Jocelyn was special, because she was chosen for something awful.

I never thought it had anything to do with me.

"The stuff I said to Gus—that was because he's a moron. I don't think that about the rest of the school."

"You sure?"

"Are you even trying to put yourself in his class?" I laugh. "Please."

"I know. But—but Jocelyn wasn't like the rest of us."

"Hey, Kelsey, look—just—she's not here, okay? So you don't have to bring her up."

"She's kind of here. The same way she's kind of in our art class. Or anywhere you go."

I feel the goose bumps on my skin and know that this girl is right. Kelsey might look younger than she is, but she knows. She knows, and she's right.

"I don't know what to say."

"It's okay, really," she says. "I understand."

We keep walking and see the lit-up house and hear the loud music. I know that this is one of those moments, and this time I act.

"Hey, hold on," I tell her.

She pauses, and this time when I look down I can see her face and her glasses lit up by the moonlight. But mostly I just see those bold eyes looking back at me.

"Look, Kelsey—I just—there's things that I can't change. Like my being from Chicago. Good or bad. Or like—well, like anything. It's just—I don't know how to say this—but there's a lot—"

Then a car comes toward us like a possessed horse galloping through the night. We move off the street, and the car screeches to a halt just beyond us.

The driver's window opens, and I hear a familiar voice.

"Chris? Is that you?"

The voice belongs to Poe.

58. THE TRUTH, FINALLY

The timing of this is really spectacularly *not* good.

"Poe?"

I can't believe it's really her. I wouldn't know if that's her car, because I don't know anything about Poe, except for the fact that she's been hating and ignoring me (Thousand Island incident excluded).

"Chris—I need to see you."

It's dark out, but not that dark. She can see that Kelsey is standing right next to me.

"Look—whatever I'm interrupting, I'm sorry—I don't mean to. I just—we have to talk, and we have to talk now."

"Kelsey—have you guys …"

"Hi, Poe," she says, answering my question.

"Yeah, hi. Look, I'm really sorry, but—Chris, you have to come with me."

"What's this about?"

"It's about Jocelyn."

I glance at Kelsey. Like I said, the timing of this is really amazingly awful.

"We were just going back to the party—"

"No, no party. I swear, Chris, you gotta get in my car and right now. You might never see me again."

"It's okay," Kelsey says.

I'm about to say something else, but I see her blond hair nodding over toward Poe.

"I'm sorry," I say to her.

"It's fine. Really."

She walks away, and I see her silhouette lit up by the stark headlights of Poe's car. This would be the moment I say "Enough" and follow Kelsey back into the party.

But of course I don't.

Of course I go toward the car and climb in.

I have no idea where we're headed.

But I know I have to go there.

We're taking a curve a bit too quickly, and I grab onto the handle above the door.

"Why don't you slow down?"

"I just want to find a place to talk."

We're in the middle of dark, desolate woods.

"Where, exactly, do you want to talk?"

"Nobody can be around."

"Poe …"

She slams on the brakes and we skid, then she gets control and pulls off on the side of the road next to a hill and a mountain of forest. I can hear the deathly quiet outside through the crack in the window.

"What's going on?"

She turns to me, and I can barely make out her face. But I think there are tears in her eyes.

"I know. I know about it. I finally get it."

"What?"

"What happened to Jocelyn. Do you know?"

"Yeah."

"What? Tell me. Tell me everything."

"Why—why now? What happened?"

She breathes out, and her breath is shaky, heavy. "I've been writing back and forth to Jocelyn."

"Letters?"

"No—emails. And texts. And I—I believed just like everybody else that she moved. Like Rachel. Except Rachel really did move. I've seen her and talked to her on Skype. She's there. But Jocelyn—the emails I got from her were strange. Weird. Just saying how you broke her heart, how she can never love again after what you did to her, how you hurt her."

"Hurt her? Hurt her how?"

Poe curses and shakes her head. "It's utter crap. Those emails and whoever was writing them. I should have come to you. I know—you tried. But something—I know something happened. Those emails weren't from her. I know that now."

"How?"

"I wanted to see how'd she react, so I brought up Stuart. I said how much I missed him and how her leaving reminded me of when he disappeared. Then I asked her what she thought had happened to him. This was the bait. And she took it, and that's when I knew—it wasn't Jocelyn."

"How do you know?"

"Because I made her once promise to never—ever—bring up Stuart's name with me. So if I was bringing it up, certainly she'd ask me why. She knew what I thought about his disappearance. She would have said something, even if she was trying to be polite or honor her promise. But instead she said that Stuart and his family moved unexpectedly—but—and here's the *but*—she's heard from him. You know. Heard from him, just like I'm hearing from her."

"Joss is dead."

The words feel cruel coming out of my mouth, but I don't know how else to share them.

"How do you know that?"

"I was there. I saw it." My mouth feels dry, the words taste like chalk.

"You saw her die?"

I nod and feel the world begin to spin and start to feel that falling, flying sensation.

Grief and fear are real.

They're real and they're like some dangerous mixture you make in chemistry class.

They're real and they taste bitter and they feel awful.

"What happened?"

So almost three months after the fact, I tell Poe. I tell her everything I can remember, and I can still remember everything.

I don't know how much time passes, but when I'm finished I smell Poe's perfume and feel her embrace and find myself holding back tears while holding on to her.

"I'm so sorry I didn't let you tell me," she says, over and over and over again.

For a long time we hold each other in the darkness of that small car. I can feel someone trembling but can't tell which of us it is. Probably both.

She finally pulls away from me. Her swollen, hurting eyes latch on to mine.

"We have to do something."

This isn't like some great idea from Poe. This is like a declaration.

"I tried."

I tell her about my conversation with the sheriff, with Staunch, with the others at the school. Then I tell her about Jared. She's the only one I've told about him.

"Do you trust him?"

"I don't know who to trust. Besides the puppy Jocelyn left for me."

"You can trust me."

I nod.

"Do you believe that?"

"I think so."

"Chris—there's—there's a lot more I can say, but not tonight. Okay? I already—I already feel watched. I don't think we should stay here."

The night that surrounds us seems to blow in the breeze like dark blankets hanging on hooks. It's like any second someone might come and pull them off their hangers and shine the big, bad, bright lights on us.

"There's one other thing," I say.

"What?"

"I discovered some emails that belonged to my uncle."

I share them with her as she starts up the car.

"Listen," she says. "This—we need to get help."

"But how?"

"I don't know. But I'll figure it out. This can't keep happening."

"Just—just be careful who you tell."

"I'm not telling a soul," Poe says. "Not yet. Not until I get a plan."

"And what do I do?"

"I think you keep doing what you're doing. Nothing. For the moment. Because if they—whoever they are—if they think that you're following orders, they might get lazy and forget to watch you. And that's when we act."

"Act how?"

"All roads lead to that freaky pastor. So that's where we start."

59. OH YEAH

Later that night, after Poe drops me off and tells me there will be lots more time to talk and then hugs me again like a dear old friend, I'm in my bed and I remember.

Kelsey.

I didn't even say good night.

If she knew, she'd understand. Of course, she'd also be packing her bags and moving to Southern California.

I think of this deep into the night. It's too late to call. I've never emailed her before.

She must so totally hate me.

I wonder what happened to Dan the Man, but that only amuses me a bit. He probably forgot that he started the evening with me.

Things were going so well with the chips and the salsa and the party. So normal.

I almost started to believe that things could be normal.

But they never will be.

Ever.

I stay up thinking about Kelsey and Poe and Jocelyn and this town and its secrets.

60. In Between

The lady in black begins walking. I watch her disappear down the long hall and through the doorway.

"Jocelyn."

My voice echoes all around. I get up and run past the ticket counter and then enter the square tube that seems to go on for miles.

She's there, standing, waiting for me in the middle of the empty Jetway.

"You're still here."

"Walk with me," she says.

She's not carrying any luggage or even a purse.

Because in dreams they don't have to, get it?

"Don't confuse this with a dream," Jocelyn—the adult Jocelyn—tells me.

"Then what is this place?"

"I told you—it's in between the two other places. That's the easiest definition I can provide."

"But I'm sleeping in my bed, right?"

"Technically, your body is. But what about your soul?"

"I don't—I don't understand."

"In your dreams you experience things that are just off. Perhaps you're doing something you've already done. Or you're in a crowd of strangers naked. Something that you fear or you remember or you regret—those get mixed in with the subconscious and turn into dreams. But this isn't a dream."

She stops and looks at me. In her high heels, she's the same height that I am.

She smiles and says, "Give me your hand."

I do what she tells me, and she places the hand on her cheek. I can feel her face move gently as she talks.

"This—all of this—it's real, Chris."

"You're older."

"No. Not exactly."

"Then—then what?"

"You can't imagine how many surround you. But those whom you do see, you have to choose to trust or not."

"Like Poe?"

"Like all of them."

"Tell me."

"I can't. It's not my place."

"Because you're like a figment of my imagination?"

She shakes her head.

"You're in a tough place, and I cannot help you. This—this right here—this is not a help. This is just a passageway, a glimpse."

I don't get what she's saying.

"There's a reason you can see this, but of course I cannot say."

We keep walking, and I can see the change of light and colors that show we're close to the plane.

"You shouldn't get on."

"I don't want to wake up," I tell her. "Let me stay here. Let me get on that plane."

God, is she beautiful.

So why did He have to take her? Why?

"This is just a shell," she says. "One day you'll understand. One day—I hope—you will see."

Then she closes her eyes, and I see everything around me do the same.

And when I open mine again, I know exactly where I am.

61. CREEPER

I don't wait for art class to talk to Kelsey. I find her between first and second periods. I see her walking with Georgia and interrupt them.

"Hey—can we talk?"

Georgia glances at me like I just walked off the set of a zombie movie. Kelsey nods, and this just seems to disgust her friend, who walks off.

"Look, I'm sorry."

"It's fine, really."

"Georgia seems really happy."

"She'll get over it."

"Kelsey—I didn't expect that to happen."

"What to happen?"

Something did happen, or almost happened before Poe interrupted us.

"Just—leaving you like that. It was rude. I can explain, but not now."

"It's fine."

"No, and I don't want—" I fully intended to apologize, but then I hear myself say, "Look, would you want to do something again?"

She glances at me and seems genuinely surprised.

"Something without Dan. Just—just us."

"Sure." Everything about Kelsey and the way she says *sure* is different.

"Great."

I walk away and wonder why I just asked this girl out when all I wanted to do was save face.

You couldn't help it.

But I could. I'm not interested and I have ten thousand other things going on right now.

You have unfinished business.

But that's crazy. I know that I just hate having someone angry or disappointed in me.

That's all and nothing more.

The clouds look threatening as we stand at the edge of the clearing and look out at the set of boulders. It looks different during the day, without the flickering of the fire coating the trees. Poe was easily able to drive here, to this place Sheriff Wells called The Grounds.

"This place has always creeped me out," she says.

"You've been here before?"

"Sure. With Stuart. He liked coming up here—he thought it was the perfect place to smoke in peace."

I gather that Stuart wasn't just smoking cigarettes.

"There was another place Jocelyn showed me, by Marsh Falls," I say. "Do you know where that is?"

"Sure."

"I saw people meeting there, a group of people. Like some underground church thing or something. Jocelyn had started meeting with them."

"Was the pastor one of them?"

"Pastor Marsh? No. I think they were meeting in secret *because* of people like the pastor. Maybe they can help us."

"Have you been back there?"

I shake my head.

"And this Jared guy—you trust him?"

"Yeah. He's been right with everything he's told me, everything I can prove anyway."

"So why doesn't *he* just go tell someone who can help?"

"He's still looking around—hoping to find his father."

Poe's eyes shift over the scene of the rocks on the top of the hill in front of us. I glance at her and count the five earrings in her ear.

"I don't think you should say anything to him for now. Until we're sure we can trust him. Okay?"

"Okay."

"We have to find some kind of proof, and then we have to tell someone who's away from here."

"I have the proof I need. I saw it with my own eyes."

"But nobody's going to believe you. I mean—Chris, I still barely believe you. It's a crazy story."

"I know."

"Everybody believes Jocelyn moved away. I mean—she sent me emails. That's how ridiculous this is. You say the sheriff is even in on it, right?"

"I don't know about that. I just know that he didn't believe me. He thinks just because I got into some trouble back at my old high school, I'm not telling the truth."

"What kind of trouble?"

"Stupid stuff. Partying. Nothing major."

"You? Partying? You seem a little too good to do that."

"You really don't know me, Poe."

"No, I don't."

She looks like she's about to say something else, then stops herself.

"How do we go about getting proof that Jocelyn was killed?"

"I want to know what the pastor is hiding," Poe says. "Because I'm betting it's going to be pretty ugly. Just like them all."

"What do you mean 'just like them all'?"

"Every week you hear of some priest caught molesting kids or some big-name preacher who condemns gays caught with some male 'buddy.' It's all a crock. They're all the same."

"I don't think Marsh is going to sit down for an interview."

"I want to see those emails from his wife."

"They're in the car. I'll leave them with you."

"I think you need to find out what he's hiding at his house."

"Are you kidding?"

Poe shakes her head, and her dark hair falls over her face. She brushes it back as if it annoys her. "Doesn't he spend all his time at that church?"

"I don't know," I say. "Probably."

"So you go when he's onstage preaching."

"What? Break into his house?"

"Why not?"

"What if someone catches me?"

"The only way we can get someone to believe you—to believe us—is to give them proof."

"And you think Pastor Marsh has some kind of proof at his home?"

"A creeper like that? Absolutely."

62. ALONE

The next day, Poe comes up to me. "Here's that book I borrowed from you. Make sure you look at it before returning it to the library."

I've never seen the book before, and I've never loaned a book to Poe.

In my English class, I open it and find a folded sheet of paper inside. It's one of the emails from the stack I gave to her. Written at the top is a note: *Did you read this?*

> I'M A PRISONER IN MY OWN HOUSE.
> I DON'T KNOW HOW MUCH LONGER I'M GOING TO BE
>   ABLE TO COMMUNICATE.
> I'M LIVING WITH A MONSTER. SOMEBODY, BUT NOT THE
>   MAN I MARRIED. NOT A MAN.

HERE'S A PERSON WHO FEIGNS HAVING A CHILD
IN ORDER TO TELL STORIES ABOUT HER IN HIS
SERMONS. WHO WOULD DO THAT? PEOPLE
BELIEVE IT, TOO. EVERYBODY AROUND HERE IS
DRINKING THE KOOL-AID.

IF YOU GET THIS—IF YOU'RE STILL THERE—THEN YOU
NEED TO COME GET ME.

WE'RE NO DIFFERENT FROM THE REST. THE
TENTACLES OF TUNNELS REACH US.

FIND THE SOUTH SIDE OF THE HOUSE IN THE WOODS,
MAYBE A HUNDRED YARDS AWAY. THERE IS A
DOOR THAT LEADS DOWN INTO THE TUNNEL.
FROM THERE YOU CAN GET IN.

IF YOU CAN GET IN, THEN MAYBE I CAN GET OUT.

I HOPE THERE'S TIME.

I HOPE HE DOESN'T FIND OUT.

PLEASE HELP.

I look up and stare at the teacher and see her looking at me, waiting.

"Chris, do you have any thoughts on this passage?"

"Yeah."

"Then please share."

"It's dark. It's brutal. It's the point of no return."

Mrs. Norton gives me a puzzled glance.

"What does it mean to you?"

"That we're all alone," I say. "That we're all alone and that nobody's ever going to get there in time to help. Nobody."

63. THE PROJECT

It seems like there have been more guests at the Crag's Inn as the weather has gotten warmer. I asked Iris about it once, but she said the inn is full year-round. I would've thought she was making that up, but I'd already realized that Iris was one of the last people in the world who would ever lie.

Today, as I show up driving my mom's car (and no, I don't have a license yet, and yes, I probably shouldn't be driving), I see a group of men standing at the side of the lodge. There are four of them, and they seem to be talking about something serious. They glance at me, then resume their conversation. I get out of my car and wave at them. I receive a couple of nods. One of the guys with longer hair and a goatee is smoking a pipe.

Inside, I find Iris ready as always for whatever my task will be today. It's been an unusual job, to say the least. Sometimes it's work outside, cleaning or cutting or trimming or hauling. Then other days it's something inside, like painting a room or boxing up belongings and bringing them out to the side of the driveway or organizing photos by the date on the back.

That last one was quite the job. It was fascinating to see all those pictures, mostly black-and-white and some of the earliest taken in the '20s. The photos were all of people, most of them taken around what appeared to be the Crag's Inn or the mountains. I might have gone through a thousand photos that day, making piles of 1920s and 1930s and so on, sorting them out by the year.

There were pictures of men and women in the woods and around campfires and walking along a dirt road and by the creek. They obviously were taken around here. But I couldn't find any pictures of the town itself.

I ended up asking Iris about it.

"I guess you're right," she said.

She didn't seem either surprised or curious.

"Who are all these people?"

"Guests."

They all looked different, from their ages to the color of their skin. It seemed like everybody came to the Crag's Inn for some reason.

"How do all these people know about this place? I mean—do you do a lot of advertising?"

Iris only smiled.

A little later I asked her why I was organizing these pictures. I could understand showing a montage of guests who had stayed with you, but none of these pictures had labels. They were all nameless strangers—some smiling, some creepy looking, some looking stoic and others looking busy.

"When you have a place as special as this one, it's important to document it for future generations."

I didn't want to insult her with the next question going through my mind. But Iris seemed to pick up on my expression and answered it anyway.

"There are many places in this world that are unique, Chris. That have a truly unusual history. Do you believe that?"

"Sure."

I just didn't believe that *this* particular place was that unique or unusual.

"Sometimes it's not what's on the outside. It doesn't have to be spectacular or impressive or ostentatious in order to be remarkable. Sometimes, the smallest of things can be absolutely exceptional. Just this morning I was visited by a swarm of hummingbirds. They surrounded me on the deck outside. It could not have been a more glorious way to wake up and see God's morning glory."

I could understand that, but I still couldn't understand these pictures.

But I still did my job and did it as well as I could.

"Do you want any coffee?" Iris asks me today.

She's never offered me coffee before, so I say sure, why not. I don't really like coffee, but I'm learning to try new things. Even if I don't necessarily want to.

"I needed to make some extra for our guests. Did you see them?"

"Yeah, outside. Talking at the side of the inn."

"Good," Iris says, disappearing and then bringing me a cup. "Would you like anything in it?"

"No. I'm not much of a coffee drinker. I'm flexible."

"You're making good progress," she tells me.

Drinking coffee is good progress?

"So are you ready for something different today?"

"Yeah."

She smiles and sits and urges me to do the same.

There is a formality around Iris that's grown to be not only interesting but kinda admirable. Most people in this world are rude and loud and obnoxious. Okay, not most people, but a lot of people.

People you see on reality shows and in the news. People who seem angry and irritated at life when they wake up. Iris is reserved and well-spoken and always seems so ... so dignified.

Maybe she's royalty from England hiding out in our creepy neck of the woods.

"How good is your composition?"

I stare at Iris and shake my head. "My what?"

"Your writing. Are you a good writer?"

"Not really. Average probably."

"Then average will do. Go on, sip your coffee; you'll need the extra caffeine."

She hands me an old book that I realize is a journal.

"I'd like you to begin a project that might take some time. But you've earned my trust, and you've shown that you're ready. I've had you do most of the labor that I need done at the moment. But this is the most important thing I could ever ask you to do."

I open the journal and see cursive handwriting in faded black ink. I try to read a little of it, but can't.

"Every innkeeper has had a journal and passes it down to the next person. The history of this inn is inside these pages."

"It's hard to read."

"Yes."

She leaves for a moment. I sip my coffee and wait. She comes back with a laptop.

"This is probably a little more to your liking."

It's a MacBook, and by the looks of it, a brand-new MacBook.

"I'm giving this to you, Chris. You will need this as you work on this project."

I hold the computer in my hand and probably have my mouth halfway open in shock.

Couple hundred bucks a day is one thing, but a MacBook ...

"For now, it will stay here while you work on this project," Iris says. "But you will be able to keep it when you finish."

"As payment for—"

"No," she interrupts. "In addition to your wages."

"This is, uh, quite a lot."

"There're no strings attached. It will be yours. But not for some time. Because this is a rather large project. And it's ultimately why I wanted you to come here and work."

The way she says *you* makes it seem like she invited me to come here in the first place. Mom was the one who pushed for me to be here. And that seemed random.

"They say that you can do things like load photos on a computer like that. Is that true?"

I nod, then think of the gazillion photos I've helped archive. I must have turned white, because Iris laughs.

"No, that's not what I'm thinking. Not *those* photos."

"Okay." I try to suppress a huge sigh of relief.

"The main thing I want you to do is to write a report. You can do that, right?"

"Yeah, I think."

"I'd like for you to write a history of this place, a kind that is easy to read and would be informative for newcomers. For people like yourself who don't know about this place and its history and can't scan messy journals to discover the truth."

"Where will I get the information?"

"There's far too much information. And that's not counting the journals. I will show you. You will work in a room that I have ready for you."

I nod again.

"I promise there will be other things to do—ways to get exercise and get away from the research and writing. But I believe that you'll find it interesting. I hope you do, at least."

"Okay."

"Are you sure?" she asks.

"Sure about what?"

"Sure about this endeavor?"

I nod.

I'm not sure about anything, not since having moved to Solitary. But it's work and I can earn a MacBook, so why not? It can't be that hard or boring, right?

As I say good night to Iris, my headache getting worse as I move, she asks how the project went today.

"I didn't get anything written. Not yet."

"That's okay. There's a lot to make sense of."

"Only about a hundred folders with scraps and pieces of stuff."

I want to say it's worse than the photo project she gave me.

"There is no deadline, Chris. Take your time."

"Sure."

"And one other thing."

I stand at the doorway as she stares intently at me.

"Take care of yourself. Please."

She says this as if she knows.

As if she's aware. Of everything.

64. AFRAID OF THE DARK

I can hear rain falling through the speakers in my room and on the trees outside, and I find I'm having a hard time seeing the difference. I'm waiting, killing time, worrying, listening to The Cure's *Disintegration,* worrying a little more. It's Sunday morning and Mom is gone to work and I'm home alone without a car or a life, but I do have a plan. Or I have Poe's plan. Now I'm waiting for a good time to leave the house and meet her downtown.

It appears I'll be riding my bike in a downpour.

The plan is to sneak and spy while the pastor speaks and lies. Maybe I should write song lyrics.

A crack of thunder gently shakes the house.

Midnight sits on the bed beside me, oblivious to the sound and the shaking. I remember Brady's dog back home and how it would go berserk at the faintest hint of thunder. Sometimes it's better not knowing the things we're supposed to be afraid of.

Maybe there are families that wake up and have breakfast together and watch television while they get ready for church. They go out and see their friends at New Beginnings and listen to Pastor

Marsh preach some inspiring sermon. Or maybe they don't listen to all of it because they have other things on their minds, like Sunday dinner and starting work on Monday and the rest of the week and the rest of their life. They don't notice how odd the pastor's words seem, and they forget how odd the whole town around them happens to be.

Some people do this.

Others get ready to break into the pastor's house.

What I'll find, I have no idea.

The clouds appear full and angry as I finally venture outside with a cap and jacket to keep me remotely dry.

I have everything I need.

I think.

"I've been waiting for half an hour."

Obviously she doesn't notice how wet I am, or doesn't care, as I sit down in the front seat of her car. The good thing is that the rain coats the windows and keeps us hidden from any outsider's view.

"I was hoping for the rain to die down."

Poe is in black jeans and a black T-shirt, appropriate for the day. The only piece of clothing that's not black is her denim jacket.

"When are you going to get a license?" she asks as she pulls away from the parking spot on the far edge of the street where she told me we'd meet.

"I don't think my mother is in too big of a rush."

"Why's that?"

"Because she probably knows if I had a license I'd get in the car and drive back to Illinois."

She ignores my comment. "You ready?"

"I think so. Not like I do this every other weekend."

"I just hope nothing weird happens, like he decides to let someone else preach today and stays home."

"You're coming in with me, right?"

"No. I'm going to be outside to let you know if anyone's coming."

"So how are you going to do that?"

"Get the bag in the back."

I open her black leather purse and find two cell phones.

"Take my iPhone. The other one belongs to my mom. So when are you getting a phone?"

"I'm not getting one around here. They'll put something in it."

Poc doesn't laugh. "If I see anybody coming up to the house, I'll call you."

"You sure it'll work?"

"These aren't walkie talkies. Yeah, it'll work."

The rain is coming down harder. As Poe drives, she turns up the music. I don't recognize the punk band. They might be current or thirty years old.

"You really think this will work?"

She shrugs. "What else can we do? You okay?"

"What do you mean?"

"You look pale."

"You're one to talk."

She laughs. This girl is a lot like Jocelyn—tough. I wonder why I'm always around tough girls.

"The biggest thing is going to be getting into the house," I tell her. "If there are passageways like the tunnels I told you about—then, who knows."

"Just use common sense."

I want to tell her there's really no common sense in the man with the empty eye sockets that I encountered in the tunnel but decide against it.

"It's hard knowing where you're at when you're underground."

"Use the compass on the iPhone."

"Fancy. Do you have an app for discovering the undead?"

She ignores my joke. "Just don't break it."

I touch her phone and see the picture on the screen. For a second I feel gutted. It's a picture of Poe standing between Jocelyn and Rachel. They're huddled up and smiling and acting like they couldn't care about tomorrow.

Tomorrow never came.

"I can't bring myself to change it," Poe says. "She was really something, wasn't she?"

I nod.

It's a nice reminder why we're here.

This isn't some silly mystery where we're trying to solve a puzzle and find out the criminal.

The puzzle doesn't need solving.

It needs proving.

And that's why we are—or I am, anyway—about to break the law.

It takes me about twenty minutes to get in sight of the house.

At one point as I'm walking through the dripping woods, Poe opens up her car door and shouts to me to hurry up. That helps a lot. Really encourages me too.

I think I expected a haunted house at the end of some deserted road, but this is quite the opposite. It's another large log cabin that's high up on the side of a mountain. There's no huge valley to see at any side, however. Just a cocoon of trees.

The driveway is paved, with plenty of space for parking. Two wraparound covered porches surround the three-level house. It looks newly built, with ornately carved trim and posts everywhere. It doesn't look daunting. In fact, it looks very inviting.

I'm pretty sure this is the south side of cabin. Poe has parked down the street, away from view. The driveway and surrounding grounds are very open, and it wouldn't surprise me if they were watched with cameras.

Maybe someone already knows you're here.

I'm about a hundred yards away from the house, but so far I don't see the doorway Heidi Marsh described in her email. Then I stumble over it. My foot hits something hard that's jutting out of the ground, and I go face-first into the dirt. It's wet and soft, and I get even muddier as I stand and pat myself off. I turn to see leaves and dirt covering a wooden door. There's a latch on the side, and though I expect it to be locked, the door opens without a problem.

I look down and see darkness.

The rain continues to pour, the trees providing a little cover but not enough. I can taste water running down my cheek and landing on the edge of my mouth. I take out the big heavy-duty flashlight that I recently bought, a 13.1-inch aluminum LED one that I paid about sixty bucks for. This sucker's not going to go out if I'm being chased. In fact, it's long and heavy enough to be used as a nice weapon to beat someone's face in.

I turn it on and am surprised again at how powerful the beam is. It lights up the entire square hole going down from this doorway. There's a metal railing on the side, this one a little more clean and visible. This tunnel or passage looks freshly built.

I wipe my forehead and then proceed down the ladder. It takes me a few minutes to reach the bottom. I wonder if this passageway is attached to the ones going out of our house and the little cabin just beyond us.

Does the whole town play games with each other at nighttime?

It heads straight ahead for maybe twenty or thirty yards. I walk for a few minutes and then test Poe's cell phone.

"You okay?" she asks.

"Just wanted to make sure this works."

"Of course it works. Where are you?"

"Underground. In a carved-out passageway."

"What do you see?"

"Dirt. Rock." I move the beam of the light and study the soft ground I'm walking on. "A footprint."

"Hurry up. I'm getting creeped out waiting here in the car."

"You're getting creeped out? Why don't you come down here?"

But she's gone. I shake my head.

The air is musty down here. I see thick tree roots sticking out from the ceiling and sides of the passageway like random curls on a head. I hope I'm going the right direction, but it's the only direction there is. I keep darting my beam back behind me. Just making sure. I hate those horror movies where they never bother to check behind them until *Oh no it's too late!* and they quickly die a grisly death.

Soon the passageway ends in a split. One tunnel leads to my left and continues going forward. The other leads to my right and seems to go back the way I came.

I get the compass on Poe's phone to see where I'm at and decide to go to the right, which is more north than the other way.

The ground is more rocky and uneven here, and the passageway is smaller. I have to keep bending my head to make sure it doesn't scrape the dirt and clay above me. The beam of my flashlight bounces off the walls. My breathing seems to echo off these shrinking barriers.

The passage bends a bit, so I can't see exactly where it's headed. It just seems like I've been walking a lot longer than the hundred yards it should've taken to get to the pastor's house.

I let out a sigh, and then hear the voice.

Are you afraid of the dark, Chris?

It's not an audible voice. At least I don't think it is.

I stop and shine the flashlight behind me, around me, in front of me.

Are you afraid of being left alone in a tiny little hole?

That's not my mind talking. It's someone else's voice. It's his voice, the voice of the pastor.

But of course I'm imagining it.

I keep walking, a little faster now.

What if something happened and nobody knew you were down here and you were left for the animals for the dogs for the maggots?

Again I stop. I shake my head, hoping the thoughts are like dead skin I can simply brush away onto the floor.

Then my flashlight goes out.

I curse and can hear my own voice loud and clear.

Then in the darkness, I hear something else.

The sickening, crawling sound of laughter.

Real laughter, not imagined.

65. HELL IS HERE

When you're running in the dark not knowing where you're really going and feeling something scraping at the top of your head and imagining you're hearing footsteps behind you, you can be as brave as possible but you're still about ready to pee in your pants.

I hear something in front of me before I actually feel it. I slow down just as I crash against a wall.

For a second, while I'm on the ground, I fumble and try to

turn the flashlight back on. My hands are shaking so badly I'm like a junkie holding a syringe. Finally I press the button.

Light. Just like that.

I wave it all around me like a deranged man.

There's nothing down there. I'm at the end of the tunnel. A door about three feet tall is at the bottom.

I find the cell phone in my pocket.

Everything's fine just stop imagining things Chris.

I feel the door and find a handle. It turns with ease.

I think I expected a dungeon or something like that. Instead, I'm walking through an ordinary—well, more like a nicely finished—basement.

The door opens up to a narrow, long, closet-like room that turns out to be a wine cellar. On both sides of the room, racks of wine bottles go from the floor to the ceiling. The door I came out of blends into the wall, not as if to hide it but more as if to keep with the decor of the room.

It's not like he's trying to hide this passageway.

But then again, I don't know what he's trying to do.

Once out of the cellar, I walk down a hallway and see a few other rooms—a bathroom and a couple of bedrooms. Then I enter an open area that appears to be a media room, with a gigantic flat-screen television on the wall and several couches around it.

Everything looks new and expensive and appealing.

I guess I never really thought I'd get into the house. But now

that I'm here, I'm not exactly sure what to do. I think of calling
Poe but then decide against it. I don't want her barking in my ear.

I quickly survey the rest of the downstairs. A wet bar, a storage room with lots of stuff like golf clubs and skis and toys rich
people have. I don't find any horse heads or dead people or upside-
down crosses.

Maybe I'm wrong about the pastor.

But that's crazy. I'm definitely not wrong about the pastor. The
question is what can I find on him. And how quickly I can do it.

I find a set of wide wooden stairs heading up. Again I think
about calling Poe, but I don't.

I start up the stairs, my legs feeling stiff and unsure of
themselves.

This place is cold. Unusually cold. I shiver and hold the flashlight that I no longer need in my hands, ready to use it like a
baseball bat. Ready to swing and then get out of here.

Upstairs is a home fit for a movie star. This could be Tom
Cruise's Carolina getaway. Everything looks and feels and smells
new. Open windows reveal the woods in the distance. Everything
looks neat and organized. Suddenly I realize what's making me so
uncertain. Besides the fact that I'm, like, breaking and entering.

There's nothing personal in this house. Nothing at all.

Even Mom has a few pictures of the two of us around the house,
along with the mementos of a life being lived. We've been here just
a little over six months, and she has more in her home than Pastor
Marsh has in his. There are no pictures of Marsh and his family, no
piles of mail, no messy counters or pillows on the floor or random
remote controls in the wrong places.

Everything seems too perfect.

I check the cell phone to make sure Poe hasn't called. Then I go down a hallway past the kitchen. I find a study that looks more organized than a library. A guest room. A bathroom. A laundry room. Then another door leading to a garage.

When I open it, I can't believe what I'm seeing. The silver Mercedes SUV, the same one the blond was driving when she picked me up. If I needed proof, here it is. The woman driving the SUV, *this* SUV, was indeed Heidi Marsh.

I go back into the main room and again look outside. It's still dark and raining.

I'm not going to find anything here. Nothing at all.

I wonder if the pastor even lives here.

All of this will be pointless if I don't find something, anything. It's still not noon and church hasn't gotten out yet. I have to go upstairs.

For a second I pause by the large stairway. There's a loft area with rails that overlooks the main room below. I take a few steps and then hear a shriek above me.

Up in the loft, wearing a white robe like some wicked witch from Oz or Narnia, stands a woman with crazed hair and an even crazier face, opening her mouth as wide as it can go and screaming at me.

I'm so startled I miss a step and stumble backward.

From my position sprawled on my back I see that it's the blond.

Heidi Marsh.

But this time I see eyes red and evil and makeup smeared and grotesque like a clown. She looks pale and sickly, at least from what I can see of her under the oversized robe she's wearing.

"Get out of here, you devil! Get out, you whoremonger! You liar! Get out!"

She screams again, and I scamper like a wounded, wet dog. I bash my hip against a couch and search for the front door. At this point it doesn't matter how I get out. I'm already in deep trouble.

Her howling is awful, and it doesn't stop. I swing open the door, and as I glance back I see the woman on her knees, bony arms hanging on the rails of the loft like a prisoner in a concentration camp grabbing on to barbed wire.

"Hell is here, and he will not die!"

Those are the only words I can make out before I reach the driveway and rain falls on my face and I run and keep running and almost run right past Poe's parked car.

66. LOVE

It takes me a while to stop hyperventilating or whatever my lungs are doing.

I tell Poe to drive.

Again a part of me wonders what would happen if we just drove and kept driving and kept driving far away from this place.

I finally manage to tell her what happened. I include everything, from the laugh I heard in the tunnel to finding a deranged Heidi Marsh demanding a housewarming gift.

"You think she's crazy?"

"What's your definition of crazy?" I ask. "A year ago I would've said yes, but I don't know. I'm beginning to think *I'm* crazy."

"I never see her with the pastor."

"You've been watching?"

"I see him all the time. He's everywhere."

"She's not right. But then again, if I were married to that weird pastor, I wouldn't be right either."

"We have to tell somebody."

"No," I say. "I'm already in trouble—she's going to tell him."

"You think he'll believe her?"

I try and sort out all the thoughts going through my mind. This was definitely *not* what I was supposed to do. This was definitely not lying low.

"We need to see Jared," I say.

"*You* need to see Jared. Don't tell him about me."

"Why?"

"The fewer people that know, the better."

The rain keeps falling and Poe keeps driving and the sound of the windshield wipers hypnotizes me.

"What are you thinking?" she eventually asks.

When I exhale, I can hear my voice shaking. "This is only going to get worse."

"You don't know that."

"Yeah, I do. That's the only way this can go."

"Not everybody around here is evil. My parents—I know they're not."

"But you don't trust them."

"I don't want them getting hurt," Poe says. "That's why I wanted something—I wanted proof."

"Shall we go back and get a picture of Mrs. Completely-Wacked back there?"

"I don't think we want to go back there anytime soon."

"What if—no." I can't believe my own thought. "What if it's a ploy. Some kind of game or something. Like a dare."

"What do you mean?"

"What if—what if we did tell someone? Like the sheriff, who already doesn't believe a word of mine. What if we brought them to this house and got there and saw Mrs. Marsh sitting there drinking an iced tea and dressed like a pretty pastor's wife and smiling?"

"You've seen too many horror movies."

"I haven't seen enough," I say. "Otherwise this might all make more sense."

"I don't think the pastor even lives there."

"What?"

"The way you described it."

"Maybe he's a neat freak."

Poe is thinking something, but I don't want to push. It was her idea to go into the house. I'm afraid to hear any more ideas.

"Talk to your friend and tell him everything."

"And?"

"And then we'll go from there."

"But don't mention you."

"No," Poe says. "As far as they're concerned, I still hate you."

"Oh, so you don't hate me anymore?"

She glances at me and then rolls her eyes. "I'd like to keep you around a little longer."

"Just a little longer, huh?"

"Yeah," she says. "Until I finally escape once and for all."

The stillness beats like a heart. I can't tell if it's the ticking of my alarm clock or the pumping of my heart or the pulse of fear.

In my room, I sit and think.

I'm doing nothing but thinking.

I'm not even listening to music.

I keep asking myself questions like *Do I tell Mom?* and *Do I leave altogether?* and *Can I trust Poe?* and *Can I trust [insert any other name here]?*

A part of me answers with no and no and no and no.

I go to my desk and find the picture of Jocelyn and me, the computer printout. I want that back, that moment, that time, that snapshot. I want to go back in time and then escape. Escape with her holding my hand.

Another photo under some papers gets my attention. It's the snapshot I found in my locker, the one where I'm in the sun, smiling, looking carefree and happy. I pick up the photo and study it.

It's starting to fade. Not just the colors, but the entire shot. It looks like it's been out in the sun too long and the image is beginning to blur and wash away.

But I never left it in the sun.

It's symbolic. Next thing I know, it's going to light on fire and I'm going to finally understand.

Yeah, Heidi, you're right. Hell is here, and I'm stuck right in the middle.

Dad's voice comes to me, but I bark back a curse to shut it up.

It's followed by another voice. Iris's voice. Proper and eloquent and sophisticated.

I think of something she said to me recently. *Want to know the most powerful thing in this world, Chris?*

The secret of life, and she was going to tell me.

Of course I wanted to know.

"Love," she said.

Of course that's what she would say.

I'm not sure what I'm supposed to do with that wisdom.

"I think you're the only person in the world that loves me now, Midnight." I scoop her up and bring my nose to her soft little head.

It's terrifying to think what's out there, beyond this door and this cabin.

But holding this little thing that I love, this precious little life that reminds me of a love I believed I held—a sixteen-year-old's notion of love—I think that maybe Iris is right.

Love is powerful. I just wish it could keep the demons out at night.

67. ONE THING

That night I'm driven around by another beautiful girl.

It's not Jocelyn or Poe or Heidi Marsh. Thank God it's not Heidi Marsh.

This is a golden-haired beauty and she's laughing and she turns up the stereo and the music competes with the wind rushing against us. We're in a convertible.

This can be yours and more she says.

You can have whatever you want she says.

She grabs my hand and then accelerates.

I'm a kid on a roller coaster. Except this time, some gorgeous girl is holding my hand.

Of course she is. This is my dream. I'm far away from Solitary.

No you're not, the driver says. *You're still here. And you're here because you belong. Because you were chosen. Because all your life has been orchestrated for you to be here right here and now.*

I feel the wind and feel her grip and feel the motion as if we're flying. Maybe we are.

Just let go and stop fighting.

She doesn't understand, of course, but dreams never do.

I understand everything, she says. *And that heavy, sickening, horrific feeling you wake up and go to sleep with every day ... it can be gone.*

I see the lights of the center of town right ahead.

There's just one thing you need to do.

I look at her and believe her and want to stay here.

I suddenly realize I'll do anything she says.

But I wake up and find I can't.

At least not yet.

68. Train Wreck

I'm heading down to the car to climb in and wait for Mom. She's running slow this morning. Guess she had a rough day yesterday too.

I open the side door and see an envelope on the seat.

We never lock the doors because nobody is ever going to steal our car. I glance around to see if anybody is watching, to see if I can see tracks or any trace of someone. As usual, nobody is around for me to see.

I climb in and close the door and then wait for a minute, listening for Mom's footsteps on the wooden stairs. When I don't hear anything, I open the envelope.

A small sheet of paper is inside. On it is a handwritten address: *49 McKinney Gap.*

No town or state or zip, though I doubt I need it.

I fold the envelope and sheet of paper in half and tuck it in my pocket by the time Mom opens the car door.

"Ready?" she asks.

I nod and look out the windows and wonder i͟
ing us.

I nod and look out the windows and wonder if someone's watching us.

If they are, I wish they'd just come out of the shadows.

For several days I try to find out where McKinney Gap is. I spend time in the computer lab looking on Google Maps, which I thought showed every single street and road in the world. But many of the roads around Solitary aren't even on the map. Even my street isn't on there.

If our address isn't on Google, does that mean we don't even exist?

Poe doesn't know. She reminds me that she doesn't technically live in Solitary and doesn't know the place extremely well. I tell her where I got the address, and she says she'll do some investigating herself.

Next I ask Newt. We don't talk very much, even though we usually are around each other at our lockers or at lunch. Sometimes I think the less he knows about me and my life, the better. He doesn't recognize the street either.

I shouldn't be surprised when he comes to my locker Wednesday morning and hands me a sheet with something drawn on it in black ink.

"There you go," he says. "Your own treasure map."

"You found it?"

He nods, acting like he's about to say something else … then nothing.

"Thanks."

"It should be obvious where you need to go," he says, in a way that makes it seem like he's also saying *so don't ask me to show you.*

Mom is working tonight, so I know what I'll be doing after track practice.

If someone will drive me, that is.

"So what exactly is your deal?"

I'm standing at my locker and am not exactly sure if Georgia is talking to me.

"What?"

"Yeah, you. Hello? Anybody there?"

I put up my hands. "What?"

"So, like, are you going to ask her out again, or was that something you just said to make yourself feel better?"

For a brief moment I honestly don't know who she's talking about. Then I remember. Kelsey.

"Because, you know, there are *a lot* of other guys she can spend her days and nights thinking about instead of weirdos like you."

I've woken up to what she's talking about. And now I'm fully aware, fully functioning, and fully irate.

"Georgia. It is Georgia, right? I keep confusing it with some other state like Florida or Oklahoma. But Georgia, right, because here's the thing—and shut up for a second and let me talk—whatever happens between me and Kelsey or me and *anybody* in this school is totally not your business and never will be. So please get out of my face and get out of this space and leave me alone."

She curses in my face. I'm guessing she's never been told off by a guy before.

First time for you, too.

I'm expecting her to spit on my face.

"I told her you're a jerk," she says before walking off.

I still have art class today.

Like I need any extra drama in my life.

I stand for a second and just look into the sliver of space in my locker and wonder if I can lock myself inside.

When I first see Kelsey, it's obvious to me that Georgia's spoken with her. Maybe in another world I'd make small talk and not get to the point, but this is not that wonderful world.

"Hey, look, can I—can we talk out in the hall for a second?"

Kids are getting their stuff ready and coming and going. Mr. Chestle is oblivious, and half the time lets kids come and go as they please. Kelsey nods and walks out, and I follow her.

We stand by a door to the outside that leads to the parking lot and the track field below.

"Look—Kelsey—this is the thing. My life is sorta—no, not sorta, it really is a train wreck. And I couldn't—there's really no way I could begin to tell you why. Or how. And the thing is, you're a really neat girl. Sorry—I mean, that sounded stupid. It's just—it's not that I don't want to hang out, because I'd like that. But the way things are now—I just—it's not really the best time."

"Would you like to have dinner at my house sometime?"

There are many responses I might have imagined from this shy blond hiding behind the glasses and braces. An invitation to meet her parents is *not* one of them.

"What?" I honestly laugh out loud, it's so unexpected.

"I know," she says, understanding my surprise. "It's just—I've been talking to my parents, especially my father, about you. He's been on me to invite you over. You don't have to, but I told him I'd ask."

Did you not hear everything I just said?

I start to shake my head, but then I look into those sweet blue eyes that look away and then sneak a peek at mine.

"Yeah, sure," I say.

Kelsey is not the only one of us who is saying surprising things.

"Just ignore Georgia. She likes to think that she's my protector or something."

"Tell her I'm sorry."

"Maybe you should."

I nod. "Yeah."

"I'll ask my parents—but maybe this Sunday."

I wonder if she's going to invite me to church, but she doesn't.

We go back into art class, and for the next forty minutes I manage to forget about the train wreck. It's still there, the embers of the fire still hot and burning, but I'm able to ignore it for a while.

It's a cool thing.

69. Getting Darker

Sometimes I think I'm growing to like girls driving me around. If I wrote a memoir about my junior year of high school, it might be called exactly that. *Riding with Girls. And Ghosts.*

"So you think this is right?"

"Definitely."

Poe waited around for me to get through track practice. I'm still sweaty and wearing my sweats and drinking the bottled water she was kind enough to give me.

"You're pretty good."

The comment surprises me. "At what?"

"Hurdles, stupid."

"Oh."

"How do you even get over those tall ones? I'd totally kill myself."

"Yeah, I've done that too."

"You gotta watch out. Unless, you know, you don't care about having children one day."

I laugh.

"That Coach Brinks is on your case a lot."

"Ray says it's because he thinks I'm good."

"Well, our school isn't exactly known for its amazing athletic program."

"Maybe if it was, then it wouldn't end up being so ..."

"Creepy?"

I nod. "I was going to say so forgotten about."

"Yeah, that, too."

She slows down at the road we're approaching. It's not like there's a street sign or anything.

"Is that a road or a driveway?" she asks.

I can't tell.

"Oh, well. Let's check it out."

The map says that we're close. But this road doesn't even look like a road. It looks like a dirt entrance to the woods, maybe a driveway that's been long abandoned or a logging trail that hasn't been used for years.

Branches scrape the top of Poe's car.

"That didn't sound good," she says.

We bounce in our seats like we're in some kind of slow, rocky ride at an amusement park. Though it's not dark out, nor is it raining, the trees still block the fading sunlight of the day.

We drive slowly for a few minutes.

"Scared?" Poe asks as she glances my way.

I shake my head in an obvious no, but then see how tightly I'm gripping the handle on the side of the car.

"Worst thing that happens, we run face-first into the pastor. Or someone worse," Poe says. "Then I just reverse and we hold on."

We narrowly miss a small tree on my side.

"That's a real comforting thought," I say.

We actually pass the house the first time, because we think it's abandoned. I hope it's abandoned, because if anyone's living in the cobweb-infested coffin we spot, I don't want to meet them. But the road soon dead-ends into nothing, just a wall of woods, so we turn around and go back to the small one-story cabin nestled behind weeds and overgrown bushes and trees blocking half of it from view.

"There's nothing in that," Poe says.

It's getting darker, and while we can still see fine here, it might be a little more difficult inside the house.

"Let's just check it out."

"*You* check it out. I'm not going in there. I said I'd drive you."

"I don't even know if I can get in."

I step out of the car and still feel sore from practice. The only bad thing about running track is that I'm prone to shin splints, which coach says is all in my head but sure doesn't feel in my head right now as I'm standing on the side of the road.

Nobody's touched this cabin for a long time, that's for certain. The porch looks caved in and dangerous to walk on. The door is missing, along with the windows. In their place are fallen wooden beams overgrown with wild vines, impossible to get through. It still has a roof, but the wood on the house looks ancient, as if a violent thunderstorm could knock it over without even trying.

"You think we missed the street?" Poe asks.

I shake my head. "I'm sure Newt gave me the right directions."

"And you trust him?"

"I have no reason not to."

"Do you see any address?"

If there was a mailbox it's long gone. Same with any numbers on the dark wood on the front of the house.

"I don't want to break my neck trying to get in there. Let me see if I can get in from the back."

I have to take a long route around the house since the overgrowth is so wild and thick right around the edges. I get near the back of the house, about twenty yards away, when I step on something smooth.

It's a trail leading away from the back of the house, and it looks like it's been used lately.

The trail cuts its way through the trees and weeds straight to the back of the house, where a door waits.

When I get to the door, I try it, but it's locked.

The front of this house looks demolished, while the back has a door that's actually locked?

I can't see Poe back here. It's shadowy, and as I try the door again, I suddenly feel watched.

I look behind me to the small incline and the dense forest.

There could be a dozen men watching and waiting back there.

Something about this place, about this door, about touching it—something doesn't feel right.

I feel dirty.

I get a sick feeling inside, but I know it's probably nerves. A collection of nerves that has been growing like a cancer inside me.

There are windows on each side of the door, dirty windows coated with grime and mud. I look in one but can't make out anything. I take the edge of my sweatshirt and rub it against the glass.

It's just light enough to make out something. A chair. A chair and a desk.

I can make out things on the desk. A computer. A big one.

I go back to the door, and then I hear the sound of an engine starting and tires spinning.

I don't have Poe's phone this time to ask her what's going on.

I bolt back the way I came, and as I approach the road I can see something.

Not a car, but a figure.

I drop to the ground and find a tree to hide behind.

For a while I remain hidden, breathing fast but as quietly as I can, not moving.

I hear something jingle and then a deep cough. No car, no voices, nothing else.

I don't know how long it's been when I peer back around. I can hear the moving and shuffling going away from me.

It's the big guy, the one in the trench coat and boots, and his dog. The German shepherd is on a leash. That's what's making the jingling sound.

They're walking away from the house, down the road.

I watch them until they're out of view.

Now what?

I need to start a to-do list.

Get a license and a car.

Get a phone.

Get a gun.

And yeah—get a life.

I wait for a little while and then step back on the road. It's a lot darker now, and it's just going to keep getting worse.

I start walking the way we came, hoping that maybe Poe will come back around. I walk for a few minutes, then stop, walk for a few minutes, then stop again, listening.

The mountain man and his dog are gone.

I reach the paved road and head back to town. I wonder if the cabin belongs to the bearded stranger I keep seeing.

If so, what's he doing in the back there? And why does he keep showing up in the middle of nowhere?

I have another scary thought, one I don't want to dwell on.

What if this guy is a ghost roaming these hills?

If he is, then Poe saw him too, the same way Jared saw him. So at least I'm not completely crazy.

It's amazing how long I walk before hearing anybody or anything. When a car finally comes from behind me with its lights on, I'm not sure whether to remain on the road or hide. Before I can decide, I see the flickering brights of the headlights and realize that it's Poe.

"Did you see that guy?" she says as I get in the car. "Tell me you saw something. Please."

"Yeah."

"He came out of the woods with that monster dog, and I completely freaked out."

"That house is hiding something."

"What?"

"I don't know. The back door was locked."

"You gotta be kidding."

"Maybe it belongs to the guy we saw."

"Who gave you the address, then?"

"I don't know."

"See what I mean? This is why you can't say anything, why we have to be careful."

"I thought that's what we're doing, being careful. Not saying anything to anybody."

"I gotta get home," Poe says.

She doesn't say much of anything else in the car ride home except that she'll see me tomorrow.

When I shut her door and watch her drive off into the night, I wonder if I'm making a big mistake involving her in whatever's happening to me.

I stand there outside in the darkness, full of so many questions. And so few answers.

70. TRULY TORTURED

I'm waiting for my mom in Brennan's after track practice. I've done this several times, coming in for dinner and then going home with her. Tonight I'm in a booth in the corner, finishing a chicken sandwich, when someone slides into the seat across from me.

"Hello, Chris," Pastor Marsh says.

I suddenly feel sick. There's no way I can find an excuse to leave, especially since Mom is still busy and I'm holding what's left of my dinner.

"Please, don't let me stop you."

I stick the rest of the chicken sandwich into my mouth. Jeremiah Marsh studies me, looking amused and without a care in the world.

"You know something, Chris. I have to tell you this. I like you. I really like you."

He says it in a way that makes it seem like he's going to follow up with *And now I'm going to eat you.*

"Would you like to know why?"

I'm still chewing. This is the longest bite I've taken in my life.

"Mmmm hmmm," I respond.

"Because you, unlike so many in this nice little pub and won-derful little town, are not a follower. Everybody else—so many, it's pitiful to even count—is just doing what everybody else does. They just march on like tiny little ants. You ever see a line of ants going to something sweet and sticky on the floor? Have you seen them all going to get just a little taste, just a little suck?"

I sit upright, my heart racing and my head unsure what to do.

"But you're not like them, are you, Chris?"

"What do you want?"

He smiles. No looking around, no wondering if my mom's going to come, no worries in the world. I look around to see if I can spot Mom, but she's not in sight.

"I was a lot like you when I was young," Pastor Marsh says. "Really. I didn't like doing what I was told. I liked figuring out things myself. I like this about you. Now, you've still got a lot of figuring out to do, right? But you're doing it on your own, in your own way."

He knows I broke into his house. He knows, and this is his way of telling me.

"Want to know the most powerful thing in this world?"

For a second, I think of Iris asking the same thing and wonder if they've been having coffee recently. He still hasn't answered my ques-tion, yet he's asking his own cryptic ones. I don't want to play along.

"Can I do something for you?"

"Yeah. You can stop trying to play games and engage with me. Don't act coy, young man. Don't try and act naive."

I hear footsteps approaching, then see my mom standing there.

"You guys okay?"

"Wonderful," the pastor says.

I nod.

"Just give me a few minutes," Mom says.

Wonderful, my brain echoes.

"Can I get you anything to drink?"

Marsh shakes his head. "No, thank you. My wife and I just finished dinner ourselves. Just wanted to see Chris. Heidi has such good things to say about him."

Mom hears someone calling her name and disappears.

"My wife, your mother—they're not so different, are they? Both can get made up and look oh so pretty, but deep down they're really truly tortured, aren't they?"

"What do you want?"

"I want you to answer my question. What's the most powerful thing in this world?"

I shake my head.

Love, Chris. It's love. That's what Iris said. Tell him that.

He waits for a moment, acting as if I'm going to respond.

"It's fear, Chris. Fear. It will drive a person to do anything. If you grow desperate and afraid, anything can happen. *Anything.*"

I swallow. I want to look away, but I can't.

"You know enough about fear, right? But imagine being able to invoke it in others. My young man—it is a taste that cannot get any sweeter."

He stands, looks around, then glances at me.

"Keep looking. Keep learning. Ultimately you'll understand. Ultimately you'll know what to do. We always do."

With that he leaves.

I sit in the booth shivering and breathless and wondering why he's playing games with me.

71. GIRLS

I sit in English class and remember looking back at Jocelyn. Some days she'd ignore me. Other days she'd give me a quick glance and smile.

Now she's not around to do either.

I still feel like an empty mug.

Day by day, something hot and bitter gets poured into that mug.

Day by day, I'm getting more full, but not particularly in a good way.

"Hi."

This isn't just a hi. It's a rehearsed hi. Like the kind you do in front of the mirror for a part in a play. But this isn't a play. It's art class.

"Hi," I say back to her.

There's something different about her today. I guess if I paid closer attention I'd know it right away. It's sorta like the months passing. I forget until someone tells me it's already April.

"I don't know if Sunday still works for you?"

I'm busy trying to figure out what looks different about her, and
I basically ignore the question.

"It can be another Sunday. They were just thinking—my older
brother is going to be in town."

"You're not wearing your glasses."

I need to be a little quicker about these things.

"Sometimes I wear contacts."

"Really?"

She gives me a polite smile that probably says *Yes, like every other
day, you idiot.*

"It's fine if it won't work."

"No—that's great. I mean—is it a formal thing?"

"No. We'll be coming back from church."

Again, I wait. She didn't ask the first time, but maybe the second.

"But we always change anyway before lunch."

Again, she doesn't ask.

"Will you need a ride?"

"No, please, come on."

I say that as if I can't believe she's asking me if I need a ride.

But, to be honest, I do need a ride.

I'm such a loser.

Girls asking me out and me needing rides.

Loser.

I manage to get to Poe, who's rummaging in her locker, before she
can spot me coming and bolt.

For a moment, I realize that she's just as alone as I am at this
school. Jocelyn and Rachel are both gone. I don't see that she's replaced
either of them.

"Poe."

She looks at me with a nervous, attacking stance.

"I'm not going to hurt you," I joke.

"Chris, you know—we've talked about this."

"I haven't heard anything since—"

"You will."

"Everything okay?"

"Yes."

"Then what's the next—"

But she takes off before I can ask her what our next step of action is.
I sigh.

There's gotta be a self-help book out there that can help me with
these—girls.

72. MEETS AND MEETINGS

"We've got a big meet coming up on the twenty-first. So I don't want
any of you doing anything stupid the weekend before, like getting
arrested or going to the hospital for drinking too much. Got that?"

He seems to be talking to Ray and me. I think he could care less
about two-thirds of the guys on the team.

Obviously Coach Brinks doesn't know me.

"The meet this Thursday will be a warm-up for Hendersonville because they're tough, and frankly, we aren't. But we still got a little game in us, right, Chicago?"

"Yes, sir," I say.

"Now let's go out and have a good practice."

As we're walking off the center of the field to the track, Ray pulls me aside. "Hey—you make a decision about prom yet?"

For a second I think prom is some kind of dish I'm supposed to try.

"No."

"Alexis really wants to go with you."

"She told you?"

I vaguely remember Ray talking to me about this some time ago, but I was winded and my shins were killing me and I couldn't for the life of me picture Alexis.

"No, not really. But, come on. She's a senior. She's hot. And she's pretty much willing."

"I don't know."

I haven't even seen Alexis, not to mention the fact that I really couldn't care less about going to this school's prom.

"I'll introduce you to her. Stef is good friends with her, and they want to double. And I'm telling you, buddy …"

Ray laughs as Coach Brinks barks out to us.

As I start practicing hurdles, I reflect that this is certainly good training for what I need to do around this place.

Run and jump.

Run far away and jump over everything in my path.

Ray is going to take me home when another voice interrupts and offers me a ride instead. Turns out it's time to touch base with Jared.

Part of me still questions whether I should tell him about Poe.

"You still keeping a low profile?" His voice has an accusatory tone in it.

"Do I still have to?" I ask.

"Look—just—some weird things have been happening, and I needed to let you know about them."

"Like what?"

And what's your definition of weird, since everything around here is weird?

"The group that meets at the falls. You said you saw them once. Do you have any idea where they might be meeting now?"

I shake my head. "I haven't been invited."

"The sheriff—has he talked with you at all?"

"Sheriff Wells? Not since calling me a liar and telling me to stay out of his hair."

"He's been doing some funny things recently. So how's that new job of yours going?"

"It's good. It pays well. And the lady there is pretty cool."

"And you haven't discovered any dead bodies in the basement?" Jared jokes.

"Those rumors are just because Iris never goes to town. You ever been up there?"

"A long time ago, I think. You'll have to take me up there sometime."

"Yeah, sure," I say. "If you want to help me do some work."

"One other thing I'm worried about."

"What?"

He pauses for a moment. "Your mother."

"Why?"

"Because of some of the people she's been hanging out with. Some of the things she's been doing when she's gone."

"She's always working."

"Not always."

I ask him what that means.

"Don't get defensive. I'm telling you what I'm seeing. I have the luxury of being able to find out things. You don't. That's okay."

"What's she doing, then?"

"There are many ways of getting involved with the wrong people around here."

I still don't get it. And maybe I don't want to.

"I have a feeling things will only get worse."

"Like how?"

For a while we drive, and Jared doesn't say anything.

"I think they know. I think that they know that things are unraveling."

"How?"

"Because of you, Chris. Because you're different in some way."

I recall Mr. Meiners getting angry at me after the fight with Gus and saying the same thing.

Different how? Different why?

"I'm not doing anything." Besides sneaking into the pastor's house and finding some little weird cabin.

"You gotta tell me everything."

"I am."

Of course I'm not.

He gets to my house and leaves the car running as if he's waiting.

"What is it?" I ask.

"You have to start telling me everything, because I'm the only person around here who can help you, you got that? Nobody else can do that. Nobody. Not even those who used to know Jocelyn."

He knows about Poe.

Of course he knows about Poe.

"She's harmless, but also stupid. Chris, you just gotta start using your head. And start trusting me."

"What do you want me to do?"

"I'll be around again. Soon. Maybe I can give you a lift to your job sometime."

"Okay."

"Stay safe."

He drives off while I head inside, not sure if Mom is working or not, not sure if and when she's ever working now.

Doubt really sucks.

73. HAROLD MARTIN

The more I work on the history of the Crag's Inn, the more random notes get added to the assorted piles.

The earliest I can find anything mentioned is a little after the Civil War. In the 1870s there was talk of the railroad being built and passing through the town of Solitary. This was meant to be an alternative to another steep railroad pass called Pace's Gap, which ended up being completed first around the end of the 1870s. For a while trains ran through Solitary, in the 1880s and 1890s, but they increasingly weren't used because of the trains used on Pace's Gap not too far away.

While Solitary itself isn't mentioned a lot in the notes I'm reading, the railroad is mentioned frequently. It seems that was how the first owner/builder of the inn found the town and the area. He got off the train and ended up buying the plot of land where the inn stands. His name was Harold Martin. At first it seemed he just wanted a place to build a business. But there's quite a bit more to Harold's story.

Something happened to his family—some tragedy. It's referred to repeatedly but never really named. His wife and maybe children? All I learn is that Harold Martin came to Solitary alone and decided to buy property and build an inn there.

One letter repeatedly says that the inn will not be in Solitary, but nearby.

It cannot be in the town, that will not work.

It seems that this Harold Martin was a religious man. He mentions following God's path and God's will over and over. He refers to whatever happened to his family as "the darkness" and the inn being a light.

I need to do something to squelch the darkness and combat the fatigue of my weary soul.

Initially he got resistance from people about buying the property, then about building. But every good thing he says is an answer to prayer—"fervent prayer" as he calls it, "prayer with petition."

Despite the resistance, he was able to build the inn sometime before the turn of the century.

It's hard to know which details I need and which ones are worthless. There are lots of notes on the building process and the costs of labor. The details of running the inn seem endless and boring. But there are little details and notes that I discover while wading through notes and letters that seem to stand out.

One of these is a note going to Maude, who may or may not be his mother, which includes the details on their first guests—

We had our first guests last night. To say I was surprised and anxious is quite the overstatement. They stayed only one night and did not talk very much. The dinner I set out was ignored. They left early in the morning without much sound. But it was the start. My hope is that it is the start of something bigger and better.

For some time it seems that running this inn and getting visitors was difficult. Some of Harold's concerns were with various townspeople who didn't want him there (why, I can't see). Other concerns were with attracting guests.

I leave these things in God's hands because I know this is where He wants me to be.

Then I come across a letter that startles me.

I have started a church with three others. We meet by the falls in the woods. It's a beautiful place, tranquil and peaceful, perfect for seeing God's hand and God's will in these dark times.

I think back to the people meeting in the woods, the ones Jocelyn showed me.

I need to find out who they are and where they're meeting now.

Just like the previous Saturdays, I have pages of notes but nothing started. Iris doesn't press me, just pays me and asks if everything is going well. She's busy today—there is a group coming in this evening, and she needs to get things ready. My mom arrives, and Iris says good night.

I wonder how long this project will last.

Holding the cash in my hand, I hope it lasts a long time.

74. Normal and Messy

On my way over to Kelsey's house for Sunday lunch, I realize what a skeptic I've become. Cynic, skeptic, critic, something with *ic* on the end of it that looks and feels like a big "ick."

I'm driving Mom's car. She came home late last night and was still sleeping when I asked her around, oh, eleven, if I could take it.

Eleven. That's one hour away from noon. One hour away from the middle of the day.

When you're at the bottom, the middle's a little harder to get to.

I get in the car, and I'm angry. I'm angry at Mom for being all wasted and wrecked. I'm angry that I don't have a license and a car of my own. That I have to ask someone who shouldn't be asked anything for permission to drive. Of course she said yes to get rid of the guilt on her back. Sleep isn't going to make it go away.

But as I drive and start thinking of things, I realize that I'm not the same kid who moved here what feels like a few decades ago.

It's true that I can't stand my father. Hate? Yeah, probably. But I'm slowly or quickly growing the same feelings toward Mom.

And toward this town.

And toward my life.

And now as I crank up the radio and can't find a decent song whatsoever, I begin to think about Kelsey and her family.

Are they trying to save my soul?

Are they going to suck me into some deep, dark secret?

Are they weird like half the town, or evil like the other half?

Why can't you think normal thoughts?

But I can't think normal thoughts because there's nothing normal about this. When you're in a prison you can't go on believing you're in the real world.

She's just a cute and harmless girl who likes you, and that's it.

But then what am I doing?

I think of Jocelyn and wonder if this is cheating.

You're whacked in the head.

I know.

That's the problem.

I'm wondering if I'm cheating on a girl I was never with, a girl taken away from me, with a girl I don't really know, a girl I don't really like anyway.

Idiotic.

Moronic.

Pathetic.

I used to drive and listen to songs and not think about any of these things. I thought about NBA players and the brands of shoes they wore. I thought about the girls on the Maxim website and I thought about Celeste the senior at our school. I thought of going away to college and going crazy and getting away from responsibilities.

You've already reached crazy without responsibilities.

I flip the station, but there's nothing to combat these thoughts.

They keep coming.

And coming.

And coming.

Thank God for something normal.

Nice people who don't smell like sickly sweet alcohol from the night before, who are awake and dressed in nice clothes for church.

A mother and a father who are unbelievably still together and still able to touch each other. Not in a weird, freaky way, but in a nice way. Kinda sweet and at the same time, normal.

A house that looks like any other suburban house. Two-story and inviting with no signs of underground tunnels or mannequins or dead animals.

An older brother named Keith who goes to University of South Carolina and who actually seems …

normal

Unbelievable.

Keith is the one who answers the door. He gives me a casual hello. Next I see Jack, Kelsey's dad, who shakes my hand and says how good it is to see me again.

Then I see something not exactly normal.

Kelsey walks in, wearing a blue dress that seems to poke at this cloudy bubble I have going on in my head and my heart.

"Did you find our house okay?"

I didn't realize that I was driving to a field full of beautiful blue lilies.

"Yeah."

She smiles and seems a lot more confident here than in the art class or in the halls of Harrington High.

I smell something like real home cooking.

You're dreaming this it's another dream come on not fair.

I actually feel nervous here.

Meeting the parents over a Sunday meal. What are you thinking, Chris?

I'm led into the kitchen and see Kelsey's pretty mother doing something at the sink. She smiles and then comes over and gives me a hug.

Do they know something I don't?

"Oh, you're such a cutie," she says. "I'm Ruth. It's very nice to finally meet you."

Kelsey's mother is an older snapshot of her, blond and tall and smiling. We stand around the kitchen talking about stuff like school and where I'm from and all that.

Normal stuff.

It's nice and refreshing and I realize that they're not going to kidnap or molest me.

At least not before lunch.

"We're having a pot roast," Ruth says. "Do you like pot roast?"

I used to when I had someone who actually remembered how to make it.

"Yeah, that's great. Thanks."

"We're just so glad you came over. Maybe next time you can bring your mother."

"Lay off, Mom," Keith says in a natural and fun way. "Don't pressure the kid."

"It's not pressure. It's just nice meeting new folks."

I glance over at Kelsey, who is still quiet despite the air of security she has about her. When I see her looking my way, I feel something that is pretty much all wonderful.

It's like ...

A breath of fresh air.

I suddenly know what that expression means.

It's the cute blond in the blue dress, smiling at me as if I've made her day.

I haven't made anybody's day in a very long time.

"So you haven't seen your uncle since you arrived?"

Ruth's question is innocent and natural, but it still seems a bit too much. I take a while to figure out an answer.

"I don't mean to pry," she adds.

"No, it's fine. It's just—we haven't—we don't know where he is."

"Oh, I'm sorry."

"Yeah. I guess—I think Mom thought that he would be around or come home eventually. But I don't know. She didn't really share what she thought about coming here except that she grew up in Solitary. And that she wanted to get away from my dad."

Kelsey obviously had told them about my parents because nobody brought up the *parents* discussion or even the word.

"I have a feeling that he's long gone," I add.

"And what about your father?"

"Ruth."

"I'm just asking."

"It's okay," I say, looking first at Kelsey, who's sitting next to me. "We don't hear anything from him. I doubt we will."

"Sorry to hear that."

I nod.

"Too heavy," Keith says. "Sorry, Chris. I told them to go light, but Mom can't help herself."

"That wasn't being too anything," Ruth says.

"We were talking about college football, and it goes to this. Give the kid a break. I mean, he lives in that creepy town. He's got enough to deal with."

That's the funny thing about people who live outside of Solitary, even if it's just right outside. It's like the dome of gloom hasn't completely penetrated them yet.

Poe and Rachel talked like this.

Now Kelsey's family.

"I hear you're pretty good at track," Keith says.

"I'm decent."

"They need as many decent guys as possible."

We talk about sports and other random things in a very fun, natural, *normal* way.

Every few moments, I look at Kelsey.

Every few moments, I realize just how much this family already knows me.

How much Kelsey's told them about me.

And I gotta admit, I really like it.

We're walking down the dirt road that leads to Kelsey's house.

To think that a year ago, I never really walked around neighborhoods. I mean, I rode my bike and I'd walk to kids' houses, but I never really just strolled around. Back home it's tiny little plots of land. Your fence and my grass and his backyard and her tree.

Here, it's just all open and free.

At least in places that haven't been spoiled by Solitary.

"You have a nice family," I tell her after we've been walking for a while, talking about art class and school.

"Thanks."

"Your brother's pretty cool."

"Yeah, I think so."

I'm ready to keep talking about him, but Kelsey changes the subject.

"Do you like Poe?"

"Poe?"

"You're around her a lot."

"I am?"

"I've seen you two together."

I wonder if she's referring to in school or out.

Please don't bring up real life. I was having such fun ignoring it.

"It's okay, you know."

"No, I just …" I laugh for a moment. "I'm not sure what to say because I'm trying to figure out how you might think that. I mean— I'm not sure if Poe and I are really even friends."

"But do you like her?"

"No," I say right away. "She's a friend. But it goes back …" *Don't bring her up, not here not now.* "It's just, I've gotten to know her."

I can see Kelsey looking at me from just a few feet away, walking next to me. She's waiting and wondering. Waiting. And wondering.

"We're just friends," I say. "That's all."

And that's all I'm going to say.

"Thanks for coming today," Kelsey says.

She says it in a way that sounds like I'm doing her some big favor.

"Thanks for asking. But you probably just do that with all the new guys, huh?"

Her slight laugh says otherwise.

"Do you think your mother would ever want to come over?"

I glance at her, and my look must say it all.

"Not for—it's just, my parents really believe in being hospitable."

"Ah, I get it," I say, my smile probably filling half my face. "So this is just hospitality. Or charity. Is that it?"

"What?"

"Your inviting me over for lunch."

"No, I told you—my parents asked."

"Yes. The decent thing to do."

"No."

"Oh, wait, there's another reason?"

I glance over and see her blushing. Suddenly I feel very mean and very stupid. "I'm just kidding."

She shakes her head in a way that doesn't really mean anything. Yes or no? Sideways? Then I see her look to the ground. I can see a faint trace of a tear.

"Hey, whoa—what? What'd I say?" I stop her before she can walk any further.

"Nothing."

"I was just kidding."

"It's fine, it's nothing. Really."

"Kelsey, look—I was seriously just kidding."

"I know. It's not that. It's nothing."

I swallow. I'm wondering what I did this time. "Look—this is—this was great. Thanks. I really—I didn't mean—"

"It's fine. It's nothing. Okay?"

And that's that.

It's fine and it's nothing.

But, then again, nothing's ever just fine or just nothing.

I'm not really sure how long I should stick around or how long I'm supposed to stick around, but before I leave, Jack brings me into his office to show me something.

"Interested in history, Chris?"

"Yeah, sure."

About as much as anything else I have to study, which isn't much.

"Look at this map. It shows the area we live in. See the X? That's our house."

The map covers half a wall in his office. Not far away from the green X is a large oval marked in red.

"That's Solitary, the official town limits as best I could designate them. I'm not a mapmaker or anything. But here—this is what I wanted you to see. You can see the town here, the train tracks going through. See this blue circle?"

I nod. At the top of the red oval is a slightly overlapping blue circle about the size of my fist.

"Here—this road leads out of the town. Right around here is the road leading to New Beginnings Church. Heartland Trail. Have you been there?"

I nod and wonder if that's where they go to church.

"We go to a Baptist church ourselves, a little one a good ways away. Good church and good people. Not as big and fancy as New Beginnings, but whatever. If you've been there, then you know where this is."

The blue circle begins right near the point where he said the church was located. A little further down Heartland Trail, right near the point where it dead-ends.

I think of that piece of paper someone put in my locker with the Robert Frost line on it.

"This is where the old town of Solitary used to be before it burned down."

"Is anything left there?"

"No. I remember—years ago when I was a kid, back when there was no church and not even a road to get out there—my older brother and I found remnants of the old town. The creepiest thing I'd ever seen. Mostly half-burnt buildings overgrown with trees and bushes. Like the forest had devoured it. We were there at dusk and got all spooked. Ever since, I've wanted to find it again. I've narrowed down the location from maps and other sources, but I've never been able to find it. Every time I go searching, I end up getting lost in the forest. It gets really dense, more like a jungle than a forest."

"Why'd they move the town?"

"I don't know. I used to think to be closer to the tracks, but the train wasn't used much by the time they moved it. Maybe the damage was irreparable."

I study the map, trying to memorize it. But it's easy to see where the blue circle is located. I know exactly where it is.

Maybe someone else was trying to tell you about that too.

"I just thought you'd get a kick out of seeing that."

"Thanks."

Mr. Page tells me good-bye as we go back into the living room. I thank the family for lunch and then end up following Kelsey outside.

"Thanks for coming."

I nod. "I'm not doing anybody any favors being here."

She looks at me as if she doesn't understand.

"I meant it back at school when I said those things about my life. About stuff going on in it. I mean—you've got a great family, Kelsey. You really do."

"Is that bad?"

"No. Not at all. Except you don't want—you don't need people like me coming along and messing things up."

"Who said you're messing anything up?"

"I might if I stayed around you for too long."

"Maybe it would be good for me to have things messy."

I shake my head.

You have no idea what kind of mess I'm talking about.

"Thanks for today," I tell her again. "I'll see you—tomorrow, right?"

"Unless you plan on skipping school. Or just skipping art."

"What are you talking about? That's my favorite part of the day."

I guess this is a good comment to leave her with. And it's the truth.

I get in my car and smile at her as she stands there and watches me drive off.

I leave her not quite sure what all just happened. But, like many things in my life, it's probably best to not think about it too much.

75. DÉJÀ BOO

I'm eating Sunday dinner, except this time I'm the father watching his wife and kids. We're sitting around a big table eating turkey when the sound of glass breaking and someone screaming comes from the other room. My wife and children keep eating and then I realize *wait a minute, I'm not actually here.*

I jerk out of bed and probably smush Midnight as I land on the floor.

The scream comes again.

I get downstairs in a couple of seconds and whip around the corner and see Mom holding a bat. As I approach, she swings it at me.

"Get away, get out of here, go on, go."

She curses, and I know that she's totally out of it. She swings the bat hard, and it thuds against the drywall.

I look to see where the sound of glass came from and see that she busted out one of her windows.

"Mom, it's Chris. Mom!"

She finally seems to get it, to wake up, to see that her only son is standing in front of her. She drops the bat and then rushes past me to the kitchen.

For a second, I'm going to follow, then I think of something. I pick up the bat and I go into the bathroom. I turn on the light, then open the doors to the cabinet and look at the back. The piece of paneling is not attached.

Someone came in here. Someone was in here and did a lousy job of covering up his tracks.

I listen but can't hear anything.

This is crazy. I've got to call someone.

I stay there for a moment, kneeling and watching, waiting. The bat next to me.

I stare into the darkness.

Waiting.

A slight chill coming over me.

Waiting.

This is the moment the bloody head pops out of the darkness and bites you.

Waiting.

This is where the bony hand slivers out of the black and grabs you with a cold grip of death.

Waiting.

But there's nothing. I eventually go into the kitchen to find Mom. She's drinking something in a cup. I don't want to know if it's spiked or not.

There's nothing to say, because we've been here before. I just sit down with her at the table, and she grips my hand. Her touch is icy.

I force a smile, but it's as bleak as the dark night outside.

Tomorrow I'm going to tell someone. Even if that means I'm going to be in more trouble.

76. PROOF

I really totally and completely don't care anymore. Not a bit.

I've just gotten off the phone with Sheriff Wells, and here's the thing. Not only do I have to go through this, all of *this,* this black pit of mess, but then I have to be treated like a liar and a loser.

If they're bugging my phone oh well.

If they're watching me now oh well.

If the sheriff is working for them …

Oh.

Well.

Mom's not home, and that's good, because I don't want to tell her about the hole in the bathroom wall that goes to whatever-that-is. I need to tell somebody, because I'm beginning to think that the hole is going to my brain, and it's sucking every legitimate and decent thing left up there.

"Am I crazy?"

The flat little furry face doesn't answer.

"I'm not crazy, am I?"

Midnight just looks at me, but I don't like that look. She knows. She knows too much. She knows I'm loony tunes.

"Look, just—just don't tell the sheriff that I'm a little ... you know. Okay?"

Midnight puts her head back on the couch and seems content to keep our secret.

The sheriff looks skeptical until he opens the doors to the bathroom cabinet and pulls off the piece of paneling. I see him look up at me with a speechless, dazed glance.

"Here," I say, handing him the flashlight.

He shines it, but I know there's nothing really to see. Then he forces himself into the opening and shines the light down.

I can't imagine what he's thinking. If, and this is a very big if, Sheriff Wells had no idea about the tunnels, then this has got to be pretty eye-opening.

He slips back out and dusts himself off as he stands. The face looking at me is grim and pale. "Your mom know about this?"

I shake my head.

"Anybody else?"

"No."

For a second he rubs the bridge between his eyes as he looks around the bathroom. Then he walks out into my mom's bedroom and into the main room. I follow in silence.

"Look, Chris," he says in a very slow and deliberate manner, "you need to keep doing what I told you to do."

The strange thing as the sheriff talks is that he's not looking at me.

"Do you understand?"

Still not looking at me.

"Yes, sir," I say.

"That's good. You keep quiet and mind your manners and stay out of trouble. Got it?"

Again I say that I do.

Again he's not even trying to look at me.

He's more interested in finding something. At the kitchen counter, he sees a notebook of mine from school, then finds a pen.

"Nobody needs to know what the owner of this cabin did to it before you guys got here. Probably your uncle, right? Probably someone just trying to have some fun."

As he says this, he's writing something down. He shuts the notebook and then walks up to me. "You leave this alone, and leave me and Ross to watch over Solitary. Do you understand?"

I shake my head and am about to ask him what he just wrote down when

"Do you understand?"

"Yes."

"Good."

He leaves me, and for a moment I just stand there hating the guy. Then I open the notebook and find the page he wrote on.

Meet me at Jocelyn's cabin at eleven tonight. Be careful. Make sure nobody knows you're coming. Be quiet.

I hold the notebook in my hand and can tell it's starting to shake.

I don't know which scares me more. Going to meet with the sheriff late at night. Or going back to Jocelyn's abandoned house.

77. A WAY OUT

I can see his car under the shadows of trees along the driveway leading up to Jocelyn's still dark and vacant house. Just as I did many thousand nights ago, I rode my bike here and slipped through the trees to wait and watch. The unmarked car drives up right before eleven. I wait for a moment, then see the sheriff roll down his window and light a cigarette.

"Sheriff?" I say a short ways from the car.

Making sure. Just in case I have to turn around and bolt. If the driver happens to be someone like Wade, Jocelyn's sicko quasi-step-uncle.

"Get in."

I recognize the voice and do what I'm told. He finishes his cigarette as we sit in silence.

"I saw you when I drove up," Sheriff Wells says. "You get an F for your covert skills."

I just sit there, uncomfortable in this old car, the smoke tickling my nose.

"Nobody's around here, not anymore," he tells me.

I wait, wondering where this is going.

"You said on the phone you went down into one of those tunnels."

I nod.

"What did you find?" He reaches over and grabs my wrist and forces me to look at him. "Chris, look. I'm not—I'm not proud of what I've done, but this is far worse than I ever—what did you see down there?"

"The passageways go for miles, it seems."

"But where did you end up?"

"I don't know."

"You saw nothing?"

"No. I—I don't know what I saw. Some creepy old man."

He lets go of my arm and looks out the front window. He rubs the back of his head and then his goatee, then lights another cigarette.

"Look, Chris. I don't know how, but every single thing you do and say and probably even think, they know. They just know."

"Who?"

The sheriff doesn't answer my question. "They're not watching me, not like you. They don't have my car bugged, and they're not monitoring my every move. But they are yours. And that's why—that's why we're here."

"For what?"

He looks at me and curses, then shakes his head.

"I'm sorry."

I don't expect these words to come from the sheriff's mouth.

"I'm sorry and I don't—I can't—look, I'm frightened and you don't—you can't believe what that can do to a man like me. I'm not supposed to be scared. I'm supposed to guard and protect guys like you. And I just—I don't know what I'm to protect you from. But I know that it's ugly and that it's everywhere and it has threatened my family."

I think of the pastor's words to me at the restaurant.

Fear. It will drive a person to do anything.

The sheriff sighs and takes a drag of his cigarette.

"I knew something was up, but when the whole thing about Jocelyn happened—when you told me what happened—I chose to believe the lie. Everything in me said not to. But they came around—men came to my house and talked to my wife and greeted my children as if they were warning me. They *were* warning me. And that warning is still there."

"So you believe me?" I ask.

"I've heard—I've *seen* some crazy things. And that tunnel. It confirms that there's evil here and it's real and it can't be stopped."

"We have to tell others."

"No. Listen to me. I mean this. We can't."

"Why?"

"I don't know how much you love your mother, but I love my family very much. Nothing's going to happen to them."

"But you can—you can take them and leave."

"It's not that easy, Chris."

"Sure it is."

He shakes his head. "No. I'm not willing to sacrifice one of my own in order to try … I can't."

"What's happening here?"

I can hear the crickets and the cicadas in the night as the sheriff waits to answer.

"Who's doing all of this?" I ask again. "Is it—does it have to do with Mr. Staunch? Or Pastor Marsh?"

"I don't know."

"You must know something."

"I know that the best thing I can do is do my job."

"And your job is to let people like Jocelyn die?"

The sheriff curses, and for a second I wonder if he's going to punch me in the face.

"I had nothing to do with that."

"But you knew?"

He shifts in his seat. "No. Everything I'm telling you is truth. I was told specifically to watch you—to watch Chris Buckley carefully—but to also give you some slack. But I knew nothing about Jocelyn. And I still don't—I still can't believe everything that's going on."

"I gave you some proof. Today. There are tunnels in our house. And I swear someone's coming in at night and terrorizing my mom."

"But why this strange interest in you? What are you to this town?"

"You think I know?"

"What did Jocelyn say?"

"The same thing everybody says. Very little. Not enough. 'There are evil people here, but oops, I can't say anything more.'"

"I'm telling you everything I can." The words coming out of his mouth sound like defeat. "I believe you, Chris, that's one thing you have to know. And I know now. It's just—I've seen people try to leave this place, and they can't. They don't. Some leave, but they come back in coffins. I don't want to be one of them."

"Can't we go to the FBI or out of state somewhere?"

"You think that Solitary is the only place where evil exists?"

"But I ... but if ..." I can't finish my thought.

"Chris, listen. Yesterday I still refused—I still chose to believe that Jocelyn moved away with her aunt. That the rumors I have a whole file on were just that—silly rumors. I chose to ignore them. Including the rumors about the tunnels."

"Others have reported them?"

"I'm surprised you haven't heard talk at school or with other kids. You haven't told anybody about the tunnels?"

"No." I leave out Poe's name. For now.

"When I got here, the stories about the underground tunnels were among the first of a whole bunch of supposed urban legends I heard."

"And what? What'd they say?"

"That underneath the town of Solitary there are secret passageways that allow vampires to come prowling in the night and slip into people's homes and drink their blood."

I wait to see if the sheriff is joking.

"That's the legend. So of course I laughed it off. I knew there were some old mines around here, but tunnels for vampires? Next thing I knew there was going to be a cave that led to that school Harry Potter went to."

"But there really *are* underground tunnels."

"I know. And that's what I'm saying. When I saw that today—I can't just ignore it anymore. I tried to. This spring—" He lets go a really nice curse word that Mom would ground me for. "It's not a good thing, living in regret. You wake up with it, Chris. You go to sleep with it. But it just picks away. Day after day."

He's lighting his third cigarette since he got here.

"What do we do?" I ask.

I watch the smoke swirling from his mouth toward the outside window. I wish I could escape from Solitary like that. Just fade away into the night.

"I'm sorry, Chris. I'm sorry I didn't believe you. I'm sorry that I—that I was scared. That I *am* scared. But you can trust me."

"Others have told me that too."

"Yeah. And you have every right not to trust me. But you gotta give me some time."

"How much time?"

"That I don't know. I just—I don't know."

For a long time we sit in the front seat in silence. I can't help looking at the shell of a house in the distance and thinking of the light that used to live there.

"I can do better," Sheriff Wells says. "I'm better than this. This sneaking around and apologizing and being scared of the dark. I'm better than that. And I didn't become a cop to hide. That's not what I'm about. If there's one thing you understand, then understand that. Okay, Chris?"

"Yes, sir."

"There's a way out. Out of here. I just gotta find it. Give me time to find it."

78. SOMETHING IN HERE

"That jerk. He could've done something, but he chose to do nothing. Nothing." Poe is lost in her own world as she faces the street ahead and drives.

"You didn't believe me either."

"That's different," she says right away.

"But you should be able to understand where he's coming from."

"He's the sheriff. The sheriff! A cop. What's he supposed to do? Huh?"

"I think we can trust him."

"I've already told you, I'm not trusting anybody. Nobody. Just me, myself, and I."

"When can I be added to the circle of trust?"

"I wish we were in *that* movie instead of *Nightmare on Elm Street*."

"Which *Nightmare*? Weren't there like twenty of them?" I ask, trying to make a joke.

"Does it matter? All of them."

We reach the turn into the woods and head right onto Heartland Trail. To the wonderful and welcoming New Beginnings Church.

I'd like a new beginning myself, starting with burning this church and town down.

Signs have been pointing me here, starting with Jocelyn's picture and poem. If there is any kind of significance, it's time to find out.

"So are you coming with me this time?"

Poe just smiles.

We stand on the edge of the turnaround where she's parked her car. Light is draining out of the sky even though sunset isn't for another half hour or so. I'm holding my heavy flashlight in my hand.

Poe brushes her messy dark hair away from her face. She's not wearing as much makeup these days, and I notice that it makes her a lot more pretty. Her lip ring has been gone for some time. I wonder again why she needs to hide behind all that stuff.

She pulls a backpack over her shoulder. "Ready?"

"You're really coming?"

"I'd rather go with you than wait on the side of the road in the middle of nowhere. You know where you're going?"

"I know the general direction. I just don't know if we're going to find anything."

But general is really just that: general.

We enter the woods.

It seems there's something in these woods that someone wants me to find.

Either that or they're warning you to stay away.

I feel the dread covering me as I start into the woods. Just a few steps in, the air feels colder.

I'm about to ask Poe if she feels it when she says, "The temperature just dropped like ten degrees."

"It's the shade."

She gives me a look that says she doesn't quite believe it. I don't either.

I grip the heavy flashlight as hard as I can. It helps. A little.

We keep walking straight into the woods, through trees and over leaves and dead, split logs and untouched bushes. It's so quiet my own breathing seems loud. The steps we make on the forest floor seem to echo, the trees around us smothering and ogling, this place for some reason feeling unwelcoming.

That's in your mind, so stop it.

I turn around and see Poe a few feet back. "Am I going too fast?"

"No." She scrunches up her shoulders and hugs herself.

"Here," I say, zipping off my running jacket and handing it to her.

"I'm fine."

"No, seriously. It's getting a lot colder. I'm fine."

It's not true, because I'm freezing, but so is Poe in her short-sleeved shirt. I slow down a bit to let her walk with me.

"What are we looking for?"

I shake my head. "Anything. Anything that looks like part of an old town. Mr. Page said that it was in these woods."

"But what then?"

"I don't know. I just—there's something in here. Something in that old town. Something I need to find."

"Like what—owww!" Poe stops for a minute and holds her foot.

"What happened?"

"Nothing, just—I just bent my ankle the wrong way."

As my mind starts to tell me what that means, that if we suddenly have to bolt out of these woods and she can't run …

"It's nothing, seriously. It's fine. See. Look, fine."

"Okay."

"You don't have to worry about me slowing you down. If we see something—anything—then I'm going to make you look like the slowest person on your track team. You got that?"

I smile. "Sounds good to me."

We keep walking, listening to our steps in these silent woods, while the light continues to drip away into the evening.

79. IN THE MIDDLE OF NOWHERE

I smell them before I see them.

And the fact that I'm using plural is not good, not in this case.

If it weren't for the stench, I don't know if we would have spotted them.

I'm already using the flashlight because there's maybe ten or fifteen minutes left of light in the sky. The beam is bouncing over the trees in front of us when I hear Poe moan.

"Do you smell that?"

A few steps later I do. It reminds me of the garbage in the back of a restaurant back home where me and a few buddies would hide out and drink beers. The dumpsters were full of rotting food that baked in the sun and ended up smelling worse than vomit. We held our noses but went there anyway because we knew nobody else would be around.

Somehow, what I'm smelling here is even worse.

If smells can produce pain, then I'm in agony.

I think of the trip to see Aunt Alice and of the poor groundhog that I saw on the road

and also saw in the bathtub don't forget about that!

and I remember that stench.

I suddenly start sweeping the ground in front of us with my flashlight.

"It's getting worse."

It almost feels like we're stepping into a pile of animal carcasses. But there's nothing unusual on the forest ground beneath us.

I hear the buzzing of flies near my head and swoop my hand to make them go away. That's when I see it. The thing near my head. The thing hanging on the tree.

Poe screams.

I bolt backward and fall to the ground, all while aiming the light at the furry thing in the tree. It's gray and black, and I swear it's getting ready to spring.

"That's a cat!"

I see beady eyes reflecting the light. Poe's right. It's a cat.

A cat that isn't springing anywhere anytime soon. It looks— attached to the tree.

I don't even want to know how.

"It's dead oh gross it's so dead." Poe curses and comes behind me as I get up and try to act like the brave guy again.

"How's it just hanging there?" I get as close as I'm going to get and examine it. It's attached by its chest, which seems to be nailed into the tree.

"That was done recently," Poe says.

"Yeah."

Thanks for the obvious and for adding to the nightmare.

I glide the flashlight around and examine other trees. I think I spot at least three more dead animals.

"Let's go," I say. I don't want her to see any more.

"Go back?"

I shake my head. "No. We're far enough out here. Whoever did this—there might be a reason why."

"I don't think I want to know a reason. I can think up a few myself."

"Come on."

We keep walking and we reach a small hill with an old, crumbling wood fence at the top. I kick it in, and the wood disintegrates. Then I look ahead and see the opening.

Even in the shadows I can see the outlines of what used to be buildings. Old houses, cabins, small one-story log cabins that now only seem like massive and grotesque building blocks in the evening light.

"This is it."

I nod at Poe and grab her hand and hold it tight. I think I just want to make sure that I have something real and normal to hold on to. Her grip is tight as we walk down what appears to be an old street, now overgrown with brush and weeds.

A handful of half-erect buildings are on each side of us. Small trees and weeds the size of me fill them in. The flashlight reveals the scarred black on the building, a kind that can only come from fire.

I see the building in front of us before Poe does. The shape is what first gets my attention. It's a rectangle, a couple of stories tall, intact. Then I see something that chills me even more than those dead animals. It's a sharp steeple pointing high in the sky.

This building is wood and stone, and it looks brand-new.

"What's a church doing here?"

The road we're on has suddenly become flat and clear, as if

vehicles have driven over it recently. We see sawdust and mud and tire tracks and ruts in the ground.

"Who's building a church here?" Poe asks.

It's crazy, because we thought we were in the middle of nowhere.

The windows aren't in, but the roof and the walls are solid and stable. I can't see anything inside except darkness.

"You think Pastor Marsh is building this?"

I nod. It makes sense. At least as much as anything else makes sense in this crazy town.

"But it's right next to *his* church."

"Yeah."

There's a door on the front, even though the main entry is still only dirt. My flashlight shows the cross on the door.

It's inverted.

"I'm not going in there," Poe says.

"We have to."

"No way. Uh-uh. You see that?"

"Nobody's here."

"How do you know?" she asks.

"I have to go inside."

"So go. I don't want to touch it. I don't want anything to do with that."

We're already way out here, so there's no way I'm not going in. I press Poe a couple more times, but she backs away from the church and folds her arms. I know her well enough to know there's no way I'm getting her to budge.

It's dark and it's cold and this is probably a very bad idea.

"Okay, just—stay there."

"I'm fine."

I scan around the church. There are woods on all sides. I can't tell where the road that we're on leads, but it's got to be a main road where trucks can come for building and supplies and all that.

Everything is silent.

Too silent.

"Just wait. I'm going to check it out."

"You're crazy," she says.

"Yeah, maybe."

I go to the door and turn the handle.

It opens with ease.

As if whoever built this has been waiting for me to come on in.

80. Upside Down

It's dark outside, but it's black in here. It's strange because even though this place is really unsettling, it has the smell of a new home. The smell of freshly cut wood as opposed to the kind that's rotting away in the forest. The whiff of sawdust instead of the gasp of dust and cobwebs. The boards underneath me don't creak like they do in spooky haunted houses.

Yet this does nothing to make me feel better.

Why are they building a new church here?

I go through what appears to be an open area that will serve as the welcome area. A wall separates it from the main sanctuary, but there's no door in the open entryway.

This isn't bigger and better than New Beginnings. So why?

There are no pews in the church, at least none that I can see. I see tools and a couple of table saws, some stacks of wood, some stone, some drywall leaning up against the wall.

My flashlight moves over these things quickly because I keep imagining that someone's going to come out of nowhere with an ancient face and hollow eyes spitting out spiders and sickly insects.

In front of me is a roped-off area where the pulpit should be. They're building a platform around the ropes, but standing ten feet tall is a statue of something. It looks like a stone sword coming out of the earth, the handle near the bottom and then the blade going up and ending in a spire.

As I get closer to the structure, I realize that it's not a sword.

You don't need any more proof this is it this is all you need Chris now get out of here.

Yet I keep walking.

I keep walking as if I was always meant to find this.

Of course you were, people have been pointing you in this direction for some time.

I feel cold and heavy, like the air is thick. I also feel something that's starting to overpower the fear inside of me.

I feel like I'm falling. No, not falling, but sitting in a roller coaster flying.

Rushing.

I can feel my heart racing and yet I also feel so deathly cold, like

I'm in the middle of subzero temperatures with no clothes on. My arms begin to shake and I rub them but can't stop the tremor.

I get to the structure and know that it's no sword.

It's a cross. An upside-down cross.

It's also old. It's made of dark stone that looks worn with time.

The ropes stand about five feet away from the stone structure on each side. I shine the light on the ground in front of me and see a plaque of some kind firmly cemented into the floor of the church.

This is a gravestone. This thing, this tall upside-down stone cross, is a gravestone.

I get closer to see what the plaque says.

Louis-Henri Clérel de Solitaire

1736–1842

And then, in a much smaller font that I have to squint to read, is something written in French. Identifying the language is the best I can do. Even if I weren't doing so horribly in French, I still bet I wouldn't understand a word of this.

Quand on parle du loup, on en voit la queue.

I wish I had a phone to take a picture of the inscription, because there's no way I'm going to remember it.

"Yessssssssssssssss."

I drop the flashlight and turn around and shield myself, since the voice coming out of nowhere sounds like it's two inches away.

"Chrissssssssssssss."

The voice, low, hungry, grave, sickly …

"Now," it says. "Right now. Now."

I reach over and scrape the floor and find the flashlight. Then I scan the area around me.

That's the voice you heard in the passageway.

I think about the time they blindfolded and gagged me and then threatened me.

"Who's there?" I shout.

I don't see anybody. But I can hear the laughter. Laughter like a razor blade scratching against skin, taking little chunks with it.

"Who's there?" My scream echoes off the walls. "Who are you?"

"The one who knowsssssssssss. The one who can set you free."

I feel like I'm in one of those theaters with the deep roaring bass that's just thumping and throttling.

That's how this voice sounds.

That's how my heart feels.

Then I see something bright blistering through this dark mess, and I squint and fall to my knees, knowing I'm in trouble knowing I'm dead knowing the end is here.

"Chris."

It's Jocelyn.

She's come to save me.

81. ECHOES

I see her outline lit up by something behind her. She stands at the edge of a doorway in the back of the church.

"This was a mistake."

I pause for a moment. It's her voice—I can hear her and see her. Yet I don't understand what she's talking about.

"Jocelyn?"

"You don't want to be with someone like me."

What's she saying?

"Joss—"

"Don't ruin yourself. I'm used goods."

I keep walking toward her. She's looking down, not at me.

"Jocelyn, it's me."

"You strip this away, and there's nothing down inside."

Then I remember. She said that once to me. Yet I can't remember when.

"God did this."

I keep walking toward her without answering.

"Ultimately God let my parents down."

What's she saying, what am I hearing?

"If—and I mean *if*—God is up there, then why?"

These are things she said to me once, but …

I reach her, and she looks up at me and smiles.

But the face looking at me and those eyes looking into mine and that smile don't belong to Jocelyn.

Up close now, I know it's not her.

The eyes are empty and black and the gaze is needy and obsessed and the smile is hateful and wanting.

"What—who—who are you?"

She moves to kiss me, and I see her smile that's transformed not into brilliant white fangs wanting to bite but rather blackened and oozing gums wanting to suck.

I scream and then see those eyes shrivel up to nothing. Nothing but emptiness. Nothing but rotting black holes.

"We don't have to die, Chrissssssssssss."

But before the rotting, sickly old man in front of me can reach over at me, I swing my flashlight and strike something hard. I think it might be his jaw or the side of his face.

I tear out of there before whatever this is can touch me.

Then I'm outside, sucking in air and sweaty and trying to find Poe to tell her to run, and I realize that I'm alone.

Poe is gone.

82. Things in My Head

I've lost someone else.

This is what runs through my mind as I'm calling out her name and directing my light in a hundred different spots trying to see her.

I've let someone else I care for get taken.

And still out of breath and still in a state of shock, my voice cracking because I'm losing it, I hear a ghost call out my name.

"Chris."

Of course, it's not a ghost. It's Poe standing at the edge of the woods we came in from.

I reach her, and she clasps on to both of my arms.

"What'd you see in there?"

"Nothing. Just—my imagination is playing tricks. I just thought—when I came out and you were—"

"I felt weird standing by the empty church."

Oh but it's not empty not at all Poe.

"Did you find anything inside?"

"Let's go."

"Chris?"

"It's already too dark, and I don't want to get lost."

"That's why I'm standing over here," she says. "To make sure we know which direction to head."

I want to tell her that it'll be a miracle for us to find our car again.

Yet just a few minutes later—ten or twenty or maybe thirty, I can't tell because my mind is too full to compute time—we're getting into her car.

"What happened?" she asks before starting it up.

"That church is like a shrine to somebody."

"What do you mean?"

I tell her to start the car and go. As she drives, I tell her what I saw.

"What did the French say?"

"No clue."

I would've forgotten even if I hadn't seen whatever it was I saw.

"We need to go back."

"Maybe in broad daylight," I say. "With others."

"Okay, fine. But this person, maybe he has something to do with everything that's going on."

"I sure hope he doesn't. Since he's, you know, *dead.*"

"That's not what I meant."

"Yeah."

But maybe you're right, maybe he's still around and haunting this place.

"Why would they stick a gravestone in the middle of a church?" Poe asks.

I don't want to tell her what I'm thinking.

But I'm thinking …

No, stop thinking. Stop thinking and leave it alone.

"Chris?"

"I don't think we want to know the reason."

"Yeah, maybe not."

The drive home seems long and quiet and troubling. I tell Poe I'll see her tomorrow.

I don't say all the other things in my head.

Things like *Make sure you lock your door tonight.*

Things like *Tell me tomorrow if Jocelyn comes to you in your dreams and suddenly turns into an old, dying man with really bad dental hygiene.*

Things like

Enough, Chris.

The voice shutting me up sounds like Mom or Dad but is obviously my own.

This whole haunting and creeping and nightmaring business sure helps a boy grow up.

83. Not Watching Anymore

Hatred doesn't forget. The longer it waits, the more it grows like some grotesque fungus.

I learn this the hard way one April day.

The end of school is not too far away, and summer is within reach. The sun is drying out the winter's harsh bite and making things seem halfway normal.

But on the day of our track team's big meet versus Hendersonville, I'm faced with the reminder that anger isn't a good thing to store up. Like perishable food in a pantry, it's going to go bad fast.

It's the end of art class, and somehow the hippie teacher Mr. Chestle has disappeared before the bell rings for us to leave. Students file out, and I'm chatting like always with Kelsey when I see her stop in midsentence.

"I was just kidding," I say, not really sure what I said that got to her.

Kelsey shakes her head, glancing toward the door.

I turn to look and see Gus coming in. And behind him, the rest of his crew.

The rest of the kids in the room quickly decide it's smart to leave.

Gus walks over to us. Kelsey's yellow painting that she's worked on for over a month is in front of her.

"Isn't that pretty?" Gus says, looking at me.

"What do you want?"

He only smiles, then looks back at the door. Riley closes it.

"We haven't had a chance to talk lately," he says.

"Cut it out, Gus. We have classes to go to."

"What's your name again?" he asks Kelsey.

I stand between the two of them as he sneers like a bull spotting red.

"I never did get that apology I've been waiting on since you attacked me in the hallway," Gus says.

I look at the pockets of pimples on his face, the way his hair sticks up like a Chia Pet, the big forehead that needs a nice rag to sop it up.

"Why don't you go," I say to Kelsey behind me.

"Uh-uh. She's staying here. You—Miss Braces and Glasses. This your painting?"

"Get out of my face, Gus."

"Or what?" he asks me. "What are you going to do?"

He laughs as he takes a knife out of his pocket and opens it. Then he sticks the canvas of the yellow painting and cuts several slits through it.

I start to yell and go toward him, but Kelsey grabs me by the shoulder to tell me to stop. Meanwhile, Riley and Burt come to flank Gus while Oli remains at the door.

"Put that away," I tell him.

"Or what? What are you going to do?"

"Kelsey, leave."

"Kelsey, huh? Nice little pretty girl. So different from your last one, huh?"

"Shut your fat face."

"Chris—"

I glance back at Kelsey and see her almost in tears. "Gus, I'm serious. Let her go."

"I'm not a monster," he says. "But I can do monstrous things."

"Gus."

"I want an apology."

He's still holding the knife by his side. I honestly have no idea if he'll use it.

"I'm sorry, okay?"

"Not good enough. Not sincere enough."

I see the gaping hole of the shredded painting Kelsey spent so much time on.

See I told you I'm no good for you. People around me only get hurt.

"Gus, I'm sorry. Now leave us alone."

"Uh-uh. Oli, guard the door."

Gus smiles. Riley and Burt chuckle.

"Maybe you'd learn if something happened to little Miss Virgin here."

I look around me. I never bring anything to art, so there's nothing to pick up and defend myself with or even to throw at him except some art tools.

"You'd learn then, wouldn't you?"

I move my arm to shield Kelsey as I try to think through what I can do and how I can protect the girl behind me.

Then something weird happens. Something not part of the suggested plot.

Oli is standing by the door and peers through the tiny slit of glass as if to check and see if the coast is clear. Then he jogs to the side of the room and picks up a large palette knife that looks like an elongated spatula.

I'm wondering what he's—

"Owwwww!"

I guess that's my answer.

The blunt tool makes a loud slap against the back of Gus's big head.

It'd be hilarious if I weren't so freaked out about the knife and the girl behind me.

Gus puts one hand on the back of his head as he grimaces. But Oli doesn't stop there. He flails down with the flat instrument and whacks Gus's hand. I hear what must be the knife drop on the floor.

Oli speaks. And this time he's not whispering to me in the locker room. "No, Riley, you stay over there."

Meanwhile, Gus is yelling and cursing.

"Shut up and get up," Oli says. He's holding the palette knife like it's an actual knife. But there's probably no one in the room who doesn't think he'll use it.

"What are you doing, you idiot?" Gus says. He's still rubbing the back of his head.

"No more. Chris, you guys can leave."

"Kelsey, leave."

"Chris—?"

"I'll be just a minute."

She gets her stuff and quickly leaves the room. I'm standing there watching the scene play out.

"Oli. Are you high?" Gus stares at him in disbelief.

"Not this time," Oli says.

Gus curses at him some more.

"I'm tired of watching you hurt people that don't need hurting, and I'm not going to watch anymore. This time I'm not going home feeling guilty that I should've done something."

"You put that thing down—"

"Or what? Huh? No more."

"That's right, it's no more. I'm done with you."

Oli nods as if that's fine with him. "You can leave, Chris."

"Okay," I say. "But after you."

He drops the tool on the floor. "You try and do anything to me, Gus, and I'll kill you," he says.

"Not if I do it first."

It doesn't look like either of them is joking around. Oli leaves, and I follow him into the hallway.

84. Happy Accidents

"Oli—dude—"

"Look, it's fine."

"What just happened in there?"

We're walking down the hall, and I keep looking around, hoping to see Kelsey.

"It's about doing what's right," he says.

"Okay. But—"

I spot Kelsey waiting for me.

"I'll explain another time. Go talk to her."

"You can come with me."

"She doesn't want to talk to me."

I nod and am about to say thanks, but he's gone.

I reach Kelsey, and she starts crying. All I can do is hug her. For a few moments, it feels like we're the only two people here. And that feels fine with me.

It's amazing how accidents seem to happen at the strangest times.

Kelsey and I are walking to our next classes after the few moments I've spent trying to calm her down. We're already late, but that's okay. It's not a big deal to be late to history class with Mr. Meiners. And I'm sure Kelsey is such a good student she could take a couple days off without getting in trouble.

I stand in front of the closed door to her class and look down at her to make sure she's okay.

"Why'd he do that?" she asks. The big, blue eyes behind the glasses are looking at me with confusion and relief.

"I have no idea."

"What'd he say to you?"

"That he'll explain later."

"It's good to know you have people looking out for you."

I laugh. "Yeah. I guess that is good. I can use it."

"I'd better go in."

Before she does, I lean closer to her and slip my hands over hers.

"Listen, Kelsey. I'm sorry, okay. I don't want—I don't want any stuff like that to come back and hurt you."

"It won't."

Even though she's shaken, she still somehow looks strong.

"It almost did."

"It's worth it." She squeezes my hands, then opens her door to her classroom and goes inside.

I'm standing there for a minute, once again surprised, not just at this girl but at my feelings for her and at how quickly they're developing when I strictly said they couldn't.

I turn to go toward Mr. Meiners' room when I face that happy accident.

Poe is standing at the side of the hallway, watching me.

"Hey," I say, actually glad to see her.

But she turns and heads the other way.

She's like a Halloween trick-or-treater in all black.

I call out her name, but she's gone.

85. PURPOSE

For the first time in a long time, I have purpose.

I don't know if I've ever felt like I had so much purpose as I do right now.

Coach Brinks is nearby on the sideline along with the rest of our team. Ray is there; so are the others. Normally they don't *all* pay attention, but right now they are.

I always feel stupid before races because I don't have some ritual. The guys next to me, two big guys from Hendersonville High, are stretching and jogging fast and looking up at the sky and doing whatever else they need to. One is a white guy with not an ounce of body fat on him. The other is a black guy who looks like he could bench-press me.

It's great that I'm stuck in between these two.

There's another school here, but everybody knows that the race is ultimately among the three of us.

The starter prompts us to get ready. I'm getting better coming out of the blocks, but that's the beauty of the 300-meter hurdles. You don't have to shoot out of them like you do with the 100 high hurdles. This race is part sprint, part endurance, part timing.

And in your case, part luck.

"Runners, take your mark."

I can feel my heart beating.

But it's a good kind of beating. It's not the kind that you get when someone is laughing at you in the mysterious passage below your house. It's not the kind you get from seeing some undead grandpa in some weird tunnel in the middle of nowhere. It's not the kind you get when pimply bully-boy pulls out a knife.

And it's not the kind you get when you're running to save someone who is already dead.

"Get set."

I know one thing.

If I could have run faster, I would have. If I could have hurdled more logs and bushes, I would have. If I could have been stronger and tougher, then maybe.

Just maybe.

The shot rings out, and I'm no longer thinking about the guys from Hendersonville. I'm not thinking about the coach who calls me Chicago or about Mr. Popular who thinks I can win this one.

I'm not thinking about this school or this place or my place in this school.

I'm running to Jocelyn.

I'm running for her.

I catch the first hurdle fine, with all the right strides.

But the right strides don't mean anything in this life. It's all random, all meaningless, all complete luck.

The big guys are ahead of me, but I don't care.

I take the second hurdle fine.

There are eight hurdles, and I'm making my way around the corner, running fine.

Then something happens.

I don't know what it is. Maybe it's just my stupid stubbornness.

But I see big guy one and big guy two start pulling away, and it makes me angry. Really angry.

Like the kind of anger that's been inside, deep inside, like a giant river flowing into an ocean, ever since leaving Libertyville.

I never wanted to move to this hellhole.

Next hurdle.

I never wanted to see your stupid marriage implode and then explode.

Next hurdle.

I never wanted to meet someone new and fall in whatever version of love I could fall into only to get slapped and beaten and thrown out of the car and left for dead myself.

Next hurdle.

I never wanted to know that evil is real and darkness is thorough and that the weird, spooky stuff of life might really be out there.

Next hurdle.

I might be sucking in air, but I can't tell. Someone somewhere might be cheering for me, but I can't hear anything. I'm just running faster now than I was at the start of the race.

I've never had this much energy while closing in on the final hurdles.

In some movies or stories I might reach the final hurdle and trip over it. But I already did that the last time I was running this fast and this steady and this hectic. I tripped over something big and discovered that she was already long gone.

Not this time not this time you soul-sucking town.

And even though I'm beginning to see little dots of stars in my vision and my lungs have been tossed over some mountain ledge like a grenade as I pass the finish line, I don't slow down. Not until I'm all the way around the track and see Coach Brinks and the others rushing toward me.

I can't breathe or even really see when Coach Brinks puts his arms around me.

"You ran like someone was chasing you there, Chicago! That was incredible."

They tell me the results, but I don't really care.

All I know is that, for a moment, I wasn't in some prison, running around in circles.

I was free and running away. I was running toward something. I was running for a reason and a purpose.

They keep telling me over and over about the results, but I just nod and try to catch my breath.

As I do, I look up in the stands, which are mostly empty.

But I see a figure in black.

I guess Poe saw me win the race.

86. BLACK LEOPARD

"Good thing I didn't know you were watching." I sit down next to Poe.

"You won the race. You were awesome."

"Yeah, but I would've probably tripped if I'd seen you."

"Shocked that I'm at a sporting event?"

"Shocked that you're at mine."

She smiles. "You beat those guys pretty bad."

"Coach says I set a new school record."

Poe looks up at me and beams. "That's amazing. Congratulations."

I shrug as if this is the sort of thing I do every day.

"You don't seem happy."

"I was happy running. Now I'm just exhausted."

The track meet is still going on down below the stands.

"A record. Now you're a jock, huh? And I obviously don't hang around with jocks."

I laugh. "Why'd you bolt this afternoon when I saw you?"

She glances out to the football field below with those eyes so heavy and so full. Poe is sorta like a beautiful animal, like a bobcat or a leopard.

A black leopard, so sleek with those eyes, but also always ready to snap or bite back.

"It's no big deal," Poe says.

"Nobody was around, so I don't know why you had to—"

"Chris?"

"Yeah?"

"Just shut up, okay? I'm watching the meet."

I give her a look that says *you gotta be kidding me,* but she doesn't look back. I take a sip of bottled water and then look down below too. I'm too tired for any kind of drama this afternoon.

The sky is beautiful with pockets of clouds and an endless blue that I wish I could sail away on.

"Guys are pretty stupid," Poe says, surprising me.

"What?"

"Just hush, okay?"

"I thought that's what I was doing."

Then the black leopard moves over and kisses me on the cheek.

87. SHE'S A GIRL

The cafeteria behind us is quiet, the lights off and the chairs and tables sleeping in the shadows. We sit on the end of a table that faces the front doors to the high school. The sun is just beginning to dive beneath the mountaintops far in the distance.

"If I had a phone—or maybe a life—I'd call my mom and tell her not to pick me up," I say to Poe.

"It's fine."

"You really don't have to stay."

She's sitting on the table while I'm standing, watching for the lights to come up the drive of the school.

"I'm not going to bite," she says.

I nod, then realize she means I can sit by her. Or maybe it means I *should* sit by her.

I'm still a little surprised at that kiss. Not freaked out or bewildered but ... curious, I guess.

Not long ago I would never have guessed that a kiss like that would come from Poe.

We're sitting side by side, and I'm quiet because I don't know what to say. Poe clears her throat and turns and faces me.

"Okay. I'm just going to get this out since I still stand by what I said earlier, that guys are stupid. You always have to be shown something. You can't just—you can't come up with it yourself."

She's talking in another language. Girl language.

Interpreter, please?

"Can't come up with what?"

"So that's why—if I don't do this, I know I'll forever probably regret it. The same way I regretted it when—when I should have at the very beginning."

"I'm lost," I say.

"You always are."

"Maybe."

"Do you remember the first time we came up to you at school? When you were wearing a Smiths T-shirt?"

"Yeah."

I think about that all the time. It was the first time I ever had a chance to talk to Jocelyn. Or talk around her.

"All you probably remember is Jocelyn, and that's fine. That's all anybody remembers, when it comes to the three of us. Which was always fine until—until you showed up."

I'm still lost.

"I wanted to come up to you, Chris. You probably don't remember it, but I called you cute."

I shake my head. Poe thought I was cute? When was that?

"I don't remember."

"Of course you don't. And then you got swooped up into the hurricane that was Jocelyn. And I knew it. I knew you would, but I always—I just thought … hoped, I guess. I thought that there might be something there. I figured we had things in common, and I knew that the last thing Jocelyn wanted was a relationship. But of course, she fell in love with you."

I look away from her glance, down at the floor.

"And who wouldn't?" she says.

I can't quite believe her words, so I look back up at her.

"Why do you think I was so irritable with you and Jocelyn?"

"I just thought it was because—because everybody else didn't want me with her," I say.

"Yeah. But my reasons were different."

It clicks.

And yeah, I guess I'm pretty clueless.

"The only reason I'm telling you this—I'm not trying to bring up the past or make you feel bad or anything. It's just—today, I'd heard about the fight and was waiting to see what happened, and then I saw you and that girl. And I just—everything came back, Chris. Everything. Those conversations I had with Jocelyn where she said she wasn't interested and that we'd make a good fit."

"She said that?"

"Early on. And then everything—who knew? I still can't believe she's gone. I still can't believe that she really knew. I think she just wanted to escape. Or leave. Or ignore it. But you came along and changed all that."

"No, I didn't."

Poe looks up at me with an expression that's as soft and comforting as any I've seen in my life.

"You did everything you could, and you did even more than that. I know what you did for Jocelyn. I just—I was angry that you chose her, even though I always knew you would."

"Poe, I just—"

"Please, no. I only bring it up because today I saw it happening again. I don't know what you think and feel toward Kelsey, but I want you to know that there's another girl here. And you've been kind enough to allow her back into your life. And that girl still—still hopes."

This is too much. It's more surprising than setting some school record.

"I never knew."

She laughs. "Why would you?"

I shake my head, my mouth slightly open, ready to say something but unable to.

Then Poe moves and kisses my lips before they can say something stupid and ruin the moment. And for the second time in a short span of hours, I'm lost and I'm free and I'm full.

I don't know how long that kiss lasts, but it feels like a long time.

When our heads part, I see the beams of light in the driveway below us.

"Perfect timing, huh?" Poe says.

"I had no idea."

"Well, now you know."

I shake my head.

Poe smiles. "I'll see you tomorrow, okay. And we can talk."

I stand and feel dazed and confused for the right reasons.

She's still sitting there.

Not some girl hidden behind black and covered with anger and angst.

She's smiling and looking at me like someone who wants me, like someone who likes me, like someone who finally has told me the truth.

"Go on," Poe says. "Listen to some songs tonight and think of me, okay, Mr. Record-setting Track Star?"

I nod and smile.

It's only in the car that I realize I was too speechless to wish her good night.

But she's not clueless, so she knows why.

Girls know.

88. THE SPACES IN BETWEEN

I've been working on this project for Iris all day and getting nowhere. I told her I'm not a writer and I really don't know what I'm doing. There are pages and pages of notes that I'm trying to cram into a school paper. Or not even that. Into some short copy for a brochure. I'm not the guy to do this.

I can't help but think about the past week.

The stuff that happened with Gus and with Kelsey. And then the track meet and the kiss with Poe.

I think about our conversation the next day. It wasn't any momentous occasion, just a passing conversation.

So I have an idea. Why don't you take me to prom?

Before I could answer, Poe smiled and told me to think about it. No pressure. *No harm, no foul,* she said.

I still never gave her an answer before the weekend came.

I'm thirsty and haven't seen much of Iris today. I go into the kitchen and decide to get a bottled water from the fridge. Then I notice something that I've been curious about every time I see it.

The pantry is at the end of the rectangular kitchen, with the refrigerator to the right, then the sink with a window above it. But to the left of the pantry there's a short, square wooden door in the center of the wall. Not really a door, maybe a half door, with a latch on it.

It seems random and out of place. I can't tell where the door goes because the house extends farther than this wall.

It's silent. Iris must be outside doing something.

The door isn't bolted. I decide to see what's behind it. Probably nothing. It's not like I'm a cat and curiosity is going to do anything to me.

As I try the bolt, I have to force it to unlock.

I swing the door open and feel a cool blast of damp, musty air.

It's black inside, but I can make out something very short and narrow. A small cupboard—no, not really a cupboard. More like just a blank room hollowed out and enclosed with wood.

It's just big enough for one or two people to hide in.

"So what do you think?"

The voice causes me to jerk and turn around and then feel guilty.

"It's okay. I'm not hiding anything. At least not today." She smiles and goes to the sink to rinse out a glass.

"Sorry," I tell her.

"Not at all. Do you know what that is?"

I shake my head. "A closet of some kind?"

"Unused space. Years ago they discovered that there was a small amount of unused space behind this wall. For some reason nothing was ever done with it—no closet or cupboard was built. Probably because it was too small to be worth it. But I call it one of the spaces in between. Every time something is built, this happens. There are small little nooks and crannies that go unnoticed, untouched."

I shut the door and bolt it back.

"How is your project going?" Iris asks.

Every day I work here, the elderly woman seems to look younger to me. Every day I see her, the lines seem less visible, her eyes and smile more apparent. It's a weird thing, but weird in a beautiful sort of way.

"Slowly," I say.

"Why don't you sit for a minute. Please."

As I sit she gets a teacup and makes herself some tea. I wait, familiar with this ritual of hers. She takes her time and doesn't rush. Soon she is sitting across from me, letting the tea cool.

"Do you remember when you first started work here, Chris? Remember when I asked you what you believe?"

I nod.

"Has that changed at all?"

I think for a moment but know my answer. "I don't think so."

I'm being nice, because actually I know it hasn't changed.

She takes a sip of her tea, looks at me as if she's trying to look through me. It makes me nervous but doesn't give me the creeps like it would if it were 95 percent of the people out there.

"Tell me what you think about Solitary."

I'm surprised by her question, because it seems as if we've never spoken about the town. I've often wondered if she's avoiding the topic.

"There're a lot of things I think."

"Such as?"

"It's a weird town." Such an understatement. But what am I supposed to say?

"If I told you it was evil, would you believe that?" she asks.

I nod.

"So it's easy to believe in the darkness, but not in the light."

"I haven't seen a whole lot of 'light' around this place," I say.

"If you studied the Bible, you would see how many times the terms light and darkness come up. 'We look for light, but all is darkness; for brightness, but we walk in deep shadows. Like the blind we grope along the wall, feeling our way like men without eyes.'"

Sounds like I could relate to that writer.

"Do you believe in the evil things you cannot see?"

Again I'm not sure what to say. I'm not sure if this is a test, or if she's trying to get something out of me. Or if she's finally going to start really preaching at me.

"I'm not sure."

"It sounds like you do."

"Why?"

"Because you don't hesitate to say the things you *do not* believe in. Your passion and your strength give you away."

"Strength?" I ask. I laugh. "Not sure about that."

"Do you want to know what I believe about Solitary?"

"Sure."

"'He will bring into the light of day all that at present is hidden in darkness, and he will expose the *secret motives* of men's hearts.' That is a quote from the Bible, not from me."

"Do you know what's happening? With the town? With the stuff going on there?"

"I know this place and my calling, Chris. And I tell you this now, because a few months ago you would have shut me out. At least you're listening. At least you know I'm not going to hurt you. At least you know a little more about this place. We're not in Solitary. We're above it. And there is a reason why. This place is a light in the darkness, Chris."

"But—how, exactly?"

"You are doubtful," Iris says.

"No, it's just ... nobody even knows about this place. The few that do think it's haunted. I just—how can you say that this place is a light?"

"That door, the one you just opened. Remember what I called it?"

"An unused space."

"A space in between. That's what the Crag's Inn is, Chris. It's always been in one of the spaces in between. But its purpose is to provide help and hope. To provide some amount of reinforcement in a dangerous setting."

I don't get this. It's a tiny bed-and-breakfast that's used by strangers visiting North Carolina. What does it have to do with Solitary, with the evil going on there, with Staunch and Pastor Marsh and all the weirdness and evil?

"You don't do a very good job keeping your feelings off your face."

"No?" I ask.

She reaches over and touches my hand.

For someone who hasn't ever really been hugged and kissed much in his life, I've sure been touched and kissed this past week.

"I want you to do something else for me. Will you?"

I nod, feeling awkward and not sure what Iris is going to ask.

"I want you to read the tenth chapter of the book of Daniel. It's in the Old Testament. Will you do that for me?"

"Sure."

"Take these words to heart, Chris. 'Don't be afraid—for you are deeply loved by God. Be at peace; take heart and be strong!'"

I nod as Iris lets go of my hand.

"Please read it. Read it and think about what I said, about this place, about the spaces in between. And Chris—you need to know something. Your coming here to this town, you sitting across from me right now—it wasn't an accident."

I almost don't want to know what else she's going to say. I'm beginning to get a little frightened.

"I have something else to show you. Something else to give you. Come on."

89. THE BIKE

There are a couple of sheds on the property around the Crag's Inn. One is full of tools and equipment and junk that I spent a couple of Saturdays sorting through and disposing of and organizing. I always assumed that the other shed was something similar.

I discover that I'm wrong.

This shed is more a garage of sorts. Inside is a car, which makes sense since I never see any cars up here and I assume Iris has to get around somehow.

You thought she could fly, right? Like witches do.

The thing I notice right away, however, is a silver-and-black motorcycle that looks old but doesn't look like junk.

"Have you ever ridden a motorcycle?" Iris asks me under the hazy orange light in the shed.

"A few times. Mom's never been a big fan."

"This one belonged to your uncle."

First we're talking about light and the Bible and the book of Daniel, and now she's talking about Uncle Robert. Both seem like crazy made-up stories to me.

"You serious?"

"Yes."

"How'd you get it?"

She folds her hands and gives me a nice, polite smile the way a politician or First Lady might. "He used to work for me some time ago."

"What?"

"In many ways, you remind me of him."

"Are you serious?"

"Yes, Chris."

"Does my mother know about this?"

"No."

"So then how—do you know where he is?"

She shakes her head.

"What happened?" I ask. "How long ago did he work for you?"

"A few years ago. The bike was something that he found and brought up here to work on. An actor that he liked once owned a bike like this. I forget the actor, but the bike is called a Triumph. He never managed to get it fixed. I got someone to finish it in case he ever came back. But he didn't."

"He quit?"

"Yes. I wasn't as … patient, I guess I should say, with Robert."

"With what?"

"With trying to teach him. With trying to let him know who he was."

She makes it sound like Uncle Robert was some Jedi warrior or something.

I know my Star Wars, and this is not Star Wars.

"I tried too hard with him. That's why—this time, I decided to back off. As opportunity permits, I've been able to talk with you."

"I don't understand. He just didn't like all the stuff you talked about?"

"Uncle Robert was confused, Chris. Probably much like you are."

"Maybe it has something to do with the place he was living in."

"It has everything to do with the place. But it also has everything to do with *him*. And that was the part he refused to accept."

"What about him?"

Iris ignores my question and goes over to the bike. "Do you want to learn how to ride this?"

"Now?" I'm picturing her getting on this and think my mind is a few seconds away from being blown.

"No. Not now. But soon. They're a little tricky to start. And of course you'll have to be careful going down the hill."

"But—"

"It's yours."

"For what?"

"For listening. And for showing up when your uncle never did."

"What do you think happened to him?"

"I wish I knew," Iris says. "I still pray for him every day and night. I pray that he is still alive and that there's still time. But I don't know. I really don't know."

90. OH MAN

"Oh, yeah, sure."

That's how I answer Poe Monday morning when she asks me if we're still going to prom.

That should show how into it I am, how much I've thought about it.

I haven't stopped thinking about the connection between Uncle Robert and Iris and my place in this.

How in the world can I think of prom when I'm thinking of bigger things? Like life and death and dead animals and gravestones and French guys with ironic last names and Triumph motorcycles I need to start riding.

How can my answer be anything other than *Oh, yeah, sure?*

But the problem isn't what Poe says next. She only smiles and nods and walks away. She knew I was going to say yes anyway. She kissed me, and I didn't run away to the nearby hills. She knew that there was something on the other side of that kiss, though I couldn't really say *what* exactly, because I don't know myself.

It's a big adjustment from thinking someone hates you to realizing they've liked you all along. I'm not just seeing Poe in a different light. It's a whole different room. No, make that a new house in a new town on a planet far, far away.

No, my problem comes when I get to art class.

Oh man.

Kelsey greets me, and I see how excited she is to see me and I instantly know I'm in trouble. Not now, of course. But once I'm found out. Once my predicament is known.

"How was your weekend?" she asks.

"Great."

At least I have a motorcycle now. One that can take me far away from all of this. Once I learn how to drive the thing.

91. AS IF EVENTUALLY

April belly flops into May, and I soon find myself drowning.

Something happens, and I can't say exactly what. It's like a full moon rises in the sky and then just hangs there, daring everybody to keep going, taunting us all with its cold color and craziness.

The craziness starts, of course, with Mom.

It started when she got the idea to come back to this crazy town and it continued once we actually arrived.

She's been working more and coming home later and acting more strange, though part of me has been too preoccupied to really notice. But when I get home one evening after practice, Ray having given me a lift, I find her in a state of panic.

Make that terror.

I get to the door and find it locked. It's never locked when Mom's home. I unlock it and hear someone bark out at me and see a shotgun pointed at me.

"Chris! What are you doing?" Mom is standing behind the couch, in front of the island in the kitchen, pointing a shotgun.

At me.

"What are *you* doing?"

I guess most kids would be calling 9-1-1 by now and saying "Yes, sir, I've got a bat in my house but it's actually in my mom's head 'cause she's gone totally batty."

She lowers the shotgun but doesn't apologize or even act like it's weird to be pointing it at me.

"Mom?"

"I thought you were someone else."

"I usually get home around this time."

"What time is it?"

I know she's been drinking. I can hear it in her voice. Her pitch is slightly higher, and even when she can say the words without slurring, they sound as if they've been coated in wine.

"It's around seven."

"Lock the door."

"What's going on?"

"Just do it!"

I lock it and put down my bag and look around the room. There's only one light on in the whole house. I don't even need to bother to look to see if dinner is ready.

"Mom?"

"I'm in trouble."

"With who?"

"You be nice to the wrong people and they'll just want to wreck your soul, that's all I can say."

For a split second I wonder if this has anything to do with Dad. She's still holding the shotgun.

"Where'd you get that?" I ask.

"It was here."

"Where?"

"None of your business."

"Mom?"

"Promise me, Chris. Promise me that when you grow up you'll not be like ninety-nine percent of the guys out there. Promise me that."

"Why don't you put that down?"

"I'm not giving this to you."

Yeah, because I can't handle it, but you sure can.

"Just put it down."

She sets it on the island.

"Should I call the police?"

"We're not calling anybody. But if someone comes through that door, he'll get an answer. I told him if he sets foot on this property, I'll shoot him. I don't care."

"Who?"

"Chris—it's not your—"

"Who are you talking about? Tell me!"

I think my voice might wake the dead, or at least the dead in the tunnels underneath our house.

"Mom?"

"A guy I met at work."

"What's his name?"

"Why?"

"Well, in case you pass out like you usually do every single night, and he knocks at the door. A name might be good. Or if he shows up at school like everybody does and pops out of my locker."

"Mike."

"What'd he do?"

"Nothing," Mom says.

"Really?"

She sees me glancing at the shotgun.

"He's a guy I met at work who I thought was one thing but was really something else. Just like every other guy I've ever met."

"Did he—?"

"Just drop it."

"Is he coming over? Seriously?"

Mom leans against the couch and looks like someone who's just finished a marathon.

"I don't know."

That's all she says. That's all I get.

Mike.

Mike who might be coming over.

Mike who was going to be welcomed with a nice shotgun blast.

And here I'd thought we might have one of those nice scenes where a kid talks to his parent about prom, kinda like in those cute eighties flicks.

But this isn't one of those films. I'm not a girl, and I'm never going to be pretty in pink.

Later that night, after Mom eventually falls into a coma on the couch with the television still on, I'm in my bed with my eyes wide open, waiting to hear anything.

I really can't remember what it's like to go to bed without worrying or wondering or waiting. I remember that I used to go to bed wondering what my friends would say tomorrow about my Facebook comment. Now I go to bed wondering if some creepy face is going to pop up by my window.

Eventually I turn the light back on and decide to read. That doesn't work, so I put on some music at a decent volume that only the conscious can hear. I decide to skip the heavy, dark, sad stuff that fills most of the record collection. Instead I put on a Duran Duran album that is bouncy and peppy at first, yet soon turns sad and reflective. Of course.

I find the leather band I no longer wear but still have. For a long time I hold it and think of Jocelyn.

If heaven does exist, is she looking down at me?

If heaven does exist, she's surely doing far more important things.

I want to cut this leather band up into a hundred little pieces.

I put it back on my desk and then see the picture, that crazy picture I found sometime ago.

It's even more blurry and faded than I remember, like a snapshot accidentally taken pointing at the sun.

I want to cut the picture up, too, yet for some reason I keep it.

The same reason I keep listening to music like this.

The same reason I keep waiting.

As if eventually, it'll all make sense.

As if eventually, it'll all be okay.

92. A Change in Seasons

Maybe ten or twenty years from now, I'll look back on this with fond memories. Fond memories that I got *out* of this nightmare. Fond memories that I left this school and this town in the dust. But at the moment I'm just wondering how to make it to tomorrow.

I really want to talk to Kelsey about the whole prom thing, but then one day at lunch I see her talking to an upperclassman.

His name is Sam, I think. He's not a jock, but he runs in the same circles as Ray Spencer. I think he might be competition for Ray, to be honest. Another good-looking, well-to-do guy who dates a lot of girls at this school.

Kelsey is laughing at him and bringing her head close to her shoulder in a way a cat might as it's purring.

I bump into someone, who curses at me, and I stop staring and find my seat next to Newt.

"That's crazy," I say, talking more to myself than anything else.

"There are two times when people get really crazy around here. May and December."

I look at Newt and wonder how he knows what I'm even talking about, then realize I'm lucky to have a friend like him. Before I can start picking at my lunch, Georgia strolls by and stops in front of us.

"You had your chance, but look who got her instead."

This girl really just needs a mop in her mouth.

"What did I do wrong today?"

"Oh, nothing," Georgia says with contempt. "Nothing at all. The news about prom wasn't hard on her at all. But she's still going."

"With Sam over there?"

Georgia nods.

"So are you going with the man of your dreams? Dan? Planning on eloping?"

"No. In fact, Ray asked me. Might've been a nice group if you had been smarter."

I thought Ray was going to ask someone else to prom. I'm going to say something, but she walks away. Newt is eating Cheetos and just staring at me.

"What?"

"Like I said," he says, shaking his head. "May and December."

Things do feel different, but it's the end of the school year and everyone is ready for summer. Poe still doesn't talk much with me at school, yet she wants to go to prom with me. Kelsey acts like a stranger, not even painting by me in art any longer.

Mom is a mess, drinking more than ever. She's no longer hiding it, which is not good since I'm no longer hiding my growing contempt at having to watch her self-destruct. This is one of those cycles that can only end badly.

I don't hear from Jared, nor do I hear from Sheriff Wells.

It's nothing except a vibe I get. Things *are* different.

All I know is that summer is coming, and maybe with it will come a change. Or at least a change of scenery.

Maybe if I could look into the future, I'd feel a little more at ease.

But something tells me otherwise. Something dark and oppressive is coming, something that's going to change everything, something that is even worse than what happened with Jocelyn.

Nothing could be worse than that.

Nothing.

93. MISS YOU

The night before prom, and I'm not thinking about Poe.

I'm thinking about you.

I miss you. I miss your smile and your spirit and your sweet touch.

I miss knowing there could have been more. Knowing there *should* have been more.

I miss the days and weeks and months we could have spent together. I miss the future we could have looked forward to and the past we could have looked back on. I miss the memories we could have built.

I miss feeling missed, feeling wanted, feeling anything.

I miss everything that we had in that blink of time. Everything that got buried and blacked out and blown into the wind.

I miss knowing there's something to fight for. Something for *us* to fight for.

I miss everything that could have been and should have been.

I miss you, Jocelyn.

No amount of time changes that. It only cements it even more.

94. SAVE A PRAYER

Uncle Robert is deejaying the prom!

That's what I think as I enter the gymnasium. There's nobody else to have a conversation with, so I'm talking to myself. The music sounds like something out of Uncle Robert's record collection. It takes me a few minutes, but gradually I notice signs of the eighties everywhere, along with the way some of the students are dressed. I get it. A themed prom.

Guess it shows how much I've been paying attention to the whole prom thing.

I'm here by myself because of the last-minute call I received from my date. Thankfully Poe didn't call and say it was all a big fat joke. No, the message was short and tense.

"I have to meet you at the school and I can explain," she told me.

"Is everything okay?"

"No."

It's always a bad sign when someone says no to that question, because even if things are bad, people usually say yes. Yes, everything's okay even though my house just burned down and my dog died. But yes.

Getting the no means things must be really, *really* bad.

I start to ask Poe for details, but she cuts me off and says she'll see me at the prom.

So here I am, feeling like an idiot because I'm by myself and because I had no clue about this eighties theme, feeling uncomfortable in the tux that I rented that seems a bit too big, feeling just overall stupid.

Meanwhile, the gym is packed.

Our school prom back in Libertyville was held on a boat in Lake Michigan.

Harrington High goes all out … in the gym.

I scan the room, but don't see Poe. I do, however, see Kelsey. And pretty much most of me wishes I hadn't.

She looks …

Wow.

She's playing up the theme with her poofy hairstyle that seems like it's holding a bottle of hairspray. She's dressed in a wild black skirt and heels and looks about ten years older. Like Madonna when she first came out.

Older. And hotter.

And of course Sam has his arms around her.

I recall the dance I came to with Jocelyn and how she ended up slow dancing with some other guy.

This seems to be my place in life. To look from the sidelines at the pretty girl that I could and should be with.

So where is Poe?

The music begins to play Tears for Fears, and the kids seem okay with it.

I should be dancing and having a fun time, but Poe is nowhere to be found.

For a while I wait near the doorway. I even head outside to see if Poe might be waiting there.

I manage to kill time by wandering around as if I have somewhere to go or something to do. I've had good training doing that in the hallways at school. But after an hour of this, I'm done.

I'm five seconds away from walking out when the girl who kidnapped Kelsey's body comes out of nowhere with a smile and a stare.

"Are you on your own?"

I chuckle and try to act all cool. "Yeah. I was just about to leave."

"Even your best buddy has a date tonight."

"Who's that?" I ask.

"Gus."

"Wonderful."

As if on cue, that song that they played at the end of *Pretty in Pink* starts to play. If there's a God above, He has a sense of humor.

"What happened?"

"Not quite sure," I say. "I didn't know it was an eighties theme."

"I can tell."

"You look—great."

"Georgia had to force me into this."

"No, really. You look great."

She glances back into the mass of people. Corny lights are set up to try and make it look like a dance floor, but the whole thing is still pretty ridiculous. The sound of saxophones blasts through the speakers.

"So, big party afterward?" I ask Kelsey.

She nods and then looks away. She's wearing more makeup and no glasses, but still—it's Kelsey. She can't hide who she is. Or what she's thinking.

"Good seeing you," I tell her.

This is my way of saying *I probably should have asked you to prom.*

I don't want her feeling like she has to come and babysit me.

The DJ announces that it's the last song of the evening. As he does, Kelsey looks at me.

I suddenly get the feeling that she didn't just happen to come over here at this particular time.

Somewhere, her date is surely looking for her.

The song begins to play.

"I better go," I tell her.

"Do you want to dance?"

I shouldn't dance with her. It's not right. Poe's not here, but she still might show up. And then there's Kelsey's date. Some guy I don't know and don't really care to know, but still. He had the guts and the smarts to ask her. I know better and shouldn't be messing with Kelsey anyway.

"Sure," I say.

She walks out to the dance floor, and I realize that this is my fate. I know better, but I do things anyway.

I want to dance with her.

And yes, I really do. But sometimes you shouldn't do things you want to do.

It's amazing that a girl as shy and reserved as Kelsey seems to have no problem locking her arms around me and looking up at me as we dance.

For a moment, as the old eighties song I've heard a bunch of times begins to play, I find myself dancing alone with Kelsey.

I'm no longer in this town and this state. I'm no longer a student in school and a teenager in life. I'm dancing alone with a beautiful lady. One who holds me close.

I can't help but get lost in the synthesizers and the strobe lights and the softness of Kelsey's touch.

You shouldn't be encouraging this, Chris.

And as it does so many times in life, in my life, the song seems to know what's happening and it speaks to me. It speaks *for* me.

"And you wanted to dance so I asked you to dance, but fear is in your soul," the singer sings.

Fear is in my soul, and this girl has no idea.

No idea.

But for a moment, I don't care.

For a moment, I want to be here.

I want to be close.

And I want to be wanted.

When the song ends, Kelsey smiles as the lights get brighter.

"Thanks," I tell her.

She doesn't say anything back, but again, I can see it on her pretty and innocent face. It thanks me back. It thanks me back and also tells me not to let her go.

As I leave Kelsey and leave the gym, the words of the last song follow me. I want to say them to Kelsey as I leave to look for Poe.

I have a bad feeling about what I'm going to find.

95. RAGE

Hope and happiness are beginning to look a lot like big bubbles blown by some kid. They drift by and then pop and disappear, leaving only sticky drops on the ground behind.

I can still hear the song that played to my dance with Kelsey when I get out of my mom's car and walk up to Poe's door.

It seems like every light in the house is on. I've never been here before, but it's pretty much what I expected. A nice, traditional two-story home in a nice little subdivision about twenty minutes away from Solitary.

I'm still in my tux and feel weird that I'm knocking on this door *after* the prom.

Poe answers, and I instantly know things aren't good. She looks behind her and then walks out, almost into me, as she shuts the door behind her.

Then she grabs me and hugs me and starts to cry into my chest.

"What's wrong? What happened? Poe?"

She sounds like she's talking with a sock in her mouth. When she looks back at me, I can hear her say sorry.

"What? What's wrong?"

"I'm sorry I wasn't there, that I couldn't go. I was going to, I really was. I was going to force them to have to send me home."

"What?"

"I was going to do it, but then my parents—my dad—Chris, it's awful."

"What?"

"They got to him. I know that's what happened."

"What are you talking about? Poe?"

She clears her throat and looks up at me with sad eyes. "I got expelled from school."

I try to make sense of what she just said.

"They found drugs in my locker. And this isn't the first time. They'd found pot on me before."

"What?"

"The first time was legit—it was my sophomore year and—yeah, long story. But this—they're saying they found heroin in my locker. Heroin. I mean—really? Look at me. Come on. It's such a joke."

"Who—when'd you find out?"

"They told me Friday afternoon. That's why you didn't see me at the end of the day."

"I usually don't anyway."

"They got my stuff and I was escorted out by Sheriff Wells."

"What?"

"Yeah. So much for that, huh? So much for alliances."

"Did you tell them that it wasn't—"

"Of course. But no. Then today my father got fired from his job. Works as a marketing something-or-other for a company that—well, basically it's Mr. Staunch. That's what happened."

"Do your parents know?"

"Know what? They don't know anything."

Save a prayer, Kelsey. Save a prayer for the morning after. Or maybe don't wait that long.

"Poe ..."

She curses. "This is what they do, Chris. They make people disappear. They did it to Jocelyn *and* to Rachel. I was afraid this would happen."

"But why?"

"I don't know. I don't. But I know too much."

"We have to tell your parents everything."

"No." She looks around, since her voice echoed off the walls. "No, we can't," she says in a softer voice. "They don't believe the drugs. They know that I didn't do that."

"Then you can tell them what's going on."

"No. Because I don't want anything happening to them."

"And your expulsion? I mean—what does that mean?"

"It means that they'll be willing to go easy on me if I go to another school and am placed on probation."

"Another school?"

She nods.

"I'm—I don't know what to say."

"We should never have come up to you in the first place," Poe says. "Even if you were the new cute guy. Your life would've been a lot easier."

"Sometimes I think it's the other way around. That this is all because of—that it's all my fault."

"It's not anybody's fault except the monsters doing this." Poe looks out to the street as a car passes. "You shouldn't be here."

"Why?"

"Just—it's not good for you to be here. I don't want—you need to give me some space, Chris. For now."

"I've been giving you space."

She finally notices the tuxedo I'm in. "You look handsome."

"I'm sorry you couldn't come."

"How was it?"

"Surreal." I'm not lying to her. It was surreal. In a good and a bad way.

"I don't know what's going to happen."

"Don't disappear on me," I tell her. "Don't move in the middle of the night or anything like that."

"We just have to get through tonight. My parents are pretty shaken up."

I give her a hug and then watch her as she goes back inside.

I feel something that's been growing and mutating inside of me for some time.

It's rage.

Rage that I'm stuck inside some invisible cell. Rage that I'm being constantly watched. Rage that every good person who comes across my path gets taken away or hurt or worse.

A rage that needs revenge.

I turn up the music as loud as it can go as I drive home.

I tell myself that I'm going to find the people who did this.

I'm going to find the reason they're doing this and then show it to the world.

96. DRIVING AGAIN

I wake up and realize what I have to do.

I need to see Iris.

I need to get answers from her.

I trust this woman. There's something different about her. Something authentic and real. Something hopeful. And whatever mumbo jumbo she might end up sharing with me doesn't matter because I'll take anything. Anything that offers a glimmer of light, even if it's barely visible through the tiny peephole.

It's Sunday morning and ... yeah, I don't even need to say it. I'm awake and Mom's asleep and she has no idea I'm taking her keys and I have every idea why she's still sleeping. Enough said.

The car that I feel like I just got out of is covered in dew. I start it and turn on the windshield wipers and let them go for a few moments, listening to the steady beat in a trance.

I head up the road on this cloudy gray morning when I see something in front of me and swerve into a ditch.

When I look back up, I see Jared walking up to me. It takes a second to roll down the window.

"Are you trying to kill me?" he asks.

"What are you doing?"

"I was coming to see you."

"Why?"

"Because it's time. Back up and let me in."

It takes me a couple of tries to get the car back onto the dirt road. Jared climbs inside and studies me.

"You're driving a lot these days, aren't you?"

I nod.

"Get your license or something?"

"No."

"Well—guess it doesn't really matter. Not around here."

The car is still in neutral.

"Where you going?"

"I was heading to work."

"On a Sunday? That's the day of rest, right? You never work on Sundays."

"I need to see Iris."

"Why?"

I haven't told him about his father working there.

"What is it, Chris?"

"Your father. He used to work at the Crag's Inn. Just like I do."

Jared waits for more information.

"He just disappeared on her."

"And she knows nothing more?"

"That's all she told me," I say. "I have a feeling she knows a lot more. About Solitary. About me."

"Drive then."

I still remain parked on the side of the road.

"What is it?"

"I'm not supposed to bring anybody there."

"Why? Because we'll invade the woman's privacy or something?"

"No, it's just—it's one of her rules. And I don't want to do any-thing against her."

"She's an old lady who's as nutty as Aunt Alice. She's just more refined. That's all. Same craziness in a different brand."

"I promised."

"What? You want me to get my car and follow you?"

"She can't see that I brought you there."

"It's not like the Crag's Inn is some secret. Everybody knows where it is."

"I don't know."

"Chris—listen. You're not the only one who wants answers. I have a right to know."

I feel the heat finally start working in the car. I stare out the clearing windshield and shake my head. "Just stay in the car until I tell her you're there," I finally say.

"No problem."

97. THE SIGN

When we make the corner to turn onto the road that winds back and forth up the steep mountain toward Iris and her mountain inn, I can almost feel the change that we drive through. Like a car wash in the middle of the North Pole. The temperature drops, and the car seems to slow down.

Then the birds start to attack.

I'm shivering as I hold the steering wheel and begin the ascent when a blanket of squirming, scratching beasts seem to cover our car. It's not like a few suddenly peck away at the window. It's more like a battalion of soldiers all attacking at the same time.

Jared curses and ducks as I pound on the brake and jerk the car to a halt.

"Keep going, man, keep going."

Jagged itching frantic obsessed crazed birds. That's what they are.

The bluebird has sent its troops down.

I can't tell what kind of birds because there are too many. Big and small and all of them one massive cluster of madness.

Jared rips at my sleeve and forces me to look at him. "Go. Get up that mountain. Now."

I get the car moving, and for a while I'm driving in blindness. It takes me a while to find the windshield wipers, and they don't do much good. Jared tries to open his window to get them away, but then he howls and shuts the window and holds his hand.

For a second the noise is unbearable and the frenetic motion is crazy.

Get out of here back up and back away.

"Keep driving, Chris!"

I jerk to a halt again, then accelerate, then shift a couple of times to try and get the birds off.

A sliver in the throbbing black mess on the windshield shows the road curving to the right, so I turn and keep going.

And then, like a blurry dream, the birds are gone. Again I stop the car and listen to my breathing.

"Keep going, Chris."

"What was that?"

He curses and says he has no idea but this isn't the place to stop.

I'm still cold and I suddenly feel scared.

You shouldn't be here. Not like this. Not with him.

"You need me to drive?" he asks.

"No."

A small shape flickers in the air above us. Then it suddenly bolts away like all the other birds did.

Whatever kind of sign that was, I know that it wasn't a good one.

98. THE SAME GUY

When I get to the top I tell Jared to wait in the car. He seems less anxious now. For a moment he just stares out at the inn.

"I'll tell her that you're here and ask if she wants to see you."

"Wonderful."

I climb out of the car and go to the door. After a few knocks, I let myself in. Iris has always said to make myself feel at home, to come whenever I'd like, never to feel like I'm bothering her.

But today's a Sunday. And I brought someone with me.

It's quiet inside, almost *too* quiet. I call out for Iris. Sometimes when I do this, I hear her voice answering from a room upstairs or down the hall. Today I don't hear anything. No voice, no movement, nothing.

I enter the kitchen. No coffee or tea made. No breakfast out. No dishes in the sink.

I wonder if there are any guests in the inn.

Again I call out her name. Nothing.

There's a reason for this.

The birds, Jared coming with me, the spooky fog outside …

Something's wrong.

But something's been wrong ever since I set foot in Solitary. Iris knows the town and knows my place in it. She knows about Uncle Robert, and it's time to get some answers. Some legitimate, real, eye-opening answers.

As I head out of the kitchen through the dining room, I hear a door open.

"Iris?"

I go into the room and see him. A face and a smile I know but suddenly don't recognize. Every inch of me goes cold.

"No."

That's all Jared says. But it's the way he looks, the way he says it. And suddenly I know. Just like that.

Just.

Like.

That.

"Let's wait for her in here," Jared says.

"I told you to wait in the car."

"She won't mind. I'm sure she won't."

I take a few steps and then stand near the wall between the dining room and the front door. Jared is by the couch, about ten feet away from me. I can smell something different, something strong.

He's holding something white. A cloth or an old handkerchief, the kind that guys used to have in the old-time movies. He uses his index fingers and thumbs to delicately turn the white thing.

"Why don't you sit, Chris?"

"You shouldn't be in here."

His eyes maul mine, then he looks around, then looks back at me. Again he smiles.

You're so stupid, Chris. Stupid.

"Do you recognize this?"

I look at him and then at the cloth.

"Jared—what—"

"Tell me. Do you recognize it?"

"No."

"It belonged to my father. It was his handkerchief. He taught me how to use it too." He pauses, looking like he's about ready to deliver a punch line.

I glance at the door.

"Uh-uh. We have to wait."

"Jared. What are you doing?"

"My father taught me to be careful about the dosage. With a strong enough dose you can knock out anybody."

I can get to the door I can make it there before he can grab me.

Jared moves a little closer to the door, reading my hand. Then he holds up the handkerchief. "You really should remember this, Chris. And so should your mom." He laughs.

And I know.

I know, but I have no idea *why*. Why all the lies? Why all the games?

You can't get out you have to get somewhere else.

"Both of you went out so fast. It was ridiculous."

I back up and then stand against the wall.

What about Iris? What's he going to do to her?

"Do you know that chloroform was used between the 1800s and 1900s? The only problem with it, then and now, is the side effects. Especially with your liver and your kidneys. But, well, we'll just have to worry about that when the time comes, won't we."

"Why are you doing this?"

He ignores my question and puts the cloth in one hand.

"Why?" he echoes. He takes a step closer. "It was my job. The icing on the cake is discovering this place. All thanks to you. "

He smiles again.

I just don't …

Go.

I bolt and stop thinking and get around the corner heading down the hall, but he's too fast.

Way too fast.

I feel a hand on my arm and another pulling my shirt and then I feel something come over my face then feel something pressed over my face and my mouth and I start to scream but I can't.

I'm trying to scream one thing over and over but I can't get it out.

Iris get out of here Iris get out of here.

I keep trying until I suddenly can't try anything anymore.

99. IN FLAMES

There it is again.

The fire and the smoke.

Blossoming in front of me, burning hot and bright and wild.

I know she's in there.

Jocelyn is in there and she's burning and I'll never see her beautiful face again.

My eyes close, then open again.

The flickers of yellow and orange and red flames wave at me.

I close my eyes again.

This time when I open them, I see them.

Animals everywhere.

Dogs and cats and deer and groundhogs and foxes and even wolves.

They're all …

I'm so dreaming. He must've slipped me something else besides chloroform.

The animals stand at the side of the fire, watching.

Then I see the black shape that's in flames.

The Crag's Inn.

My senses are having a hard time tracking and keeping up with the flickering flames. I feel weighed down, trapped, half conscious.

The inn is burning. It's really, truly burning.

I hear a song that was playing at the prom, mocking me.

Wake me up before you go-go 'cause I'm not planning on going solo.

But solo is what I am.

The inn is gone and surely that means Iris is too.

No.

I look to my left and see the window of my mom's car.

Outside it is a fluttering bird, watching.

Watching me.

I close my eyes again.

100. DRIVING

Good thing I'm not confused.

Because if I was, I might be driving really not so well on my way to get Poe and then—oh, I don't know.

She's the only one I trust.

I trusted Iris, but ...

Don't think about it don't go there don't Chris.

I don't know what happened. With Iris or with Jared or with Poe or anybody.

Iris wasn't in there there's no way there's absolutely no way.

I'd feel sick to my stomach, but I feel like I left my stomach and my wits and pretty much anything I have back there on the hill that has a still burning still raging fiery mass on top of it.

I really almost drove off the cliff when I started up the car. Not on purpose, but because I was driving so fast.

And because you don't have a license.

But really.

I mean really.

I *want* someone to pull me over.

Please lock me up and throw away the key. I'll do anything for that.

My mind races.

Jared—is that his real name? I seriously doubt he's Uncle Robert's son.

How could you be so dumb?

I replay the last, what, five months or so. I should have thought things through more carefully.

He shows up the moment I go looking for help after her death. He shows up with his stories and his lies and his advice.

Listen to me, okay? You have to lie low. For a while.

So that's what I did.

I laid or lied low. I don't know which one I did. I just know which one Jared did.

I trusted him while he *lied.*

But what does Iris have to do with any of this? And why—why do this now? Why do this and leave me there to watch?

Everybody else around me gets hurt. But nobody hurts me. Not physically, anyway.

I don't want to imagine something happening to Iris. It's impossible. There's no way. She was an old lady who wouldn't hurt anybody. They wouldn't do that to her. They couldn't.

I drive through a maze of woods and wilderness and wonder if I'm some animal trapped inside, being watched like a guinea pig.

I think back to last night, about the smile and the sweetness that made me forget. Just for a moment.

Moments like that are good. They're necessary.

They're also like dreams. You wake and find them gone. You wake and find yourself driving in a nightmare. Just like now. Just like this.

101. MAD WORLD

Then you arrive at Poe's and suddenly find that you're hovering over yourself watching in horror.

You see the cars outside, but still you park on the side of the street.

Two squad cars with lights still on.

Of course you think the worst. But you can see Poe on the lawn crying and being held by her mom.

You see her father talking to Sheriff Wells.

Someone approaches you as you walk toward them.

The sky is clear and you're out of the woods and the heavens watch you.

Deputy Do-so-very-little Kevin comes over to you and stops you before you can go any further.

Now you're screaming though it doesn't really feel like it.

You're shouting for Poe but she just looks your way.

Looks your way as if this is your fault.

But you don't know what you did.

The deputy warns you to get back in your car and leave.

The sheriff looks over with little help.

No expression.

No expression.

Something happened.

You stand and look around and your world spins and swirls and you don't go anywhere.

Kevin tells you to go home and wait. Go home and wait.

Sit and listen.

You look at Poe and see the tears in her eyes.

That's all this town is and this story is and these secrets are … just one big bowl of tears.

You find it kind of funny.

You begin to walk back to your car.

You find it kind of sad.

You start up the car and look back and then drive.

You don't want to go home.

You don't want to go anywhere.

But you do what you're told because there's nothing left to do in this very, very mad world.

102. UNKLE

The song for the rest of the day is "Rabbit in Your Headlights."

Just another find in Uncle Robert's collection.

Just another find in this little room.

Just another song played over and over.

Just another theme for another life.

103. SUMMER PLANS

I feel like a kid forced to go on those drugs for ADD and feeling now like a zombie. Motionless. Lifeless. Hollow. Spent.

Good thing that I have expulsion to wake me up.

"What?"

This is my life word. My life verse. My life summary.

"What?"

I'm sitting in Principal Harking's office once again.

Stop me if you've heard this one before.

I'm sitting there not just being accused this time, but being told.

"There are two options here, Chris. Making up for this year by taking summer school and retaking your failed classes, or being expelled."

I think of a split cantaloupe and how they scoop out the brains— I mean seeds—before slicing it.

"Chris?"

"Yes."

"Do you understand what I'm saying?"

So far, this is what I *think* the principal has told me. We're the only ones here—no cops or my mom or Gus or whoever.

First she tells me that it was reported that I pulled a knife on Gus in art. I don't yell in my defense. Frankly, I'm too tired to yell. I think I laugh and tell her the truth. But the truth is some sickly orphan around this place. Nobody wants anything to do with the truth. Nobody.

The thin red line in front of me known as Principal Harking says in an automated fashion that since she can't prove that I wielded the knife, it's simply going in my file. On my record. Blah blah blah. Yada yada yada.

"But your grades are another matter."

My grades?

She proceeds to tell me that I'm failing three classes.

Failing.

Three.

Classes.

French, which surprises me but not really.

Talk to the guy whose name is on the tombstone. He'll help.

Algebra II, which does surprise me because I've been doing halfway decent.

And English, which is crazy.

"I can't be failing three classes."

But she shows me. She's talked to the teachers. Since I'm a bad egg, they need to throw the bad egg out before it gets salmonella.

This town should be renamed Salmonella.

"So your option is to finish this week and then report to summer school the following week."

What about my plans to vacation in Maui? I want to protest, but really, how and why?

This is beyond a conspiracy.

This is like the rest of everything that's happened here.

"Poe didn't deserve to get expelled," I tell the principal.

"We're not talking about her today."

"I am."

The principal steadies herself in her chair like a pencil sharpening its tip.

"It does not surprise me in the least that the two of you are friends."

"She doesn't use drugs."

"With more of that attitude, I can make your stay at this school extremely unpleasant."

"I wouldn't say it's been wonderful so far."

She looks at me.

I suddenly feel like I'm waking up and filling in.

And once again, it's anger and rage inside of me.

She can see the look on my face.

I'm staring right at her.

She doesn't frighten me. No way. Not around here, not when there are a hundred other things to frighten me.

"You will need to fill these out for summer school. Part of that will involve detention."

"Awesome."

"Chris."

"Yes?"

"You're heading down the wrong path."

"And what path is that?"

"You still have one more year here," she says.

"Do I? Do you really know that?"

"Chris."

"I might not be here tomorrow. You might not be either. You never know, do you?"

I stand up and grab the papers from her and walk out.

I'm wide awake now.

Wide awake and feeling just absolutely awesome that I get to see this hellhole for the summer.

104. THE TWO LADIES

Kelsey and I have an intense, moving conversation in art class.

"Hey," I say.

Hey in this case means *Look, I'm really exhausted since this guy I've been trusting turned out to be a liar and knocked me unconscious and ended up burning down this inn I work at* along with *Oh, and yeah, I just learned I'm failing half my classes and need to take summer school.*

"Hi," Kelsey says back.

Hi in this case might mean *I had a really great dance with you the other night and have been thinking about it ever since and really hope that maybe we can have that dance again.*

I'm not saying this because I feel really good about myself. But I see it in Kelsey's eyes and in everything about her. I saw it on her face the other night.

The same way she saw it on my face.

That's the gist of our conversation. Deep, insightful.

At the end of the class, she continues our conversation.

"See you later," she says.

Which means *Why didn't you bother to ask me anything at all about the rest of my night or my weekend and why don't you bother talking or walking out with me because I'd really enjoy that but oh well that's your loss.*

"Yeah, see ya," I say.

Which means just that.

I'll see her again, sometime.

If I see Poe, a very big if since I have no idea what happened when I went by her house yesterday, it will end up going very differently from the limited interaction I had with Kelsey.

I take the bus home and then ride my bike out of town, heading to see Poe.

When I get to her house, I honestly expect it to be empty.

But as I put my bike on the driveway and start to walk to the door, Poe opens it and rushes toward me. She hugs me for a long time. Not saying anything, just hugging me. Then she tells me to come on inside before someone sees us.

I need to tell her about what happened, but I also need to know what happened to her.

"Who is this?"

The man speaking must be her father. I offer my hand and am about to say my name when Poe interrupts me.

"This is Steve. From school. A friend."

The guy doesn't shake my hand. He just looks at me with suspicious eyes, as if I did something or am about to do something.

Look, baldie, I'm not the problem here.

"He should leave before your mother gets back," Poe's father says to her as if I'm not even in the room.

"Fine."

She leads me to the family room, where we sit on the couch.

"I saw her. Pictures of her."

I shake my head, not understanding what she's talking about.

"Jocelyn."

"Pictures of Jocelyn?"

She shakes her head and begins to cry.

"Poe, what?"

"Somebody came here and threatened me."

"Who? How?"

So for the next ten minutes or ten hours, I can't really tell, through tears and gasps of air and confused dialogue, Poe tells me what happened. She says certain things in barely a whisper, not wanting her father to hear.

Someone sneaked into her house Sunday after lunch while her parents were gone. They came up to her room and opened the door and forced her to look at pictures of Jocelyn. Pictures of Jocelyn after she died.

I ask who and what they wanted and why, but Poe just ignores my comments and continues her story.

Whoever came to her house was wearing a Halloween mask, but she could tell it was a man. Probably a young guy. He showed her the pictures and then said that's what happens to girls who hang around with guys like me.

"They said my name?" I ask.

It was a warning. Whoever came in wanted her to stop every-thing and anything to do with me. As if they were watching. As if they knew what we were doing.

"Did you tell—"

"I told my parents someone came in and threatened me. I told them everything except the part about you."

"Poe—"

"Shhh. He doesn't know. Mom is gone to Walgreens to get some meds the doctor prescribed for my nerves. I think she's going to take half the pills herself."

I no longer want to tell Poe what happened.

I can't.

"The guy said one thing before he left, Chris. One thing that—I didn't tell the police. But you need to know."

"What?"

"He said that this is what happens to those who get close to you. It happened to Jocelyn. It happened to the lady at the inn you worked at. It'll happen to me."

"Iris?"

The word explodes like a firecracker, leaving a burning scent in the air.

"Then he told me that we're all going to die. We can be afraid, or we can embrace our last breath. Something like that."

I don't say anything.

"Chris?"

I know exactly who sent this guy to threaten her. It's as if he's begging to be found out. As if there's no mystery about who's wear-ing the mask, who's behind the dark curtain.

It's like he's wanting you to go to him.

"Chris, what is it?"

She knows. She can see it on my face.

I've made up my mind.

That's exactly what I'm going to do.

105. ONE MOMENT

I started this year angry and desperate and searching for answers. I didn't wait for them, either. I went out to search. Yet before I could get to anybody, I ended up being saved from the creepy mountain man by Jared.

Jared who happened to be there and who proceeded to fill me with lies.

I never got a chance to follow through with what I wanted to do. I wanted to not only find out the truth. I wanted to hurt whoever was responsible for Jocelyn's death.

Now, without any doubt whatsoever, I know.

That's why I'm skipping school today. What are they going to do? Threaten my life?

That's why I'm holding a rock in my hand.

That's why I'm throwing it through the glass window and then taking the rest of the shards out with a stick.

And that's why I'm climbing through the window at the back of the little, seemingly abandoned and desolate cabin. The one wearing the mask, just like everybody else around here. The one with a false front, just like the guy I'm pretty sure owns it.

I stand there with misty light coming through the windows. It rained earlier, but now it's clearing and sun is drizzling down. There's a desk and a computer and files and books.

I guess if it was the middle of the night I'd be creeped out. Maybe it should be pouring rain or something. But no. It's bright and I'm angry and the only fear that I have is what I'm going to do. What I might end up doing to hurt myself.

I find a bunch of files about the church, confirming that this office does indeed belong to Pastor Marsh.

Another drawer is full of cards—the same type of cards I saw a bunch of kids playing with at Ray Spencer's party the first time I ever went over there. They have different images on them, strange images. A leaf or a flower or an animal.

Another drawer reveals a knife, which I decide to take. I wish I still had Uncle Robert's gun.

There're a lot of things I wish.

The bottom drawer is locked. I find a letter opener that I use to unlodge the drawer and break through the wood. It's not even wood, just particle board. The lock that's hiding whatever secrets are behind it breaks easily.

Inside are folders stacked on top of each other. Ordinary manila folders. Each one is marked in black pen. The folder on top says #6.

I take them out and then look out at the woods. Nothing. Nothing but nature talking back at me and sunlight spilling in.

You don't want to see what's inside these.

But I open the folder marked #6, and I see her looking back at me. Jocelyn. It looks like a school picture. She looks younger.

You don't want to do this, Chris.

I keep going through the file. Pictures, information, copies of emails, more pictures, information on Aunt Alice and Wade. There's a stack of pages paper-clipped together that are all about my mom. Copies of a birth certificate, driver's license, family photos back when there was a family to photograph.

My hands are shaking.

I have to keep looking. I want to know. I want to see.

I want to know why they killed her.

Then the door behind me opens, and the folders in my lap spill out as I stand.

At the door is the man responsible for this. His evil eyes behind the slivers of his glasses don't appear surprised.

"Hello, Chris," he says, his voice as casual as the white polo shirt and jeans he wears.

The fan of pages that litter the top of the desk from where they spilled out show enough. For just one brief second, I see.

She's hurting and bleeding but she's still alive, at least in those pictures.

The man at the door just stands there. "I have a lot more than just photos I can show you," the pastor tells me. "I have video, too."

I swallow, but my mouth and throat are dry. My body goes numb, hot and cold, my eyes fill with dizzy red rage.

"She screamed your name, Chris. Over and over again."

With that, I find that knife on the top of the desk and take it out of its sheath.

As I do, the pastor bolts away from the doorway. I hear hurried steps rushing through the woods.

I think of Wade, the monster who was hurting Jocelyn.

I dealt with him, and I can deal with this.

I follow him, knowing exactly what I'm meant to do.

Whatever—whoever—was left of Chris Buckley after Jocelyn died stays in that little cabin next to those horrific pictures I only saw for a moment.

But one moment is all you need in this life.

And that one moment is all I need to end the pastor's.

106. THE BIG BAD WOLF

Evil wears a mask, and I can finally see its face.

The rushing waters surround us as sunlight plays tricks on my eyes. Gold glitters in these woods, damp from the earlier rain, foggy from the temperature change. My legs splash in the cool stream that comes up to my shins.

He's standing on the edge where the water drops fifty feet to the jutting rocks below. He faces me with his sick smile. "What are you going to do now, Chris?"

I'm no longer scared, no longer running away.

"It's done," I say. "You're done."

The voice talking is not mine. The hand holding this knife doesn't belong to me.

Chris Buckley is gone. Long gone.

It's been six months, but I can still taste it in my mouth. The anger, the bitterness, the absolute hunger for revenge.

You don't have to do this, not here, not like this.

He smiles. "What do you think you're going to do?"

"Whatever you're doing to this place and these people—it's over. Right now."

His laugh twists into my skin.

"There are things you need to know," he says.

"I know enough."

"You know only what you're supposed to know. That's why I brought you here."

"I followed you."

"I could break your neck if I wanted to."

I smile. Because something in me says he's wrong. Something in me believes that if he wanted me dead, I'd be dead already.

"You're not going to do anything to anybody ever again," I say.

"So what happens after you kill the Big Bad Wolf?" he asks. "There are others lurking in these woods and in this town. I'm just the obvious one. Killing me achieves nothing."

My hand shakes, but I steady it as I walk closer to him. Streaks of sunlight circle us like a laser show.

You can't really do this, Chris, no matter how you feel and how right it is.

"So the pastor stands at Marsh Falls," he says. "How ironic. How fitting. And how utterly predictable."

"You killed her," I say to him.

He laughs and looks at me through his short glasses, and I want to take them and break them just like I want to break him.

"Six months and you're still seething," Pastor Marsh says. "That's good."

"People are going to know."

"Haven't these past months taught you anything? You're smart, but you're not *that* smart. You're not here because you're some bright young star chosen because of your intelligence, Chris. You're really rather unremarkable, to tell you the truth."

I inch closer.

He's now about five feet away from me. He looks behind him, then glances back at me.

This is the first time I think I see fear on his face.

Because maybe, just maybe, he doesn't see fear in mine.

One more step.

The echoes of the falls smother all other sounds.

Hell is not dying, Chris. It's knowing and living.

Whoever said that was right.

I think whoever said that is standing before me right now.

"Do you want to know the truth?" he asks.

"I *know* the truth. The new church. I know where it is. I found the folders. The pictures. I have proof. Everybody is going to know about Solitary. Everybody is going to know what's really going on."

"Have you ever been surprised, Chris?"

"You're a sick man."

"Have you ever believed in something with all your heart, only to discover it was an ugly little lie?"

"Shut up."

"Everything you think you know about this town and about your mother and her family—all those things are pretty little lies covering up the ugly, awful truth."

"No."

"Oh, yes, Chris. Maybe this has all been some elaborate test."

I move closer.

"Maybe we never wanted Jocelyn. That sweet but dirty little thing you professed to love."

I curse at him.

"Maybe all we ever wanted was you."

My hand is steady and I know it's because I've used a weapon before and I'll do it again. Even though a gun's a lot different from a knife, it doesn't matter.

I'm not Chris Buckley because that boy died on New Year's Eve along with something far more precious.

Stop before it's too late.

"We're watching, but all you see is the scene before you," Pastor Marsh says. "You don't see anybody but a face you hate and fear and a boy you hate and fear even more."

"I'm going to kill you."

He smiles. "If you do, Chris, we will watch and applaud and await."

Then the pastor opens his arms as if giving the benediction at church.

And that's when I plunge the twelve-inch hunting blade deep into the place where I imagine his heart might have been at one time.

I see Jocelyn's face as I move the knife and feel the softness of skin and hear the gasping, choking breath as I thrust down.

I let go and see him looking surprised. Not in horror, but almost in utter delight.

"You want to know the truth, Chris?" a draining, coughing voice asks.

And then he tells me.

And suddenly I realize that he's right and I'm wrong.

I realize this just as he staggers over the falls and drops below.

107. DEFY

Somewhere in these woods I stagger. I know now it doesn't have to be night to see darkness all around you. I understand that you don't have to be drunk to be blind. I get that a single act and a single statement can leave you breathless and hopeless and reeling.

The trees watch me. Like those students in the hallways at Harrington. Like those walls in the cabin in Solitary. Like the unseen ghosts that are laughing at me. They watch as I stumble and hold on to them and walk in circles.

I still hold the bloody knife. I'm scared of what I just did. I'm scared of what I still might do.

There's no way you leave these woods. You can't run from this. You can't escape what you just did.

I hear his last words and try to will them away from my mind. But I can't. I can't.

"Where is God?" Pastor Marsh asked. "Where is your father? Tell me."

He just stood there, almost triumphant, with the blood gushing out of his chest, his face delirious and crazy.

"They call him God the Father for a reason. The reality, Chris, is that they both abandoned you. They both left you alone to live and die in this place. But I can show you—I can show you that you don't have to fear death. Look at me. What do you see, Chris? What do you see on my face? I've been waiting all this time for you to make a choice. To see what I see. To believe what I believe."

He spat out something dark and then said his final words. "We can live and die afraid, or we can live to defy, Chris. It is up to you."

Then he fell back and out of my life.

I crumble to the forest floor and lean against a big tree. I look at the knife.

For a long time I just stare at it, wondering what to do and where to go. I know it doesn't make sense, that it sounds crazy, that I should be running and sprinting and bolting out of here, but I can't.

I'm just so tired. I stay there under that tree and drift off. And sometime, maybe minutes or hours later, I don't really know—when I wake up, I find the knife that had been in my hand is gone.

Just like that.

Just like Pastor Marsh. Gone.

I'm not scared.

If someone had wanted to get me, he could have already done so.

If someone really wanted that knife, let him have it.

"I don't care!"

I hope whoever took it hears me. I hope he hears loud and clear.

108. TOO MUCH

I get back home. I always do. Somehow I just really can't seem to get far enough away from the cabin or the town.

It's afternoon, and I'm ready to sleep for twenty hours. Yet something is waiting for me in the driveway. It's not Mom's car. Of course not.

I pull up and see the silver-and-black motorcycle that was in the shed at the Crag's Inn.

Instantly I expect that Jared is somewhere around. He's dropping by to rub it in my face. Or to bring me to the cops after what I did to the pastor.

For a moment I think about taking the bike and riding away. But I'm exhausted and don't have the energy to get on it. I really just don't care.

There's a white envelope taped to the seat. I see my name on it.

I'm not going to like this.

I hold the card in my hands.

Just get rid of it, Chris. Even if it has your name on it. This isn't a birthday card.

The wind rustles. I wonder if school missed me today. Or if Mom did. Or if anybody really did.

I tear open the envelope and see the folded card inside. It's special stationary that has a picture of the Crag's Inn on it.

Iris …

I swallow. How did it get here, and why, and who—

Add them to the collection. The collection of HUH? stories that I'm starting to own.

I open the note.

> Dear Chris,
> The bike belonged to your uncle and now belongs to you. Keep it and learn to ride it. Just be careful when you do.
> You know more than you think you do. You understand more than you believe you do. But you are at a critical juncture and you have to make a choice.
> Just remember that our struggle is not against flesh and blood, but against the rulers, against the authorities, against the powers of this dark world and against the spiritual forces of evil in the heavenly realms.
> Remember those words even if you do not believe them.
> Yes, it is dark.

But the Lord is a lamp.
And He can turn the darkness into light.
Iris

I fold up the letter and look around.

The breeze still blows.

I wonder why. Why me. Why now. Why.

I take the steps up to the cabin.

I don't feel anything.

I'm too tired to feel. Too bewildered to understand.

It's all just a bit too much.

109. Sealed Shut

I hear the sound of a jet nearby. It wakes me up.

And here I am, sitting in a seat on a plane.

I know I'm dreaming, because Jocelyn is sitting next to me.

"You can't stay here," she says.

I look at her and feel myself blushing. I feel like a kid next to her. I *am* a kid next to her.

"Where is here? They use planes and airports in my imaginary heaven?"

"This isn't imagined and this is not heaven. This is just a place in between. Otherwise it's too startling."

There's that expression again. *But shouldn't it be space in between?.*

"Why didn't you tell me?"

"About what?" she says.

"About the pastor. About my uncle. About Iris."

"I can't tell you those things, Chris. It doesn't work like that."

"Then how does it work? When is any of this going to make sense? And—and why do you look grown up?"

Jocelyn only smiles. "Does everything need to make sense in your world? Did everything make sense when you lived in Chicago?"

"A lot more than now."

"Like with your parents splitting up? Your father abandoning a career after finding faith? And all the countless little moments you chose to ignore on a daily basis?"

"No."

I don't want to acknowledge what she said, because I can't.

There's no way she can know that. There's no way my dreams can even know that.

"You've felt something all your life and yet have done nothing about it," Jocelyn says. "And it's only since coming here that it's come to the surface. This empty feeling deep down. Those fears. The questions."

"Stop," I tell her.

"We don't have a lot more time."

I fumble with my seat belt and then stumble out into the walkway.

"I need to wake up."

"Yes, you do," Jocelyn says.

"And you—you—whatever you are—whatever thing you are. I want you to leave."

Jocelyn watches me with eyes that haunt and hurt. She remains quiet.

"I don't want any more maybes in my life," I say. "Any more might-have-beens. I'm tired of them and tired of thinking. Tired of wondering what might have and should have and any of that. I'm just mostly tired, Jocelyn, and I don't—I *can't*—keep seeing you here, or keep showing up here, or keep doing whatever it is that I'm doing to get here."

"Chris—"

"No. No. Please. Just let me leave. Let me be. It happened and it was magical, and then someone ripped it away from me and the world crumbled. And I don't want to wake up every day going through piles and piles of crumbs to try and find something. I'm tired of it. I want something that I know. I want something that is real. I want something that doesn't make me sick with sadness."

She looks at me and nods. No anger or frustration or confusion on her beautiful face. She nods and then looks out the window next to her.

I don't want to say anything else because there's no use.

I start walking away, not sure where I'm going or what I'm doing.

You know more than you think you do.

But it doesn't matter.

You understand more than you believe you do.

It does not matter.

You have to make a choice.

I want it back. The part of me that doesn't care. The part of me that doesn't fear tomorrow.

I just want to move on with it.

"Got it?"

I keep walking and hear the sound of the door to the airplane seal shut behind me.

110. The End Is the Beginning

"We're leaving."

Just like that, another story is over.

Just like that, another chapter ends.

"What?"

"This is how it works," Poe tells me. "I've seen it with others. I mean—it just happens. People suddenly leave. Someone loses a job, and then their family moves. Or they get a bigger or better job somewhere else."

"It's over," I say.

"What do you mean?"

"It's over."

It's been three days since it all happened. I haven't been back at school. I've done nothing the last few days. That includes sleeping. That also includes keeping my sanity.

I left it by those falls when the pastor fell over to his death.

It's graduation day, and I'm meeting Poe outside by the track field.

"What's over?"

"The pastor. He's dead."

Poe laughs.

"I'm not kidding."

"Shut up, Chris."

"No. The day after I saw you—it happened. I saw it because—because I *did* it. I killed him."

So I tell her in a hurried whisper. I tell her while she looks at me and shakes her head and keeps shaking it.

"That's impossible," Poe says. "Why are you making this up?"

"I'm not."

"It's not going to change anything."

"What isn't?"

"This—your story."

"I'm not making this up, Poe."

"I might never see you again after today, and you're doing this."

"I'm not doing anything." I don't understand why she doesn't believe me. "Listen—it really happened. Just like I said. Remember when you wouldn't believe me about Jocelyn."

"So go inside."

"What?"

"Go inside the gym. Then come back and look me in the face and tell me you're not lying."

"Poe—"

"I saw him this morning."

"You saw who?"

"The pastor."

Now it's me who thinks she's lying.

But I'm already running to the gym where the ceremony is going on, where the graduates have already marched, where somebody is probably giving them a nice pep talk before they head out into the big dark world.

Even before I enter the open doors, I hear his voice.

I stop and listen and know this cannot be happening.

It can't be.

It's not real.

I move through the opened double doors and see the crowd and the platform and then I see him.

Pastor Jeremiah Marsh.

Talking and saying something that sounds really seriously wonderful.

And as if he knows, as if he can just feel that I'm in the room, he grins.

III. A FINE ENDING

If this were a fairy tale or a story about a good person, then this would be his moment. The moment where he would seek the water for baptism. Where he would give himself up and finally give up. When he would embrace this thing that his father so fully accepted, this thing that Jocelyn so freely gave herself over to. He would stand in this flowing stream and kneel and ask for forgiveness and just let go.

That would be a good story and a fine ending.

But this forest doesn't belong in a fairy tale, and standing in this stream is no good person.

I hold an old backpack containing the items I have to offer.

A Bible that once belonged to my father. One he claimed had answers for me. A Bible I gave to someone else to use, only to receive it back with claims that echoed my father's statement.

They were both wrong.

Also inside is a leather band once given to me by someone I had just begun to know. Something that meant the world to her. It was like the Bible, a present a parent gave a child, a present with deep meaning.

Then there's the picture of Jocelyn and me, a faded color printout of another time and another life.

Faith is believing in someone or something. And this is my moment of finding faith.

You want me to make a choice, Iris? So be it.

I know what I believe now.

I believe in anything and everything that I can do.

I believe that the world is messed up and that there's evil and that there's madness and that there's mystery.

But there isn't a God up above. He can't be watching, not with all this madness around me. Not with everything happening. It's okay if He wants to abandon me, but there are too many others for Him to *not* abandon. Too many. If He is up there, He abandoned us a long time ago.

I lift the bag and then chuck it over the falls.

If the dead can be raised, then so can other things.

I stand and look out to the surrounding stranglehold of woods.

I believe that I can and will be free.

No more sadness and no more sorrow. No more secrets and no more spying.

I'm tired of trying to be a hero in a story I don't belong in.

So here I am. Here I am.

I'm a new person, a new soul. And this soul is open and free and ready to start living.

And if God is up there, then it's up to Him to hunt me down.

112. LITTLE BIRD

Sometimes I wonder if the bluebird watches me.

I've seen him too many times to wonder if it's just random. Too many times around my house and on my deck and by my window.

I know it's him. I just wonder why he's still around.

Sometimes I think the bluebird is a ghost of Jocelyn that's haunting me, trying to get me to understand its language and find the key.

Sometimes I think it's Iris looking at me with questioning eyes, wondering how I could have entered her life only to see it all burn to the ground.

Sometimes I think it's an angel wondering what happened to me and where I went wrong.

Sometimes I think it's a demon out to get me, out to corner me and pin me down and peck my eyes out.

And sometimes I think it's just a bluebird out there, flying because it has nothing better to do.

I like the last thought the best.

Yeah.

But that doesn't mean I believe it.

ALSO BY TRAVIS THRASHER

The Promise Remains

The Watermark

The Second Thief

Three Roads Home

Gun Lake

Admission

Blinded

Sky Blue

Out of the Devil's Mouth

Isolation

Ghostwriter

Every Breath You Take

Broken

40

THE SOLITARY TALES

Solitary

Gravestone

... a little more ...

When a delightful concert comes to an end,

the orchestra might offer an encore.

When a fine meal comes to an end,

it's always nice to savor a bit of dessert.

When a great story comes to an end,

we think you may want to linger.

And so, we offer ...

AfterWords—just a little something more after you

have finished a David C Cook novel.

We invite you to stay awhile in the story.

Thanks for reading!

Turn the page for ...

- **Three Recommended Playlists**
- **Behind the Book: The Empire Strikes Back**
- **A Snapshot**

THREE RECOMMENDED PLAYLISTS

GRAVESTONE PLAYLIST
#1 FOR THE WALKMAN

1. "A Forest" by The Cure
2. "Domino" by Genesis
3. "In a Lonely Place" by New Order
4. "Walk through the Fire" by Peter Gabriel
5. "The Ghost in You" by The Psychedelic Furs
6. "Millimillenary" by Cocteau Twins
7. "The Hurting" by Tears for Fears
8. "That Joke Isn't Funny Anymore" by The Smiths
9. "Someone Speaks" by Anything Box
10. "Shouldn't Have Done That" by Depeche Mode
11. "Save a Prayer" by Duran Duran
12. "Mad World" by Tears for Fears
13. "New Day" by The Cure
14. "The Seventh Stranger" by Duran Duran
15. "Song to the Siren" by This Mortal Coil
16. "Faith" by The Cure

GRAVESTONE PLAYLIST
#2 FOR THE iPOD

1. "Story" by Great Northern

2. "Reckoner" by Radiohead

3. "Keep Quiet" by Hot Chip

4. "Missing Persons 1 & 2" by OneRepublic

5. "Canvas" by Imogen Heap

6. "Norway" by Beach House

7. "This Is Who I Am" by Cause and Effect

8. "Keep the Car Running" by Arcade Fire

9. "Dissolved Girl" by Massive Attack

10. "Miss You" by Trentemøller

11. "Mad World" by Michael Andrews and Gary Jules

12. "Rabbit in Your Headlights" by UNKLE

13. "The Space in Between" by How to Destroy Angels

14. "Little Bird" by Imogen Heap

GRAVESTONE PLAYLIST
#3 FOR THE MOVIE

1. "Turquoise Mix" by Johan Söderqvist (from *Earth Made of Glass* soundtrack)

2. "Caught" by David Julyan (from *The Prestige* soundtrack)

3. "Christmas Island" by Depeche Mode

4. "The Artifact & Living" by Michael Andrews (from *Donnie Darko* soundtrack)

5. "Waves, Waves, Waves" by M83

6. "Aker" by Johan Söderqvist (unreleased)

7. "The Low Places" by Jon Hopkins

8. "Night—City Back Street" by David Lynch and Marek Zebrowski

9. "The Field of Gold" by Alexander Malter (from *Fireflies in the Garden* soundtrack)

10. "Slipping Away" by Michael Andrews (from *Donnie Darko* soundtrack)

11. "End Credit Mix" by Johan Söderqvist (from *Earth Made of Glass* soundtrack)

12. "The Long Walk" by Mark Isham (from *The Crazies* soundtrack)

13. "The Big Ship" by Brian Eno

BEHIND THE BOOK: THE
EMPIRE STRIKES BACK

When I started to dive into *Gravestone,* the second of four books in
The Solitary Tales, I began to study second installments of series. Not
just book series, but movies as well.

This led me to rewatch *The Empire Strikes Back* and break it
down.

There's a reason why so many people regard this Star Wars movie
as the best one ever made.

First off, it's action packed. The story starts off fast and never
slows.

It dives deeper into the main characters of the story, separating
them and charting their own unique journeys.

It gives us brand-new, lovable characters. "Star Wars without
Yoda, unthinkable would be, hmmm?" Okay, sorry, that's my Yoda-
speak for you. But seriously, can you imagine not having Yoda as part
of the overall story? Or how about Boba Fett, a minor character that
was so cool he made you want to become a bounty hunter?

But most of all, *The Empire Strikes Back* was dark. It ended on
quite the downer. (Need I even bother saying "spoiler alert"?) At the
end of the film, Han Solo is frozen in carbonite and taken away to
some guy named Jabba the Hutt. Luke's no better off. His dad is
Darth Vader, after all. And his father decides to lop off his hand.

So when all is said and done, the story leaves us breathless, waiting for what comes next.

With this in mind, I set out to write *Gravestone*.

Unfortunately, the scene where Chris's father comes back and cuts off his hand was axed by my editor. As was the scene where Chris meets Iris in a small hut in the swamp.

No, the universe of Stars Wars is quite different from that of Solitary. It's a whole other genre. But since this was my first foray into writing a second installment, I let *The Empire Strikes Back* help me with the storytelling.

If you're wondering where these stories are headed, let me promise you that I do know … even if I don't know exactly how we're going to get there. Or who exactly is going to survive.

So what of book three?

Well, I'm going to take a unique approach to the book that we're calling *Temptation*. It's going to pick up right where we've left Chris, but it's going to go off in a different direction. That's all I'll say. You'll be surprised, but not for the reasons you might expect.

I hope you stay tuned for the ride. Lots more to come in Chris's journey. Lots more to discover about Solitary and the people … and even the animals … who live there.

This tenth grader didn't do anything note-worthy except for one thing: sneaking into the girls' dorm and getting expelled from high school. This unfortunate event provided the catalyst for changing schools and entering a whole new existence in North Carolina. At least it would provide good material for writing many years later.

For more information on Travis Thrasher, visit www.TravisThrasher.com.

Chris Buckley's saga in The Solitary Tales will continue in *Temptation*, scheduled for publication in June 2012, and will conclude in *Hurt* in June 2013.